THE
FAMILY
REMAINS

THE FAMILY REMAINS

LISA JEWELL

CENTURY

1 3 5 7 9 10 8 6 4 2

Century
20 Vauxhall Bridge Road
London SW1V 2SA

Century is part of the Penguin Random House group of companies
whose addresses can be found at global.penguinrandomhouse.com.

Penguin
Random House
UK

First published in the UK by Century in 2022

www.penguin.co.uk

A CIP catalogue record for this book is available from the British Library.

ISBN 9781529125795 (hardback)
ISBN 9781529125801 (trade paperback)

Typeset in 11.75/16.63 pt Times New Roman by Jouve (UK) Milton Keynes.
Printed and bound in Great Britain by Clays Ltd, Elcograf S.p.A.

The authorised representative in the EEA is Penguin Random House Ireland,
Morrison Chambers, 32 Nassau Street, Dublin D02 YH68

MIX
Paper from
responsible sources
FSC
www.fsc.org   FSC® C018179

Penguin Random House is committed to a sustainable future
for our business, our readers and our planet. This book is
made from Forest Stewardship Council® certified paper.

This book is dedicated to the memory of Steve Simmonds

THE FAMILIES OF 16 CHEYNE WALK

The Lambs

Henry Lamb Sr and Martina Lamb

Henry Lamb Jr, their son, who also calls himself Phineas Thomson

Lucy Lamb, their daughter, once married to Michael Rimmer; mother
to Libby, Marco and Stella

Libby Jones, Lucy's daughter, formerly Serenity Lamb; in a
relationship with journalist Miller Roe

The Thomsens

David Thomsen and Sally Thomsen

Clemency Thomsen, their daughter, now living in Cornwall

Phineas Thomsen, their son, also referred to as Finn Thomsen, now
living in Botswana

Birdie Dunlop-Evers, musician

Justin Redding, Birdie's boyfriend

Prologue

June 2019

Samuel

'Jason Mott?'

'Yes. Here. That's me.'

I stare down at the young man who stands below me ankle-deep in the mud of the banks of the Thames. He has sandy hair that hangs in curtains on either side of a soft, freckled face. He's wearing knee-high rubber boots and a khaki gilet with multiple pockets and is surrounded by a circle of gawping people. I go to him, trying to keep my shoes away from the mud.

'Good morning,' I say. 'I'm DI Samuel Owusu. This is Saffron Brown from our forensics team.' I see Jason Mott trying very hard not to look as if he is excited to be in the presence of two real-life detectives – and failing. 'I hear you have found something. Maybe you could explain?'

He nods, eagerly. 'Yes. So. Like I said on the phone. I'm a mud-larking guide. Professional. And I was out here this morning with my group and this young lad here' – he points to a boy who looks about twelve years old – 'he was poking about and opened up this bag.' He points at a black bin bag sitting on some shingle. 'I mean, rule number one of mud-larking is no touching, but this was just sitting there, like someone had just dropped it there, so I guess it was OK for him to open it.'

Although I know nothing of mud-larking rules, I throw the young boy a reassuring look and he appears relieved.

'Anyway. I don't know, I mean, I'm no forensics expert . . .' Jason Mott smiles nervously at Saffron and I see him flush a little. 'But I thought that they looked like they might be, you know, human bones.'

I pick my way across the shingle to the bag and pull it open slightly. Saffron follows and peers over my shoulder. The first thing we see is a human jawbone. I turn and glance at her. She nods; then she pulls on her gloves and unfurls some plastic sheeting.

'Right,' I say, standing up and looking at the group gathered on the mud. 'We will need to clear this area. I would kindly ask for your cooperation.'

For a moment nobody moves. Then Jason Mott springs into action and manages to corral everyone off the beach and back up on to the riverside where they all stand and continue to gawp. I see a few smartphones appear and I call up. 'Please. No filming. This is a very sensitive police matter. Thank you.'

The smartphones disappear.

Jason Mott stops halfway up the steps to the riverside and turns back to me. 'Are they . . .?' he begins. 'Are they human?'

'It would appear so,' I reply. 'But we won't know for sure until they have been examined. Thank you, Mr Mott, for your help.' I smile warmly, hoping that this will send a signal that he must stop asking questions and go away.

Saffron turns back to the bones and starts to lift them out of the bag and on to a plastic sheet.

'Small,' she says. 'Possibly a child. Or a small adult.'

'But definitely human?'

'Yes, definitely human.'

I hear a voice calling down from the riverside. It is Jason Mott. I sigh and turn calmly towards him.

'Any idea how old they are?' he shouts down. 'Just by looking?'

Saffron smiles drily at me. Then she turns to Jason. 'No idea at all. Give your details to the PC by the car. We'll keep you posted.'

'Thanks. Thanks so much. That's awesome.'

A moment later Saffron pulls a small skull from the black bag. She turns it over on the plastic sheeting.

'There,' she says. 'Look. See that? A hairline fracture.'

I crouch. And there it is. The probable cause of death.

My eyes cast up and down the beach and along the curve of the river as if the killer might at this very minute be running from view with the murder implement clasped inside their hand. Then I glance back at the tiny ash-grey skull and my heart fills both with sadness and with resolve.

There is a whole world contained inside this small bag of bones.

I feel the door to the world open, and I step inside.

PART ONE

1

July 2018

Groggy with sleep, Rachel peered at the screen of her phone. A French number. The phone slipped from her hand on to the floor and she grabbed it up again, staring at the number with wide eyes, adrenaline charging through her even though it was barely seven in the morning.

Finally she pressed reply. 'Hello?'

'*Bonjour*, good morning. This is Detective Avril Loubet from the Police Municipale in Nice. Is this Mrs Rachel Rimmer?'

'Yes,' she replied. 'Speaking.'

'Mrs Rimmer. I am afraid I am calling you with some very distressing news. Please, tell me. Are you alone?'

'Yes. Yes, I am.'

'Is there anyone you can ask to be with you now?'

'My father. He lives close. But please. Just tell me.'

'Well, I am afraid to say that early this morning the body of your husband, Michael Rimmer, was discovered by his house-keeper in the basement of his house in Antibes.'

Rachel made a sound, a hard intake of breath with a *whoosh*, like a steam train. 'Oh,' she said. 'No!'

'I'm so sorry. But yes. And he appears to have been murdered, with a stab wound, several days ago. He has been dead at least since the weekend.'

Rachel sat up straight and moved the phone to her other ear. 'Is it – Do you know why? Or who?'

'The crime scene officers are in attendance. We will uncover every piece of evidence we can. But it seems that Mr Rimmer had not been operating his security cameras and his back door was unlocked. I am very sorry, I don't have anything more definite to share with you at this point, Mrs Rimmer. Very sorry indeed.'

Rachel turned off her phone and let it drop on to her lap.

She stared blankly for a moment towards the window where the summer sun was leaking through the edges of the blind. She sighed heavily. Then she pulled her sleep mask down, turned on to her side, and went back to sleep.

2

June 2019

I am Henry Lamb. I am forty-two years old. I live in the best apartment in a handsome art deco block just around the corner from Harley Street. How do I know it's the best apartment? Because the porter told me it was. When he brings a parcel up – he doesn't need to bring parcels up, but he's nosey, so he does – he peers over my shoulder and his eyes light up at the slice of my interior that he can see from my front door. I used a designer. I have exquisite taste, but I just don't know how to put tasteful things together in any semblance of visual harmony. No. I am not good at creating visual harmony. It's OK. I'm good at lots of other things.

I do not currently – quite emphatically – live alone. I always thought I was lonely before they arrived. I would return home to my immaculate, expensively renovated flat and my sulky Persian cats and I would think, oh, it would be so nice to have someone to talk to about my day. Or it would be so nice if there was someone in the kitchen right now preparing me a lovely meal, unscrewing the cap from a bottle of something cold or, better still, mixing me something up in a cocktail glass. I have felt very sorry for myself for a very long time. But for a year now, I have had house guests – my sister Lucy and her two children – and I am never, ever alone.

There are people in my kitchen constantly, but they're not mixing me cocktails or shucking oysters, they're not asking me about my day; they're using my panini-maker to produce what they call 'toasties', they're making hot chocolate in the wrong pot, they're putting non-recyclables in my recycling bin and vice versa. They're watching noisy, unintelligible things on the smartphones I bought them and shouting at each other when there's really no need. And then there's the dog. A Jack Russell terrier type thing that my sister found on the streets of Nice five years ago scavenging in bins. He's called Fitz and he adores me. It's mutual. I'm a dog person at heart and only got the cats because they're easier for selfish people to look after. I did a test online – *What's Your Ideal Cat Breed?* – answered thirty questions, and the result came back: Persian. I think the test was correct. I'd only ever known one cat before, as a child, a spiteful creature with sharp claws. But these Persians are in a different realm entirely. They demand that you love them. You have no choice in the matter. But they do not like Fitz the dog and they do not like me liking Fitz the dog and the atmosphere between the animals is horrendous.

My sister moved in last year for reasons that I barely know how to begin to convey. The simple version is that she was homeless.

The more complicated version would require me to write an essay. The halfway version is that when I was ten years old our (very large) family home was infiltrated by a sadistic conman and his family. Over the course of more than five years the conman took control of my parents' minds and systematically stripped them of everything they owned. He used our home as his own personal prison and playground and was ruthless in getting exactly what he wanted from everyone around him, including his own wife and children. Countless unspeakable things happened during those years, including my sister getting pregnant at thirteen, giving birth at fourteen, and leaving her ten-month-old baby in London and running away to the south of France when she was only fifteen. She went on to have two more children by two more men, kept them fed and clothed with money earned by busking with a violin on the streets of Nice, spent a few nights sleeping rough, and then decided to come home when (amongst many other things) she sensed that she might be in line for a large inheritance from a trust fund set up by our parents when we were children.

So, the good news is that last week that trust finally paid out and now – a trumpet fanfare might be appropriate here – she and I are both millionaires, which means that she can buy her own house and move herself, her children and her dog out, and that I will once more be alone.

And then I will have to face the next phase of my life.

Forty-two is a strange age. Neither young nor old. If I were straight, I suppose I'd be frantically flailing around right now trying to find a last-minute wife with functioning ovaries. As it is, I am not straight, and neither am I the sort of man that other men wish to form lengthy and meaningful relationships with, so that leaves me in the worst possible position – an unlovable gay man with fading looks.

Kill me now.

But there is a glimmer of something new. The money is nice, but the money is not the thing that glimmers. The thing that glimmers is a lost jigsaw piece of my past; a man I have loved since we were both boys in my childhood house of horrors. A man who is now forty-three years old, sporting a rather unkempt beard and heavy-duty laughter lines and working as a gamekeeper in Botswana. A man who is – *plot twist* – the son of the conman who ruined my childhood. And also – *secondary plot twist* – the father of my niece, Libby. Yes, Phineas impregnated Lucy when he was sixteen and she was thirteen and yes that is wrong on many levels and you might have thought that that would put me off him, and for a while it did. But we all behaved badly in that house, not one of us got out of there without a black mark. I've come to accept our sins as survival strategies.

I have not seen Phineas Thomsen since I was sixteen and he was eighteen. But last week at my niece's birthday party, my niece's boyfriend, who is an investigative journalist, told us that he had tracked him down for her. A kind of uber-thoughtful birthday present for his girlfriend. *Look! I got you a long-lost dad!*

And now here I am, on a bright Wednesday morning in June, cloistered away in the quiet of my bedroom, my laptop open, my fingers caressing the touchpad, gently guiding the cursor around the website for the game reserve where he works, the game reserve I intend to be visiting very, very shortly.

Phin Thomsen was how I knew him when we lived together as children.

Finn Thomsen is the pseudonym he's been hiding behind all these years.

I was so close. An F for a Ph. All these years, I could have found him if I'd just thought to play around with the alphabet. So clever of him. So clever. Phin was always the cleverest person I knew. Well, apart from me, of course.

I jump at the sound of a gentle knocking at my bedroom door. I sigh. 'Yes?'

'Henry, it's me. Can I come in?'

It's my sister. I sigh again and close the lid of my laptop. 'Yes, sure.'

She opens the door just wide enough to slide through and then closes it gently behind her.

Lucy is a lovely-looking woman. When I saw her last year for the first time since we were teenagers, I was taken aback by the loveliness of her. She has a face that tells stories, she looks all of her forty years, she barely grooms herself, she dresses like a bucket of rags, but somehow she still always looks lovelier than any other woman in the room. It's something about the juxtaposition of her amber-hazel eyes with the dirty gold streaks in her hair, the weightlessness of her, the rich honey of her voice, the way she moves and holds herself and touches things and looks at you. My father looked like a pork pie on legs and my lucky sister snatched all her looks from our elegant half-Turkish mother. I have fallen somewhere between the two camps. Luckily, I have my mother's physique, but sadly more than my fair share of my father's coarse facial features. I have done my best with what nature gave me. Money can't buy you love but it can buy you a chiselled jaw, perfectly aligned teeth and plumped-up lips.

My bedroom fills with the perfume of the oil my sister uses on her hair, something from a brown glass bottle that looks like she bought it from a country fayre.

'I wanted to talk to you,' she says, moving a jacket off a chair in the corner of my room so that she can sit down. 'About last week, at Libby's birthday dinner?'

I fix her with her a *yes, I'm listening, please continue* look.

'What you were saying, to Libby and Miller?'

Libby is the daughter Lucy had with Phin when she was fourteen. Miller is Libby's journalist boyfriend. I nod.

'About going to Botswana with them?'

I nod again. I know what's coming.

'Were you serious?'

'Yes. Of course I was.'

'Do you think – do you think it's a good idea?'

'Yes. I think it's a wonderful idea. Why wouldn't I?'

'I don't know. I mean, it's meant to be a romantic holiday, just for the two of them . . .'

I tut. 'He was talking about taking his mother; he can't have intended it to be that romantic.'

Obviously, I'm talking nonsense, but I'm feeling defensive. Miller wants to take Libby to Botswana to be reunited with the father she hasn't seen since she was a baby. But Phin is also a part of me. Not just a part of me, but nearly all of me. I've literally (and I'm using the word 'literally' here in its most literal sense) thought about Phin at least once an hour, every hour, since I was sixteen years old. How can I not want to go to him now, *right now*?

'I won't get in their way,' I offer. 'I will let them do their own thing.'

'Right,' says Lucy, doubtfully. 'And what will you do?'

'I'll . . .' I pause. What will I do? I have no idea. I will just be with Phin.

And then, after that – well, we shall see, shan't we?

3

August 2016

Rachel met Michael in a pharmacy in Martha's Vineyard in the late summer of 2016. She was waiting for a prescription for the morning-after pill to be dispensed to her by a very young and somewhat judgey man. Michael stepped ahead of her and greeted the pharmacist with a brisk, 'Is it done yet?'

The judgey pharmacist blinked slowly and said, 'No, sir, it is not. Could I ask you to take a seat? It won't be much longer.'

Michael took the seat next to Rachel. He folded his arms and he sighed. She could sense that he was about to talk to her, and she was right.

'That guy', he muttered, 'is just a delight.'

She laughed and turned to study him. Fortyish, to her thirtyish. Tanned, of course; at the end of a long Martha's Vineyard summer, there was nobody left without a tan. His hair was due a cut; he was probably waiting until he got back to the city.

'He's a bit judgey,' she replied in a low whisper.

'Yes,' he agreed, 'yes. Strange, in one so young.'

Rachel, at the time, had been conscious of the only-just-showered-off sweat of a boy called Aiden still clinging to her skin, the tender spots on her inner thighs where his hip bones had ground into her flesh, the sugary smell of his young man beer breath lingering in the crooks and crevices of her body. And now she was here, flirting with a man old enough to be Aiden's father whilst waiting for emergency contraception.

It really was time for Rachel to go home now. The summer had been desperate and dirty, and she was used and spent.

The pharmacist pulled a paper bag from a clip on the carousel behind him and peered at the label. 'Ms Rachel Gold?' he called out. 'I have your prescription.'

'Oh.' She smiled at Michael. 'That's me. Hope you don't have to wait too long.'

'Line-jumper,' said Michael with a sardonic smile.

She typed her PIN into the card reader and took the bag from the pharmacist. When she turned to leave, Michael was still looking at her. 'Where are you from?' he asked.

'England.'

'Yeah, obviously, but whereabouts in England?'

'London.'

'And whereabouts in London?'

'Do you know London?'

'I have an apartment in Fulham.'

'Oh,' she said. 'Right. I live in Camden Town.'

'Whereabouts?'

'Erm.' She laughed.

'Sorry. I'm an Anglophile. I'm obsessed with the place. No more questions. I'll let you get on, Rachel Gold.'

She lifted her other hand in a vague farewell and walked quickly through the shop, through the door, on to the street.

Two months later, Rachel was eating lunch at her desk in her studio when an email appeared in her inbox titled 'From the American Anglophile to the English Line-Jumper.'

It took her a beat or two, her brain trying to unscramble the sequence of seemingly unconnected words. And then she clicked it open:

Hi Rachel Gold,

This is Michael. We met in a pharmacy in Martha's Vineyard back in August. You smelled of wood smoke and beer. In a good way. I'm going to be staying in London for a few months and wondered if there was anywhere in Camden you'd recommend for me to explore. I haven't really been to the area since I was a teenager – I was looking to score some hash and ended up buying a stripy rucksack and a bong instead. I'm sure there's more to the locale than the market and the drug dealers, though, and I'd love an insider's point of view. If you are reeling in horror at the appearance of this missive in your inbox, please do delete/ignore/ call the police. (No, don't call the police!) But otherwise, it would be great to hear from you. And my slightly anal knowledge of London postcodes led me to your email address, by the way. I googled 'Rachel Gold' then 'NW1', and up you popped on your website. How apt that a jewellery designer should have the surname Gold. If only my surname were Diamond we'd make the perfect couple. As it is, it's Rimmer. Make of that what you will. Anyway, I'll hear from you if I hear from you, and if I don't, I'll buy something from your website and give it to my mother for her birthday. You're very, very talented.

Yours,

Michael

xo

Rachel sat for a moment, her breath held, trying to decide whether she wanted to smile or grimace. She brought the man's face back to mind, but she couldn't find the full extent of it. Michael C. Hall's face kept appearing and smudging it out. At the bottom of his email though was a company name. MCR International. She googled it and brought up an anonymous-looking website for what appeared to be some sort of logistics/haulage type organisation, with an address in Antibes in the south of France. She googled Michael Rimmer Antibes and after some hunting around, finally found him on a website for local news, clutching a champagne flute at a party to celebrate the launch of a new restaurant. She blew his face up and stared at it for a while on her screen. He looked nothing like Michael C. Hall. He looked . . . basic handsome is how she would describe it. Basic handsome. But in the way his white T-shirt met the waistband of a pair of blue jeans there was something sexual. Not tucked in. Not pulled down. Just skimming the edges of each other. An invitation of sorts. She found it surprisingly and suddenly thrilling and when her eye returned to his face, he looked more than basic handsome. He looked hard. Almost cruel. But Rachel didn't mind that in a man. It could work in her favour if she wanted it to.

She shut the email down. She would reply. She would meet him. She would have sex with him. All of this she knew. But not yet. Keep him waiting for a while. She was in no rush, after all.

4

June 2019

I go for a run the following morning. I must be honest and say that I really don't like running. But then neither do I like going to the gym and seeing all those perfect boys who don't even glance in my direction. The gym used to be my playground, but no longer. Now I dress down, keep my eyes low, grit my teeth until I feel that comforting, satisfying connection between my feet, the ground, my thoughts and the beat of the music in my ears, and I keep doing that until I've done a full circuit of Regent's Park. Then my day is my own.

But today I can't find that sweet spot. My breath grinds through my lungs and I keep wanting to stop, to sit down. It feels wrong. Everything has felt wrong since I found out that Phin still exists.

My feet connect with the tarmac so hard I can almost feel the bumps of the aggregate through the soles of my trainers. The sun appears suddenly through a soft curtain of June cloud, searing my vision. I pull on my sunglasses and finally stop running.

I've lost my way. And only Phin can guide me back.

I call Libby when I return home.

Lovely Libby.

'Hello, you!'

She is so very the sort of person who says 'hello, you'.

I return it as fulsomely as I can manage. 'Hello, you!'

'What's new?'

'New? Oh, nothing really. Just had a run. And a shower. Just thinking about what we were discussing at your birthday dinner the other night.'

'The safari?'

'Yes, the safari. Lucy says I shouldn't come.'

'Oh. Why?'

'She thinks that you and Miller want it to be a romantic get-away for just the two of you.'

'Oh, no, nonsense. Of course, you'd be welcome to come. But we've hit a snag.'

'A snag?'

'Yes. Miller called the lodge the other day to ask about an extra person on the booking and apparently Phin has . . .' She pauses.

'Yes?'

'He's gone.'

I sit heavily on the nearest chair, my jaw hanging slack with shock. 'Gone?'

'Yes. Said he had a family emergency. Didn't know when he'd be back.'

'But . . .' I pause. I'm fuming. Libby's boyfriend Miller is a well-regarded investigative journalist. He's spent a year of his life tracking Phin down (not for me, you understand, but for Libby) and then five seconds after finally tracing him, Miller's clearly done something utterly stupid that has resulted in Phin taking flight, the journalistic equivalent of stepping on a twig during a stag hunt.

'I don't understand,' I say, trying to sound calm. 'What went wrong?'

Libby sighs and I picture her touching the tips of her eyelashes as she often does when she's talking. 'We don't know. Miller could not have been more discreet when he made the booking. The only thing we thought is that Phin somehow recognised my name. We assumed, you know, that he would only have known me by my birth name. But maybe he knew my adopted name. Somehow.'

'I'm assuming, of course, that Miller made his own booking under a pseudonym?'

There's a brief silence. I sigh and run my hand through my wet hair. 'He must have, surely?'

'I don't know. I mean, why would he need to?'

'Because he wrote a five-thousand-word article about our family that ran in a broadsheet magazine only four years ago. And maybe Phin does more than just sit on jeeps looking masterful. Maybe he, you know, uses the internet?' I clamp my mouth shut. *Nasty nasty nasty. Don't be nasty to Libby.* 'Sorry,' I say. 'Sorry. It's just frustrating. That's all. I just thought . . .'

'I know,' she says. 'I know.'

But she doesn't know. She doesn't know at all.

'So,' I say, 'what are you planning to do? Are you still going?'

'Not sure,' she replies. 'We're thinking about it. We might postpone.'

'Or you could . . .' I begin, as a potential solution percolates, '. . . find out where he's gone?'

'Yes. Miller's doing a bit of work on the reservations guy. Seeing what he can wheedle out of him. But seems like no one there really knows much about Phin Thomsen.'

I draw the conversation to a close. Things that I cannot discuss with Libby are buzzing in particles through my mind and I need peace and quiet to let them form their shapes.

I go to the website again, for Phin's game reserve. It's a very worthy game reserve. Internationally renowned. Unimpeachable ecological, environmental, social credentials. Phin, of course, would only work in such a place.

He told me when he was fifteen years old that he was going to be a safari guide one day. I have no idea what route he took from the house of horrors we grew up in to get there, but he did it. Did I want to be the founding partner of a trendy boutique software design solutions company, back then, when I was a child? No, of course I didn't. I wanted to be whatever life threw at me. The thing that I would be after I'd done all the normal things that people do when they haven't grown up in a house of horrors and then spent their young adulthood living alone in bedsits, with no academic qualifications, no friends and no family. I wanted to be *that thing*. But, in the story that this spinning Rolodex of endless and infinite universes gave to me, this is where I am and I should be glad and grateful. And in a way I am. I guess in another of those universes I might, like my father before me, have sat and got fat whilst waiting for my parents to die so that I could claim my inheritance. I might have lived a life of boredom and indolence. But I had no option other than to work and I've made a success of my life and I guess that's a good thing, isn't it?

But Phin, of course, Phin knew what he wanted even then. He didn't wait to be formed by the universe. He shaped the universe to his will.

I head into work and find the same lack of focus plagues me through a conference call and two meetings. I snap at people I've never snapped at before and then feel filled with self-loathing. When I get home at seven that evening, my nephew Marco is wedged on to the sofa with a friend from school, a pleasant boy I've met before and have made an effort to be nice to. He gets to his feet when I walk in and says, 'Hi, Henry, Marco said it was OK if I came. I hope you don't mind.' His name is Alf and he is delightful. But right now I don't want him on my sofa, and I don't even spare him a smile. I grunt: 'Please tell me you're not planning to cook?'

Alf throws Marco an uncertain look; then they both shake their heads. 'No,' says Alf, 'no, we were just going to hang.'

I nod tersely and head to my room.

I know what I'm going to do. And I really do have to do something, or I'll explode. I can't sit around waiting for the lugubrious Miller Roe to sort this out. I need to sort it out myself.

I go on to Booking.com, and I book myself a four-day, all-inclusive 'Gold Star' stay at the Chobe Game Lodge in Botswana.

For one.

5

October 2016

At thirty-two years of age, Rachel tried not to dwell too much on the fact that her entire adult existence was a mirage. Her flat was owned by her father, who also bankrolled her business. It had happened so gradually, this reliance on her father's adoration and generosity, that she hadn't noticed when it had tipped over from being 'what parents do to help their kids get started in life' to something she was too embarrassed to talk about. Her jewellery business was making money but was not yet in profit. She could fool herself that it was in profit once a month when her allowance arrived and tipped her accounts over from red to black. But really she was at least a year away from making a proper living, and even then it would depend on everything going right and nothing going wrong. In six months she would be thirty-three, a long way from the benign shores of thirty, the age she thought she'd be when she finally became fully independent of her father.

But to the objective onlooker, Rachel Gold cut an impressive figure: five foot ten, athletic, groomed, slightly aloof. She looked like a self-made woman, a woman who made her own mortgage payments and paid for her own gym membership and had her own Uber account.

On a Friday evening in late October, a week after the unexpected email from the American guy, to which she had still not replied, Rachel went for drinks after work with the woman from the studio next door in her complex on the cusp between West Hampstead and Kilburn. Paige was twenty-three and still lived with her mum, but made her own money, enough to pay her mum some rent, enough to pay for her own holidays and her own drinks and her own eyebrow tinting. Paige made jewellery from base metals, unlike Rachel who used gold and platinum. Paige lived below her means and saved. She'd left art school only two years earlier, but she was already more of a grown-up than Rachel.

In the pub Rachel got the first round: a bottle of Pinot Grigio. There were heaters on the terrace, so they drank it outside, with blankets draped over their knees. Rachel asked Paige about her love life. Paige said, 'Nil. Nada. Zero. Zilch. You?'

'A guy,' Rachel began, hesitantly at first and then with an unexpected swell of certainty that this was a conversation she needed to have. 'I met him in the States, this summer, then he stalked me down on the internet and wrote to me via my website. Said he's going to be in London for a few months and wants to meet up. I kind of . . .' She placed the wine bottle into the cooler. 'I kind of can't stop thinking about him. At first I was like, I dunno, thought maybe it was a bit creepy. He's older, as well.'

'God. How much older?'

'Like, maybe, ten years? Early forties, I'd say. Here.' She turned her phone to face Paige, showing her the photo of Michael Rimmer she'd saved into her camera roll.

'Hot.'

'You think?'

'Yeah. In that way. You know?'

'What way?' She narrowed her eyes at Paige, not wanting her to echo back her own strange thoughts about this unexpected man.

'Looks like he'd fuck you hard. Then lie there, bollock naked, with his arms behind his head and ask you to get him a drink.'

'Fuck.' She snatched the phone back from Paige's hand.

'Which could be, you know, a good thing? Yes?'

'God. I don't know. Yeah, maybe. But no. Good and bad, I reckon. I'm going to be thirty-three next year. Is that what I want?'

'I dunno – you tell me?' Paige peered at her quizzically, a challenge in her gaze.

'No. No. I mean, yes. For fun. But not for marriage, babies, all that.'

'Is that what you want?'

'No, not really, but I might want it and I don't want to be stuck with a guy who doesn't do nurture then, do I? You've got to have a guy who nurtures if you're doing babies. And this guy' – she cast her gaze down again at Michael Rimmer clutching his champagne glass in a tacky Côte d'Azur restaurant – 'he does not look like a nurturer.'

'Well,' said Paige. 'If you're not ready for babies and marriage, why don't you just go for him as your last one that's not "the one". He's only in London for a few months. Just use him.'

A surge of nervous energy passed through Rachel at Paige's suggestion. She'd just put Rachel's own thoughts into words.

'Yeah,' she said. 'Yeah. Maybe I will.'

6

June 2019

Lucy approaches a young man in a tight grey suit clutching a folder. She puts a hand out towards him and he shakes it.

'Max Blackwood,' he says. 'You must be Lucy. Lovely to meet you. Did you find it all right?'

'Absolutely,' she replies, 'just popped it into Google Maps. Getting about is easy these days, isn't it?'

'Very true,' he replies and then regales her with stories of Google Maps getting it wrong and guiding people up dead-end roads and into meadows full of sheep and people's back gardens. While he talks, they walk slowly towards the house. Lucy tries not to betray her awe and excitement. She's wearing clothes picked out for her by Henry, her brother. He said, 'If you're looking at million-pound houses you need to look like you have a million pounds.' He'd dragged her up and down Marylebone High Street, in and out of trendy French boutiques, and made her buy a house-hunting wardrobe of soft T-shirts and tailored trousers and sweeping maxi dresses and blazers and bright white trainers with metallic patterns. Then he put her into a salon for three hours with a man called Jed who chopped eight inches off her sun-frazzled hair and streaked the rest of it with strands of vanilla blonde.

Henry had made her have her teeth whitened shortly after she moved in with him. She'd noticed him flinching every time she smiled and eventually said, 'Is there something wrong with my teeth?' and he'd said, 'I suppose it's easy to lose sight of things like that when you haven't had regular access to a mirror for so long.'

Such a shit, her big brother. He hid it with a mischievous veneer of dark humour, but she sometimes suspected that the darkness ran much deeper.

She flips up her sunglasses from her nose to her hair and looks at the house in front of her. It's a four-bedroom former vicarage just outside St Albans. It has an orchard and a wooden swing set and a trampoline and a two-hundred-foot lawned garden with a ramshackle gazebo at the end. It has stone-mullioned windows with gargoyles stationed above. It has a double front door with brass knockers and boot scrapers and built-in benches either side. It's scruffy and a bit tired. The curtains she can see through the windows are sun-bleached and shredded. But it is essentially one of the most beautiful houses she has ever seen in her life. She maintains a poker face and says, 'It's lovely.'

'It really is,' he says, sorting through the keys in his hand to find the one that unlocks the front door. 'Not the sort of place that comes up very often. Are you familiar with the area at all?'

'Yes,' she says. 'My daughter lives in St Albans, near the centre.'

The words still give her a shiver of pleasure. *My daughter*. Libby Jones. Serenity Lamb. The daughter she had to leave behind as a baby, and then found again a year ago, when she'd just turned twenty-five. She has soft blonde hair, Libby Jones, and pale blue eyes, and she holds your gaze when you talk to her in a way that makes you feel you can say anything to her and she will absorb it without judgement. She has a London accent: not a cut-glass English accent like Lucy, who went to a school where they made her wear a straw boater and a blouse with a pie-crust collar, but an accent with the edges cut off and flattened, bits missing at the ends of certain words, an accent formed at comprehensive schools and in suburban terraced houses. She has freckles on her arms and wears her hair in a side parting; she tucks it behind her ear every few minutes, and sometimes she touches the tips of her eyelashes with her finger, as if checking that they're still there. She smells of vanilla. She washes her hands a lot. She likes fruit. Her handwriting is very neat. She is amazing.

'Oh,' says Max, now, turning to smile at her. 'That's good. She'll be happy to have Mum up the road, I'm sure.'

The house is empty. The owners have already downsized to a new-build apartment. They've left the bare bones of some furniture behind, to create the impression of a much-loved family home, but in effect the spareness of it serves only to highlight the fact that the intense universe which once existed within these four walls has come to an end: children flown, the noise and chaos of a family unit truncated down to two middle-aged people in a flat somewhere, existing quietly in the spaces between visits and phone calls.

'It is a bit of a doer-upper,' Max says now, searching for light switches as he goes. 'The owners did spend quite a lot of money on it when they bought it, but obviously that was over twenty years ago. So, it is a *little bit* last century, let us say.'

Lucy already knows she's going to buy it. She knew she was going to buy it the moment she saw the details on the internet. It has an unconventional layout. Lucy was brought up in a house with symmetry at its core: a central hallway with evenly sized rooms that mirrored each other on either side. She does not want symmetry. She wants nooks and crannies and funny little alcoves and unexpected passages leading to rooms that don't make sense.

Upstairs the bedroom doors still bear the names of the children who once slept behind them. Oliver. Maddy. Milly.

They're soft names but the damage those children appear to have wrought in their house doesn't back that up: ripped wallpaper, felt-tip scribbles, something neon green stuck to the cheap carpets underfoot – slime probably.

After a year living in Henry's immaculate apartment, having to remove her shoes at the front door, having to use special sprays to mop up benign spillages, adopt a coded system of cloths for different surfaces, having to constantly police her children to make sure they aren't about to drop anything or stain anything or damage anything, she wants this – a house to bash about in, a house to drop slime in, a house to absorb them and their imperfections.

She ignores the rust stains in the sinks and the toilet bowls, the green water marks around the bath taps, the missing pane of stained glass covered over with brown chipboard in the laundry cupboard. She will happily pay a million pounds for a house that is scuffed up and kicked about, for dirty carpets and broken windows and a trampoline with moss growing on it. She will pay anything to put walls around the small family that she has brought up on streets, on beaches, on sofas, in temporary accommodation – and, for the first few years of Marco's life, in the home of an abuser.

Once the tour is over she walks back to her car and takes the particulars from Max, shakes his hand again and bids him farewell. She places the papers on the passenger seat, then puts Henry's address into Google Maps. But before she pulls away, she types a quick text to Libby:

Just seen the house in Burrow's End. It's perfect. Going to make an offer. Eek!

Then she sets the phone into its holder and pulls away, watching her house in the rear-view mirror until it's completely swallowed up by trees.

7

October 2016

Later that night Rachel worded her reply to Michael Rimmer. She was not entirely sober, but neither was she too drunk to negotiate her keyboard.

Dear Michael,

It was MOST surprising to find your message in my email. MOST surprising INDEED. But not unpleasant or unwelcome. And thank you for your kind words about my designs. For context and colour, I live in an apartment overlooking the canal, on the way towards King's Cross. I live alone. I have no pets. I drink and sometimes I smoke. Yes, I am Bridget Jones, thank you so much for asking.

I'd love to take you out carousing in the area. Here's my mobile number – send me a text when you're free and we'll hatch a plan.

Yours,

Rachel

She read it through just once, before pressing send and propelling it forcefully, wantonly, thoughtlessly into the universe, where it would change the course of her life in ways that she could not possibly have imagined.

A reply from Michael was waiting for her when she awoke the next day. It was almost midday. She'd missed a yoga class. She always missed her yoga class. She'd booked and prepaid for twelve classes eight weeks ago and thus far had been to only two. She grabbed her phone and tugged out the charging cable, switched it on, and there he was. Michael Rimmer, the man she'd rashly invited into her life the night before with a bottle of wine, a vodka shot and a small bowl of stuffed olives inside her.

Hello Rachel!

So good to hear back from you! And I think you can probably guess that Bridget Jones is just about my dream woman, so we're good there. I'm flying in on the 8th, so how about meeting up one night that week? I'll text you when I'm here. And I am so looking forward to spending some time with you. Truly.

Yours,

Michael

Rachel sighed. Was she having second thoughts? Not quite. Maybe a thought and a half. But still, the 8th was ten days away. Michael Rimmer might have died by then. She might have died by then. His plane might come down over the Atlantic. No point stressing about it. No point worrying. If Michael Rimmer was meant to be, then Michael Rimmer would be.

Ten days later, a text arrived:

Hi! Rachel! It's Michael Rimmer! I just got into London. How are you fixed for tomorrow night?

Rachel felt her insides jolt. She hadn't heard a word from Michael Rimmer since he'd replied to her drunken email. She'd been chatting to a guy on Tinder, a bit younger than her, but quite mature. Charlie. A medical supplies courier. Lived in south-east London somewhere. God knows. South-east London was a mystery to Rachel. But they'd been chatting quite intensely. They'd covered family and dreams and ambitions and regrets, even a smattering of politics. But Charlie still hadn't asked to meet her and, frankly, Rachel was too long in the tooth to sit around waiting for boys called Charlie to suggest getting together for a drink. And there was Michael Rimmer, brazenly elbowing his way to the front of the queue with his four-sentence text message, straight down to business in a way that suggested to Rachel that she might be having sex by this time tomorrow. And she really wanted to be having sex by this time tomorrow.

She scrolled through her camera roll to find the photo of Michael Rimmer she'd screenshot after he'd first written to her, the one where he was holding champagne, looking well fed and self-possessed. She zoomed it open with her fingers and rolled the image around the screen awhile, imagining him.

Then she switched screens to his text message and typed in fast:

Yes. Sure. Come to mine, we'll head out from here.

Michael Rimmer appeared in her doorway at 7 p.m. the following evening, glowing with a tan from a country where it was still summer. He had flowers. He had champagne. She put the flowers in water and the champagne in the fridge and took him out for cocktails because if they opened the champagne now they'd be having sex within twenty minutes and she wanted to enjoy the lingering experience of a proper date, the building up of unbearable sexual tension, before they crossed that line.

He was more handsome than she recalled. Less basic. He wore a pale blue shirt and jeans and trainers. He smelled of clothes just taken out of a suitcase and a light aftershave cologne that Rachel couldn't identify. He held doors for her and pulled out chairs for her in a way that Charlie the medical supplies courier would have been very unlikely to have done.

Michael ordered himself a Margarita, Rachel a Dark 'n' Stormy, and then they talked.

'Do you have any kids?' he asked her.

She started slightly. Being asked if she had kids felt as odd to her as being asked if she still had all her own teeth. Rachel still felt young, far too young to be viewed as a mother. But Michael wasn't the first man to ask her this over the past year or two; somehow, without even noticing, she had crossed some invisible line into the 'mother' zone. She tried not to blanch at the question and said, 'No, no. Not yet. How about you?'

She saw his face light up. 'Yeah,' he said. 'Yeah. Just the one. A boy. Marco. He's . . . well, he was born in 2006, so God, he must be about ten, I guess?'

'You don't sound very sure.'

'It's complicated. I haven't seen him for a while.'

'Divorced?'

'Yes. Divorced. And my ex . . .' He let out a puff of air that signified his ex was problematic. 'Well, you know, it's messy, it's complicated, my ex knows where to find me, but she chooses not to. She has a chaotic life. I offered to support her, her and the boy. But she pretty much ghosted me. So yeah. It's sad. Marco, my God if you saw him, just the most exquisitely beautiful boy. But living a life that isn't going to end well.'

Rachel saw Michael's eyes glaze with tears, and felt the encounter shift into another gear, a shift that seemed as if it might impinge on the unspoken promise of inevitable sex that had laced every moment of their previous communications, but might also take them somewhere else, somewhere completely unexpected, somewhere grown-up and real.

She put her hand out to cover his. He turned his hand over and curled his fingers around her palm.

'It's OK,' he said, his eyes dry once more. 'It's just a shame, you know, the way life can take you away from the things that matter.'

'Did you ever try to get custody?'

'No,' he replied, caressing her hand gently. 'No. It was a quickie divorce; she didn't want anything from me. I thought we'd work things out in the fullness of time. I saw Marco a lot at first. But then I went back to the US for a few weeks, on business, and when I returned to the south of France . . .' He pulled his hand from hers and used it to describe a puff of smoke.

'So, you live in the south of France?'

'I live in a lot of places. But yeah, I have a house in Antibes. It's pink. I have a pink house. You'd love it.'

'What shade of pink? Not, like, hot pink?'

'No. No. A very subtle pink – my ex used to say it was the colour of dead roses.'

'Dead roses? Wow. That's kind of bizarrely poetic.'

'Yup, well, Lucy is a kind of bizarrely poetic woman.'

Lucy, Rachel thought. *Lucy*. That is the name of the woman. The woman who came before.

8

June 2019

Lucy turns the key in the lock of Henry's front door, her breath held hard inside her as it always is when she returns. Not because she thinks anything bad will have happened, but because she knows that Henry would rather never hear the sound of her key in his lock ever again and that the very fact of her walking into his apartment, of resting her bag upon his table, of calling his name, of opening his fridge, of drawing and exhaling her breath within the area formed between the four walls that delineate his own, very private space, will cause him pain of the sort that will translate into a sharp comment, or a pedantic complaint, or just a brooding presence behind the door of his bedroom, a door that stays shut more and more frequently these days.

Stella is on a playdate at Freya G's (they call her Freya G

because her other best friend is also called Freya) and Marco is playing some kind of video game on the big plasma screen in the living room with his nice friend Alf. Lucy casts a nervous eye at the passageway that leads to the bedrooms, hoping that the sound is not carrying to Henry's room.

'Turn it down a tiny bit,' she asks gently. Marco doesn't glance up, but reaches for the remote and turns it down.

Alf turns round and smiles at Lucy. 'Hi, Lucy,' he says, 'how are you?'

'I'm fine,' she says. 'How are you?'

'I'm good. I'm . . . Oh, shit—' He's gone, his attention back on the game on the screen, and Lucy goes to the kitchen and pours herself a glass of wine.

She wants to tell Henry about the amazing house in St Albans, but she knows he'll take one look at the particulars and tell her that she is mad, that she is wrong, that she is about to make a huge mistake. He will tell her that it is a money pit, that she doesn't understand property, that she will regret it. She doesn't want to hear those things.

Before Henry has a chance to make her question her judgement or change her mind, Lucy emails the estate agent and makes an offer.

The following morning Lucy notices that Henry's bedroom door is still closed at eight fifty when she gets home from dropping Stella at school. Normally he is just leaving for work at this time, sometimes she even crosses paths with him on the pavement out-side the apartment block. She tiptoes down the hallway and very quietly pulls down the handle of his bedroom door, then pushes it fully ajar when she realises that there is no one in his room, that his bed is made, his blinds are open.

She calls out to him, in case he is in his en suite, but there is no response.

Henry must, she assumes, have had an early meeting. But she's only been out of the house for twenty minutes. His shower is dry. There is no condensation on the mirror. He was definitely not up when she left; he can't possibly have awoken, got ready and left in the time she's been out of the house. Henry would never leave the house without showering.

She is about to type a message into her phone when she notices something: Henry's toothbrush is not in his bathroom. He has a fancy electric one that charges on a base via a USB cable. It has multiple settings and a blue light and usually sits on the marble surface of his vanity unit, flashing on and off. It's not there.

Something grips Lucy's gut then. She remembers something: a shard of a moment, awaking from a deep sleep when it was still dark outside, Fitz, at the foot of her bed, ears pricked, a low growl rumbling at the base of his throat. They'd both lain for a while, absolutely still, heard the dull hum of the lift going down the shaft in the corridor beyond the apartment, and then fallen back to sleep.

She'd assumed that someone outside the apartment had woken them up, but maybe it was someone inside.

She switches on her phone and words a message to Henry:
Where ru?

She stares at the tick. It stays single and grey. According to the app, Henry was last seen online at 7.45 a.m.

She pulls open his wardrobes and his drawers. She doesn't

know what she's looking for, but she knows what she thinks. She thinks that Henry left the apartment in the middle of the night to catch a flight to Botswana, to look for Phin. And for some deep-seated and sickening reason, the thought of Henry finding him fills her with fear.

9

Business-class travel. If you haven't done it, then you can only imagine it. And once you have done it, you can never unimagine it – you are ruined for life. It is probably the single greatest reason to be wealthy that there is.

I sip my champagne. It's barely nine o'clock in the morning, I've been up since 3 a.m. and my palate is nowhere near ready for the sour audacity of it, but I drink it nonetheless because I can. I picture Lucy in London, returning from her school run, wondering why I'm not bustling about in the kitchen, wondering where I am. I suspect she will guess, and quickly. We may be very different, Lucy and I, but our connection runs deep, even after twenty-five years apart. You find that with children who've shared a childhood trauma: it's like a fine wire that runs between you; you can feel the tug on it from time to time. And I feel it now. I know that she's about to call Libby, that Libby will call Miller, that my disappearance is about to become a thing, a drama. But hey-ho. I'm in the air. By the time I get off this flight, they will not have a clue how to track me down.

They will think I've gone to Botswana. But I have not gone to Botswana. I am on my way to Chicago.

It's all a bit last-minute. Obviously.

I had booked a flight to Victoria Falls Airport and a hire car to take me on to the reserve. I have lost a lot of money but thankfully the hotel booking was cancellable so at least I have that back. And frankly, I'm rather glad I don't have to go to a game reserve in Africa. It's not really my idea of a good time, whereas Chicago very much is.

So, why Chicago?

Well, late last night I went on to Tripadvisor to look at reviews of the Chobe Game Lodge. I thought it would be good to have a better idea of where exactly I was going and what exactly I was letting myself in for. And I came upon a review from a very jolly, chatty woman who'd stayed there as a single person two weeks earlier. Her review was full of name checks for members of staff she'd found particularly helpful and kind and she sounded like the type of person who would be more than happy to share her experiences with a complete stranger messaging her out of the blue. And indeed she was. Nancy Romano from New Jersey. So chatty. I asked if she had any recommendations amongst the tour guides; was there someone in particular maybe I should look out for who was more knowledgeable than the others?

Yes! she replied. *Look out for Finn! He's English, like you, quite quiet, but so insightful and knowledgeable, has a lovely way with words and really brings the scene to life. Such a nice man.*

I replied along the lines of what a shame as someone else had recommended him but according to the reservations team, it seemed he'd disappeared on a family emergency.

Oh, yes, Nancy had replied. *He has family in Chicago, I believe. I hope nothing terrible has happened.*

Who knows whether the 'family in Chicago' is fictional or real?

The four of us – me, Lucy, Phin, his sister Clemency – we've all had to live covertly and dishonestly, we've all had to fly under the radar, change our names, build fake lives and backstories for ourselves. I didn't have a passport until ten years ago; I used to pretend I had a phobia of flying to get out of invitations to go abroad with friends, which I then had to extend into a phobia of tunnels when someone suggested going to France on the Eurostar. So it's highly possible that Phin has a stock narrative that he uses to explain himself to strangers. But I don't know, I have a strong feeling that this other life in Chicago might be true. And either way, I suppose I'm about to find out.

10

November 2016

Rachel turned and quietly sniffed the crown of Michael's head. If you liked the smell of someone's scalp, she'd always theorised, then you were probably sexually compatible. And she did like the smell of Michael's scalp. It had the scent of someone who shampooed daily, who never slept on grubby pillowcases or pulled on a sweaty baseball cap or ate a cheap burger and then ran their fingers through their hair. It had squeaky clean tones of sandalwood and citrus, but just enough musky hormonal tang to differentiate it from a spray of cheap room perfume.

She examined Michael's face. Interesting to look upon the face of a man past his first flush of youth. Some open pores in the creases of his nostrils, deep lines in the forehead, and a sharp line down each side of his mouth, but his skin still soft and plumped up. She wondered if he used any products; she strongly suspected he might go for professional facials. She didn't have a problem with that.

The night had been a success inasmuch as they had had good conversation, good food and good sex. And now it was nearly 8 a.m. and here she was, sniffing his scalp, examining his pores, finding him attractive even as he slept. Rachel could count on one hand the number of dates she'd had which she could describe in such glowing terms.

Details of the previous night came back to her in shards. She remembered talk of his house in Martha's Vineyard ('no pool, but a hot tub with a view to die for'). She remembered talk of a boat moored in the Antibes harbour. The boat had a name; something to do with diamonds? Or silver? There was talk of a chalet in a ski resort. 'Well, it's more of a condo, I guess you'd say, but feels bigger than that.' Rachel had never skied but the name of the resort had sounded familiar, so she assumed it was one of the expensive ones.

'Do you like skiing?'

'No,' she'd replied drily. 'But I do like drinking and I do like eating.'

'Well then, you'd like a ski holiday.'

'That's what I thought.'

They'd left after two cocktails and a shared platter of char-cuterie and wended their way back to her apartment where they'd opened the champagne and stood for a while on the balcony over-looking the canal, laughing about the stench of it, each finding more and more outlandish language to describe it: 'Cheap pork sausage with a hint of rancid mackerel and an undertone of last night's jism.'

Then he'd said, as their laughter died away, 'I want to kiss you; let's go indoors.'

She'd been expecting it to be harder, more urgent, more *all fours*, less *staring into his eyes*. She'd been pleasantly surprised by the emotional intensity of it.

Surprised, but also unnerved.

Michael Rimmer was meant to be her 'last hurrah'.

Not her first husband.

Rachel met her dad for lunch later that day. He wanted to know all about her date with 'the American guy'.

She played it down. 'He was nice,' she said, leaning out of the way so that the waiter could place her Prosecco in front of her. 'You'd like him.'

'I would?' Her father raised an eyebrow at her.

'Yeah. I reckon. He's smart, charming, successful.'

'Old.'

'Old-ish.'

'How old, exactly?'

'Forty-six.'

'Hm.'

'Hm, what?'

'Why isn't he married?'

'I don't know, Dad. Why aren't I married?'

He laughed out loud as he tore a bread roll in half, then rubbed his floury fingertips against the linen napkin on his lap. 'Well, just watch out. A man his age who's never been married . . .'

'He has been married.'

'What? But you just said—'

'I said he isn't married. He has been married. He's divorced. He has a son.'

'Baggage.'

'Well, sort of. But not really. He doesn't see the son. The ex won't let him.'

Her father collapsed back against his chair theatrically. 'Oh, Rachel.'

'Look,' Rachel interjected. 'It's not serious. OK? He's only here for six months. It's just some fun. Don't overthink it.'

'Someone has to overthink things, Rachel. Someone has to think about things, full stop.'

The conversation moved on then, as it always did, to the business.

These conversations had once been exciting and energising when she'd been a twenty-something whose dad was 'helping her get it off the ground'. Now that he was basically bankrolling her, the conversations made her feel inadequate and edgy.

On her phone she opened the app she ran her business through to show her dad her latest orders. But something looked wrong about the lines of figures in the columns, out of proportion. She clicked on the newest order and stared at it numbly for a moment.

Someone had ordered £54,000 worth of jewellery. In one order. Including the white gold eternity ring with yellow diamonds that was the most expensive single item of jewellery available on her website at £8,500.

'You OK, sweetheart?' her dad asked.

'Er, yeah. Just had a big order. Like a really big order.' She turned the phone to show him. She watched his face light up, his hands clap together.

'There. You see? All along. What did I say? You just need one big order and then you'll be flying.'

She was only half listening to him. Mentally she was calculating how long it would take her to fulfil the order, how quickly she could get hold of the gems – she kept only a small amount in stock – and her heart raced gently with the beginnings of stress.

'I'm not sure,' she said, scrolling down the items on the big order. 'I'm not sure I'm going to be able to fulfil this, not in six weeks. Not on my own.'

'Well,' her father replied, 'you need to bring someone in. Maybe someone from college? Or is there anyone else in your studio complex? That nice girl next door?'

'Paige?'

'Yes. Paige. Here's what you do. Write to the customer. Advise them that because of the size of the order it will be closer to eight weeks than six weeks for delivery. Tell them you'll need a fifty per cent deposit up front. Bring Paige in, on a ten per cent basis. Work every hour of every day. Fulfil the order. Simple. Yes?'

Rachel nodded, but her heart wasn't convinced, and neither was her gut. She pressed the back button on her phone and then the 'Customer details' tab. And then she breathed in sharply.

Michael Rimmer
Flat 4, Moynihan Mansions
Radcliffe Gardens
London
SW6 2AS

'Rachel?'

She glanced up at her dad.

'It's going to be fine, you know. You can do this. You can totally do this.'

She quickly shut down the 'Customer details' page on her phone and smiled at her dad. 'Yes,' she said. 'Yes, I think I can.'

11

June 2019

Lucy's phone trills and she glances at it where it sits on the dining table in front of her. It's not the estate agent and it's not Henry. It's a text from Stella's school. Something to do with a cake sale. She ignores it. She can't think about cake sales when her head is full of houses and Henry.

She picks up her empty plate and takes it to the dishwasher, making sure to stack it in size order with the ones already in there: biggest at the back to the smallest at the front. Sometimes, when she fails to do this, she can hear Henry rearranging them, once at three in the morning when he'd just got in from a night out. Then she remembers that Henry is probably halfway across the world and that she can stack the dishwasher however she chooses, so she takes the plate out and slots it at the front with the small plates.

Her phone trills again. It's Stella's school again. A PS to the previous text about cake sales.

Could all volunteers arrive through the back gates which will be opened for you at 3.20 p.m. Thank you!

Lucy is still baffled by English schools. In France the teachers want nothing to do with the parents; they'd rather children didn't actually *have* any parents, she'd sometimes thought. Here the parents virtually live at the school: reading sessions in the classroom, special assemblies for parents to attend, cake sales every five minutes it sometimes seems.

It's two o'clock. Lucy has nothing to do until she collects Stella but worry, so she pulls a recipe book down from Henry's small collection on a small shelf in the kitchen and flicks through it for inspiration. The children of Havering Primary School, W1, she suspects, will not be interested in a lemon and pomegranate roulade, or a beetroot and cream cheese loaf cake, so she googles 'fairy cakes' on her phone, finds a recipe called 'world's easiest fairy cakes' and starts to gather the ingredients together.

At ten past three she says goodbye to Fitz and carries a Tupperware box around the corner to the school. She smiles politely at some of the other mothers gathered by the back gate, all clutching shopping bags and their own Tupperware containers, as they wait for it to be opened. She has held back from getting to know the parents at Stella's school; she doesn't linger at the gates in the morning, or in the playground. There will be questions she doesn't want to answer. And besides, her time in this area is almost coming to an end. But she knows how happy Stella will be when she leaves her classroom this afternoon and sees her mum with all the other mums behind the trestle tables.

The caretaker appears at the gate, and they file through into the school's tiny, urban playground. A mother in a silk robe and head scarf smiles at her and says, 'Which year is your child?'

Lucy has to stop and think, she's so used to the French system. Then she says, 'Year one.'

'Yes. Me too. This is our table.' They unload their cakes; the other mother has brought three trays of cupcakes from Tesco. As she unpeels the packages she says, slightly defensively, 'We don't have an oven in our room, just a microwave.'

Lucy nods. She wants to say, 'Please don't be apologetic, I once lived in a single room with my children, without an oven. I once lived on the street with my children.' But that's a conversation she doesn't want to have. She looks down at the trainers Henry made her buy from Whistles and she thinks of the two million pounds sitting in her bank account and she feels a wave of horror and disgust at her own good fortune pass over her. She wants to give her money to this woman, so that her life can be changed and transformed. She wants to give her money to everyone who lives as she once lived.

She takes her cakes from their box and lays them out on a tray. Each one is iced either pink or blue, with a chocolate button on the top. She thinks of the mess she's left in the kitchen, the sink piled with bowls and spatulas and baking trays. She thinks again of Henry, wherever Henry is, and feels a strange wave of discomfort pass across her consciousness. More mothers arrive and add their cakes to the display; they all chat to each other over Lucy's head, then classes begin to spill out from the school building and Lucy scans the playground for the golden ringlets of her daughter. And there she is, her girl, her face lighting up at the sight of her mother. She runs from her friends, the Freyas, and to the front of the trestle table. 'Did you make cakes?' she asks breathlessly.

'Yes,' says Lucy. 'These ones.'

Stella gasps slightly at the sight of the pinks and the blues. 'Can I have one?'

'Yes, but we have to pay for it.'

'How much?'

Lucy turns to the woman in the headscarf. 'How much do we charge?' she asks.

'For those?' She gestures at Lucy's cakes. 'Fifty p?'

There are twelve cakes. That's six pounds. She thinks about how far six pounds would go in a school like this where 90 per cent of the children are on a pupil premium and she unzips her wallet, pulls out a twenty-pound note and surreptitiously slides it into the money box before handing Stella a fairy cake.

The cake sale passes in a blur of outstretched fingers and sticky coins and suddenly there are no cakes left and it's nearly 4 p.m. and the caretaker is helping to put away the trestle tables. Lucy holds open a black bin bag and Stella fills it with litter and used paper napkins. There is a sense of camaraderie as the mothers file from the playground and on to the pavement. Lucy finds herself chatting in French to a woman from the Ivory Coast about the maths homework that had been set the week before which appeared to have a number missing. She manages to sound as though she cares, but she really doesn't.

The mothers disperse in four directions and Lucy takes Stella's hand and they are about to turn to head home when she feels her phone buzz in her handbag and a sixth sense makes her stop and pull it out.

And there it is, as she'd expected.

A message from Henry.

It's a photo of him on an aeroplane clutching a small glass of champagne and the words:

Sayonara, little sister. I'm off to Phinland!!

Lucy feels a cold slick of dread pass through her. Henry's tone is light-hearted, but his intent, she knows with a terrible certainty, may be anything but.

12

I have booked myself a double room in the best hotel in the North-alsted district of Chicago. I chose it mainly at random but also with a sprinkling of logic. Northalsted used to be known as Boys-town and is the most inclusive LGBT district in the whole of the USA. I have no idea if Phin is actually gay; he never said that he was. But I have always assumed that he was and although he may not live in this specific area, he or people who know him may frequent it.

I lie down on my lovely hotel bed and look at my phone. There's a message from Lucy. In fact, there are multiple messages from Lucy and I realise with a kick of anxiety that at some point during the nine-hour flight, I had drunkenly sent her a text telling her what I was doing and it must have sent automatically when I switched on my phone at O'Hare.

Where are you going?

Do you know where he is??

Henry? Where are you? Please talk to me before you talk to Phin.

Henry. WTF are you up to????

I sigh. Sober Henry would not have let Drunk Henry send that message for precisely this reason. This *mild hysteria*. This idea that I am *up to no good*. I can't possibly deal with Lucy now. This has nothing to do with her and everything to do with me. I block her number with a flourishing hand gesture and go instead to my camera roll, where I click on the only photo I have of Phin, the one I downloaded from the safari website.

I had been quite taken aback when I saw this photo for the first time last week. Phin had been so immaculate when we lived together. The slick of blond hair that always hung just so, slightly over one eye. The clear, poreless skin. The tightly defined cheek-bones, smooth jawline, softly sculpted lips. That was the face I had been chasing my whole life; with every visit to every cosmetic surgeon, with every beauty treatment, that was what I'd been hoping to recreate. But Phin was not that person any more. Phin has not remained, like me, a creepy boy-child, just on the cusp of curdling, he has embraced his adulthood, his manhood, allowed his soft skin to crisp in the African sun, allowed lines to etch themselves into his features, and hidden over half of his beauty with a large sandy beard.

I shower and re-dress and make myself smell good and look approachable. I exit the foyer of the hotel and wander towards a strip of trendy bare-brick bars and teal-velvet brasseries and chichi restaurants with one syllable names. It's 6 p.m. and the warm night air is full of anticipation, possibility, sex.

I'm following my instincts here, entirely. I don't have a game plan. I don't have any kind of plan really. I push open the door of a bar called The Gray Area and I go to the bar and order a shot of Mezcal, for my nerves, and a glass of Pinot Gris, for something to hold on to. And then I approach a group of men, who look to be in their late thirties to early forties, and I ramp up the English accent to the max and I say, 'Sorry to be so rude. My name is Joshua Harris and I'm looking for an old friend who might have gone missing. His name is Phin. Phin Thomsen.'

Their heads dip together towards the image on my phone. One of them uses his fingers to draw the image closer. They shake their heads and apologise.

I repeat this a dozen times, and a dozen times I get shaken heads and apologies. I move to the bar next door; this one is a little rougher and has a bearded DJ on a graffitied platform playing the sort of music that I cannot bear. I order myself a second glass of Pinot Gris and ask the girl behind the bar if she has ever seen Phin Thomsen, the man in the photo on my phone. She says no. I take my wine glass and I tour the bar, interrupting conversations here and there, having to shout somewhat now to be heard over the music. I see another bartender appear and head back to the bar to show him the photo. I show the DJ the photo. I leave this bar and head to another bar. I stay out until 3 a.m., I show Phin's photo to a hundred, maybe two hundred people. Nobody knows him. Nobody has ever seen him before. It's fine. I don't know what else I could have expected, really. And tomorrow is another day.

13

November 2016

Rachel kept her finger pressed hard against the brass button at the entrance of the red-brick mansion block in Fulham. Then she stopped and waited. No reply. She pressed down again. No reply. She pulled her phone from her handbag and stabbed at the screen with shaking fingers, then slammed the phone to her ear and waited for him to pick up her call.

'Well, hi. How are you?'

Rachel moved the phone to her other ear and said, 'Not good. Not good at all. Where are you?'

'I'm just heading back to my apartment from the shops. Where are you?'

'I'm outside your block.'

'Oh. Fantastic. I will pick up my pace. Wait right there.'

She felt a little disarmed by the lightness of his response to hearing she was standing outside his apartment. Many of the men she'd dated in recent years would have classified it as stalking and been quite keen to keep away from her as a result.

A moment later he appeared from around a corner, clutching coffee in a takeaway cup and a canvas bag of shopping with the tip of a paper-wrapped baguette standing proud. He had a face full of stubble and was wearing a very nice woollen overcoat. She was struck for a moment by the sense that he was already familiar to her in some way, that he was more than just the guy she'd hooked up with last night.

His face broke into a smile when he saw her, and he approached her with outstretched arms. Rachel brought herself up tall, remembering her rage, her disgust, her horror.

'What the fuck?' she began. 'What the actual fuck? What do you think I am?'

'Er . . .'

She turned her phone to face him. 'This,' she said, pointing at the screen. 'What is this? What the fuck gives you the idea that you needed to pay me for sex? What did I do to give you that impression?'

Michael blinked at the screen of her phone and then looked at her. 'I don't really get—'

'I thought last night was kind of nice,' she interjected. 'I thought we'd found a nice sort of balance with each other. I mean yes, of course you *did* spend half the night telling me about all your houses around the world, while sitting in my tiny flat over a stinking canal, so yeah, maybe I should have picked up on the *Pretty Woman* vibes then. But for some reason I felt comfortable with

you, I felt seen and respected. So what the fuck is this?' She waved
the phone in his face again. 'What is it?'

Michael sighed and his head flopped heavily towards his chest.
'Christ,' he said. 'Rachel. I'm sorry. Please. Come in. Let's talk
indoors.'

Rachel sighed loudly and shoved her phone back in her handbag. 'Fine,' she said. 'Fine.'

They shared a mirrored lift with highly polished brass buttons
silently to the third floor and then she followed him down a thickly
carpeted hallway to his front door.

In his kitchen he unpacked his canvas shopper and plugged his
phone in to charge.

'Tea?' he said. 'Coffee?'

Rachel shook her head.

Michael sighed. 'I fucked up, didn't I?'

Rachel nodded. 'Yup.'

'I just didn't – It didn't occur to me that you'd see it that way.
I just, God, I just loved your jewellery and I just wanted to buy
some to give to people—'

'What people?'

'I don't know. Friends.'

'What for?'

'Birthdays.' He shrugged sheepishly.

'But fifty-four thousand pounds' worth? In one order? I mean,
that's insane.'

'Yes. I know. But, in the . . . *context*—'

'Of being a millionaire.'

'Well, yes. Of that. It seemed like . . . Oh fuck.' Michael slapped
his hands to his cheeks and growled softly. 'I'm a dick. I dunno.

I just got home this morning and felt so euphoric. I think maybe I was also still a little drunk. We just had such an . . . well, to my mind' – he put a clenched fist to his chest – 'such an incredible night. I was buzzing. And I remembered what you said about still finding your feet with your business and I imagined your face as you opened up your laptop and saw the big order sitting there and I just . . . *didn't think*. I didn't think. And no. I do not think you should be paid for sex. I think you are extraordinary and magical and beautiful and . . . and . . . magnificent. And I will cancel the order right now.' He swung open the lid of a laptop on his kitchen counter. 'Right now.'

Rachel stood and watched him with her arms folded.

He pressed some buttons and then closed the laptop again. 'There,' he said. 'It's gone. Please. Give me a chance to make it up to you. If you do, I *promise* I will never do something that crass and undignified ever again. I swear, Rachel Gold, that I am not what you think I am. I'm a feminist.'

Rachel let out a short bark of dry laughter.

'Well, maybe not a feminist. But I am a good guy, I swear. I've never treated the women in my life with anything other than the utmost respect. It's how I was brought up. C'mon. Please? Dinner, maybe? Tonight? If you're free?'

Rachel felt it open up inside her then: a gap, a space. A place where she could be nice to this guy, where she could let him in, this 'good guy' who'd been brought up well. She could give him another chance. And she was free tonight and she had already made the journey halfway across town. She glanced around at his apartment now that the red mist in her head was lifting and saw a nice kitchen; black metro tiles, battered cookbooks, mismatched utensils in a red enamel pot, a tall sash window at the far end over-looking the river. She could imagine padding in here barefoot in the morning and making herself an espresso from the big shiny machine over there. She could imagine Michael walking up behind her and those strong arms around her, the smell of him on her, his clothes folded neatly on a bedroom chair, his sweet breath in her ear, his world coming together with hers. She wondered briefly about 'Lucy', about the ex-wife. She wondered what she might have to say about Michael's assertion that he had only ever treated women with respect. Why had it ended? Who had been at fault?

But then she shook the thoughts from her head. Nobody ever knew what had happened inside a marriage apart from the two people in it. It was no business of hers. She looked up at Michael and she allowed her face to soften and she said, 'Fine. Fine. Dinner tonight. Yes. But you'd better be on your best behaviour.'

Michael put the palm of his hand to his chest and said, 'I swear, I will now be on my best behaviour *forever*.'

14

June 2019

Stella skips to keep up with Lucy as they walk back to Henry's apartment. 'Why are we walking so fast?'

Lucy holds her key card to the panel outside the block and ushers Stella through the heavy chrome doors into the foyer. 'I just need to make some calls, that's all.'

'Calls to who?'

'To Clemency.'

Clemency is Phin's younger sister and Lucy's best friend.

'Why is it so important? What's happening?'

'Nothing's happening, baby. It's fine.'

They exit the lift and enter Henry's apartment, then Lucy gives Stella the bowl she'd made the butter icing in to lick and takes her phone into her bedroom.

'Clem. It's me. Listen. Something weird's going on. Phin's left the reserve and nobody knows where he's gone.'

There's a small, brittle silence and Lucy feels a jolt of understanding pass through her.

'Oh my God. Clem! Was it you? Did you call him?'

'Of course I called him! He is my brother, after all.'

'But the trip was meant to be a surprise. We agreed that we weren't going to say anything to him.'

'No. You agreed. But I know Phin and he would have hated a surprise. Hated it with a passion. And the thought of Henry being there too . . .'

'You told him Henry was coming?'

'Of course. He had the right to know. I just – I'm sorry, Lucy, but I thought the whole thing was a terrible idea. I know Phin, and I can guarantee that he doesn't want to be found by anyone, let alone Henry.'

'Henry? Why do you say that?' Lucy asks tentatively.

'Oh, come on. You know why. The way Henry was with Phin, back then. The way he was obsessed with him. Then what happened. At the end.'

They fall silent, then. Their shared history is so big that it's sometimes as if mere words cannot contain it and that it exists only in the pauses and the silences and the unfinished sentences. Twenty-six years is long enough for memories to grow cobwebby, abstract. Twenty-six years is long enough to doubt your recollection of things, to wonder if maybe things really did happen the way you think they happened. And in the house of horrors that Lucy, Henry, Clemency and Phin were brought up in, the truth was constantly warped and distorted through the filters of their

parents, the people who were supposed to care for them and protect them and the people who instead allowed them to suffer abuse
and depravity.

Was Phin in danger from Henry back then, Lucy wonders, and
is he in danger now?

Lucy sighs. 'So, do you know where Phin went?'

'I have no idea. I didn't even speak to him. He was out on the
range when I called so I just left a message for him.'

'Saying?'

'The Lambs have tracked you down. They're coming to see you.'

'And you don't have any inkling where he might have gone?'

'None. No. I've given him my number, given him Mum's
number. Haven't heard a word from him yet. And who knows if I
ever will. He was always a loner, my brother. Never a pack animal.
Maybe that'll be it for another twenty-six years . . .' She sighs,
loudly. 'Fuck,' she says. 'I'm sorry. I didn't think he'd do a runner.
I just wanted to warn him, that's all. I just wanted him to be prepared. Not to disappear. Is Henry really fucked off?'

Lucy clears her throat, then says, 'Henry's gone.'

She hears Clem's sharp intake of breath. 'To where? To Africa?'

'I guess.'

'But what for? If he doesn't know where Phin is?'

'I have no idea. I mean, maybe he got a lead? A clue? But he's
on his way there now. He sent me a text just now. Him on a plane.
And I tried to call him, tried to message him, but he's blocked my
number.'

'He *blocked* you? Oh my God.'

'Yes.' She pauses. 'What shall I do?'

'I have no idea. Have you searched his apartment? For clues?'

70

'No. No, not properly. But even if I did find out where he was, then what?'

'Well, maybe you could . . . I don't know, go?'

Lucy laughs hoarsely. 'Right,' she says. 'With two kids, a dog and a fake passport.'

'Yes. Maybe not. But I'll keep calling the reserve. See if anyone knows anything more. And hopefully, maybe, Phin might call. You never know. Fuck, Luce, what a fucking mess. I'm so sorry. I really am.'

They end the call and Lucy goes back into the living room where Stella has blue butter icing all over her chin. She opens drawers and cupboards. She goes through the pockets of Henry's clothes in his bedroom, the pockets of his coats in the hallway. She calls his office, and they tell her that he's told them he's not coming back for at least a week, but that they don't know where he is. She asks Oscar in the foyer of the apartment building if he knows where Henry might have gone, and he says no. She goes on to an app that shows her which flights left London at 7.45 a.m. and turns it off when she discovers that at least twenty flights leave London every fifteen minutes. She tries to message him, but her message is bounced back. She thinks of her first sighting of Henry last year, the strange, smiling man waiting for her in the empty shell of their childhood home with his hair made blond, his face made pretty, leaving her to guess if he was Henry or Phin, and an image floods her consciousness, bright as a flash: Phin, somewhere in this world, opening a door to Henry, a pair of hands pushing him hard across the room, and a chill runs through the core of her.

15

December 2016

By Christmas of that year, Michael was officially Rachel's boyfriend.

It felt surprising to Rachel both in its unexpectedness and its predictability.

When she caught sight of herself and Michael in a shop window or the mirrored wall of a restaurant, she would note that they made a good couple: both tall, both olive-skinned, both with recently whitened teeth and thick brown hair. Their age gap was cancelled out by their physical similarities. Michael's Americanness was tempered by his Europhilia; Rachel's Englishness was tempered by her cosmopolitan upbringing. In spite of the ocean and the years that had kept them from having shared experiences to bind them together, they made a strange sort of sense.

A week before Christmas, Rachel took Michael to a party. It was the party of Rachel's best friend, Dominique. She threw it every year in her converted loft in Kentish Town. It was legendarily messy, drug-fuelled, loud and late. But Dominique was currently pregnant with her first child and guests had been warned that this year things would be a little more sedate; *Ubers @ midnight*, the invitation stated.

Michael seemed a little nervous as they got ready at her place that night.

He had met a handful of her friends already over meals for four with other couples, but he had not been required to socialise with Rachel's friends on a large scale and it was here that Rachel felt a disparity, a difference between them beyond age and nationality. In London, Michael was a lone ranger. He had a few business associates and a couple of ex-girlfriends, but he didn't have a rooted circle of friends with the conversational and emotional shorthand that comes with having rattled around together in the same city for all of your life.

She felt protective of him that night, watching him button his shirt, check his teeth, fuss with his hair. She imagined him worrying about what people would think of him, worrying about the impression he would make. She sidled up to him in the bathroom and kissed his cheek.

'What was that for?' he asked, turning to smile at her.

'Nothing,' she replied. 'Just like kissing you on the cheek.'

He kissed her on her cheek and then returned to fussing with his hair in the mirror. 'Is there anyone there I need to watch out for? Any rogue exes or crashing bores?'

'No rogue exes, possibly more than a couple of crashing bores. I'll point them out to you.'

'And remind me? Dominique? Is your friend from high school?'

'Primary *and* secondary. I've known her since I was four.'

'And she is married to? No, don't tell me. I can remember. She is married to Jonathan. Who is a tabloid journalist.'

'Correct. High five.'

'She is five months pregnant, due in April?'

'High five again.'

'And she's a . . . a . . . a visual merchandiser at Matches, the boutique for rich ladies?'

'Wow, you are good! Yes. She is. And she will most likely be in a bad mood because she can't drink and she's at that awkward phase of a pregnancy where you look fat, not pregnant, so she won't be able to wear anything nice, and she's tired all the time.'

Michael nodded sagely. 'Oh, yuh,' he said. 'Yup. I remember that phase. I remember it very well.'

Rachel flinched slightly at his words. Michael didn't talk much about Lucy, about his marriage and the family he'd lost touch with, but whenever he did, she felt it like a small spiteful pinch to her insides. Michael was box fresh to her: a fragrant, well-maintained man with no ties and no commitments beyond the occasional business call or meeting. Yet, beneath all that, she had to keep reminding herself, there was a brief mysterious marriage to a woman who could play the violin, who talked in poetry, who was fluent in French and had given birth to his only child. Beneath all that was a life that she would never ever be allowed to understand or experience, secret places she would never be allowed to go. She felt the smile freeze on her face and then snapped herself out of it.

'Well,' she said. 'I don't know about you, but I'm thinking maybe a glass of something before we leave? Just to take the edge off?'

'One hundred per cent *yes*. I will join you in a minute.'

She kissed him again and left the bathroom, uncorked a bottle of wine and poured them each a glass. She'd intended to wait for Michael but found herself picking up her glass and taking a large slug, her psyche telling her to pour something numbing over the hot ashes of jealousy smouldering inside her. Rachel was not a jealous person. She had never felt like this before about any other man's history. She didn't like the feeling; it made her feel lesser, somehow. It made her feel as if Michael was now somehow in control of her happiness, could switch it on and off with a careless comment or a throwaway anecdote. She took another sip of wine and then turned on her phone.

Dom, she typed, *can you get Jonathan to do a bit of sleuthing with Michael tonight? Find out stuff about his ex and his kid and stuff? Don't want to keep asking him stuff and he's v cagey. THANK YOU!!! See you in an hour.*

'He's fucking gorgeous,' Dominique hissed in Rachel's ear. 'God, the way you were describing him I thought he was going to look like your dad. Which . . . well, he kind of—'

'Don't! Do not even!'

'Well, only in as much as your dad is a good-looking older man.'

'My dad is sixty-three, for fuck's sake, Dom! He's old enough to be Michael's dad!'

'I'm teasing, Rachel. Anyway, this guy is veh, veh handsome.'

'Maybe a bit *too* handsome? Do you think?'

Dominique had always selected her boyfriends on the basis of their quirks. The more quirks the better. Jonathan was a walking litany of unusual features and idiosyncrasies. She would not look twice at a cookie-cutter guy like Michael.

'No! Of course not. Well, not for you, obviously. He's perfect for you. You look great together. Cheers!'

They clinked their glasses together.

'What have you got in there?' Rachel asked, eyeing Dominique's glass of something pink.

'Urgh. Sparkling water with Angostura bitters. Bloody hell. It's so shit, this not-drinking thing.' She glanced down at her stomach, housed inside a floaty gold tunic top with gold chain straps, and smiled faintly. 'The things I do for you, little one. The things I do for you.' Then she glanced up at Rachel and said, 'Talking of little ones, I've briefed Jonathan. He's going to go into full journalist mode. Ask the right questions. I will have a comprehensive report for you tomorrow. What is it that you're worried about, exactly? Looks like he's one hundred per cent into you?'

'Yeah. Yeah, he is. It's just I kind of hit a brick wall when I try talking to him about his ex-wife and his kid and I don't want to keep pressuring him. I just feel like there's something he's not telling me. That's all.'

'Well, if there's anything he's hiding, Jonathan is the man to get it out of him. Leave it with him.' She winked and tapped the side of her nose. 'Right, I should mingle. I will see you later . . .'

Rachel topped up her wine glass and wandered out of the kitchen area and across the loft space towards Michael, who was chatting to a woman called Ella whom Rachel knew vaguely from Dominique's extended social circle. Ella was small and blonde and effervescent in a way that Rachel, who was not at all effervescent, had always found slightly challenging.

She saw Ella's face cloud a little as Rachel approached her, since Rachel would never normally approach her at a party, and then she saw Ella's gaze go to Michael and a flash of realisation pass across her heavily made-up eyes.

'Hi!' Rachel pitched in brightly. 'Ella! Nice to see you! I see you've met Michael.'

'Yes, although I didn't actually know his name was Michael. We hadn't got that far.' She let out a nervous laugh.

'No,' Michael interjected. 'We kind of hit the ground running with stories of worst ski injuries ever.'

'Oh!' said Rachel. 'Hilarious!'

'So, you're . . .?' Ella waved her hand vaguely between Rachel and Michael.

'Mmhm,' said Rachel, nodding. 'Yes. We're together.'

'Oh, good!' said Ella. 'Lovely. That's great!'

'Yes!' said Rachel. 'It really, really is.'

Then she found herself grabbing hold of Michael's arm and kind of pressing herself against him and for a brief flash she saw herself from the outside looking in and realised she was behaving appallingly. She was being someone she couldn't bear. Clingy, simpering, insecure. She saw the smile freeze on Ella's face, and then saw her eyes pass across her shoulder to another point in the room before she said, 'Well, lovely to meet you, Michael. Enjoy your time in London. And Rachel, so, so lovely to see you – you look gorgeous, by the way. As always.'

Then she left the two of them standing together, a strange feeling building between them.

'Did you just get a little jealous, Miss Gold?'

'Fuck off.'

'Oh, come on. I think you did?'

'Seriously. Fuck off.'

'I like it, I think. A little bit.'

'Stop it.'

'Seriously. It's cute. I mean, Jesus, look at you and look at me. You are out of my league in a hundred different ways. *I'm* the one who should be feeling insecure. I like that you think I might just bin you off for Little Miss Eyelashes over there.' He rolled his eyes in the general direction of Ella, who was laughing loudly at another man's jokes a few feet away.

'I didn't think that. I was just surprised, that's all, that you hadn't mentioned you were with me.'

'Christ. She didn't give me a chance! That girl is a motormouth. And also drunk. If she'd slowed down for even a second I would have been straight in there with *oh, by the way, small woman with annoying voice, I think you'll find I'm dating the most beautiful woman in this room, her name is Rachel Gold, do you know her?'*

Rachel couldn't help a smile forming on her lips then, and Michael smiled too, dipping his head towards hers and capturing her gaze with his. 'You're the only one, Rachel. The only thing. In the whole world. OK?'

She nodded, submitting to his adoration, even as she felt it diminishing her somehow, making her less.

16

June 2019

I awake the next day with a sharp headache. Not quite a hangover, I didn't drink enough for a hangover, but more of a shrill prickle of jetlag and dehydration and stress. After breakfast I find a print shop around the corner from my hotel and I get the photo of Phin blown up to A4 size. I cannot bear one more stranger dragging their dirty fingertips across the screen of my phone. Then I put on my sunglasses and begin my day's quest. For three hours I sweet-talk porters and concierges and stop busy people as they try to get in and out of their apartment blocks to get on with their lives.

I pause for lunch at a brunch restaurant with a vaulted ceiling hung with silk wisteria blossom and I order a Salvadorian quesa-dilla, a masala chai and a turmeric and saffron sparkler. I find I have a hearty appetite after feeling a little queasy earlier and scrape my plate clean. Halfway through, a boy with peroxide hair asks me how my breakfast is tasting. I tell him it is tasting very good and he looks delighted for me.

And then I am back pounding the streets, a sheen of sweat beginning to bloom on my skin. I feel so far from home. I've never before been further afield than the Canary Islands. But Chicago feels pleasantly European, and I can pretend that I'm in a cool corner of Paris maybe, or Berlin.

By 4 p.m. my phone tells me that I have walked nearly eighteen thousand steps since awaking. I sit on a bench with a bottle of water and take stock. How long can I keep this up for? How many more steps can I take? I'm starting to look bedraggled and slightly alarming. I really should head back to my hotel and take a shower. But I've invested so much time and energy into my search today, I can't stop now. I take my phone from my pocket to check my email and see that I've missed a call. I do not understand how I've missed a call, but then I notice that I've had my phone on silent all day. I call up voicemail messages.

'Er, hi. This is Lyle. We met last night? You were looking for a guy named Finn? Well, I don't know if this means anything to you, but I have a friend named Joe who rents an apartment from a guy named Finn who lives in Africa? I described the guy in your photo and he said it sounds like him? I can give you his number? If you like? Call me.'

I blink. A huge smile is trying to break out all over my slightly sunburned face, but I rein it in.

I find Lyle's number in my missed calls, and I press it.

17

Lucy's phone rings while she's cleaning Henry's kitchen the following morning. Her heart stops and starts again at the thought that it might be Henry. But it's a St Albans prefix and it's not Libby, so it must be an estate agent. She replies slightly breathlessly. 'Hello?'

'Hi! It's Max Blackwood, from Raymond & Cobb. Have you got a minute?'

'Yes,' she says. 'Yes. I do.'

'Well, I've been going back and forth a bit with the vendors and they have said that if you can stick another fifty K on the end of your offer, they will take it off the market for you.'

'So . . .' She can't arrange the numbers in her head into anything that makes sense.

'Yes, that's one million and fifty thousand.'

'Right. OK.'

It seems crazy to her, how little the extra fifty thousand seems in the context of all those other zeros. She should fight it. She should object. But she wants this house and she doesn't want to do anything to delay getting this house so she finds herself replying, very quietly, but resolutely, 'Yes. OK. That's fine.'

'So you're happy for me to say that you'll accept?'

'Yes. I am very happy for you to say that. But on the understanding that they will do everything within their power to push this through as quickly as possible. Please.'

'I will absolutely mention that to them, Lucy. Absolutely. I cannot see any reason for them to drag their feet.'

After the call ends, Lucy rolls her head back on her neck and says a silent prayer to the gods of house buying. Please, she thinks, please after all these years and years and years, give us a home where we can finally be safe. *Please.*

18

December 2016

Dominique's party emptied out, as directed, at midnight. Dominique stood at the front door, seeing people into the lift, her high heels long kicked off, yawning theatrically. Rachel leaned into her ear and said, 'Text me tomorrow.' Dominique said, 'I sure will.' Then they hugged and waved goodbye and Michael and Rachel climbed into an Uber and headed back to Michael's apartment.

It was a mild night for December, and they asked the driver to drop them by the river. The still surface shone with reflected street-lights. Behind them the tall sash windows of big Victorian houses glittered and glowed with lit-up Christmas trees. Rachel pulled her coat tight around her and nestled herself against Michael's shoulder as they walked. Her feelings were muddled and strewn in random places, as though she'd been ransacked. She felt intensely that she was in love with Michael, in love with him in a way that she'd never imagined being in love with anyone, let alone a rather cocky older man with baggage and secrets who was leaving the country in three and a half months. All she wanted when she was with Michael was to touch him, smell him, be held by him. In shared spaces she wanted his gaze upon her, his attention, his arm around her, his thoughts consumed by her. She missed him with an ache on the rare occasions when they were not together. If he took too long to pick up a call or reply to a message she fretted over it, convinced that he was having second thoughts about their relationship, that her lustre had dimmed somehow, that their bond was fading. The relief she felt when the text reply came or the call was answered or the flowers were handed to her with a flourish, when his fingers were in her hair, his arms around her waist, his lips against her lips, was so powerful that it sometimes made her gasp.

She would look at herself in a mirror occasionally, after one of these pathetic, desperate interludes, and wonder who she was. Was she still Rachel Gold, the ice princess, the ball-breaker, the statuesque brunette who could never find a man to meet her high ideals? Or was she now somebody completely different? Had there in fact never been one finite version of herself? Had she always contained multitudes? Had Simpering Rachel who clutched men's arms at parties in order to repel a competitor for his attentions been there all along? How awful, she thought to herself. How absolutely awful.

But now she pulled those feelings into some semblance of order.

Of course she was still Rachel Gold. She was just Rachel Gold who'd finally met someone she needed a commitment from. That was the only difference.

And as if he could hear her thoughts, Michael stopped and turned her towards him so that they were face-to-face. 'I liked it', he said, 'when you were jealous earlier.'

'I was not jealous.'

'You were jealous. I loved it. The idea of you, being jealous around me. Ha! I mean – wow. Any man should be so lucky. Any man should be so honoured. And I do not know what I have done to deserve the jealousy of a woman like you, but man, I would like to keep hold of it. Forever. Because I tell you what, the thought of another man making you feel jealous makes *me* feel jealous.'

They laughed then, and Rachel stared into his eyes and said, 'No other man has ever made me feel jealous. Not ever. I usually just want men to fuck off out of my face, to be completely honest. But with you . . . it's just . . . different.'

Michael grabbed his heart theatrically and made a pleasurable groaning noise. 'Stop,' he said. 'I cannot take it. You're going to give me an uncontrollable monster ego and I'm going to leave you for a Hollywood film star. Talk down to me, please, remind me who's in charge. It can't be me. Don't let it be me.'

He was playing with her, he wasn't being serious, she was certain. She smiled and said, 'OK, loser, show me that you're worth keeping around. Or I'm going to go off and find someone decent-looking with some money and a good personality.'

Michael laughed, rocking back slightly on his heels before straightening and leaning in towards her. 'You,' he said, 'oh God, you. You are just, just too, urgh, too beautiful. Too everything. I am – fuck, Rachel, I am fucking insanely in love with you. I do not want to think about being without you, not ever. And listen. I know it's only been a few weeks; I know we've barely gotten started. But I already know that this is it. This is me. And I want to stop, right now, stop everything and . . . I want to marry you, Rachel. Will you? Will you marry me?'

And there, there it was. The thing, the elusive, flighty thing, the small fluttering bird that had been trapped inside her all these years, crashing into the walls of her psyche, her notion of who she was and what she was meant to be. She wanted to be Michael's wife. There. Simple. The window opened; the bird escaped.

'Yes,' she said, clutching Michael's hands in hers. 'Yes! Fuck! Of course. Of course. But where shall we live?'

'Everywhere,' said Michael. 'We will live everywhere.'

At work on Monday Rachel steamed straight into Paige's studio.

'I have a commission for you,' she said theatrically.

Paige pulled her black-framed reading glasses down her nose and peered up at Rachel through her eyelashes. 'Oh. Cool. What sort of commission?'

'An engagement ring.'

'Right. OK. Not my usual thing, but tell me more?'

'It needs to be white gold. A solitaire. Very simple.'

'Well, that sounds more like your kind of thing than mine. Why don't you want to undertake it?'

'Because' – she could barely keep her voice even – 'it's for me.'

Paige's eyes grew wide. 'You mean . . .?'

Rachel nodded, feeling half ecstatic, half ridiculous.

'Michael? The American guy?'

'Yup.'

'Fucking hell, Rach, that's immense. That's – what's it been? Two months?'

Rachel nodded again.

'Shit. I mean, that's amazing. But are you sure? I thought he was just going to be a six-month thing?'

'Yeah. Well, me too. But seems he's a keeper.'

'Oh. God. Well, then get over here and bring it in.' She opened up her arms and Rachel walked into them and let her friend squeeze her hard. 'He's a lucky, lucky man,' she said. 'I hope he knows that?'

'Yes. He totally does. That's kind of what it's all about really. He has no side, no game, no bullshit. He just thinks I'm amazing. And I think he's amazing. And—' She broke off at the sound of her phone pinging three times in quick succession and switched on the screen with her thumb.

Three messages from Dominique:

Jonno's got the lowdown.

Some stuff you should know.

Call me.

'Sorry,' she said to Paige. 'I need to make a call. I'll pop back in a minute.'

She unlocked her studio door and dropped her bag on her bench. Then she pressed in Dominique's number and cleared her throat while she waited for her friend to pick up.

Some stuff you should know.

She cleared her throat again and stood up straight when she heard Dominique answer. 'Dom,' she said in greeting.

'Rach. Hi. You OK?'

'Yup. All good. You?'

'Super trouper. Just felt the baby move for the first time.'

'Oh. Oh! Wow! That's—'

'Weird, actually. It felt weird. Like having a goldfish in there. Anyway. Listen. I finally got Jonno's full report. On Handsome Michael. Wanna hear it?'

'Yes. Well, yes, I suppose. I mean – it's nothing bad, is it?'

'No. God. No, nothing bad as such. Just a couple of little what you might call *red flags*.'

'Red flags?'

'Yes. So apparently he said his ex-wife – Lucy? Yes?'

'Yes.'

'Apparently Michael described her as "a freak".'

'Right . . .'

'And said that he *picked her up off the street* when she was twenty-one.'

'Sorry, he said he picked her up . . .?'

'Off the street. She was busking.'

'And how old was Michael at the time, did Jonno say?'

'He didn't. But let us assume, given the house in Antibes, etc., that he must have been quite a bit older than her.'

Rachel moved the phone to her other ear. She was not sure what she was meant to be feeling about the red flags presented to her thus far. 'What else?'

'Well, this is less about what Michael said to Jonno and more about what Jonno has unearthed from the internet, but apparently his business, MCR International, is not what it seems.'

'OK . . .'

'Yes, it appears to be a kind of cover operation for a few

different business concerns, some of which Jonno said look a bit . . . shady.'

'Shady? In what way?'

'I don't know. He didn't really go into detail. He just said that. Shady.'

'You mean like drugs? Money laundering? What?'

'He's not sure. Just weird addresses, kind of storage units in back streets in Algeria, storage units in industrial estates in Belfast. Jonno did Google Map Street View searches, said the places looked suspect.'

'So, you mean maybe just financial shenanigans then? Nothing actually illegal?'

'Yes. I reckon that's it. Just financial stuff. Not, like, child sex trafficking. Though, God, actually, all those weird lock-ups in the middle of nowhere – you know . . .'

'Fuck! Dom! Stop it!'

'I'm kidding!'

'I know you are. But still . . .'

'You don't actually think . . .?'

'No! Of course I don't! Jesus!'

'Anyway, look, Rach. The bottom line is that Jonno thought he was a decent enough guy. Maybe not marriage material, you know, but decent enough.'

Rachel gulped drily. 'Right,' she said. 'OK. Was there anything else?'

'Er, no, that was all Jonno got. The young woman he *picked up off the street*, referring to her as a freak, and the weird business set-up. And – oh, yeah. He's fucking nuts about you.'

Rachel's stomach roiled pleasantly. Yes, she thought, yes. He is. And I am mad about him. And that is all that matters.

'Well,' she said, wanting to end the call, her head spinning with children in lock-ups and engagement rings and buskers and the incongruity of everything smashing together like furniture on a boat in a storm. 'Please say thanks to Jonno. Tell him I'm really grateful. And you, take care of yourself and your little goldfish.'

She ended the call and breathed in hard. She corralled her thoughts before they made her any dizzier; lined them up and examined them. So, Lucy was quite young when Michael met her. That didn't necessarily mean that they started a relationship then. Maybe he just took care of her, kept her safe, and then something deeper blossomed between them. The business thing: well, business was weird. The world was full of strange operations, and companies carved into odd shapes to fit through loopholes and avoid taxes and make more money for less output. So what? Michael had told her that he oversaw a few operations, mainly import/export. He'd been honest with her about that. He'd told her about Lucy being a busker, about taking her in off the street. He'd told her she was a nightmare. There was nothing new here. There was nothing to worry about.

Rachel went back to Paige's studio. 'So,' she began, opening a sketchbook and placing it in front of her, 'I've made a few rough designs.'

19

June 2019

Samuel

'Hi Saffron.'

'Hi, Sam. Results are back. Can you talk?

I grimace a little. I don't like to be called Sam. But I like Saffron very much, so I let it pass.

'Sure.' I put my sandwich back into its paper container and touch my lips with a paper towel. 'Go ahead.'

'Well, looks like our girl was roughly twenty-seven to thirty-three years old. Five foot two. Small build. That's the easy bit.'

'OK,' I say. 'What's the difficult bit?'

'Dichotomous results re the condition of the bones. It looks like they may only have been in the water for a relatively short amount of time. A few months. Maybe a year. But the bones themselves are at least twenty years old. Probably closer to twenty-five.'

'So . . .' I pause, unable to locate the second half of the question as I'm still pondering the first.

'So, it looks like the bones had been stored somewhere for a very long time. And then moved. We found traces of foliage in the plastic bag. Traces of cobweb. Some insect matter. That's all being tested now, separately. We should have results in an hour or so. There were a couple of other things.'

'Yes?'

'Bunions. The female had bunions. And signs of wear in the knee joints. The sort of wear and tear often seen in intensively trained dancers, ballerinas. Could be something to explore? And also, some fabric fibres. Possibly from whatever the bones had been wrapped up in before they were transferred to the plastic bag. You never know. They might yield something we can use. Particularly if it's an unusual fibre.'

'Any signs of what might have been the cause of death?'

'There's that slight fracture to the left side of the skull, on the temporal.'

'Caused by?'

She pauses briefly and I hear her exhale her breath. 'Blunt force trauma.'

I close my eyes and sigh. 'So – an act of violence?'

'Yes. I would say that with ninety-nine per cent certainty.'

I feel the weight of this land hard on my shoulders. We are now officially dealing with a murder case. A murder case with barely any physical or circumstantial evidence.

But on the plus side, time is not of the essence. Whoever this poor woman was, she's been dead for over twenty years. I can take my time. Nobody breathing down my neck. On the downside, this is the sort of case that could have me chasing shadows into corners for months and months and into infinity. This is the sort of case that nobody will be interested in. At least, not until I can find out who this girl might be.

Not until I can tell someone who it is that we're looking for.

20

Phin's place is across the other side of Chicago in a gentrified, upmarket, very unfunky area peopled by well-to-do young families with SUVs in their driveways. The houses are mainly Victorian red brick with bay windows and terracotta-tiled pathways. Phin's apartment is a conversion in one of these; it's on the second floor, up two flights of polished wooden stairs, nice art hanging from the communal walls and a brass chandelier dangling above the staircase from the top landing. Joe greets me barefoot, in blue shorts and a black polo shirt. Joe is very, very, very young. I cannot imagine how he can possibly afford to rent such a beautiful apartment. But then, I am not in a position to ask anyone questions about how they got where they are.

'Hi,' he says, allowing me to enter. His voice is a little high-pitched. If he were a dog he would be one that quakes and quivers, or one that sits in a bag and growls occasionally.

'You are too kind,' I say, making my voice sound as deep and honeyed as I can, to alert him to the fact that I am a fully grown man but also that he is safe with me. 'I really, really appreciate you letting me come and talk to you.'

'Can I get you a juice?' says Joe, standing against the kitchen counter, one bare foot balanced upon the top of the other. 'Soda? Water?'

'Water would be great, thank you.'

I lean against the back of a sofa and glance around. It's a beautiful apartment: lots of neutral colours, the odd bit of big-game-philia – etchings of tigers and elephants, watercolour maps of Africa. It's absolutely nothing like my apartment, the apartment I had designed with Phin in mind, and once again I realise that I have been chasing a ghost all these years, living my life in the slipstream of a young man who doesn't exist any more. But rather than dampen my need to find Phin, this realisation only serves to increase it. Joe passes me a glass of water and I say, 'So, have you ever met Phin?'

'No.' Joe shakes his head. 'I've never met him. I have spoken to him, though. He's British, right, like you?'

'Yes. Yes he is.'

'I've seen photos of him, also; there are a couple in the apartment. So I knew what he looked like and he—' He stops and his gaze flicks up to me and down again. 'How well do you know him? I mean, are you like super-close?'

'Well, yes and no. We knew each other as children and then I knew he'd gone to live in Africa and work as a safari guide. And we were all set to go and visit him – "we" being me and my family, his family – when he disappeared. And we're all terribly, terribly worried about him.'

'So, you haven't spoken to him in a while?'

'No. No. Sadly not. The whole family lost touch with each other for a very long time. This was meant to be a reunion. Of sorts.'

He throws me a nervous glance and says, 'I hope this doesn't sound strange, but there are a few photos of him in the apartment and me and my friends, we have this joke about him, because he's kind of hot, you know, and kind of mysterious and we make up stories about him? You know? About Hot Finn, the Game Ranger. So that's what rang a bell with Lyle, I suppose. When you were asking about him last night. I hope that doesn't sound disrespectful?'

'Oh God. No. Not at all. I totally get it.'

'It's just fun. You know.'

'Yes, of course.' I smile widely. 'And how long have you lived here?'

'Couple of years. Since I graduated. My parents pay for it. In case you were wondering.'

I shake my head firmly, as if the thought had never occurred to me. 'And it's just you here?'

'Yeah. Just me. And the occasional sleepover. I mean – not that kind of sleepover. I mean, you know, like *friends*.'

I smile reassuringly. My goodness me, if you can't sleep around when you're twenty-two, cute as a button and living rent-free in a gorgeous one-bed apartment in a smart suburb of Chicago, then when can you? I want to tell him to crack on with it, stop with the platonic sleepovers and get busy. I want to tell him that this bit doesn't last long, that it's a beautiful blowsy rose which blooms and dies so quickly that you barely have time to catch your breath. But of course, I don't. I just say, 'And have you spoken to him lately? To Phin? Has he been in touch?'

'No. No, I haven't spoken to him for a few weeks. I had to write to him a while back about some works to the roof. Some scaffolding. But nothing since then.'

'And this was his apartment? I mean, he used to live here?'

Joe squints up at the ceiling and then back at me. 'I suppose he must have lived here. At some point. As some of his things are still here.'

'Like the photos, you mean?'

'Yes, like the photos. They were in a drawer in the desk in the bedroom.'

'Could I see them, do you think?'

'Yeah. Sure. I mean, I already got them out for you. Here.' He turns and scoops a small pile of photos from a shelf behind him and passes it to me.

I leaf through them, my cheeks sucked in hard against my teeth with the effort of not shaking, not betraying my excitement and anxiety. I clear my throat and glance down.

There he is. There is Phin. Not beardy and sun-crisped as he is in the photo I've been staring at obsessively since the night of Libby's birthday, but clean-shaven, young. What – late twenties, early thirties? Sporting a variety of haircuts from shaven-headed to long and floppy. Suntanned here, pale there, in jumpers and padded coats, in shorts and vest tops. He has a tattoo, I see, just one, on his bicep – very old-school, like a sailor – I can't tell what it is. Phin smiles, he frowns, he laughs, he eats, he drinks, he faces the camera, away from the camera. He has his arm around girls, his arm around boys. He drinks beer. He drinks champagne. He sits in restaurants and on beaches. He looks beautiful in each and every one. His looks have lasted him all the way through from twelve years old to over forty. It's appallingly unfair. I look for a sign that one of the supporting actors in these photos might be someone of some intimate significance; I look for something to tell me about his sexuality, about which way he's landed in the world after his ambiguous beginnings. But he is sexless, flawless, impossible to read, like a children's TV presenter.

'Do you happen to know, if he . . . well, was he in a relationship with anyone that you knew about?'

Joe shakes his head, sadly. 'Not that I know of. He never mentions anyone, at least. And I guess his lifestyle, out there in Africa, it's probably a single guy's existence, y'know?'

'Yeah. I suppose it is. Could I – Would you mind? If I just took some photos of these?'

'Oh. Yeah. Sure. Go ahead.'

I get out my phone and arrange the photos on the kitchen counter. 'And you said that you had an email address for him? I don't suppose you'd be able to give that to me?'

For the first time, Joe looks uncertain. 'I mean' – he strokes his chin – 'I mean, I could. I guess. But I wonder if maybe he's trying to lay low? On purpose? Would it be an infringement of his privacy?'

'Oh, Joe. What a sweet thing to worry about. And you're right to think about it. Absolutely. But no, he's definitely not lying low on purpose. He was desperate for this reunion, desperate for us all to get together again, after everything we've been through, as a family. It was all he ever wanted.'

'But you must have it, right? If you've been talking to him? You must already have it?'

He's lost me. 'Have what?'

'Finn's email address?'

'Ah!'

Good question.

'Good question,' I say. 'We, er, we always talked on Whats-App, actually. Never on email. But his messages aren't landing now. And he's not answering his phone. And it's all . . . a bit of a worry.'

Joe still looks uncertain, but I can see him wavering. 'Sure,' he says, picking up his phone. 'Sure. Here. It's finnthomsen@chobe-lodge.com.'

I want to ask him how Phin has spelled his name, but realise that that will sound alarm bells, so I write it as I've been told Phin now spells it and smile gratefully. 'Fantastic,' I say. 'Really fantastic, thank you. And I don't suppose you know if there's anyone in the city who might have more of an idea about him? Or his whereabouts? I mean, does he use an agent to rent you this place? Or do you rent it through him directly?'

'Yeah. Through him directly. Or at least, my parents do.'

I can tell that Joe is starting to tire of this. I'm asking too many questions and he's not sure he should be answering them. Asking for his parents' details now would be pushing him way outside his comfort zone so I clap my hands together and say, 'Well, I think it's time to leave you be. I've infringed on your time far too much as it is. But thank you. Thank you so much, Joe. If I find anything out, I'll be sure to let you know.'

I smile and bow my head slightly, sling my bag across my chest and then I say, 'Would you mind terribly' – I never use the word 'terribly' in England, but I feel it has a certain power here – 'if I used your bathroom before I hit the road?'

'Sure. Yeah. It's just off the hallway.' He points me in the general direction. I ape his movements and he nods.

The toilet is opposite his bedroom. I can't help but poke my head around the door, just to see – just to let my gaze come down upon Phin's bed, where he once slept, with God knows who, maybe some of the people I now have images of on my phone, the ones he has his arm around, the ones he drank with, ate with, laughed with, loved. The bed is neatly made: grey sheets with Moroccan-style cushions and a cream throw with knotted edges. It sits in a bay window, overlooking the street. I close my eyes and picture myself there, in that bed, unfurling myself after a night spent curled into Phin's solid back, running my fingertip over his solitary tattoo. I open my eyes again and see the empty bed. Joe is the only link I have to Phin, I realise. If I walk out of here, I'm back to square one.

I use the bathroom and then return to the living room, where Joe is putting my water glass in the dishwasher.

'I'm in town', I say, 'for another couple of nights. I'm staying in Northalsted. If you wanted to meet up, maybe, for dinner? Or just drinks? You have my number, I suppose. In your phone. Just call. Or message.'

I read his face for his response. I see something flicker across it: a kind of dark dread. It makes me want to slap him.

'Oh,' he says. 'Yes. Maybe. Though I'm kind of booked up. But if I think of anything else, about Finn, I'll drop you a message.'

I smile grimly. No more of the Hugh Grant. 'Yeah,' I say. 'Well, anyway, thanks for your time.'

I leave Joe there loading his dishwasher in his bare feet and I let the door slam closed loudly. I picture him on his phone, calling Lyle, saying, 'Whoa, that guy was intense. I think I'm gonna block him.' I feel a throb of rage across my temples. I breathe it away and I order an Uber.

While I wait for it to arrive, I stand across the street and stare up at the bay window inside which, I now know, sits Phin's double bed. A moment later I see Joe's face appear at the bay. I raise a hand to him. Just for fun.

21

February 2017

Rachel and Michael honeymooned in the Seychelles two months after Michael's proposal. 'I'm not getting any younger' had been his rationale for a short engagement. They had a small wooden house on stilts over an azure sea filled with colourful coral and rib-boning fish, a private plunge pool on the deck and a double-ended bath with a glass bottom. They drank champagne every morning with their breakfasts of fresh fruit and fish and slept the days away on hammocks and loungers. And, as any good honeymooners, should – particularly honeymooners who have known each other only a few months – they spent quite a lot of their time having sex.

Sex with Michael had always been calmer than Rachel had anticipated during those heady few days of expectation before their first date. She had appreciated this at the outset as it had helped build her trust in him, helped her to feel safe and secure with a man who'd appeared in her life from nowhere. But now, three months into their relationship, with a ring on her finger and actual paradise on their doorstep, Rachel had hoped that things might start to develop into something more . . . *complex*, something that more met her needs. Because Rachel was fine with vanilla sex on the whole, but she did not want to spend the rest of her life having sex only one way. And yes, she should probably have had this conversation with Michael before she agreed to marry him, but things had still been so sweet then, in those early days, so precious and delicate. And then her focus had switched to the exact filigree of her antique-lace wedding dress, the last inch she wanted to carve off her hips, the precise cut of the yellow diamond of her engagement ring and the carat count of Michael's wedding band. It had been on scouring the internet for the most perfect Seychellois resort and trying to find shoes in a size nine to fit Dominique's late-pregnancy-swollen feet. Sex had been an afterthought, a nice thing that she and Michael did at the end of every day that soothed and reassured them both that they weren't doing anything stupid, marrying so soon after meeting.

But now there was nothing left to think about other than sex. Sex and food. And she was bored now, bored of the soft thrusting and gentle caresses and his face buried lovingly in her hair. She thought about the man she'd seen on the internet, the man in the photo who looked as though he expected to be in control of everything and she thought that surely he would like to be in control of her. Sometimes. Not all the time. But sometimes.

After dinner on their third day, Rachel felt the bottom of her suitcase for the package she had brought with her from London.

The silken ropes. The switch. The underwear that didn't come from Victoria's Secret. She took out the objects – all brand new – and she laid them by the side of the bed.

Then she waited for Michael to appear from the shower. His gaze didn't alight upon the objects for a few moments and there was a messy episode of banal conversation that threatened to deaden the mood. But then his gaze found the objects and she watched him closely to gauge his reaction. First of all, an uncertain smile; then a small burst of laughter. Then a wide-eyed glare of recognition, followed by a 'Whoa!'

Rachel couldn't tell what the whoa meant. She waited a beat.

'Are you . . .?' He looked from the objects to Rachel and back again. 'Is that . . .?'

'I just thought . . . I mean . . . Is it something you'd like to try?'

Michael put a hand against his chest. 'Me? You mean, you tie me?'

'No. You tie me.'

'And then I—?' He picked up the switch and ran it across the palm of his hand. 'I do this?' He swished it against his hand, once, then twice. 'To you?'

'Erm. Yeah.'

'Whoa,' he said again, before unleashing a throaty laugh. 'Well, my goodness me.'

Rachel held her breath. She could not tell where this was heading but she knew that it would end up somewhere different to anywhere they'd ever been before and that there'd be no going back to the innocence of earlier days.

'Have you ever . . .?'

'Er, no. No, no. Never. I never have.' He shook his head decisively. 'Nope.'

'And how would you feel? If I were to put that on?' Rachel glanced at the underwear. 'And we could just give it a try? See if it's something you like?'

Immediately, Rachel felt something in the atmosphere curdle and warp. She watched as Michael lifted the underwear, dangled it on his fingertips and examined it warily. 'You wear this?' he said. But it wasn't a casual enquiry.

'Yes. If you'd like it.'

'And . . . have you? I mean, is this something you've done before?'

The question landed between them like a thrown dagger. Rachel knew what she should say. She should say no, this would be my first time. Because she knew, in every atom of emotional energy in the room at that moment, that Michael did not want to know about her doing this with other men. And that Michael was not what she'd thought he was. But she could not lie. Rachel was incapable of lying. And so she said, 'Well, yes. Once or twice. Not often. But yeah.'

'And you liked it? You liked being tied up? And being . . . what? I don't know – spanked?'

'It's not spanking. It doesn't hurt. It tickles.' She tried to add lightness to the situation, but she already knew it was too late.

'Wow. Rachel. Fuck. I mean . . .' He dropped the piece of underwear and paced back and forth across the wide teak floorboards for a moment or two. 'I feel – Jesus. I feel like I don't know you, Rachel. I feel like I married a *fucking stranger*.'

There followed a moment that was so darkly silent and so tense that Rachel could almost taste it.

She attempted to lighten it. 'Ah well. Just a thought. No biggie.'

'Well, I'd say it clearly *is* a "biggie", Rachel. I mean' – he gestured at the objects – 'these came all the way from the UK. On to our honeymoon. That took some forethought. Some planning.'

'No. Really. It was nothing, I brought a million things I don't need, just in case. I even brought a cardigan.' She laughed, but it sounded hollow. 'Seriously. Just forget it. Forget this ever happened.'

She strode across the room and started to gather the objects that she now wished to douse in petrol and set alight. She hoped that Michael might touch her as she passed him, might grab her arm and pull her to him and say something to ameliorate the situation. But he stood, rod-straight, pinched-faced, hard. She took the objects to her suitcase in the dressing area and zipped them tightly into an inside pocket. When she turned back, Michael was no longer in the room and the door to the terrace rattled gently on its hinges.

The rest of the honeymoon was tainted, ruined. They still talked over cocktails at dinner, they still held hands to walk along the beach, they still took photos of each other and selfies in front of sunsets. But there was no more sex. No more sex at all. Bright, aqua days faded darkly into moody nights of rejection and cold shoulders. Each night Rachel fell asleep tucked into herself on her side of the bed, swamped with sadness, and resentful of the sound of his snores, snores that should have been post-coital, blissed, the result of a spent libido, but instead were merely the snores of a middle-aged man who'd had a big dinner and too much beer.

They got home to the frozen tail end of February and spent the night at Michael's place in Fulham. Still no sex. The following day was Sunday. They had lunch at an Italian where the proprietor forced complimentary champagne on them when he learned they'd just returned from their honeymoon and made unwelcome jokes about babies coming now, yes? and as darkness drew over the afternoon and turned it into evening, Rachel said to Michael, 'You know, I have a huge day at work tomorrow, I'll want to be in early. I might just spend the night at my place.'

She chewed the inside of her cheek and held her breath, waiting for him to thaw, to melt, to say, no, no, please, stay, I want you. I'm sorry.

But he did not look up before saying, 'Sure, baby. Sure. Makes sense.'

She wheeled her honeymoon case out on to the pavement and lifted it into the boot of an Uber, cast her eyes up to the balcony of Michael's apartment, searching out the familiar solid shape of him, maybe waiting to wave her off or even to call her back. Her gaze searched the windows for a blur of movement, a waft of hitched-back curtain, but nothing; the façade of Michael's apartment remained still and cold. She clicked her seatbelt locked and held on to her tears until thirty minutes later, when she closed her apartment door behind her and wept.

22

June 2019

Samuel

'Sam.' It's Saffron. 'We've got the results back from the textile fibres.'

'Right. Great.'

'Towelling, apparently. Cotton towelling. Which suggests that the body was wrapped in towels after death. But, more importantly, there are traces of matter on the fibres. Some blood. And, amazingly, some hair.'

'Hair? Oh my goodness.'

'Yes. Exactly. And also a small shred of another fibre. Lab thinks it might be manmade. Probably part of a label from the towel. Traces of text printed on it. Not enough to read full words.

But it's being analysed right now; we might be able to get a brand off it. So we have hair, blood, and possibly a brand of towel. And all in all, I'm pretty fucking ecstatic about that.'

I don't like the sound of swearing. It bothers my ears. But on this occasion, I fully understand the need for it. This is more than we could ever have hoped or dreamed of.

'Fucking amazing!' I agree.

Saffron laughs. 'Never heard you swear before.'

'I've never felt the need before. That's truly great news, Saffron. Truly. Keep me posted. When are you expecting more updates?'

'Within the hour. They're fast-tracking everything. Watch this space.'

'I'm watching it, Saffron. I'm watching it like a hawk.'

I end the call. Then I turn to make sure I'm not being watched, and punch the air with a fist, very, very gently.

23

I study the photos on my phone, the ones of Phin's photos that I took in Joe's apartment. I establish that at least four of the photos have been taken in the same bar; it has tongue-and-groove walls painted black and hung with black-and-white photos of rock stars. The windows are plate glass and through them I can see the outline of a row of motorbikes and behind it a food shop called Organic something beginning with a D. I google Organic plus a D, and a shop called Organic Delightful comes up. There are four branches around Chicago. One of them, according to Google Maps Street View, is opposite a bar called the Magdala that has large plate-glass windows and a row of motorbikes parked outside. I order an Uber.

The Magdala is most categorically *not* a gay bar. It's a biker's bar, a pub. I feel hideously self-conscious as I enter. A couple of guys at the bar turn to appraise me and I feel glad that I look a little wilted and not the daffodil-fresh thing I was when I left the hotel this morning. 'Take My Breath Away' by Berlin is playing on the sound system, which I find strangely comforting. I get a beer and drink it in the precise chair that Phin is sitting on in one of the photos. It feels strangely emotional. I try to imagine what sort of life he was living when the photo was taken. Had he bought his beautiful apartment yet? Had he become a game ranger? Was he happy? Was he loved? Was he lonely? Was he rich? Poor? Where was he living? What, I wonder, was he thinking? What was playing on the sound system? I try to plant myself into his moment, transport myself there by some magic energy he may have left deposited in the cracks of the leather of the chair.

But, of course, there's no such thing as magic energy.

I finish my beer, and I order another.

I feel, very strongly, that tonight I will get drunk.

When she walks in an hour later, I have had four beers and the world looks very golden and fun. She looks almost exactly the same as the girl in Phin's photo. She is wearing a black T-shirt that is small and tight enough to see that she is not wearing a bra. She looks young at first, but then, as she gets closer, not so young. Late thirties, I'd say. Her hair is tied back with a patterned scarf. She has good legs in a denim mini-skirt and tanned feet in flip-flops. In her hand is a bike helmet. If you like dark-haired, thirty-something women who ride motorbikes, she's probably a solid ten.

I start to get to my feet but stop myself when I see that she is being followed at close quarters by a large man with sleeves of tattoos on both arms and a shaved head. He bumps fists with the two guys sitting at the bar as he passes them and then he and the woman take what look like their 'usual' seats at the bar and order drinks.

She looks at her phone while he talks to the bartender and I gaze from the photo on my phone to her and back again, checking that my eyes have not deceived me, that this is the woman in Phin's photograph. But my eyes have not deceived me. They never do, of course. I should have been a detective.

I finish my beer and take my empty glass to the bar where I stand alongside the woman, who smells of dry shampoo, and say, in my best Joshua-from-Zone-5-London accent, 'I'm really sorry to disturb you. I've been trying to trace my old friend? He's called Phin and he's been missing for a few days. I have some photos of him taken in this bar, and there's one taken with a woman who looks a lot like you? Would you mind if I showed you?'

The woman bristles. I see a trail of uncomfortable energy work its way through her entire physiology as I wait for her to respond. She glances abruptly at the man to her left, who is chatting with the other men, and then down at my phone. 'Sure.'

I open the app and show her the photo. I watch her closely. 'Yeah,' she says. 'That's me. But I have no idea who that guy is. I mean' – she leans in to look closer – 'this must have been about six, seven years ago, judging by the length of my hair and the way I'm dressed.' She pushes my phone back towards me and sniffs. 'You know what it's like. You have a few drinks. You get

chatting to a stranger. Someone takes a photo.' She sniffs again
and shrugs.

'So, this guy, he's a stranger to you?'

'Er, yeah. Basically. Sorry.'

The guy with the tattoo sleeves has been growing increasingly
interested in our exchange. He turns away from the other men and
says, 'Hey. Everything OK?'

The woman puts a hand against his forearm. 'Yeah. It's nothing. This guy's just trying to track down his friend. Apparently he
used to come here. But I don't recognise him.'

He looks at me warily. Then he says, 'Let me take a look. I've
been coming here for years. Maybe I'll recognise him.'

I feel something radiating from the woman, something I recognise, something that almost has a smell to it, a hormonal musk.
It's fear. Instinctively I go to the photo of Phin with the baseball-
capped man instead of the photo with her in it. I hold the phone
tightly in my hand and point out Phin to the tattoo man. He stares
at it. 'Nope,' he says, tersely. 'Never seen the guy. But . . .' He
uses his fingers to zoom in on the face of the other man in the
photo. 'This guy.' He taps it. 'I feel like I know this guy.' He looks
at the woman. 'Do you know this guy?'

She looks down quickly and then up again. 'Erm . . .'

'It's him!' He taps his finger hard against the screen of my
phone and I snatch it away. 'The guy. The guy you were having
the thing with when I met you. Kris. Kris Doll.'

'Is it?'

'Yes! Look!'

He snatches my phone back from my hand and shoves it in

front of the woman. 'There,' he says, zooming into the man's face again, stabbing it with his finger again. 'See. Kris Doll. Your ex.'

'Oh,' she says unconvincingly. 'Yeah. It is. I didn't recognise him.'

I want to get away from these two, now. Their energy is so toxic, I'm virtually choking on it. And I've had enough of this guy continuously banging on my phone screen with his big meaty finger.

'So,' I say, 'Chris Doll? Is that D-O-L-L?'

'Yeah. And Kris with a K. K-R-I-S.'

'And do either of you have any idea where I might find him?'

They look at each other and then at me. 'No,' says the woman. 'No. I haven't seen him for years. We lost touch after I got together with Rob.' She touches his arm reassuringly as she says this.

'You don't know where he lives?'

'Well, I know where he *used* to live. But obviously he may have moved since then. And I know that he used to work down on the lake, doing the tourist row boats. But again – *long* time ago.'

'That's actually really helpful. Thank you so much. Sorry, I didn't get your names?'

'Er, yeah. Sorry. I'm Mati. This is Rob.'

'Thank you, Mati. Thank you, Rob. I'm Josh. Josh Harris. Look, here's my phone number. Just in case you remember anything later. About Phin. Or about Kris.'

'What's the deal?' says Rob. 'You lost somebody?'

'Yes,' I say. 'Yes. I have lost somebody. Someone very important to me. But hopefully I'm a step closer to finding him now. Thanks again.'

I shake their hands, I tap my forehead at the bartender, and I leave. Off to find Kris 'with a K' Doll, the row-boat guy, the ex, the key, maybe, to the strangely unfurling mystery of where the hell Phin Thomsen might eventually turn out to be.

24

Samuel

Thanks to the efforts of my remarkable colleagues in the forensics department, I am now enjoying a plethora of facts about the bones that were found by Jason Mott on the shores of the Thames. I pin the facts to the cork board in my office and gaze at them.

- Young woman, 27–33, possibly with training as a dancer, bunions on both feet
- Date of death roughly 1995
- Blood type A
- Body wrapped in a dark-coloured cotton towel from *Yves Delorme*. A similar towel today would cost around £200. Logo in use between 1988 and 2001

- Leaves mainly from London plane trees and trees of heaven (often planted along avenues), but also some dead <u>summer</u> blossom from the PERSIAN SILK TREE, **rare in London**
- Hair colour dark blonde
- Small fracture to skull around the left-hand temporal bone

Currently a team of five officers is trawling the missing person records from 1988 to 1999 for a slight young woman, possibly a dancer, with dark blonde hair and, according to the forensic facial reconstruction sculptor currently working with the young lady's facial bones, a rather pronounced weak chin. Given the quality of the towel which had once been wrapped around her body, they are particularly looking at those missing from well-to-do areas or families. Although of course this poor woman may have stumbled into the path of someone rich enough to spend two hundred pounds on a towel without being well-to-do herself. Another officer is briefing a so-called 'tree-detective' to find a point in London where the London plane and the Persian silk might coincide. And me . . . I am waiting. Waiting for my office door to burst open and for one of my team to walk in with a look of hope and possibility and say, *I think I might have found her.*

Because it is only a matter of time, and the only thing that stands between success and failure is the possibility – and it causes me genuine pain to consider it – that nobody ever reported this poor woman missing in the first place.

25

March 2017

Rachel waited three days before finally messaging Michael. Three days of going to sleep alone, waking up alone, checking her phone six times a minute. Three days of pretending that everything was fine whenever she saw someone she knew. Three days of 'Yes! The honeymoon was *amazing*. Yes, married life is *bliss*. Yes, we will definitely have you over for dinner soon!' Three days of feeling as if Michael had ripped her heart out of her chest in the Seychelles and still hadn't given it back.

M, began her message. *I don't know what's going on. I miss you. Please please can we talk?*

Within seconds a reply appeared:

Hey beautiful. Miss you too. It's been a crazy busy week. Dinner tonight? I'll cook.

Rachel gasped as she read it. After three days of existential hell, that was how he came back to her? *A crazy busy week?* While she was slowly dying inside? She rolled her engagement ring around her finger a few times, trying to decide how she felt, how to reply. And then she breathed in deeply and typed:

Sure. I'll be there at seven.

She didn't mark the message with a kiss or a love-themed emoji. She hoped he would notice and feel appropriately concerned about her.

That night she packed a few things into her shoulder bag; she didn't want to arrive with an overnight bag and give Michael the impression that she was prepared to move back in so easily after what he'd put her through.

She felt nervous as she put her key into the lock of his apartment at seven o'clock, so pulled it out again and knocked on the door instead. Her heart raced at the sound of his footsteps coming down the hallway. She had spent so many hours consumed with thoughts of Michael, picturing Michael in various states and various scenarios – with his ex-wife, with other women, on a flight back to the USA – that the idea of seeing him in real life, of him standing before her in human form, seemed almost impossible to assimilate. And yet the door opened and suddenly there he was; tanned, loose-limbed, jolly, in a pale blue shirt and navy suit trousers, bare feet, a glass of wine in his hand and a smile wreathing his handsome face.

'Baby.'

Baby.

Just that. What? What did it mean? What did any of it mean? Did it mean he was sorry? Did it mean she should forgive him? Or that he had forgiven her? Who was right? Who was wrong?

Suddenly she was in his arms, a light embrace. Not the embrace she felt the need for, not the desperate embrace of newlyweds not long back from their honeymoon reunited after their first post-nuptial row. But just a normal, perfectly average embrace between a husband and a wife.

Then just as quickly he was walking away from her and towards the kitchen where Rachel could smell good things cooking and he was saying something to her that sounded like 'I have a really nice Sicilian white. Or a chilled vodka? But I'm all out of tonics, so it would have to be orange juice' but she couldn't be sure because she wasn't really listening.

'Rach?'

'What? Oh, er, sorry. White. Please. Thank you.'

In the kitchen she took a stool and then the wine he offered her, and she stared and stared at him, this man she'd married two and half weeks ago on one of the most romantic and remarkable days of her life, this man who'd called her a *fucking stranger* on their honeymoon and then stopped touching her, this man who was acting as if they hadn't just spent three days apart from each other with no communication. For minutes and minutes, Rachel felt a kind of numb muteness.

'How's your week been?' he asked.

'Oh, you know, it's been . . . *the worst week of my life.*'

She watched his reaction. His wrist stopped turning the wooden spoon in the pot he was tending on the hob. He looked up at her and said, 'Oh, baby. What's been happening?'

And then the muteness passed, and rage arrived.

'What's been happening?' she asked in a voice reeded with disbelief. 'Are you serious?'

He narrowed his eyes at her and made a face of confusion.

'Fucking hell, Michael. We got back from our *fucking honeymoon* on Saturday. I went home on Sunday and it is now Wednesday and this is the first time I've seen you or spoken to you. We didn't have sex for the last ten days of our holiday, you said you thought you'd married a fucking stranger, and now you're acting like none of that ever happened. You're . . . you're . . . offering me wine and . . . and *stirring things*. I just don't understand. I don't understand what's happening?'

She paused and looked up at him. He put down the wooden spoon on a rest and used the heels of his hands to lean against the counter. She saw him sigh. 'You', he said, 'have got this all the wrong way round.'

'Excuse me?'

He sighed again. 'Why do you think we didn't have sex for the rest of the honeymoon?'

'Because I had disgusted you with my distasteful suggestions.'

He threw her an infuriatingly patronising look and said, 'That is not what happened.'

'Then what? What happened?'

'Well, you made a suggestion. I didn't like the idea of the suggestion. You went cold on me. How do you think I've been feeling?' He asked this last question in a neutral tone of voice, rhetorically, almost, as though he didn't really expect her to think about how he'd been feeling.

Rachel opened her mouth to respond but then realised she didn't know what to say. After a second, she said, 'I did not go cold on you. You went cold on me.'

'Well, that's your interpretation of events. I just seem to recall seeing a lot of your back in bed at night.'

'What! Michael, Jesus. NO. That is not how it was. You know that's not how it was. You literally stopped touching me from the night I made the suggestion. I tried, every night I tried. I offered you neck rubs and cuddles and you kept saying you were too tired, too hot, too whatever.'

'Well, like I say. That is your interpretation of events. I just recall a girl who was disappointed and pissed off because she wasn't going to get to do the things she wanted to do, and a brand-new husband left feeling a little inadequate and scared that the girl would rather leave him and find someone who *did* want to do the things she wanted to do.'

Rachel gasped. 'Wait. No. No, that's absolutely not true. That's not what happened. I could not have made it more clear that I still wanted to have sex with you. I could not have been more blatant. And the thing, the thing that I suggested was just *fun*, Michael. That's all. That's not who I am. That's not *what* I am.' She pressed her hand to her chest. 'It was just meant to be fun. It was just . . .'

Michael sighed, picked up the wooden spoon, started to stir again. 'And then the girl takes her suitcase and disappears for three days and doesn't get in touch and leaves the brand-new husband thinking that maybe, just maybe, he is now single again. That it is over. And then the girl deigns to send a message and the brand-new husband is too scared to think what this might mean and so he goes to the grocery store and buys organic chicken breasts and the most expensive tomatoes he can find and busies himself with the distraction of chopping them all up and making them taste good and the girl arrives and tells the husband that actually, this is all, all of this sadness and fear and worry, it is all somehow, in fact, his fault.'

He stopped stirring again and stared hard into Rachel's eyes. She had been mesmerised by the singsong intonation of his words but now they had sunk in and she shook her head slightly, as if trying to dislodge a blockage, a lump of something that would make sense of everything. She thought back to every moment of agony she had lived through since she left Michael's flat on Sunday evening. She thought back to the space between them in the huge bed in the Seychelles. Her shrugged-off touch. The wall of ice that emanated from him, every single night. She shook her head again.

'Well,' she said eventually. 'That is not how I remember it, Michael. It really is not how I remember it at all. I thought you hated me.'

'And should I?'

'What? Hate me?'

'Yeah.'

'No! Of course you shouldn't hate me. I haven't done anything wrong!'

'Yes, well, neither have I.'

'No. And I never said you had. I just . . .' She sighed. 'What happens now?'

'Now,' he replied, pulling open a packet of fresh parsley, 'we eat. We drink. And then . . .'

'Yes? Then?'

'Well, let's just see, shall we? Let's just see.'

The conversation was strained at first, but as the wine softened their moods, it became livelier, almost skittish in its attempts to steer clear of anything incendiary or controversial. They talked about their jobs; they talked about plans for the summer. Michael was going to get the house in Antibes repainted and deep cleaned, the pool emptied and refilled, so that they could spend the summer there. They discussed the possibility of buying new bedding and towels, so that Rachel could have a proper fresh start as the wife of the house. She resisted asking any questions about Lucy, about what sort of bedding she had left, what sort of towels, had she used the swimming pool, had she overseen her own renovation of Michael's house? She kept her questions neutral. And then, after they'd eaten, the atmosphere ripened and deepened with the uneasy anticipation of what happened next.

'Well, I guess . . .' She looked at the time on her phone. 'It's nearly ten. We should . . .?'

'Bed?'

'Yes, I think so.'

'Great. Well then . . .'

Michael got to his feet and put his hand out for her, which she took, with an uncertain smile, and then followed him into the bedroom.

Here he gently removed her clothes and ran his fingers across her skin and did all the soft, gentle, Michael things that Rachel had started to take for granted and which now felt like abundant golden gifts. He removed her bra from behind and then turned her around and kissed her on her mouth, a deep, endless kiss that made her shudder from her scalp to her fingertips. They moved to the bed and Michael laid her down, then stood above her as he removed his own clothes, and Rachel watched, wide-eyed with want, with relief, with love. When Michael was naked, he straddled her and kissed her again and Rachel put her hands on to his hips and moved him closer, guiding him towards her, ready, so ready after all these days and days without. She pushed her groin towards his and then pulled away again at the sensation of nothing where there should be something, where there was always something.

For a few minutes this continued, but no matter what Rachel did it became apparent that Michael was not going to be able to do what she so badly wanted him to do. Michael growled with frustration and Rachel touched her hand to the side of his face and said, 'It's fine. It's OK. Don't worry about it.' But as the words left her lips, she felt herself being forcibly, roughly shoved across the bed, hard enough to make her yell out, and Michael was off the bed and striding towards the bookshelves where he grabbed a handful of books and threw them across the room with a primal scream. Rachel instinctively brought herself into a foetal bunch, her arms wrapped around her knees, and then, as another handful of books arced across the room in her direction, she pulled the duvet up as high as she could get it.

'Michael,' she said, peering through a gap in her arms. 'Fuck. *Michael!* Stop! I told you. It doesn't matter.'

Michael spun round. His face was hot with violence. He looked at her and he said, 'It does *fucking matter*, Rachel. It does matter. This is . . . this is *you*. This is *all your fault.*'

'What?'

'You. You and your fucking "tie me up" bullshit. You and your other guys. Guys who've done that to you. Every time I shut my eyes, there they are. Lined up. And I can't, I *cannot* get them out of my head, Rachel. You put them there. Bunch of fucking *creeps.*'

'But, Michael, no! There was no "line of guys". It was just one or two boyfriends, that's all. Just . . . nothing serious.'

'That is not the *point*, Rachel. Jesus Christ. That is not the point.'

'Then what is the point?'

'The point is . . . *you*. You're the point. I thought I knew you. I thought I knew who you were. That golden girl in the pharmacy. That girl with the lustre, the class, the elegance. The girl who'd been waiting for her prince.'

'Waiting for her—? Oh, come on, Michael. You know that's bullshit. You know it is. You knew I'd had other boyfriends. Loads of boyfriends. I mean, Jesus Christ, when you saw me in the pharmacy that first time, I was a total mess. I had a hangover, and I was waiting for the morning-after pill, for God's sake.'

She saw a muscle twitch in his cheek as he assimilated this reminder into his rewriting of their story. 'Yeah,' he said. 'Maybe I should have seen what I was getting into right there and then.'

'What you were *getting into*?'

'Yeah. Damaged goods.'

Rachel felt a punch to the back of her gut at these words and the burn of bile at the base of her throat. 'I'm sorry?'

'Yeah. I guess I was duped by the English accent. Fooled into thinking it somehow equated with class. *Yet again.*'

Yet again. He meant Lucy.

'I never, ever told you I was classy. Not ever. I fucked you on our first date. What on earth made you think I was classy?'

He flinched at her language. 'That's a really good question, Rachel. A really good question.'

He'd been pacing the room during this exchange, but he stopped then and glanced at Rachel. 'Bend over.'

'Sorry, what?'

'I said, bend over.' He took a step towards the bed.

Rachel inched away from him towards the bedhead. 'Michael—'

'Turn around. Get on all fours.'

'But—'

'Do it, Rachel. Do. It.'

Rachel did as she was told. Maybe, she thought, maybe this would fix things. If she just let him do it to her this way. Just this once. He'd get over whatever weird insecurities he'd been nurturing since that night in the Seychelles. Maybe it would blot out the 'line of men' he'd allowed to take residence inside his head. Maybe it would get them back on track. Because, Rachel realised, very strongly and with a pathetic sense of shame, all she wanted was for things to be back on track. Back to normal. Back to morning hugs and late-night dinners in wine bars and hand-in-hand walks down the riverside and Michael breathing into her hair and telling her she was beautiful, that she was divine, that she was out of his league in every way.

Slowly, silently, she turned around and put herself on to all fours.

What happened next was hard and fast and brutal. He tugged on her hair so hard that it made her wince. He gripped her hips with fingers sharp enough to leave small, finger-shaped bruises the next day. Afterwards, when he was done, he pushed her roughly to one side and stalked to the bathroom.

'Well,' he called through to her over the sound of the tap

running in the sink. 'I can see why you like that kind of thing now. Rough sex. Isn't that what they call it? Maybe you can dig that stuff out of your suitcase, Rachel. For next time. Yeah?'

She listened out for a hint of softness in his voice. A hint of playfulness. But there was none.

26

June 2019

It had taken me roughly thirty seconds the night before to locate Kris Doll using just my thumb and a search engine. He appeared to be running some kind of city tours company from the back of a huge motorbike, quite possibly the biggest motorbike I've ever seen. There was a photo of him on his website, sitting astride the huge bike, wearing jeans and leather boots and a white T-shirt. On the panniers on either side of the bike were bottles of champagne chilling in ice. The text above the photo announced 'The Five Star Way to See the City'. Underneath it said:

Exclusive, one-on-one tours of the lake and the city on a fully customised Honda Gold Wing in the company of a city guide with over twenty years' experience of living in, working in and riding the streets of this magnificent city. Create your own tailor-made itinerary, or work with one of Kris's classics. The tour lasts for three hours and can be upgraded to include a final stop for champagne as the sun sets over Lake Michigan. Please fill in the form to make your booking or call the number below.

Yes, I think, looking at his picture again now, oh, *yes please*. Please put me on the back of your huge motorbike, Kris Doll, and transport me around the city and pour me champagne at sunset and tell me stories. Please.

I dial in the number at the bottom of the page and leave a message on Kris Doll's voicemail: 'Hi! Kris. My name is Joshua Harris. I don't know if it's rather short notice, but I'd love to book in for one of your city tours, maybe today? But if not, then any time tomorrow. Please give me a ring back when you get this message.'

His call comes through a moment later. 'Sure,' he says (he sounds sweet, much nicer than Rob with his tattoo sleeves and his air of turgid rage), 'I just happen to have had a cancellation tomorrow. How does five thirty work for you?'

'Oh,' I reply, 'yes! Perfect! That works beautifully!'

He talks me through what I need to do and when I need to do it ('Sunscreen – even with a helmet on you'll be amazed how much sun you'll soak up and it's set to be blue skies all the way tomorrow. Oh, and wear pants. I'm not going to tip you off my bike' – I laugh – 'but if I do, then you'll want to avoid the need for skin grafts. And as it's the afternoon spot, would you be interested in the sunset champagne upgrade? It's an extra twenty dollars?').

We agree on a champagne upgrade, a meeting spot and a rough shape for the tour and then I end the call, my face wreathed in smiles.

I go to a bar that night with the express intention of finding someone to bring back to my gorgeous hotel room. It's been months since I slept with anyone. Actually, longer. But here I am, in a vibrant city, far from home, far from work, far from Lucy. I feel I have covered a large amount of ground today, and I feel I deserve to let my hair down, have some cocktails, find someone nice to make me feel better about myself after the Joe interlude, which is still playing on my mind, twenty-four hours later.

I take a long shower and work my way through almost all the miniature hotel products in the process. I run a hand over my stubbled chin, but decide not to shave. Afterwards I open my laptop and browse the listings for 'best bars near me'. Then I put on black Levi's and a black Muji T-shirt, brown leather John Lobb loafers and a soft flannel shirt in an inky blue with a dark green overlaid check. I'm going to be Phin tonight, not the old Phin, but the new rugged one. I open the mini-bar and pull out a bottle of fancy microbrewery beer, bash off the lid, drink it from the bottleneck. *I AM PHIN*, I think to myself and the thought sends a charge through the core of me and I find myself, alone in a hotel room in Chicago, punching the air and saying, 'Bring it on.' Like an absolute weirdo.

I come back with a boy called Nicholas. Not Nick. Nicholas. He is twenty-eight but appears younger. He is not much to look at (my apologies to Nicholas's mother), but after two hours of standing around trying to look manly and being roundly ignored by all the hot men, I took what I could get. He smells nice and, frankly, that's often the main thing. I tell Nicholas about 'my' childhood, about my sociopathic father, the con artist David Thomsen, who took over people's homes, who raped teenage girls and stole money from naïve people and locked children in their bedrooms. His face is a picture. 'Oh my goodness,' he says, 'oh my goodness,' his hand clasping my kneecap in solidarity.

I find, when it comes down to it, I'm not actually that interested in the sex act itself. Use it or lose it, as they say. I have clearly left it too long. It is perfunctory and afterwards, it seems that I get more from the feeling of a person in the space next to me, the warm breath in the crook of my neck, the thin leg wrapped sweetly around my hips, the voice in my ear saying, 'Phin, is it OK if I sleep over?'

I bring Nicholas's hand over my shoulder, towards my mouth, and I kiss it, and then tuck it under my chin. 'That would be nice. Yes. Please.'

And we fall asleep entwined, and I feel almost, but not quite, at peace.

The following morning Nicholas has gone. He has not left any traces of himself, no note, no business card. I spend some time on Grindr, seeing if I can maybe find him there, but no sign of him. I don't know his surname, so I can't google him. And that is that. We may have spent an entire night wrapped around each other's naked bodies, but clearly Nicholas, dear, plain, doughy-faced boy that he was, was not keen to take things further. And as ever, I have no idea why.

But I have other things to think about today. I have my afternoon on the back of Kris Doll's Honda Gold Wing with champagne cooling in panniers and another big step in my search for Phin. So I push Nicholas from my thoughts, and jump out of my empty bed and into the new day.

27

Samuel

Then comes the breakthrough.

Bridget Elspeth Veronica Dunlop-Evers.

Reported missing by her parents in 1996.

Her parents had not heard from her for years, had only filed the report when she failed to materialise at a sibling's deathbed reunion. After a few months they had let it go. Theorised that Bridget – or Birdie as she was known to all and sundry – must have decided to cut her ties and make a life for herself far away from the family she had grown up in.

From the transcripts of the interviews with various members of Birdie's family, it sounded as though Birdie had been something of a black sheep, as if she had probably been better off without them.

I adjust the collar of my shirt, straighten the paper on the desk in front of me, clear my throat, and press in the last known phone number of Birdie's mother, Madelyn Dunlop-Evers.

'Hello?'

The voice is frail, as you would imagine the voice of an eighty-year-old woman to be.

'Hello. Is that Mrs Dunlop-Evers?'

'Speaking.'

'Good afternoon. My name is Detective Inspector Samuel Owusu.'

'Samuel *who*?'

'Owusu. Detective Inspector. I'm calling from the special crime unit at Charing Cross Police Station in London. I was hoping to talk to you about your daughter Bridget?'

'Bridget. No. There's no Bridget here. There's a boy though. In the other room. I could have a look for you?'

I sigh, close my eyes slowly and open them again.

'Is there someone there, Mrs Dunlop-Evers? Someone who could maybe answer some questions for me?'

'About the boy?'

'Yes. About the boy.'

I hear the phone being passed around, the muffle of hands over the speaker, different voices in the background, and then a man saying: 'Who is this?'

'My name is Detective Inspector Samuel Owusu. I'm calling from Charing Cross Police Station. From the special crime unit here. Who am I talking to?'

'I'm Philip Dunlop-Evers. Madelyn's son.'

'OK. That's great. I wondered if I might be able to talk to you about Bridget? Or Birdie? Your – I assume – your sister?'

'Yes. Er. Yes. Of course.'

'Could I ask you – was Bridget ever a dancer?'

There is a small silence.

'Yes. She was. She studied ballet until she was quite old. At least eighteen.'

I feel my stomach clench and unclench, a wave of drunken relief pass through me.

'Would you, do you think, be able to come to us, here in London? To discuss some . . . things?'

'Things?'

'Yes. Things that might be related to your sister's disappearance.'

'This is . . . well . . . wow. After all this time, I mean. Yes. Of course. Of course, I can come. When would you like me?'

'As soon as possible, please, Mr Dunlop-Evers.'

'Please. Call me Philip.'

'As soon as possible, Philip.'

28

Marco's mum has been in a weird mood all weekend. Marco's mum is *always* in a weird mood, but she's been even weirder than usual. Uncle Henry has disappeared, and she won't tell him why or where. Marco assumed he'd gone to Africa to find Phin, Libby's dad, but apparently Phin's not in Africa any more and Mum won't tell him why. She's been banging around the apartment since Friday, obsessively checking her phone every thirty seconds, snapping at him and Stella for minor infractions, forgetting to walk the dog and letting Uncle Henry's flat get really messy. Every time Marco tries to ask her about it, she pretends she's too busy.

On Sunday evening he notices Fitz staring longingly at the door of the apartment and he knocks on his mum's bedroom door.

'Mum?' he says. 'I think Fitz wants to go out.'

'Oh,' comes her reply. 'Could you take him?'

'I'm doing my homework.'

He hears her sigh. 'OK. I'll take him in a minute.'

'He's doing that circling thing though, Mum,' he says, his eyes on the dog. 'You know? When he's about to take a dump.'

She sighs again and then she appears. 'OK,' she says. 'OK.'

Marco gives a yell as he sees Fitz begin to lower himself into a squat. 'No! Fitz! No!' and the dog jumps back to standing. He watches his mum clip the lead to his harness. 'Why do you keep forgetting to take him out?' he asks.

'I have a lot on my mind, Marco.'

'About Henry?'

'Yes. About Henry.'

'Mum. Please. Just tell me what's going on.'

'I don't know what's going on.'

'Yes. But you must know *something*? I mean, can't you just call him?'

His mum stops for a second then and he sees her resolve crack a little.

'He's blocked me, Marco.'

'Uncle Henry?'

'Yes. Uncle Henry. He's blocked me.'

That is massive, thinks Marco. That is a really big deal.

'Well, why don't we try calling him from my phone?'

A glimmer of understanding passes across her features. 'Oh,' she says simply. 'Yes.' Then she looks down at the dog and says, 'Let's try when I get back.'

Marco awaits her return eagerly, his phone in his hand, his uncle's number primed and ready. He passes it to his mum when she returns, and she presses call. He can hear the foreign ring tone and exchanges a look with his mum. It rings out into a flat beep and she hangs up and sends his uncle a message instead. It says:

FFS HENRY. What's going on???

Then she goes on to WhatsApp and calls him from there. Again, it rings into nothingness. She sends him another message from the app:

Henry. It's Lucy. PLS CALL.

Almost immediately, Henry has blocked Marco too.

'Have we done something wrong?' Marco asks his mum, his voice cracking slightly. 'I don't understand.'

His mother smiles at him sadly and says, 'No. We have not done anything wrong. But listen, Marco. Your uncle. He's not . . .'

'What?'

'He's complicated. Remember when we first got to London last year? Remember how I wasn't quite sure who Uncle Henry was? Because he looked so much like Phin?'

Marco nods.

'Well, the thing is, Uncle Henry used to be slightly obsessed with Phin. When they were younger. He used to follow him about and stare at him all the time and then . . .'

Marco nods again, but his mother shakes her head. 'Nothing,' she says. 'Nothing.'

'No! Tell me. What was it you were going to say? What does that have to do with Uncle Henry blocking us? You have to tell me!'

'It's . . . urgh. Marco, listen. I know you're very fond of Henry. And it's important to me that you have that bond with him. I don't want to damage your relationship with him. And what I'm about to tell you, I promise, it in no way means that Henry doesn't adore you and that Henry is not an amazing person. Because he is. In so many ways. But when we were children, when all the bad things were happening to us in the house in Chelsea, Henry sometimes wasn't very nice to Phin. He once pushed him into the river when Phin wouldn't kiss him, and Phin could have drowned. And then, the night we escaped, Henry tied Phin to a radiator and . . . well, he could have died again. The way he was about Phin, it was a bit twisted. And Phin found out from Clemency that Henry was coming to Botswana and left the same day. And now, well, I think maybe Henry's found out where he is and is on his way to . . .'

'To what? You think he might hurt him?'

'Well, not hurt him as such. But make him feel uncomfortable. You know, make him feel unsafe.'

Marco's brain went mental, as though sparks were flying off it, as he tried to assimilate this information. Uncle Henry was kind of strange, but not in the way that his mum was describing. He was weird in a way that was cool and acerbic. He was funny. He made Marco laugh. He got things that other grown-ups didn't quite get. But all this Phin stuff . . .

'We need to find him,' he says.

'Yes. I know. That's what I've been trying to do all weekend. I mean, I found all his old devices. But I have no idea how to get on to them.'

'Give them to me.'

She sighs and gets to her feet, goes into her room and comes back a minute later with two old iPhones, an old Apple Mac, an old iPad and a handful of chargers.

'I've tried everything,' she says. 'Every combination of dates and birthdays and house numbers. Can't get into any of them.'

Marco taps the edge of the dining table with his knuckles, his head spinning with conflicting thoughts. 'I could get Alf to try.'

'Alf? What is he, like a hacker?'

'Yeah. Kind of.'

'Hm. Henry is pretty tech-savvy, remember. He's virtually a hacker himself. I doubt very much he'd leave anything that wasn't completely impenetrable.'

'Yeah. But he's old. Alf's young. Young hackers trump old hackers.'

He glances at his mum and sees her smiling wryly at him. 'You could try, I guess.'

Marco nods sagely, takes out his phone and messages Alf.

29

I stride across the parking lot towards the man standing next to the huge motorbike.

'Hi!' I say, my hand extended forcefully, 'I'm Joshua Harris. You must be Kris.'

Kris grips my hand inside his and crunches it slightly. I try not to wince.

'Yes! Kris Doll. Really great to meet you!'

He eyes me up and down and for a moment I think maybe he's checking me out, but then I remember that he used to go out with sexy Mati from the Magdala so that is highly unlikely, and I realise he is simply making sure I'm sensibly dressed for the back of his bike. He nods approvingly and then brings some paperwork out of a shoulder bag.

'Okey dokey,' he says, peeling through the papers with his fingertips. 'I just have to ask you to sign a few things, if you wouldn't mind. Just disclaimers. Housekeeping stuff. Ts and Cs. If you want to take the time to read them, please feel free, we're in no rush.'

He hits me with a super-smile. He is very attractive but could, in my opinion, take more care over his skin; it's very dry. And his dark shaggy hair is in dire need of deep conditioning and a good cut, but I suppose if he spends all day in a crash helmet, it probably doesn't feel worth the effort. I age him at around thirty-eight. I take the papers and I sit on a bench and flick through them, sign them *Joshua Harris* with a flourish, pass them back to him.

He peers at them briefly. 'Fan-tastic. Super. Right. Let's get you set up. You ever been on a Gold Wing before?'

'Nope. No, never.'

'Any kind of bike?'

'Well, yes. Once or twice. Been given lifts by friends. But never as a hobby. Or as a thing.'

'I don't suppose you can remember the names or the makes of the bikes you've been on?'

I shake my head apologetically. I have let him down. 'I'm sorry,' I say.

He rallies. 'No problem. That's OK. Anyway, this is the *most* comfortable ride you can ever have, believe me. You will never want to ride pillion on anyone else's bike, ever again. Let's get you up there.'

He gets me up there and I sit up high, like a little princeling about to be carried aloft on a golden sedan. He talks me through our route for the day, but I'm not listening. I stare at the back of his head as he takes his seat at the front of the bike and puts on his own helmet; then I stare at his shoulders: they are as broad as befits a man who once rowed people across lakes for a living. I am feeling the one degree of separation that exists between me, him and Phin, wondering if I will find the moment to scatter my connection to our mutual friend into the path of our conversation. It needs to be natural. A bizarre coincidence. He cannot feel interrogated. I must not tread too fast.

Kris drives us down the so-called 'Magnificent Mile', a fine avenue of skyscrapers abutting the banks of the Chicago River.

'Where do you live in Britain?' he turns to shout to me.

'London,' I shout back.

'Cool,' he says.

'Have you ever been to the UK?'

'Yeah. A few years back. I was seeing a British girl.'

'Whereabouts did you stay?'

'At her place. She lived in Milton Keynes.'

'Ah,' I say. 'That's nice.'

He points things out to me, churches and whatnot, but I can tell he's not interested, and neither am I. Eventually we descend into a companiable silence, and I watch the moving scenery and inhale the scent of petrol streets and the slightly musty inside of a crash helmet (heaven knows how one cleans the inside of a crash helmet – I try not to ponder it too deeply), and then, as the street-lights flick on and the city peters out into the banks of Lake Michigan, the bike comes to a stop next to a sandy beach and we dismount.

Kris takes a blanket from the pannier and unfurls it on to the sand. He grabs himself an alcohol-free beer from the ice bag and the half-bottle of champagne, which he uncorks and pours into a plastic glass for me. The sky across the lake is turning sugar pink; the tall buildings of the city beyond are black paper cut-outs. The air is soft June warm, and I have had a wonderful afternoon on the back of Kris's bike, looking at a city that I have never seen before. There has been an unexpected intimacy about the experience, as if we are now somehow bonded in a small way, and I wonder if everyone who takes one of his tours feels the same way or if it's only lonely, damaged people like me who take such strange comfort from them. I've barely eaten and the cheap, not-quite-cold-enough champagne goes directly to the bottom of my stomach and into my bloodstream and I find, as my eyes take in the beauty of Chicago's skyline reflected in the rose-gold mirror of the lake, that I am crying.

I turn my head a few degrees so that Kris won't see, and surreptitiously rub my cheeks against my shoulders.

'Isn't it beautiful?' he says, and I nod, not trusting myself to speak. I am awash with emotion for which I have insufficient language. A churning in my soul of loss and emptiness and lack and incompleteness. I am *incomplete*. I have always felt incomplete. And I have thought at various points throughout my life that just around the next corner would be the thing that would complete me. I thought finding Libby would complete me, that returning to my childhood home would complete me, being rich and successful, being buff and pretty, having good sex with bad men, bad sex with good men, love affairs with no love, a stunning kitchen with touch-to-open cupboard doors – I have thought that all of these things would complete me and none of them has. And now I am here on the shores of Lake Michigan with a handsome man called Kris Doll sitting by my side thoughtfully sipping alcohol-free lager from the bottleneck and the sky is on fire and nobody loves me and I love nobody and I am alone, I am so, so alone and Jesus fucking Christ I have to find Phin. I have to find Phin and if finding him doesn't fix me I swear to God I will swim across this lake and throw myself into that acid-orange sun and let myself burn to a smudge of ash.

I clear my throat and straighten my back. 'How long have you been doing this?' I ask Kris.

'Oh, you know. A few years. I was on the lake before, doing boat rides, excursions, that sort of thing.'

I act as if I did not already know this. 'So you're from Chicago? Originally?'

'Yup. Born and bred. What about you? Are you a born-and-bred Londoner?'

'Yes. Yes I am. I was born in a hospital room overlooking the Houses of Parliament. Brought up on the banks of the River Thames. And now I live in central London. I am very much a born and bred Londoner.' I pause as I try to think of a way to steer the conversation towards the information I need. Then I have it. 'What happened with the girl from Milton Keynes?'

'Ah, we broke up. Couldn't hack the long-distance thing. Plus she . . .' He pauses. 'Well, she couldn't hack my sexuality.'

My breath catches. Kris Doll is not straight?

'You mean, you're not just into girls?'

'Correct.' He runs his palms down the side of his lager bottle. 'Yeah. I thought Brits were meant to be so liberal and tolerant. At least, *all* the ones I ever met before were. But not her, it transpired.'

'Do you know a lot of British people?'

'A few. Yeah. Guys, mainly, you know. When I'm out at bars and the like.'

'What sort of bars do you go to? I mean, is there a particular scene for queer boys who like big bikes?'

He gives a wry laugh. 'No. Not really. There's a biker bar I used to go to a while back. But then I got into a kind of messy situation with a girl there and now I tend to just go to normal bars. You know.'

'A messy situation?'

'Yeah.' He laughs again. 'I was really into her, but she was really into this other guy and she played us off against each other for months and then . . . well. Plot twist – turned out he was bi too and he and I, well, you know . . .' He laughs and grimaces. 'She was not pleased. So, yeah, I kind of stopped going there.'

I pretend that I am still listening but I'm not. I'm busy swallowing down the fireball of shock that has just jumped from my gut to my throat at the revelation that Phin is bi, actively bi, and that Phin, *my Phin*, has slept with Kris Doll, this man who I am currently sitting just a few inches away from, and that if I were to touch Kris, right now, it would be almost as if I were touching Phin and I should feel jealous, maybe, or angry, but I don't, I just feel filled with wonder and a need to be close to someone who has been close to Phin.

'What was he like?'

'The other guy?'

'Yeah. The other guy.'

'Oh, he was British too, actually! Ha! From London. Kind of . . . posh.' *Pash.*

I swallow hard. 'Oh, yeah?'

'Yeah. He was kind of, *possibly*, the most interesting person I've ever met in my life.'

'In what way?'

'Oh, just in . . . He was kind of beautiful, but not vain. And he had this way of seeing the world, y'know? Just very . . . pure. But he also had this crazy backstory.'

'Ooh,' I say playfully. 'Was he a child wizard?'

Kris laughs. 'No. Ha! Not quite. Though he was locked in a room by his psycho dad.' He checks to see that I'm suitably shocked by the revelation, which I do a good job of pretending that I am, before continuing. 'He lived in, like, this mansion. Over-looking the Thames. And his dad was some kind of con artist, bamboozled this wealthy family out of all their worldly goods and then went mad, started locking people up. He escaped from there when he was a teenager and has been on the run ever since.'

'On the run from his father?'

'No, not from his father. I think he died, somehow. But there were other people in the house while all this was going on, people he didn't want to know any more. Like, some guy who handcuffed him to a radiator or something.'

I swallow again, hard. 'Sounds gothic.'

'Yeah. Super-dark. But somehow this guy – Finn, his name was Finn – he managed to kind of rise above it. Radiate goodness, you know. Other people might have let the damage taint them. But he didn't. He just ploughed his own furrow. Did his own thing.'

'He sounds inspiring.'

'Yes. He is.'

My ears prick up at Kris's sudden use of the present tense. 'What happened to him?'

'Got a job on a game reserve in Africa somewhere. That was always his passion. Animals. Conservation. All of that kind of thing.' He turns his beer bottle slowly between the palms of his hands and says, 'Apparently he's back.'

'He's—' I stop and pull myself back from appearing too excited.

'Yeah. Just got in a few days ago.'

'Here? Chicago?'

'Yup. I bumped into a mutual friend yesterday, who said he'd seen him around. He was just about to check into an Airbnb apparently. I might see if I can hook up with him; he's always a balm, y'know.' He sighs and tips the dregs of his beer into the beach. 'Anyway. I think it's getting about time . . .'

'Yes,' I agree immediately. 'Yes, it probably is.'

The sky is dark blue now, the black rectangles of the skyscrapers across the lake glow gold through their lit-up windows.

I quickly finish the rest of the cheap warm champagne and take the empty bottle to a bin. My brain spins in circles as I mount the Gold Wing and put the helmet back on. It's a fifteen-minute drive back to my hotel. As we pull up outside the hotel I unbuckle my wristwatch and slip it into the pannier of his bike.

Then I pass Kris back the helmet and I wave him goodbye. He thinks he'll never see me again. But he's wrong.

30

Samuel

Philip Dunlop-Evers is a small man with thinning hair and a weak chin. He wears a white polo shirt with blue jeans and cheap leather shoes. I button my suit jacket and stand to greet him with an outstretched hand.

'Thank you, Philip, for coming at such short notice,' I say.

'It's no problem at all. I mean, it's my sister, after all. I can't think of a better reason to cancel a few plans and get on a train.'

'Take a seat. Please.'

He sits and peers at me. He looks as if his head is spinning with thoughts. Hardly surprising.

'Philip. We recently received a call from a mud-larker. Do you know what a mud-larker is?'

He nods.

'He had found some bones washed up. A full set of human bones. We believe, Philip, that they may belong to your sister, Bridget.'

'Birdie.' He says this in a whisper.

'Yes. Birdie. Of course. So if you don't mind, if you're OK, I wanted to run through some details with you. Just to confirm. Tell me, Philip, what happened the last time you saw Birdie? Can you recall?'

'Yes. Very clearly. She was sort of famous at the time.'

'I hear she was once in a pop band.'

'That's right. They had a big hit; it was number one for weeks. She was jetting off all over the place. It was . . . We're a musical family, but it wasn't quite the thing, you know, to be so . . . *visible*. We were all a bit taken aback by the whole thing. She and the band were doing a gig at the Corn Exchange so she spent the night with Mum and Dad rather than in a hotel with the band. I was, what, fourteen? Fifteen? I remember it clearly. There was a big row between Birdie and my mother. There was *always* a big row between Birdie and my mother. My mother doesn't really like girls, you see. She had six boys and two girls and never got on with either of them. After that Birdie didn't come home. Not once. I know my sister saw her from time to time – she would know more about that period of Birdie's life – but she passed away a long time ago.'

'Ah. Was this perhaps the sibling deathbed request that alerted your parents to Birdie's disappearance?'

'Yes. Jenny's death. We tried everything to track Birdie down, but nobody seemed to know anything. None of the band members. She'd had a boyfriend, Justin. No sign of him, and obviously this was the mid-nineties. Nobody had social media. Nobody had mobile phones. No internet. We just hit a wall. We didn't know what else to do. We all sat with Jenny until she passed and then, after the funeral, one of us – my brother Dicky, I think – reported Birdie missing to the police. And, well, you know the rest.'

'And Justin. The boyfriend. What can you remember about him?'

Philip shrugs, as if it's the first time he's ever given a moment's thought to his sister's boyfriend.

'You never thought that maybe . . .?'

'What? That he had something to do with Birdie's disappearance? Well, yes, of course. Of course we all thought that. But when the police couldn't find him either it just seemed more likely that they'd either absconded together or died together. And Justin was a softie. A lapdog. He wasn't a killer. I mean, at least that was *my* impression.'

'What did Justin do? As a job, I mean?'

'He was a . . . well, he claimed to be a musician. A percussionist. He played the tambourine in Birdie's band. Clearly that's not exactly a career as such. I assume he had other skills. He was a bit of a hippy. Scruffy. Outdoorsy. A bit flaky.'

'So, Birdie and your mother had an argument. Birdie left. And do you know where she was living at this point?'

'In London. That's all we knew. With Justin. And a cat.'

'She had a cat?' I make a note in my notebook.

'Yes. I seem to recall she got the cat without checking with her landlord. He was going to kick them out and so they were house-hunting.'

'And you don't know where she ended up?'

Philip sighs. 'She had a plan, she said. She knew someone with a big house who might be able to put them up for a short while.'

I feel a muscle in my cheek twitch. 'A big house?'

'Yes.'

'You don't happen to know where this big house was?'

'No. Sorry. All she said was that she had made a new friend who lived in a huge house and the friend had offered them a room as a temporary measure.'

'And what year was this?'

'The same year she and my mother stopped talking, when I was fourteen. So it would have been 1988; the year she and her band were at their most famous.'

'And the band, they split up in 1990?'

'Yes. Around about then.'

I sigh and stretch my shoulders apart slightly. 'So, the skeleton that our forensics team have assembled, it is roughly twenty-five years old. Which puts us at about 1995 on the timeline. And your other sister, Jenny, passed away in—?'

'Nineteen ninety-six.'

I change position in my chair to relieve the ache in my back. 'So. Philip. We found fibres attached to these bones. Shreds of a label from a bath towel. A very expensive brand. Which makes me think, if she wasn't wealthy enough herself to afford a two-hundred-pound bath towel, that she must have been with someone who was. It makes me wonder about this big house and the new friend. Is there nothing else you can recall about this arrangement?'

'No. None of us can remember anything about it. We were all asked about it at the time of the original investigation. But nobody knew any more than that. We don't even know if she and Justin ever actually took up the friend's offer of a room.' He shrugs, then he looks up at me, very suddenly, and I see that his eyes are wet with tears. 'How did she die? My sister? It is my sister, isn't it?'

I stare at Philip and nod. 'We believe it is. Yes.'

I feel appalled with myself for allowing my need to find out why she died to distract me from my responsibility to break this news to her brother. I clear my throat and sit a little straighter.

'There appears to have been a blow to the head,' I say. 'She then appears to have been left to decompose inside a cocoon made of fabric and towels, outdoors. The bones were taken out of the towels and transferred into a black bag, which was tied in a knot and dropped, we assume, into the Thames, at some point in the past few months to a year.'

'You mean, the murderer came back for her?'

'Yes, it looks that way.'

Philip's head drops. When he raises it again, there are tears on his cheeks.

'Why would someone want to kill her?'

'It might have been an accident.'

Philip shakes his head. 'No. It doesn't sound like it, does it? Leaving her in a shroud. Then coming back for her twenty-five years later. Disposing of her. It doesn't sound like an accident.'

'No,' I agree. 'No. It doesn't.'

I watch realisation dawn across his face.

'Someone killed my sister,' he says. 'And they're still out there. To this very day.'

'Yes. I'm afraid it would appear that way.'

Philip looks at me. His eyes are wide. 'You are going to find out who did it, aren't you? You are going to catch them? And make them pay?'

I want to say yes, but I cannot, for I know that there is only so far a case like this can stretch, that the passage of time obfuscates and complicates, that history swallows evidence in its wake. But I know that I will do my very best and that my very best is all I have to give and so I say, 'Philip, I give you my word, I will do everything I can.'

31

April 2017

'Baby. You look tired. Have you been getting enough sleep?'

Rachel looked up at her father from her desk where she was tapping numbers into her accounting software. Her father appeared to her through a haze of bleary eyes, bleary thoughts, a darkly shifted perception of the world.

'I'm fine,' she said. 'Absolutely fine. Just been a long week.'

'Well, you need to get that husband of yours to whisk you away somewhere. To one of his many houses. I can't believe he still hasn't taken you to Antibes and you've been married for two months. I can't believe he's not . . .' He sighed and she felt the weight of unsaid words and unasked questions in the air between them. 'But everything's all right, is it? Between the two of you?'

Rachel nodded. 'Of course,' she said. 'Everything's fine.'

She was at home. Not her home, but her parents' house, the house she was brought up in, the house where she once lived with a mother and a father and a rolling succession of small dogs that her mother rehomed every time she needed to go away for more than a month. It was a beautiful house, with tall windows and a gated driveway, lacy jasmine tumbling over the front wall and her father's valet-fresh Range Rover parked outside. Her father lived now alone, since Rachel's mother died five years previously. For five years Rachel and her father had been a tiny team of two, meeting for breakfast dates at the Wolseley, for tea and cakes at his favourite patisserie in Soho, for shopping expeditions to seek Rachel's opinion on his sartorial choices, which inevitably ended with Rachel carrying home silky-handled shopping bags from out-of-her-budget boutiques. Rachel and her father had always been compatible, more than Rachel had ever been with her mother, whom she found infuriating and unpredictable. Her mother's death had served to bring Rachel and her father even closer together, but ever since Rachel had met Michael she'd felt her father drifting away from her, becoming vaguer and smaller, an outline, a sketch. Even here, standing over her, a cup of coffee cradled inside his hands, his socked feet sinking into the thick cream carpet that her mother favoured and that had to be shampooed professionally once a year, even now, mere inches from her, she couldn't locate him. As if the signal was poor. *You're breaking up.*

Her father squeezed her shoulder and said, 'You would say, wouldn't you? If anything was worrying you?'

Rachel nodded tersely. 'Of course I would.'

'I just think . . . your mother, she would have asked more questions, maybe, you know. She might have urged a little more caution. Possibly. I mean, three months. Even with a catch like Michael. Quite quick. When you think about it.'

Rachel typed noisily. 'Everything is fine. Honestly. Don't over-think it. You're being like mum.'

Being like mum. It was always the most galling thing that Rachel could say to him.

'Sorry.' Her father took his hand from her shoulder. 'Sorry.'

She heard his footsteps, muted in the velvet carpet, moving away from her, the smell of his coffee lingering in his wake. She breathed in hard to stop the tears, turned the pages of her paper-work, started to type in another row of numbers.

She left her father's house an hour later. It was starting to rain. 'Wait,' her father said decisively from the doorstep. 'Wait. I'll drive you, let me just grab my coa—'

'No. It's fine. I'm happy to walk. I've got an umbrella.'

'I can drive you.'

'No. I'd rather walk.'

She glanced at him. Brian Gold. In his navy lambswool and his socked feet and his hair still thick and dark even in his sixties, his soft face full of concern. She felt something hot and liquid rush through her, a sickening jolt of love and sadness. 'Bye, Dad.'

She took the long chrome escalator down from pavement level at St John's Wood tube station and stared into the terrifying drop below, imagined herself hurtling from the top to the bottom, land-ing as a mass of broken, splintered bones, people's mouths wide with screams, while she would be free.

Her phone beeped just before she ran out of signal. It was Michael.

Hey, beautiful. What do you want for dinner? I'm just heading out to shop.

She typed fast, before she lost signal. *Pasta wd be nice. W prawns?*

She pressed send and stared at the phone, willing it to get to Michael's phone, breathing a sigh of relief when it went. It would set the evening off on the wrong footing if he didn't hear from her before he went to the shops. He would come back with something she didn't like, deliberately, and say, *Well, I didn't hear from you, so, y'know?* He'd be clipped. He'd withhold his bonhomie. And if there was one thing that Rachel wanted to maintain, at all times, it was Michael's bonhomie. The darkness that existed beyond Michael's bonhomie was immeasurable and she thought, as she did so often, of a parallel world in which she had not brought the sex toys on honeymoon, had not answered Michael's question about whether she had used them before with other men, and had contented herself with their perfectly good vanilla sex for another fifty years, and felt anger with herself for changing the track of her marriage so completely for something which now seemed so unimportant.

On the tube she sat blankly rolling her engagement ring round and around her ring finger. She looked up at the shadowy impression of herself in the window opposite and sighed at it. It had stopped raining by the time she got off the tube at Fulham Broadway, the pavements stained petrol grey, the traffic hissing through dark puddles. She checked her phone and saw a smiley face from Michael in her text replies. She felt her mood shift, her gait lighten. He was unpacking shopping in the kitchen when she entered the apartment. He beamed at her. 'Hey, gorgeous. How's your dad?'

'My dad is just great.' She went to him and lifted her face to his and let him kiss her on both her cheeks, felt the suggestion of evening stubble against her skin. She moved away from him. 'He sends his love.'

'And how were the accounts looking?'

'The accounts are looking rosy.'

He beamed at her again. The setting sun burst through the thick cloud outside and cast itself all over him. He looked golden. 'That's great. That really is. Because, y'know, I am going to need some help this month.'

Rachel felt a slick of ice down her spine. 'Oh,' she began carefully. 'I thought you were getting an income now? From the house in Antibes?'

'Well, yeah. Kind of. But it's low season. Bookings will be sporadic. And I still have to pay the cleaner. And the pool guy. Things will pick up next month. But this month, things are still tight.'

He slid a tray of prawns into the fridge. She noticed that they were the small, pink, cooked prawns, not the big raw pearlescent ones he always used to buy. She noticed too that he'd shopped at Tesco, not at Whole Foods as he usually did.

The sun sank down behind the cloud and Michael was normal-coloured once again.

'What do you need me to do?' she asked.

'Well, I guess maybe we could start with paying me back for the shopping?' He gestured at the food items on the kitchen counter.

'Sure,' she replied, trying not to let her concern show. 'How much was it?'

He pulled a receipt from the bottom of the shopping bag and peered at it. 'Twenty-six pounds.'

'Sure,' she said again, pulling a twenty and a ten from her purse and pushing them across the counter towards him.

He took the notes and slipped them into his back pocket. 'Thanks, honey. This won't go on for much longer, I promise you.'

It was something to do with a missing shipment of parts. They were worth, according to Michael, 'not a million. But not far off.' And he was required to pay for the missing shipment out of his own pocket. 'All of my savings, Rachel. Everything.'

He'd cried and buried his wet face in her shoulder and told her that he was not worthy, that she could leave him, that he wouldn't blame her, that this was not what she'd signed up for, less than she deserved. She had stroked his hair and soothed him and told him that she was not with him for his money, that she was with him because she loved him. She loved him. She loved him.

He'd been on a hair trigger ever since, determined to make her feel every single pulse of his self-loathing. He'd put his house in Antibes on to a holiday rental site and was toying with the idea of selling his Fulham flat and moving into Rachel's Camden apartment. 'It won't come to that, I'm sure,' he'd said. 'It won't. But if it did . . .'

She'd nodded. 'Oh. God. Yes. Of course. Of course.'

Nights once spent deciding where to go for dinner were now spent at home deciding what to watch on TV. Even this was now fraught with tension as Michael explained exactly how much each streaming package was costing him per month.

'What time do you want to eat?'

She glanced at the clock. It was six o'clock. 'Maybe seven?'

'You got it.' He flicked a tea towel over his shoulder and pulled a saucepan from a cupboard, filling it with water from the tap.

In bed later that night, Michael clutched the duvet to his chest inside his fists and stared at the ceiling. They'd just got to the end of a very unsatisfactory sexual interlude, Michael's penis growing flaccid every minute or so, having to be brought back to life either by Rachel or by his own hand and ending with Rachel on all fours and Michael thrusting soullessly for over ten minutes before ejaculating without any suggestion of enjoyment.

'It's the money thing,' he said after a short, murky moment of post-coital silence. 'It's . . . I'm not used to this. I'm not used to being poor. I'm not used to having to take money from the woman I love. I'm just . . . I'm emasculated, Rachel. I'm fucking emasculated.'

Rachel looked at him thoughtfully. She wanted to remind him that he'd been having problems maintaining an erection since long before he'd lost all his money. He'd been having trouble maintaining an erection since their honeymoon, since she'd stupidly suggested extending their sexual repertoire. 'That's just silly,' she said, knowing as the words left her lips that they were the wrong ones.

He turned sharply. 'Silly?'

'No.' She flinched. 'Not silly. Just—'

'Fuck, Rachel. *Fuck*. Do you not see what is happening here? This isn't silly. I'm fucking broke. I might have to sell this apartment. I have people – God, Rachel, you do not know what kind of people – breathing down my neck. And you – you get to swan off every day to your precious little studio, and make your pretty little necklaces with your lovely daddy at the end of the fucking line ready to bail you out every time you go into the red and your lovely little mortgage-free apartment and – and your *youth* and you have no idea, you literally have *no idea about anything, Rachel.* You're a fucking child.' Michael ripped the duvet away from himself and stalked to the bathroom.

Rachel blinked slowly, to calm herself. She looked at his white naked buttocks pistoning angrily away from her. A voice inside her head was screaming at Michael. It was using foul language and it was telling Michael that he was an idiot, that he was an arse-hole, that he was shit in bed and poor and old and that she hated him, that she wished she'd never married him, that she wanted her old life back, the one that didn't involve tiptoeing around a middle-aged man's fragile masculinity, bringing his flaccid penis back to life like a paramedic every night.

But she sucked it all back down inside her, lay silently on her back and waited for him to return. When he did, she tenderly wrapped an arm around him and said, 'I love you.'

But even as she said the words, she wondered if they were true because she was pretty sure that love was not meant to feel this way.

'I'm going to turn this around, Rachel. I promise. I am going to turn this around.'

She nodded, but said nothing.

It was safer that way.

32

June 2019

I give it an hour after I get back to my hotel, and then I call him.

'Kris. It's me. Joshua. From earlier. I'm so, so sorry, but I think I might have left my watch on your bike.'

'Your—?'

'My watch. It's a vintage Cartier. My father's. I took it off and put it in one of your baskets and stupidly forgot to grab it back at the end of the trip.'

'Ah. Right. OK. Cool. The Gold Wing is in the garage for the night. I rent a space for it, two blocks down. I can't get to it right now, but I can look later on? If you're OK waiting a while?'

'Yes. Yes. Absolutely. No rush. I'm here for a few days more. I can meet you somewhere. Anywhere. At your convenience.'

'Or I could just drop it at your hotel lobby?'

'No, I don't want to inconvenience you. Just let me know where you'll be and I can meet you there.'

'Yeah, sure. Whatever. Of course. I'll message you when I've found it.'

'Great. Thank you so much, Kris. I'm so sorry for being a pain.'

'Not at all, Joshua. Not at all.'

It's ten o'clock and I should flip open my laptop and catch up with my emails. I have absolutely been neglecting work. I've told the team that I've caught a bug and am laid up in my hotel room and will check my emails intermittently, but I have not looked at them at all. Not once since I got here. And now I have a couple of hours to myself but I just can't. I am smouldering inside with the know-ledge that he is here, in the same city as me.

Phin is in Chicago. Phin has an apartment in Chicago but is not staying in it. Phin is bisexual. I have spent the afternoon with a man who has had sex with him, but who doesn't know where he is. But there is another friend who might know where he is. Sexy Mati from the bikers' bar.

I shower and change and half an hour later I'm back at the Magdala.

'The girl, Mati, she was in here Saturday night with a big guy with the—' I run my hands down my forearms to describe the tattoo sleeves.

The bartender narrows his eyes at me and nods.

'Has she been in tonight?'

He shakes his head. 'During the week, she has the kids.'

'She has kids?'

'Yeah. Two of them. She won't be back here until Friday.'

'Ah. Right. That's a shame. I'll probably be back in London by then.'

'What do you want with her?'

'We have a mutual friend. A friend of mine from London. I heard he was back in town, but nobody seems to know where he is. I just thought she might have a clue.'

'The Finn guy?'

I glance at him in surprise. 'Oh,' I say. 'Yes. That's right, the Finn guy.'

'He was in here about half an hour ago. You just missed him.'

My vision blurs. My fingers grip the counter. I feel an icy bullet pass through my gut.

'Are you sure?'

'Yes. Finn. The British guy. With the beard. Yes.'

'Did he, erm . . .' I step from one foot to the other, run the palm of my hand hard down my mouth and chin. 'Did he say where he was headed?'

'Nope.'

'Was he – *with* anyone?'

'Nope.'

'Did he, I mean, was he . . .?' I don't know what to ask.

'Are you OK?'

'Yes. I'm fine. I'm just – annoyed that I missed him. I just – I wanted to see him, he's very . . . *important to me* and now I feel like—' I am starting to crack and I can see the bartender is becoming concerned. I pull myself back into shape and smile. 'Never mind,' I say. 'Never mind. I'll come back another time. I'm sure our paths will cross eventually.'

'You want me to say anything to him? If he comes back?'

'No. Don't say anything. It'll just—' *It'll just freak him out*, is what I want to say. Because that's exactly what it will do. It will freak him out and he will run for the hills. I ramp up my smile. 'Thank you. Anyway. I'm Joshua. By the way.'

'Joshua. Great. Can I get you anything?'

'No. Thank you. I think I'll head home.'

'Sure. Have a good night, Joshua.'

On the street I stare left and right. And then I stare straight ahead. There is a man leaving the organic supermarket opposite. A tall man. With sandy blond hair and a clipped golden-brown beard. He has a tan. He is wearing a khaki T-shirt and black shorts and a pair of horn-rimmed glasses. Two large bags of shopping hang from his hands. He stops as he leaves the store and he glances across the street.

I see that he is peering through the windows of the Magdala. Looking for someone.

And it is only then, with a kick to my gut so hard that I almost fall back into the doorway of the bar, that I realise I have found him.

PART TWO

33

Samuel

The Times

Monday, 24 June 2019

The Metropolitan Police are investigating the discovery of human remains found by a mud-larker on the shores of the River Thames just under a week ago. They have been identified as those of Bridget Dunlop-Evers, also known as Birdie, who was reported missing by her family in 1996 when she was thirty-two years old. She had been a member of the band *Original Version* who enjoyed a handful of pop hits in the late 1980s. She left the band shortly after their last hit and has not been seen since. According to Miss Dunlop-Evers' family, she had been briefly homeless, along with her boyfriend Justin Redding, who played percussion with the same band, but they might have found lodgings with a new friend who lived, according to Miss Dunlop-Evers, 'in a large house'. Attempts to track down Miss Dunlop-Evers and Mr Redding when they were reported missing were unsuccessful and their fate has remained a mystery for nearly three decades. Anyone with any information regarding Dunlop-Evers' and Redding's whereabouts at the time of their disappearance is asked to contact the Metropolitan Police at their earliest convenience. Additionally, anyone with any information regarding the location of the house where the couple may have been living is also invited to make contact.

Accompanying the article is a photograph of Birdie taken during her time with the band. She is wearing a floral bandana around her neck and is holding a fiddle to her shoulder. Her hair is light brown, fine and very long, with a back-combed fringe. Her eyes are small and narrowed at the camera. Her mouth is hard and painted pink, and as predicted by the facial reconstruction artist, her chin is weak. The text underneath says: 'Birdie Dunlop-Evers, whose remains have been found on the banks of the Thames.'

I click on the readers' comments section underneath the article.

They are full of slightly harsh reminiscences of the summer in which their hit had been a number one for too long, when it appears everyone had heard the song too much. A few strike a more respectful note; some remember the story of her being missing in the mid-nineties. Some remember seeing the band playing live in the 1980s. One remembers meeting Birdie: 'She was tiny. Kind of cool. She signed my hand. She smelled like that White Musk from the Body Shop that everyone used to wear. She was actually a very talented violinist, you know, classically trained. Such a great shame. Her poor family.'

I get to the end of the comments. It's not being greeted as a big news story. It's a footnote. An oddity. It's just one big news story away from sliding out of the BBC's top ten Most Read stories. It's now or never in terms of it hitting the right people, the people who might know what happened to Birdie.

I stare at my phone, willing it to ring. It doesn't. I go back to my browser and continue the research I'd been doing into Birdie Dunlop-Evers and her band, the Original Version. I have read the interviews with her former band members transcribed from the period after she was reported missing. It felt to me that she had only been brought into the band because of her musical prowess, not because of camaraderie or a bond of friendship. None of her bandmates back in '96 seemed to have any idea where she might have been for the preceding two years. None of them seemed to care. They described her as cold and secretive, difficult and demanding. They described Justin as a hippy, a space cadet, as too nice for Birdie.

I flick through the small array of images of Birdie on the internet. She disappeared just before the internet was born so there isn't much trace of her to be researched. There's one photo that keeps recurring though. Birdie, in a velvet hat and a huge satin pussy bow, her chin held tight against the rest on her fiddle, her eyes flashing at the camera, her lips pursed. I've studied this photo in detail and have observed in the background a large red chair that looks like a throne, a wood-panelled wall with velvet shaded lights on it and the suggestion of the head of a stuffed beast of some description.

A thought occurs to me and I do a reverse Google search on the image to see where else it has been posted. It comes back with eighteen hits and I go through them in order. They are on nostalgia sites mainly. The Whatever Happened To sites. But then I click the ninth image and it takes me to a site that includes a link to a video on YouTube. It appears that the photo of Birdie playing the fiddle in front of a throne is in fact a still from one of their videos. The one for the song that was a huge hit. I wasn't here in 1988. I was five years old in 1988, and still in Ghana. I wasn't particularly aware of pop music. Not until we arrived in London when I was thirteen years old, by which point *Original Version* had come and gone and so I had never before seen the video to this song that seems to have bugged the life out of everyone in the UK that summer long, long ago. I make the screen large, and I press play.

The band are all dressed alike, in flounces and cloaks and velvet and make-up. They swagger down a set of mahogany stairs that curves towards a large hallway. In the hallway are two red velvet thrones. One of the band members jumps up into the throne and slams his sticks against a drum tied around his neck. The camera pans around the hallway and follows two more band members as they stamp into a room that looks like a private bar; a woman behind the bar hands them tumblers of some kind of alcohol, amber in colour. One of them jumps up on the bar and I see they are wearing knee-high boots with laces. The song is kind of snappy and fun. I can see why it was so popular, and the video is high-octane and exciting. The camera follows the two men out of the bar and into a room with oil paintings on the walls and a huge brass chandelier with what look like candles but are in fact light-bulbs in the shapes of candles. Then we are out again and back in the hallway and there is Birdie in her velvet layers and her hat and her red lips and violin and there . . . I pause the video. *There* is the precise moment that has been captured in the photograph.

I wonder about this building as I press play and continue to watch the video; the private bar gives the impression of it being a club of some sort. I wonder where it is. And then suddenly the front door swings wide open and we are in a manicured garden with small mazes carved into low hedges and a pair of cannons on stone pedestals, and the band heads down this path still play-ing their instruments. The lead singer has his face in front of the camera for most of the time, leaning down into it as if it is held by a very small person. And then the camera turns and we are, I see, by the River Thames – in Chelsea, I would hazard, the Embankment maybe.

The camera turns and I see the building in full: a double-fronted house, with three rows of windows; four on the bottom, six in the middle, six on the top.

Something inside my gut kicks out against my spine, hard. I hit the pause button again and I stare at the house. This video was filmed in 1988. The same year that Philip Dunlop-Evers claims his family fell out with his sister; the last time his family says they saw her; the time that she was about to be kicked out of her flat because she'd acquired a cat without permission; the same time a friend with a big house had suggested she might be able to stay with them for a while.

I take a photo of the image of the house paused on my screen and I leave my office, collecting my colleague Donal on the way.

'Where are we going, boss?'

'We're going to Chelsea, Donal. We're going to Chelsea.'

34

It's five o'clock on Monday afternoon and Alf has just arrived at Henry's apartment after an after-school club. They bump fists at the front door and Alf follows Marco in.

'Yo. What's going on?'

'Fam. I cannot tell you. But bottom line: Henry's gone and he won't tell us where and he's blocked me and he's blocked my mum and we need to find him. Like, really badly. Can you do anything?' Marco spreads his arm out across the display of Henry's tech on the dining table.

Alf unloops his schoolbag from his torso and puts it on the back of a chair which he pulls out and sits on. He looks around the apartment. 'Where's your mum?'

'Out with Stella.'

He shrugs and turns his attention to the devices. 'These all his?'

'Yeah.'

He tries switching them on in turn. Two of them are dead and he sends Marco to get the chargers. The other two come to life and he starts tapping at their screens.

'Want anything to eat?' Marco pulls open the fridge and looks at all the food that was left there before Henry disappeared which has not been replenished because his mum hasn't been to the shops and is starting to look a little sad after four days. But there's some unopened ham and a bag of grated cheese with no green bits and some eggs and Marco makes an omelette for each of them while Alf taps at Henry's devices.

'I'm in,' he says. 'His password is 0000. Can you even believe that? I mean, that's, like, psychopathic.'

Alf taps and swipes and Marco brings the omelettes, a packet of fancy tortilla chips and two cans of Coke to the table.

Alf has accessed Henry's email and is scrolling through it. 'What is it you're looking for, exactly?'

'I dunno. Searches for flights, I guess. Hotel bookings. That kind of thing.'

'Hold on.' He double clicks on something and turns the screen towards Marco. 'Look. He was chatting to someone on Tripadvisor. Someone called Nancy.'

They join heads to read the message. It seems to be a friendly chat about the woman's experience at the game reserve where Libby's dad Phin was working. But as they read the message thread, Marco sees that Henry has been asking her leading questions about Phin – or Finn, as the woman spells it – and that she has told Henry that Phin may have gone back to Chicago, where he has family. Marco and Alf shoot each other a look. Marco's heart is pounding.

'He's gone to Chicago, hasn't he?' says Marco.

Alf nods.

'Chicago is big.'

Alf nods again, then zooms up and down Henry's inbox, but there's no confirmation emails from hotels or booking engines.

'Fuck,' says Marco. 'Where else could we look?'

'I dunno. I dunno.'

Marco turns his attention back to his omelette and Alf puts his hand into the tortilla bag and pulls out a handful, which he throws into his mouth and crunches loudly.

'Um, um, um,' says Marco. 'Let's think.'

'Browsing history? We could see which hotels he'd been looking at?'

'Yeah. But he'd have been browsing on his main laptop. Not on this iPad.'

Alf shakes his head. 'Doesn't matter, if he's logged in on both devices. Which it appears he is. So, let us have a look.'

And there it is. Henry's browsing history. Bang up-to-date. The last thing he'd googled was a company that offered motorbike tours of the Magnificent Mile and Lake Michigan. Alf clicks on the contact link, where there is a phone number for a guy called Kris Doll.

'Shall we call him?'

Marco shakes his head. 'No. Shit. No. Don't.'

'Why not?'

'I don't know. Won't he think it's weird? And what would we even say?'

'We'd just say: Have you heard of a guy called Henry Lamb? Do you know where he is?'

'But why would we be asking for Henry? We'd need to have a reason.'

'Erm. Sick relative? Maybe? His dad's really ill or something?'

'But why wouldn't we just call him?'

'Not answering his phone? Then we say it's an emergency. His dad's got like days left to live.'

'We don't even know if Henry's met this guy.'

'No. We don't. But it's the last thing in his Google history. So it could be important.'

Marco sighs. 'OK then. But you do it.'

Alf groans and scrapes the last chunk of omelette on to his fork, pushes it into his mouth, washing it down with some Coke. Then he belches and clears his throat before making the call.

'*Voicemail,*' he whispers with his hand over the mic. 'Oh, yeah, hi. I'm trying to track a man called Henry Lamb. He's British. He's in Chicago. His father is very ill – dying, actually. He needs to come home but he's not answering his phone. We found your website on his browsing history. Did you happen to meet him? Please call me. I'm—' He flails his hands at Marco. Marco shrugs. 'I'm Phin.'

'*What!*' mouths Marco. '*What the fuck!*'

'Sorry. Not Phin. Mike. I'm Mike.' Alf shrugs, helplessly. 'Call me on this number please. Thank you. Sorry.'

'Fucking hell, Alf.'

'Fuck. God. I'm sorry OK. I just—'

'Whatever. It's fine. He won't know who Phin is.' He leans towards the screen again and says, 'What's next?'

Alf clicks on the next search term. 'Here we have a search for a shop called Organic Delightful. And look, there it is on a map.

So, yeah. I reckon he must be staying somewhere near this place. We're closing in, Marco. We are closing in.'

The last hotel in Henry's search history is called the Dayville. 'Call them,' Marco urges.

Alf groans again but dials up the number and says, 'I'm looking for a guest called Henry Lamb. Do you know if he's staying there?'

'Hold the line, sir.'

'*Sir.*' Marco stifles a laugh.

'I'm afraid we don't have a guest of that name staying here, sir.'

'Oh. OK. Never mind. He's British. Do you have a British man there?'

'We have lots of British men here, sir.'

'OK. Well. Thanks anyway.'

'You are welcome, sir. Have a great day.'

Marco and Alf look at each other. They've gone as far as they can go. They need to wait for the man with the big bike to call them back.

He calls an hour later as they're halfway through a game of FIFA and one of Henry's expensive chocolate bars.

'Hi,' he says, 'this is Kris Doll. Is this Mike?'

'Yeah,' says Alf. 'This is Mike.'

'You left me a message. It was kind of garbled. But something about a British guy named Henry?'

'Yeah.'

'Well, look. I don't know. I'm taking a guy out this afternoon. He's British. But his name isn't Henry. It's Joshua.'

'Oh. And you've never heard of a guy called Henry Lamb?'

'No. I'm really sorry. I have not.'

'Oh. Well. Anyway. Thank you. And if you do hear from anyone with that name, would you call me?'

'Yeah. Sure. Of course I will.'

'Erm, just quickly,' says Alf. 'This British guy. Joshua. He's not by any chance staying at the Dayville, is he?'

'Er, yeah. Actually he is.'

Alf and Marco look at each other, wide-eyed.

'Oh,' says Alf. 'Right. OK. Well, don't worry. But thanks anyway.'

'Sure. No problem.'

Marco and Alf turn to each other, smiling, and give each other a high five.

35

April 2017

Rachel put down the phone and stifled an urge to laugh out loud. She clapped her hands over her mouth and then pulled them away again. Her smile was so wide it felt almost as if she might swallow herself. She picked up her phone again and pressed in her dad's number. No reply. Her finger loitered momentarily over Michael's number in her contacts, but she removed it. No, she thought. No. This moment was so precious she did not want to risk Michael tainting it in some way by making it about him. Instead she called Paige.

'What are you up to?'

'Why?'

'I just had some amazing news and I want to drink champagne with someone.'

'Well, you've come to the right place. Give me half an hour. I'll be here waiting for you!'

Rachel locked her studio behind her and headed up the road to Marks & Spencer where she bought a bottle of champagne and a six-pack of Colin the Caterpillar cupcakes. In Paige's studio she popped the cork, poured the champagne into water glasses and passed one to her.

'So, what's the scoop?'

'The scoop is that . . .' Rachel mimed a drumroll in the air. '. . . Liberty have just phoned to confirm that as of October the seventeenth, they will be stocking a bespoke Rachel Gold Jewels range in their jewellery lounge, right between Dinny Hall and Annoushka.'

'No!'

'Yes!'

'Oh my God. Oh my goodness, *cheers*!' Paige pressed her glass against Rachel's and then leaned in to hug her. 'That is the most, most amazing thing. I mean, just *wow*! What did Michael say?'

'Oh. I haven't told him yet. I was going to wait 'til I got home.'

'He'll be so happy. Oh my goodness! It's just awesome! You'll have to get a bigger studio.'

'Yes. I guess I will. I mean, lots will have to change. I'll need a bank loan. An assistant. More stock. More space. Yes. But fuck it, I'm not going to worry about that right now. Cheers!' They knocked glasses again and Rachel finished her glass in three large swigs.

Her phone vibrated then, and she saw her father's name on her screen and held the phone away from her ear as his excited screams whistled down the line. She absorbed his excitement, his pride, his absolute certainty that this was always going to happen, that he'd known all along.

'What took them so long?' he said. 'What took them so long?'

Through the rusty, metal-framed windows of Paige's studio she saw the day darkening. It was gone six. Around now she would normally let Michael know what sort of time she'd be home. It had started as a form of bonding behaviour, tied in with the novelty of having someone to go home to, but was now tied into the logistics of planning meals which was all Michael seemed to concern himself with recently. She couldn't face it today though. She was halfway through her second glass of champagne and the delight of success was so pure and so golden and the thought of Michael resentfully trudging out to the shops without a consensus on dinner was not one she could currently entertain. She didn't want to tell Michael what time she was going to be home. She wanted to be home when fate took her home. When she felt like going home. When she was ready to go home, not when Michael was placing food on the table, food, frankly, she didn't even really want to eat.

As she thought this her phone vibrated and there it was. *What time are you back? What do you want to eat?*

She sighed. She didn't want to eat. She wanted to drink champagne and eat Colin the Caterpillar cupcakes and then go to a bar with Paige and talk about boys and maybe order some chips later on to soak up the wine and then roll home and kick off her shoes and snuggle up to Michael and tell him her news and watch some TV and go to bed with him and have proper sex, the sort of sex she didn't have to micro-manage, that just happened and was silly and sensuous and glorious.

She stared at the message for a few seconds, then turned off her screen, topped up her glass with more champagne and said to Paige, 'Fancy going out somewhere?'

Rachel got home at ten o'clock. She had finally replied to Michael's text at about eight thirty and said, *Sorry, only just seen this, I'm out with Paige, won't be eating. See you later!* He hadn't replied which she'd found strange. In the hallway she took off her shoes and left them by the door. The apartment was in darkness. She walked to the end of the hallway and into the kitchen. Immediately she felt something skewed. A sense of things not being where they should be. She felt for the light switch and turned on the overhead halogens and there behind her, like a strange abstract painting, was an ugly splat of food, crawling slowly down the wall towards the skirting board. On the floor beneath were six jagged shards of white china. Closer inspection revealed the food to be some kind of risotto dish. Pumpkin maybe. The rest of the kitchen was absolutely spotless. The dishwasher hummed gently in the background. The chrome tap gleamed. The tea towel was folded neatly and hanging from the oven door.

For a moment Rachel stood and swayed slightly, both with the effects of four hours of drinking and with the shocking ugliness of the tableau confronting her. And then, unexpectedly, she laughed. She laughed because she was picturing Michael, sitting, brooding, forking risotto into his mouth, slamming her plate into the wall and then carefully picking his way around the aftermath as he cleaned his kitchen, making sure to leave it for her to see, and she found it strangely and painfully ridiculous to think of it, almost as though she were watching a clip on YouTube, posted for comedic value: Husband Goes Crazy When Wife Misses Dinner.

She decided to sleep on the sofa. She couldn't bear to face Michael. She pulled off her sweater and her jeans. Her pyjamas were in the bedroom but she did not want to go into her bedroom so she decided to sleep in her underwear. She brushed her teeth quietly in the bathroom and pulled a throw from the back of the sofa. She plugged her phone in to charge and pushed a cushion under her head. The curtains in the living room didn't quite meet and for a while she stared at the stripe of shimmering navy-blue light sluicing through the gap. Her thoughts shimmered in rhythm, a slightly nauseating dance between the excitement of her good news, the wine in her bloodstream, the imprint in her mind of the food smashed against the kitchen wall, the gleaming chrome tap, the humming dishwasher, the sickening, furious silence pounding at the bedroom door.

At some point later that night she awoke with a start, the feel of thick flesh against her mouth, her nostrils jammed painfully up her face. She felt weight on her hip bones, on her femurs, on her ribs. And then more flesh and sinew against her throat.

She pushed but it was like pushing against a metal girder. For a brief moment she thought it was an intruder, something spirited into the third-floor apartment via a drainpipe, up and over the balcony, through the slice in the curtains, liquid, shimmering, turning to flesh and bone against her own flesh and bone. But the smell was too familiar. The smell of her husband. She wrenched his hand from her mouth and said, 'What the fuck, Mi—'

But the hand came back to her mouth, this time harder, and the other hand was on her underwear, yanking at the waistband.

Rachel tried to sink her teeth into the flesh of Michael's hand but couldn't open her mouth wide enough against the pressure. And then he was in her, and his hands were around her throat, his head up, his gaze somewhere on the ceiling, pushing her head further and further inside the cushions of the sofa with each thrust, and Rachel counted the thrusts to calm the roil of her emotions and it was fourteen. Fourteen thrusts. His hands around her neck. Her eyes pulsing and watering. Her legs cycling against the force of him. And then he was done. He was out of her. Off her. His hands gone from her throat. He stood over her, his hair ridiculous, his chest pumping, his eyes burning dark.

Rachel got to her feet and stood eye to eye with Michael. Her breath came fitfully through the tears burning her throat. 'You raped me.' Her voice didn't sound like hers. It was broken and raw. 'Michael. You raped me.'

Michael's lip curled. 'Your breath stinks.'

She felt him start to leak from between her legs and pushed past him to get to the bathroom.

'You liked it,' she heard him call out behind her. 'I know you liked it. Don't fucking pretend that you didn't. I felt you come, Rachel. I felt you fucking come.'

She sat on the toilet and emptied herself of everything inside. Her bare flesh rippled with goosebumps. She wiped and she wiped and then she wiped again. She soaked a flannel in hot water and cleaned herself with that. She washed her hands, her throat, her mouth, her face. She looked at her reflection in the mirror and she thought of all the times, *all the times* when she had followed the rules: paid for the taxi instead of walking, tipped the drink into a plant pot rather than take a risk that it had been spiked. All the men she'd wanted to tell to fuck off but she'd smiled at politely for fear of making them aggressive. She thought of all the convoluted plans, the longer routes home, the bogus phone calls, the text messages to say she'd made it home safely, all the dates she'd told her friends about so that they'd know where she'd been if she didn't come home. She thought of how she'd contorted herself and her habits and her behaviour for twenty years to be a person who would not be raped, and now she had been raped in the place where she was meant to be safe, by the person who was meant to protect her. She felt the artifice of the last twenty years of her life, the pointlessness and futility of it. She might as well have taken the shortcut, worn the tarty top, flirted with the shady guy. She might as well have lived her life free.

Black rage crept through her psyche. She stalked into the bedroom and took her pyjamas from under her pillow. Michael stood and watched her as she pulled on the trousers angrily. 'There's no coming back from this, Michael. You know that, right? We're done here.'

Michael laughed drily. 'Right.'

'Right?'

'Yeah. Whatever, Rachel. Paint yourself the victim.'

'I'm sorry?'

'You.' He extended a finger towards her, a hard, pointing finger. 'You creep in here, stinking of booze, *fuck knows* where you've been. You left me here, no word—'

'I messaged you.'

'Oh, yuh. *Eventually*. Yeah. When I'd already cooked for you. When I'd already planned my whole evening around you.'

'Go to bed, Michael. Please.'

'Out looking for it. No doubt. Well, there you go . . .' He arced his arm across the sofa. 'You got it. You got it hard and you got it good and don't ever fucking pretend that that's not what you want. Because it fucking is. *I felt it*, Rachel. And now we both know what you are and what you want. Don't we?'

She left the bedroom, letting the door slam behind her. For a moment she had no idea what to do. She stood, looking around her, as if an answer might present itself to her from one of the dark corners of the room. Then she snapped out of it. She threw a coat on over her pyjamas, pulled on her trainers, grabbed her handbag and left the apartment, letting the door click shut softly in her wake.

36

June 2019

Samuel

It has rained and now it is sunny and the surface of the road dazzles back at us as we head down the Embankment. We have the blue light turning lazily, silently, not because there is an emergency, but so that other drivers will know that there is a reason why the car in front of them is driving at twelve miles an hour.

And then I see it, set back from the main road behind a small strip of railinged gardens, a row of imposing flat-fronted houses of varying sizes and colours. I have my phone in my hand, looking at the photo of the house from the music video.

'Can you pull in there, Donal? Is there a turning? Yes, there. Thank you.'

We drive up the space between the large houses and the railinged garden and Donal parks up. On a sign attached to a low wall is the name of the street: Cheyne Walk.

'Which one is it?'

I show him the photo on my phone and point at the house further up the street.

The house looks nothing like the house in the pop video. It is overgrown with creeping plants and the garden is full of rubble and the windows are grimy and covered in dirt.

Donal and I climb from the car, and I straighten my jacket, my cuffs. Donal is not wearing a proper jacket or cuffs, just a bomber jacket and trousers that are a little too tight for his figure, in my humble opinion.

We approach the front door of the house up a pathway littered with rubbish and overgrown with grass and moss. A dog barks and a man comes to the door. He is dressed in black and grey exercise clothing. The dog is large but seems calm, for which I am relieved.

'Good afternoon, my name is Detective Inspector Samuel Owusu; this is Detective Sergeant Donal Muir. We're from the special crime unit at Charing Cross, investigating a historical murder, and we have reason to believe that this property might have played some part in events leading to the death of the victim. Are you the owner, Mr—?'

'Mr Wolfensberger. Oliver. And yes, this is my house.'

He has an accent. It sounds slightly African to me. I assume him to be South African as he is white.

'Do you want to come in?' he says.

I see immediately that Oliver Wolfensberger knows nothing

about anything but is keen to find out more. A person who lets you so easily into their home has either nothing to hide, or everything to hide. I suspect strongly that in Oliver Wolfensberger's case it is the former.

Inside, the house looks very different to the house in the music video for Birdie's pop group. There are no dead animal heads attached to the walls. No shiny golden chandeliers, no patterned carpet running up the central staircase, and no red velvet thrones. It is stripped bare, the air thick with dust and mites that spangle in the sunshine. Silk wallpaper hangs in shreds from the walls; broken floorboards creak underfoot.

'It's been virtually derelict for over twenty years. We just got the keys a couple of weeks ago and are about to start a huge reno-vation. I'm meeting the architect here any minute, in fact. But yes, this is what it has looked like for the past twenty-five years. Kind of sad, isn't it?'

Oliver Wolfensberger leads us into the kitchen, the only room with furniture: a battered table and two long benches. We sit and he smiles at us.

'So,' he says, his hand upon the crown of his dog's head. 'I'm agog. What is it you need to know exactly?'

'We are investigating the possible murder of a young woman called Bridget Dunlop-Evers, around twenty-five years ago. Her remains were brought up on the beach further along the Thames a week ago, but she had been dead for much longer. Her family don't know anything about her disappearance; they were estranged at the time she went missing. But they did know that she had been invited to stay with a new friend who had a very big house. Miss Dunlop-Evers was a pop musician, and it seems her band had recorded a music video here, in this house, a couple of years before she went missing. See.'

I turn my phone towards Mr Wolfensberger and press play on the video I have lined up on YouTube.

He bristles with excitement. 'Oh my goodness. Yes. That is my house. Yes! Oh my word!'

'Do you remember this song?'

'No. No, I can't say that I do. But my wife might. Kate. She works in the music industry. She's very knowledgeable. I can't wait to show her. She'll be so excited!' He points at my phone. 'Which one is it?'

I pause it as Birdie comes back into shot. 'This is Bridget. Playing the violin.'

'Wow. That's amazing! But now . . .?'

'Yes. Sadly now we know she is dead. And we are looking into the possibility that this might be the house she told her family she was moving into. And we wondered if you had any insight into the history of this house. For example, from whom did you buy it?'

'It was a young woman. A very young woman. Only twenty-five. Her parents had left it to her in a trust when she was a baby and they – Oh my goodness, yes. They died. Here. In the house. And she was found upstairs all alone. A tiny baby.'

I see Oliver Wolfensberger shiver slightly.

'The saddest story,' he went on. 'She was adopted and only found out about this house on her twenty-fifth birthday. It was on the market for quite some time because it was in such a bad way. And possibly because of its associations. You understand?'

I nod because I am very much beginning to understand. 'What do you know of the death of her parents?'

'Not much. I think they committed suicide. A pact? Awful. Just awful. And I know some people might feel like that was some kind of a curse on a house. But I don't believe in any of that. I have a very positive mindset, you see. I have come here to overwrite that bad history. Overwrite it all. But I do still think about it. The sadness of it. That sweet baby girl, left all alone. Someone wrote an article about it, you know? A long investigative piece. I didn't read it because I didn't want it to stain my consciousness, but I believe it was in the *Guardian*, a few years ago. We weren't living in the UK at that time so I don't know anything more than that, but I'm sure you could find it.'

'Guardian', I write in my notebook.

'Thank you,' I say. 'And the name of the young woman that sold you this house? Would you be able to tell me that?'

'Yes. Of course. Her name was Libby Jones.'

'Libby Jones', I write in my notebook.

'Do you have any contact details for her?'

'Sadly, no, I don't. She didn't live in London, though, I don't think. Maybe just outside somewhere?'

'Outside London', I write in my notebook.

'Would you mind if I had a look?' I ask. 'At the house? Just for my own' – I tap the side of my head – 'my own sense of place?'

'Of course. Yes.'

Donal and I follow him to the hallway

'Please, just wend your way. Go wherever you like. Open anything you like. I'll be down here if you need me.'

The grey and white dog follows us eagerly. It is almost as if he is showing us the house himself. Donal fusses the dog, but I find him a bit big for my liking. If he were a foot shorter, I would feel more comfortable.

The house has poetic symmetry. Everything mirrors everything so it is easy to feel our way from room to room and floor to floor. There are four bedrooms and four bathrooms on this first floor. From the back windows I look out at the garden. I look up at the trees and I take some photos, for the arboreal forensics guy, because of course I do not know what a London plane or a tree of heaven might look like.

A smaller staircase takes us to the top floor. Here the ceilings are lower and doors open from a narrow landing that goes from one side of the house to the other. Each door opens to a small bed-room with a sloped ceiling and windows overlooking either the garden or the street. Donal calls to me from one of the other bedrooms.

'Look, boss,' he says when I enter, pointing at a spot on the skirting board.

There is something scratched into the wood here. I crouch down to look and see the words: 'I AM PHIN'. I take a photo.

In the long hallway outside a small metal ladder stretches up towards a hatch in the ceiling. I follow Donal's large behind up the ladder and we emerge on to a tiny roof terrace. I take more photos of trees and of the roof itself.

There are a couple of channels up here, running between the pitched roofs. Although it is summer, they are filled with dead leaves, and I use the toe of my shoe to gingerly sift them. Mulch is underneath. I walk through the mulch to a chimney pot and peer behind it. Another channel filled with more dead leaves and mulch, but here the mulch appears to have been displaced and moved about. I take more pictures and then we make our way back through the house and to the hallway.

Oliver Wolfensberger sees us off at the door, expressing complete willingness to help us in any way possible. He furnishes us with the name of the firm of solicitors who had been in charge of the trust that Libby Jones had inherited, and then he allows me to take more photographs of the front of the house and the trees in the gated strip of garden just opposite. Then we return to the car.

Donal pulls his seatbelt across in the driver seat of the car.

'Helpful?' he asks.

I make a noncommittal noise and say, 'Well, I am ninety per cent certain that that is the house where Bridget Dunlop-Evers met her end.'

'You are?'

'Yes. What do you think?'

'It had that vibe. It's definitely a possibility.'

I nod. 'I'd like you to drop me at the solicitors' office please, Donal. It's just over in Pimlico, not far. And if you could head back to the station after that and do some research into this *Guardian* article, that would be great. Right now, I'm going to get these photos off to the trees guy and hopefully, by the end of today we will have accelerated our investigation. Hugely.'

37

I have Phin in my eyeline for a full thirty seconds before he gets swallowed up by a group of young men loitering outside a music venue. By the time I get to the other side of the group, Phin is gone. I look right, I look left, I look upwards. To the right of the music venue is a pair of ornate wooden doors with brass art nouveau curlicues and a stained-glass fanlight. Through the stained glass, I just catch the shadow of a figure leaping up a staircase. I step away from the building to improve the angle of the view and see that I am looking at a grand apartment block that flows in both directions over the bars and shops below, all with leaded, bowed windows topped with swagged ribbons of sage-green Portland stone.

I see a figure pass across the stained glass of the central window on the first floor. I watch the windows in the apartments

on that floor until one lights up. I see the suggestion of movement, but I do not see a figure. Across the street is a bar with a
decked terrace. I sit here and I order a glass of champagne and
I stare and I stare but I see nothing and who even knows what
I'm looking at. But my gut tells me that it is Phin up there. That
he is unpacking his organic groceries, unscrewing the cap from
a bottle of organic wine, making small talk with some shadowy
imagining of a person who may be a friend or an Airbnb host,
chopping up vegetables, cubing tofu. (I assume that Phin is vegetarian as he loves animals. And of course we were all forcibly
vegetarian in our house of horrors; to this day I have a phobia
of dhal.)

The champagne arrives and I smile at the waitress and thank
her.

'How's your day been?' she asks as she places the glass in front
of me.

'Oh,' I say, 'it's been . . . nice.'

'Great,' she says. 'Are you just visiting?'

'Yes, I am. I'm trying to track down an old friend.'

'Wow.' Her eyes grow wide. 'Any luck?'

'No. Not yet.'

'Well, keep looking. I'm sure they'll be so excited to be found!'

'Yes,' I say, my eye still firmly on the first-floor apartment
across the street. 'I'm sure they will.'

Then my phone vibrates, and I see a call coming through and
I smile at the nice waitress apologetically and pick it up. It's Kris
Doll.

'Hey,' he starts. 'Joshua!'

'Yes. Hey. Speaking.'

'Joshua. I have your watch and I'm heading into town first thing tomorrow. I can drop it at your hotel if you're still there.'

'Oh, that's great. Thanks, Kris. I'm very grateful! What sort of time do you think it would be?'

'Oh, like eight o'clock, I guess?'

'Eight o'clock. Great. I'll see you then.'

'You don't need to get up. I'll just drop it behind the desk.'

'I'm an early riser, Kris, I'll be up. See you tomorrow!'

I can hear the timbre of his voice change slightly. 'And oh! Joshua! I meant to say to you, but it completely slipped my mind. I had a strange phone call before I took you out yesterday. From someone called Mike? A British accent. Do you know a Mike?'

'Oh, probably, doesn't everyone?'

'Yeah. That's what I thought. It sounded kind of fake. But they said they were looking for a guy called Henry Lamb? Does that ring a bell?'

My grip on the stem of my champagne glass tightens. I leave a beat and a half, barely a nanosecond, but still a potential give-away. Then I say, too fast, with too much emphasis, 'No. No it doesn't.'

'Yeah. I thought it was probably nothing to do with you, it was just that they said something about a Finn? Right before he said his name was Mike. He said it was Finn, and then he corrected himself and I didn't think much of it at the time but then we were talking about my British friend Finn earlier and it just seemed . . . *weird*. You know. Kind of strange. I mean, first off, I haven't heard anything from Finn for, like, months and months, then within like forty-eight hours I hear he's back in town, then I get that phone call from the guy in the UK and then he comes up in conversation with you and it was, I dunno, *weird*.'

'Yes,' I say. 'That is very weird. What did he want? This Mike guy?'

'Oh, he said he wanted to tell this "Henry Lamb" that his father was dying and that they couldn't get a hold of him and that they'd found a search for my bike tour on this guy's search history and wondered if he'd ever called me.'

My search history.

I blanch. My search history. I have not logged out of Google. That means that anyone with access to any of my other devices would be able to see what I've been googling. Including, possibly, although I cannot entirely recall, the hotel I'm staying in.

'But anyway,' Kris continues, 'it's clearly something completely unconnected, just the universe fucking with us, I guess. So yeah, I'll see you tomorrow!'

'Actually, Kris, I'm thinking I might check out of my hotel tonight? It just occurred to me that it would be nice to mix it up a bit, you know? Get a sense of a different neighbourhood. So, give me a minute and I'll text you the name of the next place I'll be the moment I'm checked in. Is that OK?'

'Sure! Sure, that's fine. Just message me and I'll see you wherever you may be. Sleep tight, Joshua!'

'You too, Kris. You too.'

I stay at the bar opposite the apartment block until all the lights go off, one by one, and the building is almost completely dark. Then I head back to my hotel, throw my things in my suitcase (well, that's a lie, I fold them very neatly because I really don't want to have to iron them; I have enough on my plate right now, quite frankly, without ironing T-shirts) and check out. I jump in an Uber to take me to the next hotel, which I booked over the phone, because I am clearly not to be trusted not to leave a stinking trail of internet-based clues in my wake. It's a few doors down from the Magdala bar, and what I believe to be Phin's place of residence. I WhatsApp the name of the hotel to Kris from the back of the taxi at one in the morning. In my room I unpack, and then I open a beer which I drink in the shower. By the time I am dry, I am too tired to do anything other than put my head on the pillow and sleep.

My alarm wakes me the next morning at 7 a.m. I throw on some clothes and head down to the breakfast room. I speed eat two croissants, suddenly ravenous after nearly a day without food. I slurp back two foamy cappuccinos and I make a bacon sandwich which I fold into a paper napkin and put inside my shoulder bag for later. Then at exactly 8 a.m. I pass nonchalantly through the foyer, my eyes on the plate-glass window to the street beyond, but I hear him before I see him: the animal thrum of his huge bike as it pulls up outside. I watch him unstrap and pull off his helmet, tuck it under his arm, then head towards the hotel. I go to the desk and ask for the Wi-Fi code, even though I already have it, and then I turn from the concierge and beam at Kris as he strides across the foyer and I say, 'Oh, hello! Kris! Hold on, I'll be right there.'

I pretend to put the Wi-Fi code into my phone and then I go

over to Kris. He is more handsome on second viewing, and I feel strangely shy. An adolescent blush leaches from my chest to the lower half of my face and I breathe in to contain it. 'How are you?'

'I'm great,' he says. 'Just about to pick up a customer across town. But this is a nice place.' He looks around at the hotel. 'I mean the other place was nice, but this is little more . . . homey. And this is a great neighbourhood. Funnily enough, you're just up the street from the bikers' bar I was telling you about yesterday. Anyway. Here's your watch.'

I take it from his outstretched hand. 'Thank you.'

'And if there's anything else you need while you're in town, just message me. Yes?'

'Thank you,' I say again. 'Thank you. You're too kind.' And then I go in for the main event, my voice finely poised at precisely the right tone. 'Oh, by the way, did you ever hear from the friend you were telling me about when we were by the lake? The British guy called Finn?'

'No. Not yet. Still trying to track him down. But my friend thinks his Airbnb might be somewhere near here actually.'

'Really?'

'Yeah. Just think, you and he might even cross paths! Fellow Brits! You tend to kind of attract each other, I've noticed.'

'Yes,' I say. 'Yes, we do.'

I stare at my face in the mirror on the dressing table in my room. I try to superimpose the face of old Henry over the top. The Henry before he had that little jawbone shave, the cheek implants, the eye lift, the hair transplant, the two hours a day at the gym. Not the Henry who styled his expensively highlighted hair into a foppish cowlick over his forehead and wore perfectly chosen designer clothes with impeccable attention to collar angles and trouser length and buttons and linings, but the Henry who wore plimsolls and prissy corduroys, whose hair would never sit right, whose knees stuck out like potatoes, who had no idea what to do with himself. But I can't get that person to overwrite the person in the mirror. The new improved Henry is just too strong. Would Phin, I wonder – would he even recognise me? If, for example, I were to stand face-to-face with him in the vegan food aisle in the organic supermarket up the street, if I were to say, 'Have you tried these plant-based fake chicken tenders? Are they any good?' then smile and say thank you as I tucked them into my basket and wished him a good day. Would he know it was me? Or would he just think I was a slightly odd-looking, slightly camp, early middle-aged man with a British accent whose teeth were too white, whose highlights were too obvious, whose clothes were too, too just so? And the answer hits me like a truck.

Of course he would.

He would recognise me immediately. He would recognise me dressed as a pantomime horse because, I strongly suspect, I have haunted his dreams for the last twenty-six years, ever since we all escaped from the house of horrors, ever since I did what I did to him. I am Phin's living, breathing nightmare and he hates me. And when you hate someone, it leaves deeper scars on your psyche than loving someone ever can.

But still, I think, I should make an effort. Maybe a hat would help. I put on a baseball cap and eye myself in the mirror. Then sunglasses. It will have to do. I forgot to pack a false moustache.

The nice waitress at the bar opposite Phin's apartment block is there again. I say something about 'Do you actually get to go home ever?' and she laughs obligingly. I order a coffee, my third of the day and probably a bad idea in the circumstances, but since everything I'm currently doing is a bad idea in the circumstances, I can't really get stressed about an extra shot of caffeine. I glance up at Phin's building, which is bustling with movement. The front door opens and I watch a young male couple walk out, each carrying a French bulldog puppy. A moment later an elderly couple exit. Her bag slips from her shoulder, he pushes it back up for her and she scowls at him. A mother and her teenage son are the next to leave, then an older father and two small girls.

My coffee arrives and I thank my waitress profusely. While I wait, I go on to the Airbnb app and look for places near me. I find a one-bed apartment with leaded bay windows. It is in the same building and it is booked up for the next ten days. So now I can picture Phin even more clearly, with the background details of cushions with Frida Kahlo's face embroidered on them, a six-foot cactus, a ceiling light shade woven from raffia, a white tiled bathroom with black taps and handles, a grey kitchen, jazzy tea towels, a bar of lime green soap tied with string to a sprig of lavender on a vintage tea saucer.

In the photos I look for clues to where in the building the apartment might be located and I notice the outline of trees in the bedroom window. There are only two trees on the avenue outside the building and only four windows that would have a view of them. I go back to the search results and find another apartment in the same block. This one, unlike Phin's, is currently available. It is not as nice as Phin's but it's perfectly pleasant. I send a booking request. Twenty-five minutes later I have paid for it and have the access instructions. No key, but a code. I can let myself in any time after midday. It is currently 9.10 a.m.

I am getting close now, so close that I can smell it.

38

'Why did Dad choose us such lame names?' says Marco, staring at his passport disdainfully.

'He didn't choose the names. We got what we were given.'

'*So* shit. Antoine. I mean, do I look like a fucking *Antoine*?'

The evening before, Marco and Alf had told Lucy that they'd tracked Henry down. Apparently someone in a Tripadvisor chatroom had told Henry that Phin might be in Chicago. And a guy who ran a tour company said he was about to pick up a British guy from a hotel called the Dayville. She'd made one last attempt to contact Henry, this time using Alf's phone, but when Henry blocked Alf's number two minutes later, she'd known immediately what she had to do.

Libby had lost her adoptive father when she was a child and the thought that something might now happen to her birth father, before Libby had even had a chance to meet him, was too much for Lucy to take. So she drove Fitz to Libby's, asked Oscar the building porter to feed Henry's cats, emailed Stella's and Marco's schools to say they would not be in for a few days and then booked three one-way flights to Chicago.

Now it is 8 a.m. and she and her children are standing in the check-in line at Heathrow, clutching small, hastily packed bags and fake passports. When Henry had first seen the passports that Lucy's ex-husband had had made for them, he'd said they were some of the best quality he'd ever seen. But Lucy's confidence in the passports wavers now, momentarily. The check-in woman seems to be looking incredibly closely at the passports of the family in front of them and Lucy's heart races frighteningly in her chest; her palms sweat lightly.

Finally it is their turn and she slides the passports across the counter to the woman who opens each in turn and smiles warmly as her eyes find the face of the relevant child. She says, 'Antoine?' and Marco nods furiously. Then she says, 'Céline?' and Stella nods shyly. The woman opens Lucy's passport, catches her eye but says nothing. Lucy holds her breath hard inside her lungs. Then the woman closes the passport and smiles. 'Thank you,' she says, sliding the passports back to Lucy. 'Have a safe journey,' and Lucy smiles back at her and says, 'Thank you! You too!' and realises a beat too late that she has spoken nonsense.

In the departure lounge they mill around anxiously. They are painfully early: their flight is not for over two hours. They eat breakfast and Lucy buys Marco a designer backpack from a sportswear shop and Stella a sequinned shoulder bag from Accessorize and she lets them fill them with snacks and trinkets, colouring-in books, sticker books, magazines, wireless earphones and phone accessories. And then their flight is boarding and it is time for Lucy to show the passports once again and her breakfast churns in her stomach and her head hums with blood and her mouth is dry and her heart is pounding but this time the woman doesn't even look at their passports, merely slides their boarding passes under the scanner and waves them through, and they walk down the carpeted tunnel and Lucy feels a sense of nauseating lightness tinged with disbelief. Five minutes later they are in their seats and she is flicking through an in-flight magazine and passing objects to Stella and to Marco and a man across the aisle is smiling fondly at Stella and saying that he has a little girl at home who looks just like her and forty minutes after that they are in the air and through the window London grows tiny, impossible, and then is gone, behind a reassuring blanket of cloud.

Lucy is astounded to find herself in Chicago. She has never been to America before. As a child they went to the Black Forest in Germany every summer to stay with their grandmother. They went to Istanbul once or twice for family weddings on her grandfather's side. One year her father took them to Bali. It was her mother's idea; she'd seen an article about a luxury resort where there were rose petals on the beds and baths run with warm milk, and champagne served for breakfast and daily massages by limber-wristed young girls with begonias behind their ears, and had somehow persuaded Henry Sr to take them all there despite his great dislike of long-haul travel and of foreign food. And then, of course, the travel had stopped for many years until Lucy came to France at the age of fifteen. And now she is in America and the man at border control did not press a big red button at the sight of their passports but gruffly waved them through, and they are in the back of a taxi, moments away from the Dayville Hotel, moments away from Henry.

'I miss Fitz,' says Stella and Lucy squeezes her arm and says, 'Yes. Me too.'

She really, really does. Fitz has been at Lucy's side almost permanently for the past five years, since Stella was a baby. Fitz is with Libby. She'd offered to keep hold of the children too, but Stella suffers from severe separation anxiety so travelling without her isn't an option and Marco, *of course*, wouldn't have stayed home for all the money in the world.

'Henry thinks he's found Phin,' she'd said to Libby, as casually as she could. 'We're going over to help Henry persuade him to come back to the UK. We won't be gone long, just until we've found your dad, I promise. And if you can't cope with Fitz, I know your lovely friend Dido would be happy to have him, she loves him so much.'

Lucy has no idea if Libby could hear the awful note of panic underlying her glib words, but frankly that is the least of her concerns, the very least of them right now.

'Here you go, the Dayville.'

The driver pulls up outside and Lucy peers upwards through the window.

Henry, she thinks, *Henry, we're here.*

'I'm sorry, Miss Caron. I'm afraid we don't have a Henry Lamb staying here.'

'I think he may have checked in under another name. Here.' Lucy shows the photo of Henry on her phone screen to the woman behind the desk. 'This is Henry. Is he here?'

'I'm not really supposed to . . .' she begins cautiously, before glancing down at Stella and smiling indulgently at her. 'Is that your daddy?' she asks her.

Stella shakes her head shyly. 'No,' she says, 'he's my Uncle Henry.'

'Your uncle?' she says, smiling warmly. 'I see. And yes. Your uncle was here actually. But under a different name.'

'*Was* here?' says Lucy.

'Yeah, he checked out yesterday.'

'Oh.' Lucy's stomach lurches with disappointment and vague panic. 'Did he – did he say where he was going?'

'Yes. He said he wanted to explore another part of town. But I'm afraid he didn't say where, exactly.'

Lucy exhales slowly. 'Are you able to tell me what name he was using? For his booking?'

The receptionist's eyes go to a door behind her, and then back to her screen. She lowers her voice and says, 'Sure. It was Joshua Harris.'

Lucy nods. 'Great. Thank you. Thank you so much. I'm so grateful to you.'

'Joshua,' Marco hisses in her ear as they head towards the lifts. 'That's the name. The name that guy from the bike-tour place said. Joshua Harris. It's him!'

'Well,' says Lucy, watching the lift doors open and sliding through, 'we'll get in touch with him soon. But first, let's go and check out our lovely room.' She can't think about it now. She just needed him to be here. To be here *now*. She doesn't want to search for him, to wait for him. She needs him just to be here and needs to know that Phin is safe.

Their room is beautiful. She booked the most expensive room they had; the Aurora Suite is its name. It's four times the size of the room they used to live in in Giuseppe's building in Nice. Marco gets his own sofa bed in a separate section of the room. They also have a terrace and a kitchenette. It is decorated in shades of aqua and washed-out ochre with framed botanical prints on the walls and an ice-blue neon light over a sideboard formed of the word 'aurora'.

Stella scoots about the room, enjoying the sense of space. Marco unloads Henry's iPad and laptop from his fancy new back-pack and climbs on to his sofa bed with a bottle of Coke from the mini-bar and a packet of nuts. Lucy sits in an upholstered chair, her hands hanging between her knees, her head heavy on her neck, and allows the stresses of the journey, of the last four days, of in fact every living moment since she received that text message from Henry on Friday afternoon, to pass through her from her gut to her lungs and then out to her extremities, and she sighs so loudly that Stella and Marco both look up at her.

'You OK?' says Marco.

She finds a smile. 'Yes. I'm fine. I'm just very, very tired indeed.'

She sends Henry a message, although she knows it is futile. *Henry. Who knows if you'll ever see this. But we're here. We're in Chicago. We're at the Dayville. Please please call. PLEASE.*

She glances up and sees Marco smiling at her. 'What?'

'Wanna know where Henry is?'

'Yes,' she begins, 'of course I do. But not today, not yet, we'll start looking for him tomo—'

But then she stops. Marco has turned around the screen of

Henry's iPad and is showing her a hotel in another part of Chicago called the Angel Inn. He taps it with one finger and smiles at her from underneath his overgrown curls. 'About ten minutes from here, in an Uber.'

'I don't understand?'

'The guy with the bike. Kris Doll. I just WhatsApped him. I said that the man we were looking for also goes by the name of Joshua Harris and we were still trying to find him to let him know his dad was dying. And Kris said that funnily enough he'd just seen Joshua this morning at this hotel.' He taps the screen of the iPad again. 'Kris said he thought something seemed off with him. He asked him about Henry Lamb but he pretended he'd never heard of him. And get this, Mum, *get this*. The guy with the bike told me that he is friends with Phin. *Our* Phin. He actually knows him. And not only that, but Phin is in Chicago right this very minute.'

Lucy gasps. 'Seriously?'

'*Oui, maman,* seriously.' Marco's face is alight with triumph. 'Shall we go?' he says. 'Shall we go now?'

'Go where?'

'To the Angel Inn?'

'No, Marco. Not now. We're all shattered. Let's—'

'No, Mum. Let's go now. What if Henry moves again? What if he finds out we're here and decides to run off? We might never ever find him again. Come on. It's not even five. Please.'

Lucy sighs again, then straightens her neck and her back, slaps her hands against her thighs and says, 'Yes. Of course. Yes. Let's go.'

39

April 2017

It was nearly three in the morning. Despite the warmer weather by day, it was cold now and Rachel could see her breath. She turned the corner to the place she'd arranged to meet the Uber and watched the driver's progress anxiously on her phone until he finally arrived, his headlights cutting holes into the night-time mist, and she climbed into his back seat and said that yes, she was fine, thank you, how are you and then watched London through the window, the sleeping curves of it, the drawn curtains, the occasional pixel of light here and there, the gentle stretches of empty road, the calm waits at red lights for nobody and nothing, the soft pulsing click of the driver's indicator and then the lights shining off the filthy dark water of the Regent's Canal, white fairy lights strung across a barge, the peculiar shape of her building, the upended fridge, the glow of the nightlight in the entrance hall, her key in her front door, the smell of a neglected home, a fan of mail on the doormat. She dropped her bag at her feet, then collapsed on to her knees, tears running down her face, down her neck, into her pyjama top.

Rachel woke up a few hours later. She was in her own bed. The sheets had a dull, musty tang. She should have left her bed with clean bedding before she'd moved to Michael's but she hadn't thought. And last night she had been too broken to think about changing them. She had stood for half an hour in the shower, the pressure turned high, as high as it would go, tears mingling with the water as it poured down over her head. Now she was wearing pyjamas that she had not worn for many, many weeks, which still smelled of the fabric conditioner she used here in her own home. Her skin felt tight and raw from the hour of sickened, nauseated, rageful crying she'd done the night before.

As she awoke, she passed through a clear white moment of innocence, as fleeting as a snowflake, before she remembered that last night her husband had raped her. Then it exploded inside her mind's eye, the feel of him on her, his hand over her mouth, around her neck, the blood pulsing through her eyeballs. In the mirror she could see burst blood vessels in her eyes, a livid red streak on her throat. Between her legs there were bruises that hurt even without her touching them. She stood in the shower for another half an hour, until the water ran cool. She made coffee without milk and drank it on her balcony in her towelling dressing gown. The day was bright and soft. A flower-bedecked barge passed lazily down the canal below with two brown spaniels sitting on the foredeck with their legs stretched out. She hadn't looked at her phone yet. She did not want to look at her phone ever again. She did not want to see his words. His lies. His filth.

She went to her laptop instead, the back-up one she'd had for ten years which looked fatter and bulkier with every year that passed. She opened up her private business email account, the only one that Michael didn't have an address for. There was an email from Lilian Blow, the fine jewellery buyer at Liberty:

Rachel, I'm ccing Rosie Havers in here. Rosie is the Director of Buying and Merchandising here at Liberty. I.e. the big boss. I've been chewing her ear off about your stuff and now she's a massive Rachel Gold fan too. I thought we might get together for a lunch sometime this week, just to get this off to a fun start, get to know you a bit better and talk long-term plans, hopes and dreams. What do you think?

Rachel blinked at the words on the screen. They were words that belonged to another world. Another person. Another version of her life. She caught herself in the mirror across the room. She tried to envision the person she saw in the reflection sitting in a chichi Soho back-street restaurant with Lilian and Rosie from Liberty. She imagined them fussing over the cocktail menu and then deciding to order water instead, or complicated tea infusions. She imagined statement wedding rings and teenage children with interesting names, and manes of glossy hair that had never been held tight inside the fists of their husbands as they raped them. She saw herself between them, rope-haired, stinking of victimhood and stale bedsheets.

Then she shook this out. Shook her head hard.

'No no no no,' she muttered to herself. 'No no no no *no*.'

She slapped her own cheek and cleared her throat and ran her hands down her hair. 'NO!' she said again. Then she typed: *This sounds amazing. I'd love it! Just name a time and a place and I'll see you there. Really looking forward.*

She pressed send and watched it jump from her screen, imagined it appearing in the gilded inboxes of Lilian and Rosie. She would be fine by then, she told herself. Absolutely fine. She just needed to get through today. Get through today, one minute at a time. Get dressed. Get to work. Get lunch. Get a lawyer. Get Michael out of her life.

She opened a new email, addressed it to Dominique:

Hey fatty. 'Shit has gone down. I need an email address for your lawyer friend, the one with the red hair, I can't remember her name. I think I might be getting divorced. Please don't say a fucking word to anyone. And please only contact me on this email address. I'm not using my phone at the moment. Love you.

Then she went to her bathroom, pulled open the cabinet and took out her old make-up bag. She made herself look nice in the mirror. She covered the mark on her neck with foundation. She combed her hair out and then pulled it back into a bun. She put on perfume and some nice clothes and then she walked to her father's house.

'Baby girl! Come in! What a wonderful surprise! I wasn't expecting you!'

She returned his embrace fulsomely, breathing in the smell of Dad.

'You looked tired.'

'Oh, thanks, Dad. And I made such a special effort not to!'

'I'm sorry, darling. I'm sorry. What was it? A late night?'

'A very late night. Yes. And . . . other stuff.'

'What other stuff?'

'Make me a cappuccino and I'll tell you.'

Nothing made Rachel's dad happier than using his expensive coffee machine and she saw the bounce in his step as she followed him towards the kitchen.

'Semi-skimmed, yes?'

'Yes please, Dad.'

'Any syrup?'

'No thanks. Just basic cappuccino.'

'Chocolate on top?'

'Of course.'

They didn't attempt to talk over the din of the machine grinding beans. When it finally issued its last hiss and the final drop of coffee hit the froth, Rachel took a deep breath and said, 'Dad. I've left Michael.'

He stopped and then spun round towards her. His eyes were wide, and he emitted a slightly camp gasp of shock. 'You've—'

'Yes. Last night. Late last night. We, uh, we had a big fight. Things have been bad for ages. Things have been bad since the honeymoon, Dad. I mean really bad. There's so much—' She stopped and brought herself back to an even keel. Then she began again. 'So much has happened, Dad, that I haven't told you about. Michael lost all his money.'

'What!'

'Yes. I know. He's lost everything. I've been supporting us financially. And he's – well, he's shown me a darker side of himself.'

'Oh my God, he hasn't hurt you, has he?'

'No, Dad. Nothing like that.' She felt the sore spot on her neck burn hotter with the lie. 'No. But I sometimes felt like maybe he would. And I'm done, Dad. And I'm so, so sorry. I'm so sorry I made you spend all that money on the wedding. And I'm so sorry that I am such a loser. That I make such shit choices all the time, that I am fucking thirty-three and I don't own anything and that you have to keep propping me up and bailing me out and that I can't even make a marriage last for longer than two months.' She sniffed and wiped tears from her cheeks. 'And I'm sorry that I'm all you've got. You deserve better than me, Dad, you really, really do. I'm so sorry.'

'Oh my God. Rachel. Oh, no. No! Never say that. Please. You are the single best and most remarkable thing in my life. You always have been and you always will be and there is nothing you could do or not do that would ever make me feel differently. Nothing.'

'But I feel such a fool, Dad. That wedding. All that fuss. All that money. All those people thinking that I knew what I was doing. When I didn't, Dad. I didn't. I married a prick, a stupid, arrogant, narcissistic prick and I fell for all his bullshit like a prize idiot when the red flags were there all along. It's not like we don't know about men like him. It's not like there aren't a thousand TV shows, a thousand novels, a thousand news stories every day about women being groomed and gaslighted by abusive men. Yet still, Dad, *still*.'

'If it makes you feel any better, my darling, he completely hoodwinked me too. I thought he was wonderful.'

'Well, he's not wonderful. He's a dick. A spineless, disgusting, pathetic little dick.'

'Well, you live and learn, darling.' He leaned towards her and wrapped his hands around hers. 'At least he hasn't hurt you.'

She snatched her hands back. 'Yes,' she said, too fast.

'Has he?'

'No, Dad, I told you. No. But it felt like he might. And the whole thing was just getting more and more toxic, and it was time to go.'

'Will you be instigating a divorce?'

'Yes. Yes, I will. I've asked Dom to send me the details of her friend. She's one of the best divorce lawyers in London.'

'I'll pay, darling. You know that. Whatever it takes to get you out of this mess. You don't need to worry about that.'

She took his hands back in hers and caressed them. 'Thanks, Dad. Thank you.'

And then for a while they talked about Liberty, about the contract, about the range they wanted her to design for them: twelve rings, ten necklaces, ten bracelets, twenty earrings.

As they spoke her father looked at her seriously. 'Rachel,' he said. 'Whatever you do, do not let Michael know about this new venture. Let him still believe that you are struggling. That you need him more than he needs you. Do not let that man get his nose anywhere near sniffing distance of your imminent success. Because that will be your escape route, my darling, from this awful man: your business. Your talent. Your . . . *je ne sais quoi* . . .'

She stared at him for a moment and then she smiled and from

inside the smile a laugh exploded, so hard and unexpected that it made her father jump.

'*Je ne sais quoi!*' she reiterated in a silly accent. 'Ha!'

And she knew then that she would never tell anyone what had happened the previous night on Michael's sofa. Never. She would take it to her grave. Because she was Rachel Gold and Rachel Gold did not get raped. She *did not* get raped. She would strike this from her personal history: the marriage, the man, the rape, all of it. She would erase it and start over again.

40

June 2019

My apartment smells of bleach and damp towels. It's at the back of the building, facing out on to the rear ends of the buildings behind, a criss-cross lattice of ironwork fire escapes, and huge metal dumpster bins huddled grimly in courtyards below. The owner has left a jar of what look like homemade chocolate truffles on the kitchen table next to a single tulip in a vase, which is very sweet of course, but doesn't really do much to take the edge off the unprepossessing feel of the place. I think of Phin's apartment with the Frida Kahlo cushions and sigh. Of course he would get the superior Airbnb. Of course he would.

I have deduced that Phin's apartment is two floors below mine and three apartments to the left. I head down the echoey stone staircase that threads the building together. I count down the doors to the third and see that Phin's apartment has a door that is painted a gorgeous dark teal and has a golden knocker in the shape of a fox's head. I can almost smell the scent of the neroli and pomegranate reed diffuser that I saw in the photographs wafting under the door. I put my ear to the door, but I can hear nothing beyond.

Back in my apartment I open my suitcase and hang my clothes in the musty wardrobe, mentally writing the review of this place that I will post when I go. *Somewhat tired fixtures and fittings. Needs a little tlc.*

And then I am confronted, suddenly, resoundingly, horribly with the result of all of the decisions that I have made since I left London. I am alone in a sad apartment in Chicago staking out the apartment of a man I have not seen since I was sixteen years old, a man who despises me, and I have no idea what I do now. This is as close as I can get to Phin without physically breaking into his apartment and being there, arranged against the Frida Kahlo cushions, when he gets back from wherever he is and that is – well, no, that's too much. I fear where that might lead. I fear what I might do. I fear what he might do. I fear the power of everything that has kept us apart for all these years and I fear what that power might lead to if it found itself trapped in an Airbnb behind a closed door. And then I feel a pall of despondency descend upon me. Why am I here? What am I doing? What the hell do I want? But, suddenly, I have it and I sit up ramrod straight as it comes to me in a flash.

I grab a notebook from my laptop bag and a pen. I scribble a note.

Dear person at apartment 12. I am a person at apartment 35. I really don't like the apartment I'm in and I see on Airbnb that your booking ends in ten days and I'd love to take it over once you're gone. Would you be willing to let me have a look at it before I book it? No worries if not, I totally understand. But if you're happy to oblige, just give me a knock or drop me a text on this number. Thanks.

I pause. I was going to say Joshua, but if Kris has tracked Phin down, he might have said something about a strange British guy called Joshua asking questions, so I think for a moment and then I sign it 'Jeff'.

I fold the note into a square and I go back down to Phin's apartment and leave the note pinioned under the fox's chin. Then I head out to a perfumery I noticed earlier three blocks down and I spend seventy dollars on room sprays and scented candles.

There is no message from Phin by the evening. I'm hungry, the day is growing dark and I'm feeling a terrible thumping, throbbing urge for something, and I do not know what it is. I don't know if it's sex. I don't know if it's alcohol. I don't know if it's exercise or violence or loud music or junk food but there is something in my gut and it's roiling and agitating and I have a sense that I would like to punch the wall, but I have done that before and it was incredibly painful – the scuffs and cuts took three weeks to fully heal – and frankly it was not worth it.

I pace this apartment which now smells of lilies and mandarins and, apparently, sea foam. My hands clench and unclench. My breathing solidifies. I watch some porn on my phone, but it just makes me cross. I decide I need to go out. I take the echoey central stairs and cut down the corridor on the first floor. I pass Phin's door and see that the note is still there. I thunder down the last staircase and I burst through the front door and on to the street and immediately I feel myself plugged straight into the energy of the balmy Tuesday night, of the streets filled with office workers cut loose from desks and tedium, with tourists and locals and old people and young people, and I walk where they walk, in their slipstream, like an invisibly coupled train carriage, and I think I probably look mad and I think I probably am mad, and the lights sparkle and refract and make me feel dizzy and drunk although I am entirely sober, and at some point I decouple from the crowds and stop outside the doors of a brasserie with six-foot parlour palms in front of heavy velvet curtains and a maître d' in fitted black shirt and trousers and a smile to charm the birds from the trees as well as the mad lonely man from the street, and I am ushered into a booth and given a menu, and I order the porterhouse steak for $90 and the onion rings and a Tibetan wine called Shangri-La *can you believe it* for $450, and I drink the wine as if it is fruit juice and barely touch the steak because I'm not actually very hungry after all and my eyes cast across the room towards the pavement and I look at the men going by, at the boys, and I want all of them, all of them. But then my heart fills with rage because they don't want me so I order a bottle of Ruinart champagne for $195 and eat the onion rings with my hands and swipe through Grindr with my greasy fingers, and the agony of being so close to Phin is excruciating, it's eating me up from the middle out like a disgusting piece of fruit and I can't do anything with any of these feelings, all the things I want to do right now would end with me in a police cell so I get the bill and I pay it, adding a 50 per cent tip, and I get up and find that I cannot balance and have to grip the table and the waiter who was the recipient of the $300 tip takes me by the elbow and guides me sweetly across the restaurant, and he is not even cute but I cannot help but say, 'You're very cute, what's your name?' And the way he smiles at me, as if there is maybe a globule of sick in his mouth, might well be one of the worst moments of my life, and believe me when I say there have been many.

I career around the pavement, and I want to kiss someone, hit someone, shout at someone, kill someone, stick my hand down the front of someone's trousers and squeeze them until they squeal. I realise in some base way that this is me, this has always been me, but that I have sat on it, stifled it, trapped it in a cage, sedated it like a pet tiger, and it seems at this moment in time that the line between me killing someone and not killing someone has always been so much finer than I'd ever realised, and I want to stab someone through the heart and punch someone in the face, I want to commit a mass killing, to shower these crowds of shiny-faced people with the contents of a semi-automatic and watch them scream and scatter and fall to the floor, clutching their wounds as their life forces leave them. I want to do that. I really, really want to do that.

But also, I want to do drugs. I want some coke. And some vodka. I find my way back to the Magdala and make myself as sober as possible before I ask the barman if he knows anyone, and thankfully he gets the inference immediately and points me in the direction of a woman in the far corner of the bar who looks about fifty. She is drinking beer, alone, and I walk towards her and she gestures me towards the private area in the far left corner and says, 'Are you OK? You look pretty wired.' And I say, 'Yeah, I am pretty wired.' I tell her that I've drunk a bottle of wine and a bottle of champagne and that I feel like I'm losing my mind and I need something, I just need something, and she says, 'Well, you don't need coke, that's for sure.' And she gives me some ketamine and some Valium and I give her fifty dollars and she goes back to her beer and I pocket the pills and the powder and I leave.

Immediately I'm annoyed that I let her talk me out of the coke. But I don't want to go back so I go into another bar and drink three shots of tequila in a row and send a text to Kris Doll.

I'm drunk and horny. Come and find me on your big bike.

(Although actually it says: *Im dunk and horn comr adn find em On your big bike*, with a bike emoji.)

I try to get into a club but the security guy won't let me in and I tussle with him, physically, slam my hands into his chest, feel the futility of it as he pushes back with his own steroid-pumped forearms and peels me away from him like a wet leaf, and then I am free-wheeling for a while, shouting things out to strangers now who stare back at me with disgust and wry amusement. I hand the ketamine and the Valium to a pair of teenage boys. 'Here. Have some drugs.' They take the baggies with slack jaws, and then I am outside my apartment block and I look up and I see the light is on in Phin's apartment and my gut is burning, my heart, my head are burning, flames of fury are licking up through me and threatening to swallow me whole and I need I need I need . . .

I buzz myself into the building and I storm the stairs to the first floor and I know I should wait and I should plan and I should do this properly for God's sake do it properly but I just can't and I bang on the teal door with the fox-head knocker and I hear a voice saying, 'Er, hi?'

'Hi,' I say, using an American accent. 'This is Jeff. From upstairs. Could I have just a minute of your time?'

There is a pause. I shuffle from foot to foot and then I hear the chain unlatch and the door open and I put my foot right there, in the gap and I leave it there and I look up and there is Phin looking down at me and I see it, the split second that he goes from thinking I am Jeff from upstairs to knowing that I am Henry from his nightmares, but it is too late, because I am in his apartment and there is absolutely nothing he can do about it.

PART THREE

41

Samuel

I learn a lot from the story in the *Guardian*. But also, I learn nothing. The piece was written in 2015 by a journalist called Miller Roe and I track him down via Google within about five minutes. However, he does not answer his phone and no email response is forthcoming and there is no address for him and so, while I wait for him to reply, Donal and I take a drive into the countryside to talk to Libby Jones.

She lives in a nice house just outside the city of St Albans. I think it is Georgian, possibly, part of a terrace with some pillars and steps that are creamy and curved and a curtain of ivy climbing the walls. The solicitors in Pimlico told me that the house on Cheyne Walk had been sold for over seven million pounds and this house looks like it did not cost even half or a quarter of that and I wonder what she did with the rest of the money. I cannot help but let my mind spool through the myriad things I would do with a sum of money such as that. I am thirty-six, I am unmarried and I have no children. I would spend some of it, maybe, on an apartment in Florence overlooking the Uffizi in the Piazza della Signoria and maybe some art to furnish it with. I would give my mother most of it, of course, to buy a house that doesn't leak and creak and has buttons to do everything for her, and then I would invest heavily in pensions because I have no intention of living as my mother does on what the high street bank for whom she worked for thirty-five years deems to be a living sum. Lastly, I would pay off my mortgage and celebrate with some champagne that cost more than my monthly repayments.

It is with these thoughts in my mind that I exit the car and follow Donal to the front door of Libby Jones's attractive but modest home. And then I am confused to find not one doorbell but four, and I realise that this is a converted house and that Libby Jones, the multi-million-pound heiress, lives in a flat. I put my finger to the doorbell with her name on it and a moment later a woman appears at the front door, but I do not think it is Libby Jones because she looks to be much older than twenty-six. She has dark hair cut to her shoulders, very thick-framed black glasses and a square face and is wearing what appears to be a boiler suit in green but may in fact be a current trend.

'Good morning,' I say. 'I am Detective Inspector Samuel Owusu, and this is Detective Sergeant Donal Muir. We are look-ing for a Miss Libby Jones.'

'Crikey. Is everything OK?'

'Yes, everything is OK. Could I please ask your name?'

'Dido Rhodes. What is this about?'

At this moment a small dog appears behind her, much more the sort of dog that I like, a dog that can be carried and managed, that cannot jump and lick your face. It growls quietly as if deciding whether or not it wants to bark, and then it stops and sits at Dido's feet.

'We need to talk to Libby Jones. Is she at home?'

Dido Rhodes collects the small dog into her arms. I look him in the eye. The dog returns my gaze. This dog appears to contain wisdom. In his eyes I see a story. He has lived some life and if he could talk, I think, he would tell me everything I needed to know.

'Yes. Hold on. *Libbs! Libby!* There are some policemen here to see you.'

Her eyes do not leave mine as she calls, as if she thinks I might do something untoward if she were to take them off me.

Then Libby appears. She is small and neat and very blonde and very clean. She wears narrow grey jeans with a green vest top and green flip-flops. She blinks at me.

'Hello?'

I introduce myself and Donal again.

'OK,' she says. 'Can I . . .? Do you want to come in?'

The dog recommences its low growl as we cross the threshold. I smile at him reassuringly, but it doesn't seem to work.

'Sorry. He's not my dog. He belongs to my mother. I'm just looking after him for her. He's a bit over-protective.'

I nod. 'That is his job. A dog needs a job to be happy and if they don't know what their job is, they make one up.'

Libby Jones issues a small note of laughter and leads Donal and me through a door behind her and into a tiny flat on the ground floor. The flat is very pretty, a reflection of Libby in its neat shelves and ordered surfaces, its bland attractiveness. We are seated in the living room on cream linen sofas and given glasses of water by Dido in the boiler suit.

'So,' I begin. 'Miss Jones. I was given your details by Smith-kin Rudd & Royle solicitors in SW1. They tell us that you inherited a property at number sixteen Cheyne Walk around a year ago?'

'Yes. That's correct.'

'And that you sold it recently?'

'Yes. The sale completed about ten days ago.'

'To Oliver and Kate Wolfensberger?'

'Yes. That's right.'

'And I understand the house once belonged to your parents?'

I notice Libby gulp before clearing her throat and I know that her answer to this question will be a lie.

'My birth parents. Yes. That's correct.'

'And you'd never met your birth parents?'

'No, never. They died when I was a very young baby. Can I ask what this is about?'

I feel myself on a tightrope across a crevasse. Libby Jones has already lied to me once and I don't want to put her on the spot and make her lie again. I want only honest answers from her.

'We are investigating the possible murder of a young woman called Birdie Dunlop-Evers in the late eighties to early nineties.'

I see a flicker of recognition pass across her face. But she shakes her head, signifying that she has never heard of Birdie Dunlop-Evers.

'It is possible that she was living at number sixteen Cheyne

Walk at the time of her death,' I continue. 'I've read an article, in the *Guardian*, about the history of the house and of the terrible tragedy that befell your parents. I have read how you were found in a crib alone upstairs. I have read that there were other people in that house. Teenagers. Some reports say there were two teenagers. Some say three, some say four. Some reports say that there had never been any children living at the house that they could remember. A delivery man thought the house might be a nunnery? So many conflicting reports, in fact. Have you read this article too?'

'Yes. Of course. Yes. It was one of the first things I found online when I discovered that the house had been left to me. Before that I'd never heard of the house or of any members of the family. It's a very confusing article.'

'Indeed. Many questions. Few answers. And so it felt possible to me, when I read this article, that in a house with such a chaotic and tragic back story, maybe a young woman could be subsumed into the fabric of that house without anyone noticing. Disappear entirely.'

It is not a question. It is a statement. Libby Jones cannot agree or disagree and I leave it there for a moment, to settle in the silence.

Libby Jones rearranges all her limbs, both legs and arms. 'I genuinely have no idea,' she says. 'I only know what was in the article. I don't know anything else.'

'You saw the house though? Before you sold it?'

'Oh, yes. Of course. I spent quite some time there after inheriting it. Exploring. Getting a feel for the place.'

'And you never saw anything? Found anything? Anything that

might have given more insight into what happened the night your parents committed suicide?'

'No. Sorry.'

Her hand goes to her throat as she says this.

Damn. She has lied again. But this time it is a useful lie because it makes me believe that she has in fact found out something beyond the story contained in the newspaper article; that she does know something and that she is choosing not to share it with me; and if she is choosing not to share it with me, then she is trying to protect either herself or somebody else. And who could she possibly want to protect in this bizarre scenario other than another person involved in the story of that house?

The brother, perhaps, or sister?

Henry and Lucy were the names of the other Lamb children, according to the article. Is it possible, I wonder, that they had known of the date of the trust's maturity and tracked Libby down to claim their share? After all, they had both been named on the trust, too, and neither had come forward on their own twenty-fifth birthdays. Might they have been waiting for a 'clean' person to claim the inheritance on their behalf? Someone who existed above the radar, unlike themselves? And if they couldn't exist above the radar, then why not? Possibly because one of them had been responsible in some way for the death of Birdie Dunlop-Evers? But why? That is the question that I now know I must find the answer to. Why would a teenager, or even two, three or four teenagers, wish to kill a thirty-year-old woman?

'I saw the house yesterday,' I tell Libby. 'Mr Wolfensberger let me look around. It's quite characterful.'

'Scary, you mean?'

'Yes, I suppose. A little scary. It's hard to imagine that a normal family ever lived there.'

'Well, maybe they weren't a normal family.' Libby shrugs her shoulders. 'I mean, normal families don't tend to carry out suicide pacts, do they?'

I nod. This is true.

'I was lucky,' she continues. 'Lucky to have been taken out of that environment and raised in a normal family.'

'And now you are lucky because you have a lot of money?'

She smiles. I can see that this money has made her happy. And it makes me wonder what she has done with all that money. If the brother and the sister had tracked her down for their share of the money and tried to take it from her by force or blackmailed her into giving it to them, then she would not look so relaxed about her change of fortunes. But she is relaxed. So I think that maybe she has shared the money, happily, equally; that she is at peace with the money because she has comported herself in a reasonable and fair-handed way.

'So, will you buy a larger property now?' I ask.

'Yes. I mean, I'll keep this place. Rent it out for a very low rent to a young couple or a single person, someone who is struggling. I won't need the income, but I know how hard it is to make ends meet for young people. Everything is so expensive. And I've been looking at a place further out in the country. With a bit of land. Somewhere I could run an interior design workshop. Maybe a barn or an annexe, something like that.'

'So you will still work?'

'Well, it's early days. I haven't got it off the ground yet. But my friend, Dido' – she points to the door – 'she's the head designer and franchise owner of the kitchen showroom in town where I used to work; she's going to help me get set up.'

Dido is waiting outside the living-room door. She thinks she is invisible, but she is not. I can hear her breathing, hear her bare feet against the wooden floorboards, a slight clearing of her throat. I wonder how much Dido knows about the mystery that her friend is part of. Maybe as much as the dog, who has stopped growling, but is very much staring at me.

'Well. That sounds like a great plan and a great use of your inheritance. And what of the rest of it?'

'The rest of it?' She looks somewhat startled.

'Yes. A house in the country. A barn. A business. You will have plenty left over?'

'Well, not really. I mean, I'll give some to my mother. Of course. And maybe, you know, some charities. Investments. That kind of thing.'

I nod. I need somehow to get into Libby Jones's bank account. I'll need a warrant but I will worry about that later.

'Do you ever fear that one of your siblings might come to you, once they hear of the sale of the house? It is on the internet after all; soon the land registry will post the selling price and the whole world will know. Including your brother and sister, Henry and Lucy. What would you do? If they came to find you?'

I hear Dido break out into a strong cough behind the living-room door.

'They won't,' Libby says.

I don't respond to this with words, but a raised eyebrow.

'They're probably dead.'

I try to look as if there is a small chance that I believe what she has just said, but it is hard. 'Dead?' I say. 'That seems a dramatic conclusion to have reached.'

'It's the only thing that makes any sense though, isn't it? Like you say. Teenage children, here one minute. Gone the next.'

'Ah, well, yes. You may think that. But it is easier to keep a living person hidden than a dead body. As a detective, I know this only too well. A change of name. A change of appearance. A different country. Very easy to do. So they may not be dead at all, Miss Jones; in fact, and in all probability, they are much more likely to be alive. Have you ever tried to trace them?'

A very firm shake of the head follows my question. 'No. No I have not.'

'Would you want to?'

'No.'

'You're not curious to know what became of them? To have them in your life?'

'I just assumed they were dead. It never occurred to me . . .'

I sigh. This conversation has gone as far as it can go. But as I get to my feet the dog begins once more to growl and I look at the dog and I realise that there is one more question to ask.

'Your mother's dog, you said?'

She nods.

'So this is your *adoptive* mother's dog?'

'My—?' All the colour leaves her face. 'Yes.' She rallies. 'Yes. My adoptive mother's dog.'

'And where is she, your mother?'

'She's in Spain. She lives in Spain, or well, at least she sometimes lives in Spain. She has a place. She sometimes comes back. We – It's kind of a dog-share thing, I suppose.'

Libby Jones is gabbling. Lying. Or covering up a lie. I think of the photo in the *Guardian* of her birth parents: the exotic, dark-haired, half-Turkish mother. The squat, bulldog-faced father. She looks like neither of them. Not in any respect. I am leaving Libby Jones's home with more questions than I arrived with.

42

Lucy and the children climb out of the Uber outside the Angel Inn. It's a 1920s building, on the cusp of deco and nouveau, with metal-framed windows and an ornate chrome revolving door. It's not as slick as the Dayville, but it is more charming, more to Lucy's taste; less, she imagines, to Henry's.

In the foyer, Lucy grasps Stella's hand and heads towards the reception area.

'Hi,' she says. 'We're looking for my brother. He goes either by the name of Henry Lamb, or Joshua Harris. This is him. Is he staying here?'

She turns her phone to the receptionist. The receptionist smiles and nods. 'Yes,' she says. 'That's Mr Harris. He was staying here. But he checked out at lunchtime.'

Lucy feels a punch of surprise in her gut. 'Lunchtime today?'

'Yes. I'm so sorry you missed him!'

'And you don't know where he went?'

'No. I'm so sorry. He didn't say. But he left on foot? If that's of any help?'

Lucy turns to Marco and Marco nods. 'Yes,' she says. 'That is helpful. Very helpful indeed. Thank you so much.'

They leave the hotel and stand for a while on the pavement. It's still light and the streets are busy; early diners at pavement tables are being served large glasses of wine that catch the long golden sunrays. They look around themselves for a while, as if they might just see Henry pulling his suitcase along behind him at any minute.

'Now what?' asks Marco.

Lucy shrugs. 'God knows. I mean, he left on foot. Not by taxi. So he must still be here somewhere.' She looks around again, her eyes searching for a dash of blond highlighted hair, the curve of his shoulders, the distinctive slap of his feet in designer trainers or expensive leather shoes. But of course he is not there. Of course he isn't. 'Shall we get some dinner, maybe?' She casts her eye again across the cafés and the pavement tables and the glasses of cold white wine glittering in the evening sun.

But Stella is yawning. It is gone midnight in London. She's been awake for nearly a day. They take an Uber back to the Dayville and they order room service and by 8 p.m. all three of them are fast asleep. Even Lucy.

The following morning, Lucy awakes inside the dark heat of an anxiety dream, and for a moment when she opens her eyes she has no idea where she is, feels almost as though she is upside down, that the ceiling is the floor and the floor is the ceiling, and that the walls are sliding in towards her. She sits bolt upright and catches her breath. She sees Stella's curls on the pillow beside her and hears Marco snoring gently from around the corner in the living area. She grabs her phone to check the time. It's just gone 8 a.m. She has slept for twelve hours but still feels exhausted.

She rubs her face and has a shower, one of those showers that doesn't make her feel any cleaner, despite the heat of the water and the tang of grapefruit extract in the body wash. She sits on the edge of the bed in a hotel robe with her hair wrapped in a towel turban and picks up her phone.

Her heart skips a beat and then races. There is a barrage of messages from Libby on WhatsApp. The dog, she thinks at first, something has happened to the dog. But no. It is not the dog. It is something far, far worse.

Mum. I don't want to freak you out and I'm sure it's nothing, but some police came to see me yesterday.

They were asking questions about you and about Henry. Asking if you were alive, if you'd ever been in touch with me about the inheritance.

I lied as best as I could.

But I fucked up a bit. I said that Fitz was my mum's dog. Then I had to pretend it was my other mum's dog but I could tell he knew that was wrong. I could tell he knew I was lying about everything.

But it's Libby's final message that sends a stab of sheer panic through her gut.

They said they were looking into the murder of Birdie Dunlop-Evers. I just made out like I'd never heard of her. I think they believed me. I think it's going to be OK.

Lucy lets the phone drop on the bed.

Birdie Dunlop-Evers.

The sight of her name in Libby's text messages is enough to make her flesh crawl. Her vision grows black, her head fills with dark fog, her nostrils fill with the smell of Birdie's scalp, the stale heat of her breath against her cheek as she sternly moved her fingertips up and down the strings of the battered violin she taught Lucy to play on.

She remembers the games that Birdie played with Lucy's head towards the end, the way she brought Lucy into her relationship with David, made Lucy feel special with hair ties and nail polish and time spent doing illicit activities away from the gaze of the others; she remembers sitting on Birdie's mattress eating Maltesers out of a family-sized bag while Birdie watched her with greedy eyes. She remembers a copy of *Smash Hits*. A packet of fruit-flavoured chewing gum. A squirt of designer perfume from a bottle with a gold bow on it. A pair of claret suede shoes with kitten heels which she modelled for David Thomsen while Birdie preened over her. She remembers how David had encroached a little closer into the space that she and Birdie inhabited every single time they were together; first a distant observer, then an active observer, then a part of her and Birdie's team until one day Birdie was gone and she was alone with David. At the time she had felt honoured and thrilled that David wanted to spend time with her without Birdie. She'd felt it as a tingling necklace of ice around her neck, a roil in her stomach, a dark glow in her body, a thing that she wanted even though she didn't know what it was: attention, maybe, but more than that. She wanted love. She wanted love so much she ached with it. And that was what David Thomsen called it. He called it love.

And though she has thought of David often across the years, she has rarely thought of Birdie – she sidled off the pages of Lucy's interior story a long time ago. A footnote. A smell. A shred of something. But now Birdie is filling her whole head, every atom of her being, every thread of her psyche. Birdie with her waist-length hair and pretty hands, her small teeth and clipped English vowels; Birdie with her dead blue eyes. And now that Lucy is a woman, a mother three times over, now that she is older than Birdie will ever get to be, she knows that the precious little gifts and secret whisperings and perfume spritzes were all designed to make her feel comfortable enough and special enough and important enough to believe that having sex with a forty-six-year-old man when she was only thirteen was a good thing. Lucy knows now that Birdie groomed her on behalf of David, she knows that Birdie was a monster. And she knows that Birdie died from a blow to the head and she knows that it was all to do with Henry. The three bodies in the kitchen. Birdie dead in the bedroom. Phin tied to the radiator. The dead cat. The baby her mother lost at five months gestation. That it's all tied in with Henry, all of it, but she's never quite been able to work out how. She just remembers the shock of seeing Birdie without her life force, without her power, a flaccid puppet, a nothing, the unworldly weight of her body as she helped Henry carry it on to the roof of the house on Cheyne Walk . . .

And now, somehow, Lucy has no idea how, a policeman in London has discovered that Birdie is dead and has decided that it must have something to do with the people she once lived with, and she has no idea how this policeman in London has made this connection and how things have got to the point of this policeman arriving on her daughter's doorstep in St Albans and asking her uncomfortable questions about her family set-up, but she knows that those questions won't stop once they start, that more questions will follow like steps in a dance until they get to the point in Lucy's life, almost a year ago, when she did something shocking, something terrible, and she feels the noose around her neck growing tighter and tighter until she almost cannot breathe.

43

April 2017

Rachel finally switched on her phone again a week after she left Michael. There was nothing from him. No missed calls, no messages. She was both surprised and relieved. Each day she awoke in her apartment in Camden Town and opened her eyes and wondered for a second where she was in her life. Her dreams every night were vivid and confusing. In her dreams she married Michael again; she slept with Michael again. In her dreams she told Michael that she loved him, that she missed him, that she wanted him. She kissed him and held him in her dreams and then she would awake and soon remember reality and feel glad and unburdened, climb off her bed and greet the day in the soft embrace of benign solitude. The days were growing warmer, longer, kinder. She kept the doors open to her balcony for as long as the sun shone through them, drank her morning coffee out there and reconnected with all the weird and wonderful people in her canalside community, some of whom had barely noticed that she'd been gone, some of whom were full of curiosity about her absence.

On the Monday after she left (this was how she phrased it in her head: she left him – that was it, nothing more) she met with Dom's friend, Thea, the shit-hot divorce lawyer. Thea lived in Primrose Hill so they met halfway between them in a deli on Gloucester Avenue, abutting the canal. Dom told Rachel that it was to be a freebie, a favour, a fifteen minute-er, so Rachel didn't waste any time with small-talk. She said, 'I met this guy in August, we had our first date in November, got engaged in December, married in February and from the fourth day of the honeymoon it's been an absolute disaster.'

'Disaster,' said Thea, unpeeling a curl of pastry off a cinnamon roll. 'What sort of disaster?'

'Emotionally abusive.'

Thea narrowed her eyes at Rachel, then popped the pastry into her mouth between rose-tinted lips. 'In what way?'

'Well, we experienced a moment of – sexual incompatibility on our honeymoon. I suggested trying something new. He was appalled. Ever since, he's used it to punish me. He's been having problems with – well, with maintaining an erection. He's lost all his money—'

'How much money?'

'Oh. I don't know. He's cagey about his finances, but over a million. Yes, definitely over a million. So, I've been paying for everything.'

'So you married him thinking he was wealthy?'

'Yes. Yes I did. Turns out the condo in the ski resort was a time-share, the house in Martha's Vineyard was a summer lease and he's renting out his house in Antibes to cover the mortgage repayments on his flat in London. Everything else he had was cash, and he's lost it all.'

'So, since you married, he's lost both his money and his erectile function?'

'Essentially. Yes.'

Thea breathed in hard through her tiny nostrils and leaned back in her chair. Her fingertips ran over the flakes of pastry on the rim of her plate. 'Some might be tempted to refer you to your wedding vows, Rachel. For richer, for poorer, etc.' She cocked an eyebrow at Rachel, and Rachel felt her fists clench under the table.

'It's more than that, though. He became controlling.'

'In what way?'

'As in always wanting me straight home after work for dinner, that sort of thing.'

The eyebrow cocked again. 'And what would he do if you weren't home after work for dinner?'

'He would . . . well, I don't know really, because I always was. And then once, last week, I wasn't, and he threw a plate of risotto at the wall.'

'Was he aiming it at you?'

'No. I mean. I wasn't actually there. I just got home and found it there.'

'And what else? What else did he do when you didn't come home for dinner?'

Rachel could feel where this conversation was going. She could see how threadbare her case was without the horror of what

Michael had done to her on the sofa the previous week. She glanced up quickly at Thea, absorbed the two fans of perfectly mascaraed eyelashes, the fresh-out-of-the-specialist-dry-cleaners'-bag cashmere crewneck, the squared-off fingernails, the simple gold wedding band and Michael Kors sunglasses perched on top of improbably shiny red hair, and she thought: This woman would not let that happen to her. This woman has never been violated like that. Her body never used as a piece of meat. And she knew that the only way she could persuade this woman that she had a good case to divorce this man was to throw the rape down on the table between them. But she could not. She simply could not. So she sighed and she said, 'Nothing. Just that. Just the thrown risotto.'

'And you left?'

'Yes. I left that night.'

'And has he been in touch?'

'No. Not a word.'

'Is that what you might have expected?'

'No. Actually. Not really. I thought he'd be angry. That he'd stalk me.'

'Stalk you?'

'Yes. Pursue me. You know?'

'Did you want him to?'

'No! Oh God, no! I'm happy he hasn't. I'm happy not to be with him. I'm happy he's gone. I'm really happy. I never ever want to see him again!'

And there it was. The petulant edge to her voice. A marriage made in haste to a rich man who turned out not to be rich, to a smitten, adoring man who turned out not to give a shit, who was happy to let her walk out of his life, a manly man who let her down in bed, and Rachel saw how it looked. She saw it clearly and painfully. She was a princess and her prince had turned out to be just a guy, and she was disappointed that her fairy tale had turned out to be so numbingly pedestrian, and now she wanted out and her rich daddy was happy to pay the £500-an-hour, shit-hot divorce lawyer to make it happen.

'So, you know, you could just talk to him and sort this out between yourselves,' said Thea. 'I mean, there are no joint finances? Mortgages?'

'No. We own our own properties.'

'No children? Debts?'

'No.'

'Does he have any of your property?'

'No. Well, just clothes and toiletries. Nothing big.'

'And you have none of his?'

'No.'

'Anyone else involved?'

'No.'

'I think, to be blunt, Rachel, that you should try to keep this as civilised and simple as possible. Buy yourself a DIY divorce kit and start the ball rolling.'

'But what if he refuses?'

'Then you'll have to go to court and prove that the marriage had irrevocably, irretrievably broken down. Or you could wait.'

'Wait for what?'

'Wait for a two-year separation.'

'You mean stay married for another two years?'

'Yes. But live separately.'

'And then I wouldn't have to prove anything?'

'Uh-huh. Exactly.'

'Or explain anything?'

'Correct.'

Rachel nodded, a small jerk of her head, as this option landed and settled. It had taken her nearly thirty-three years to find one man to marry. She was pretty sure she wouldn't find another any time soon. In fact, she was pretty sure she had no intention of ever marrying anyone ever again. She would focus on the business. On her friendships. She would go to yoga every week. And spend time with her dad. She would stop using dating apps and stop pursuing relationships. She would, she decided, be celibate. For two years. She could do that. She was sure she could do that. She would come out of the other side of her separation from Michael cleansed of the shittiness of men and of the ways in which she behaved when she was around them.

'I think', Rachel said, the display on her phone telling her that they were about to hit the fifteen-minute mark, 'that that is what I will do. Yes. That's what I will do.'

Thea's face softened. She clearly felt that Rachel had made the right decision. 'But in the meantime,' she said, 'make sure that you and Michael remain civilised. Or, ideally, estranged.'

Estranged.

The word filled Rachel's head with a kind of calm. 'Yes,' she said. 'I will. I will have nothing to do with him at all.'

Dom's baby was born on 28 April, right on her due date, an eight-pound baby girl they called Ava. Spring turned to summer and still Rachel did not hear from Michael. In June, Rachel went to Ibiza with Dom and Jonno and the baby and another couple who were pregnant. She was the only single person there, but she did not mind. Other people's relationships looked tainted to her eyes now. She imagined the reality of their lives behind closed doors. She saw, in her mind's eye, a smashed plate of pumpkin risotto smeared on all of their walls, if not now, then maybe soon. She felt the ripples of tension in the ways the couples addressed each other, especially Dom and Jonno as they tussled gently back and forth over who should do what for the baby and when.

One night, as midnight moved towards 1 a.m., Dom and the other couple had already gone to bed and Rachel found herself up with Jonno drinking tequila and sharing a spliff. Jonno, who had never once said anything to her about her split from Michael back in April, narrowed his eyes at her and said, 'I found out other stuff. You know. About Michael. But Dom said not to tell you. Once you said you were engaged to him.'

Rachel blinked at him. 'Oh, yeah?'

'Yeah. Do you want to . . . I mean, shall I tell you? Or are you—?'

'Tell me. Please. I want to know.'

Jonno squinted into the smoke he'd just exhaled and passed the spliff to Rachel. 'Sure?'

'Yes. God. Just tell me.'

He breathed in and then laid his hands out on the table in front of him. 'His business ventures. What did he tell you about those?'

'Oh, like transport logistics? Industrial equipment? For making boats? Something like that?'

'Yeah, right. So not *quite*. More like industrial equipment sold to high-volume drug manufacturers.'

'Drugs? You mean, like illegal drugs?'

'Correct.'

'And, sorry, what was Michael doing exactly?'

'A middleman, essentially. He procures the equipment from legitimate suppliers and then sells it on at vast profit to the drug manufacturers. He also has some involvement with their trafficking systems.'

'He traffics drugs?'

'Well, tangentially, yes. Not directly. In a very hands-off way. And all of this of course would be very hard to prove.'

'He's a criminal.'

'Neegh.' Jonno shrugged and grimaced. 'Not exactly. But criminal adjacent.'

'He lost all his money.'

'Shit. He told you that?'

'Yes. He said a shipment of equipment went missing in transit. He'd paid for it up front and the people who lost it refused to take accountability for it. A million pounds, or more.'

Jonno sucked in his breath and dropped his chin. 'Fucking hell. And it was his money?'

'Well, yes. I suppose so.'

He sucked in his breath again, this time through his bared teeth. 'Might not have been though.'

'What do you mean?'

'I mean it might have been money that was . . . *fluid*. I.e. money that was meant to be repaid somewhere along the line. Did he seem extra stressy?'

'Well, God, yes. I mean, that's pretty much why I left him.'

Jonno nodded. 'Well,' he said, 'I reckon there's more to come of this sorry story. Definitely more left to tell.' Then he tipped the tequila bottle towards her and said, 'Another shot?'

Rachel smiled and said, 'Sure. Why not?'

In July Rachel moved out of her studio in Kilburn and into a much bigger studio in Holloway, closer to her flat. Paige had agreed to work alongside her part-time in parallel with her own jewellery business and the bank had agreed to a loan of £150,000 to finance the materials for her first exclusive range for Liberty. Her father had taken out the loan on her behalf, but Rachel was going to repay it herself, every penny. This was it. No more handouts, bailouts or loans. She had a 50 per cent off everything sale on her website and used the cash raised from that to employ two professional goldsmiths to work alongside her and Paige on three-month contracts. By the end of July the sample range was ready: one of each item. She and Paige wrapped them in suede pouches and took them in an Uber to Liberty to present them to Lilian and Rosie in a wood-panelled room with tea served in a pot and macarons on a floral plate and there was laughter and lightness and excitement for the future.

'They are *exquisite*. Oh my God, Lils, look at this pendant.'

'Oh, wow, Rosie, I am absolutely getting one of these pink stacking-ring sets. Just stunning.'

'Rachel Gold, you are a beautiful little genius. You really, really are.'

Back in the studio, Paige and Rachel drank champagne and toasted all the work they'd done and all the work that was yet to come and they tucked the sample range away inside the extra-secure safe that Rachel had bought for the new studio, then clicked off all the lights and locked up the studio behind them. On Monday the contracted goldsmiths would start work; the days would be long, the nights would be longer. Five of each piece ready to put on display in Liberty on 17 October for the big launch.

Rachel went to bed early that night, even though it was a Friday, and fell asleep thinking of plans, of numbers, of cash flows, of a safe full of diamonds and gold.

By September Rachel and her new team were in a rock-solid routine. The display signage and branding had all been designed and produced. And still Rachel had had no contact from Michael. And then, one glowering, stormy afternoon, when a bullying wind was stirring the first few fallen leaves in circles around her feet, and she was wearing a coat for the first time since before the summer, Rachel was halfway between her studio and a meeting in town with Lilian and Rosie when she stopped dead in her tracks outside a shop selling tartan and felt her breath catch in her chest cavity. There, heading briskly towards her, his hand in the hand of a woman who looked a lot like Ella, the tiny blonde woman she'd found him talking to at Dominique's Christmas party the year before, was Michael. He was wearing a grey woollen overcoat and a burgundy-and-navy-striped scarf, had grown a beard and was beaming at her from ear to ear.

'Oh my God. Rachel! Hi!'

Rachel's body felt numb. Her gaze tracked briefly to the woman who looked like Ella and she saw a flash of horror pass across her face and realised that it was, it was Ella, and how, she wondered, how had Ella and Michael come together? When? Where? They'd only met once, so briefly, and he hadn't even liked her, and what

was Michael doing holding hands with her and why was he smiling at Rachel as if she were an old friend and not the wife who
he'd raped on his sofa five months ago and not seen since? She
could not find a reaction that was appropriate to this situation. Her
face didn't know what to do. Her body wanted to run.

Eventually she said, 'Erm. Hi. I mean, I can't really . . . I need
to, I'm late for—'

'Sure. No worries. It's great to see you though. You look
amazing.'

'Thanks. I—'

She made an 'I gotta go' gesture and smiled grimly.

He let her go with another megawatt smile and then, just as she
passed him, he said, 'Hey! By the way! Ella tells me you've scored
a big contract. With Liberty. I mean, that is immense! Totally!'

Rachel's mouth went dry. She stopped and turned back and
looked from Michael to Ella and said, 'How – how did you know
about that?'

Ella dropped her gaze to the pavement. 'Dom told me.'

'Dom—'

'Yeah, I saw her last week. She told me about it.'

'Dom? Erm, hold on – does she know? About you two?' She
flapped her arm at them.

Ella flushed slightly and looked up at Michael. Then she shook
her head.

'So, you went out with my best friend and let her tell you
things, personal, private things about me, and she doesn't even
know that you're' – she flapped her arm at them again – 'whatever it is you're doing?'

'Oh, come on now. It's no big deal,' said Michael. 'We're

257

keeping this quiet for now. That's all. There's no big conspiracy. I mean, would I have come over to you and said hello if we were trying to hide anything?'

Rachel did not respond. Michael cocked his eyebrow at her patronisingly. 'Anyway, Rachel, it's great to see you looking so well. And congrats on the Liberty thing. Seriously. You totally deserve it.'

And then they were gone, and Rachel was left on the pavement, her feet rooted to the spot, her legs unable to move, her heart chilled as ice.

44

June 2019

Samuel

It took a full twenty-four hours for us to obtain a warrant to look at Libby Jones's bank details. During those twenty-four hours, we received the report from the arborist. He confirmed that the trees overhanging the house on Cheyne Walk were indeed London planes, trees of heaven and Persian silk, the exact trees that had formed the basis of the mulch found attached to the remains of Birdie Dunlop-Evers.

We had what we needed. Proof that Birdie's body had been kept on the roof of number sixteen Cheyne Walk. I experienced a warm feeling of euphoria and sat at my desk smiling for a while.

Donal and I return to Cheyne Walk now, to join the crime scene detectives and Saffron Brown, the forensic investigator.

'Hi, Sam,' says Saffron. 'Good to see you.'

'Good to see you, too,' I say and I notice Donal mouth the word 'Sam' at me and smile strangely whilst wriggling his eyebrows. I roundly ignore him and turn back to Saffron.

'I am very sorry for leaving footprints on the roof. I hope it hasn't hindered your operation?'

'Not at all, Sam. No problem. But come and look at this.'

We follow her to the bottom of the garden, just past a tree with a circular bench built around it. Here there is a tall wall, grown over entirely with a thick, ropey wisteria. Another forensic investigator is crouched down over a flower bed, pulling items from the soil on to a sheet of plastic. My stomach lurches with shock and I hear Donal gasp.

Bones.

Small white bones.

'Not what you're thinking, Sam, don't worry,' says Saffron. 'They're actually cat bones. Look, here, the skull?' She picks it up and shows it to us. It is clearly the skull of a small animal and I breathe a sigh of relief.

'And look,' she says, guiding us to a spot closer to the back of the house. 'See this?' She points at a rectangle of soil. 'This is where Justin Redding's herb garden used to be. And these' – she indicates a pair of large terracotta pots – 'are the pots that the *Atropa belladonna* was grown in, that the owners and the mystery man used to poison themselves with back in 1994.' She beams at me and I can tell she is loving the unfurling gothic narrative almost as much as I am.

Donal and I leave Saffron and her team there and return to the station, where we re-examine the police reports from the time of the 'suicide pact' bodies being found.

PCs Robbin and Shah had been the first to enter the house the day of the anonymous phone call. They had been followed later on by a crime scene team, and a special family liaison officer called Felicity Measures who dealt with the baby, and the two older Lamb children, Henry and Lucy, had never been traced. The house, according to the police reports, had been filled with strange suggestions of a somewhat cult-like history. The suicide note had been initialled by the dead: ML, HL, DT. Missing persons reports had been extensively trawled at the time looking for someone with the initials DT who matched the mystery corpse's approximate age and appearance, but no one had ever been found and the search was abandoned three years later.

Miller Roe's article in the *Guardian* suggested a similar dead end during his own investigation in 2015. Although the last line of the article held a glimmer of tantalising hope:

And then, just last week, I found a possible DT. A family man, arrived from France in 1988 at the age of forty-two with his wife and two children, but never heard from again. Only when his mother was close to death in 2006 was a missing person report filed, but the police were unable to trace him and now in 2015 neither am I. So, another dead end, another unpassable road, another mystery to add to the unending mysteries in the case of Serenity Lamb and her rabbit's foot.

But Miller Roe has still not replied to my email, and he is still not answering his phone. In desperation I ask for his address to be brought to me from the system. I am told he lives in South Norwood, and I waste an hour of my life driving there and back only to find his flat locked and empty. The upstairs neighbour tells me that Miller Roe doesn't spend much time at home these days, that he lives mostly with his girlfriend. I ask the neighbour if he knows where the girlfriend lives, and he does not but he tells me that he will be sure to tell Miller that I came, if he ever sees him again.

But finally, an hour ago, the financial report came through and although I am alone at my desk behind a closed door when it arrives, I cannot help but shout out and punch the air and spin in a circle on the toes of my left foot while making strange sounds because there it is, in monochrome on the screen of my computer. On the same day that Libby Jones had the princely sum of £7.45 million paid into her current account, she transferred two separate payments into two other bank accounts of £2.48 million each.

The name on the first account is Miss Marie Valerie Caron. The name on the second account is Mr Phineas Thomson. The name Phineas rings bells. I feel I have heard it before recently and I flick through my notebook, urgently, trying to dislodge the memory. And there it is, written in capitals and underlined: 'I AM PHIN'. These are the words that Donal had found scrawled on a skirting board at Cheyne Walk, the words I photographed. 'I AM PHIN'. At the time the words meant nothing. But now they mean everything.

I stride from my office and into the investigation room towards my colleague, Maura. I bring the banking report up on to her screen and I show her the names.

'Maura,' I say. 'I need you to find out everything there is to know about these people. Absolutely everything. Including on social media.'

Then Donal and I get back into a car and head out to St Albans once again.

Libby is not at her flat. But I remember her mentioning that her friend Dido is the head designer/owner of the kitchen showroom in the centre of the town, so we drive over there and park outside. After we enter the showroom, Dido comes out to us from her office at the back and looks at me with that same wary gaze she had two days before.

'Oh. Hello?'

'Good afternoon, Miss Rhodes. I'm sorry to disturb you at your place of work, but we are looking for Miss Jones and she is not at her apartment and she is not answering her phone and we really do need to talk to her as a matter of some urgency. Do you happen to know where she might be?'

The kitchens displayed in Northbone Kitchens' showroom are very beautiful. I find that I am running my hand unthinkingly along a creamy marble countertop and quickly remove it. I think of my own kitchen counters which are made from a plastic material designed to resemble small blocks of wood and feel suddenly that they are looking dated and that maybe it is time for an upgrade. I pick up a card from a small box on the creamy marble counter and hold it between my thumb and the tip of my middle finger.

Dido shrugs. In fact, she does not just shrug but she heaves her entire upper body up towards her ears, turns up her hands, palm first and protrudes her lower lip. 'No idea.'

'You don't know where she is?'

'Not a clue. Maybe she's shopping?'

'Yes. Maybe she is. Where does she shop?'

'I have absolutely no clue. Waitrose, probably.'

I narrow my eyes at Dido Rhodes, wondering why she seems to dislike me so. I wonder if maybe she is a racist. But I think it is more likely that she dislikes me because she is scared that I am going to hurt Libby in some way. Which is, of course, entirely possible.

'Well, please, Miss Rhodes—'

'Ms.'

'My apologies. Ms Rhodes. If you hear from her, please will you let her know that DI Owusu and DS Muir would like very much to talk to her at her earliest possible convenience?'

'What about, exactly? Didn't she already tell you everything she knows? Which is, of course, precisely nothing.'

I inhale and arrange my face into a pleasant smile. 'Yes. It appeared on Tuesday that she knew nothing, but further investigations have proved that she may know more than she thought and, in fact, Ms Rhodes – you are a very close friend of Miss Jones, are you not?'

'Yes, I am.'

'In which case, if she had somehow made a connection with her long-lost siblings, she would have told you?'

'I suppose so,' she replies, her tone more guarded now.

'Has she ever mentioned to you a person by the name of Phineas? Phineas Thomson?'

I spin the business card on its axis between my thumb and finger while I watch Dido's response and as I watch I realise quickly that she is about to lie. For such a cool customer she has some very pronounced tics. Here they show up in the way her gaze finally detaches itself from me and reaches for the ceiling, one shoulder rolls slightly forward to the right, her hips to the left. I see a tiny indent in her cheek as she clenches her teeth before she speaks.

'No. Never heard of him.'

'OK. Well, then, thank you anyway.'

I look once more around the dazzling showroom, an unexpected need for shiny new things opening up in me that is stupid and yet quite thrilling. Then I nod my head at Dido Rhodes and we leave.

'Where to, boss?'

'To Dido's house,' I say.

'Seriously?'

'Yes. Of course. Where else would she be?'

'Do we have an address?'

I flash Donal a smile. 'We do. It is right here on this business card.'

I give Donal the postcode and we leave.

45

Lucy is in a fast-food restaurant called Quik E Burger picking at a carton of fries. Marco had insisted that they come here for breakfast. They have no branches in the UK and it's all over TikTok all the time and they have a 'secret menu' just to up the cult aspect and he is mauling a burger that is described as 'The Beast', which seems an apt description as it falls apart in Marco's hands and drips down his chin.

Marco got a message from Kris Doll the day before saying that he'd had a garbled text message from Henry on Tuesday night who had sounded 'incredibly drunk' but that he had not replied to it and did not know from which location it had been sent but that it contained an invitation to join him for a drink; therefore they were able to conclude that at least as of Tuesday night Henry was still very much alive and in Chicago and thus it had been worth every minute the three of them had spent pounding the sun-baked pavements of Chicago together looking for him the previous day.

'He might be wearing a disguise,' Marco says now. His tongue appears briefly to lick away a smear of red sauce from the side of his mouth.

'Who?'

'Henry. He might be in disguise. You know, we're looking for blond hair, etc. He might have dyed it. Or be wearing a hat.'

'I doubt it, sweetheart. We've shown his photo to two separate people now and they've both recognised him.'

Marco shrugs. 'I guess.'

Stella is sucking at a strawberry milkshake and eyeing them both thoughtfully. 'When can we go home?' she says eventually.

Lucy gazes at her, wondering what Stella means when she says 'home'. Stella has known so many in her short life: the flat on the outskirts of Nice in which she was born and where she lived for the first two years of her life; then the flat of Mémé, Stella's paternal grandmother, on the seventh floor of a tower block, all three of them squeezed into the box room together, kicked out after two weeks because it 'wasn't working'. There followed three rooms in three hostels, three days on a beach, then a year at Giuseppe's bed and breakfast, another week on the beach, more nights at Giuseppe's, three nights in Henry's rented Airbnb in Battersea, a year in Henry's apartment in Marylebone and now here they are in Chicago and God knows where they'll be next, but Lucy feels very strongly that it won't be Henry's apartment in Marylebone and it won't be the old vicarage in St Albans and it might not even be with her, that Lucy is moments away from a hand on her shoulder and a voice in her ear telling her that she needs to go somewhere, with someone, and explain what happened in Antibes last year and then explain what happened in Chelsea in April 1994, and then what will happen to Stella and Marco?

She holds back tears and covers Stella's hand with hers. 'Soon,' she says. 'We'll go home soon. When we find Uncle Henry.'

'Why doesn't Uncle Henry want us to find him?' Stella asks.

Lucy exchanges a look with Marco and sighs. 'He's sorting stuff out in his own head. He needs to be alone for that. But he doesn't realise tha—'

She stops when her phone buzzes. She sees that it is Libby calling and her heart jumps.

'Hi!' she almost shouts into her phone.

'Mum! They were here again. The police were here. They found me at Dido's and I wasn't expecting them and they saw me through the window and I couldn't hide and they've seen my bank accounts, Mum. They've seen that I put the money into your account and Henry's account and because Henry goes by Phin's name they've put two and two together with the graffiti that Henry left at Cheyne Walk and they know that there's a connection, they totally know that there's a connection, and I'm pretty sure they know that the bank accounts belong to you and to Henry and that I've been lying and lying and lying and I feel sick, Mum! I don't know what to do! What shall we do? What shall we all do?'

'Wait. Just breathe. Have they gone?'

'Yes. They left about two minutes ago. They said they'll need me to come into the station for some more questions.'

'When?

'Tomorrow.'

'What time is it there?'

'It's – hold on – it's just after four.'

'Right. So. You need a lawyer.'

'But – won't that make me look guilty?'

'I don't know. No. I mean of course not. You're not guilty.'

'But I lied. I totally lied. I said that Phin Thomson and Marie Caron were *old friends*. I mean, who gives old friends two and half million pounds each?'

Lucy pauses, her head dropping into her chest briefly. She looks up and sees Marco and Stella both staring at her with wide eyes.

'What does Miller say?'

'I can't get hold of him. He's recording a podcast all day. He won't be done until this evening.'

'Well, what does Dido say?'

'I haven't spoken to her yet. You're the first person I called. Mum, they know your passport names now, they know you go by Marie Caron and that Henry goes by Phineas Thomson, they'll be able to trace your flights to Chicago. Your hotel bookings. Everywhere you've used your debit card. They'll be coming for you now, Mum. You need to get out of there as soon as you can. You need to forget about finding Phin. Just find Henry and get out!'

Lucy ends the call and looks from Marco to Stella. She forces a smile. 'OK!' she says. 'We really, really need to find Henry today. In fact, we really need to find him right now! So, let's eat up, shall we, and get back on to the streets.'

Then Marco looks up at her from his phone with wide eyes and says, 'Mum. I just got another message from Kris Doll. You know, the motorbike guy? He said he's worried about his friend, Phin. He can't get hold of him and he says he wants to meet up with us. What shall I say to him?'

'Tell him yes,' Lucy replies. 'Tell him yes.'

46

September 2017

Rachel paced up and down the pavement outside the tacky tartan shop, the phone pressed to her ear.

Dominique picked up on the third ring. 'Yo.'

'Dom, it's me. I just saw Michael. He was with Ella.'

'Ella who?'

'Fuck. I don't know. The small blonde annoying woman. She was at your party. Went to school with Darcy?'

'Oh, yes, right, that Ella. God. He was with her? Like, *with* with?'

'Yes. Holding hands. Like a couple. But, Dom, she knows about my Liberty contract. She said you told her. You didn't tell her, did you? I mean, why would you?'

There's a beat of silence, just long enough for Rachel to know that yes, Dom did tell Ella.

'Fuck. Rach. I was at Darcy's baby shower. Like three weeks ago. Someone asked how you were. I mean, I don't even remember her being part of the conversation. I don't even really remember her being there. She's such a little fucking nobody. I didn't have even the slightest clue she was seeing Michael. God, if I had I would never have said anything. Of course I wouldn't. I'm so, so sorry, Rachel.'

'Did you – did you say anything else about me?'

'No. I mean. Not really. I just said you were doing brilliantly. That you were fine. Oh, and that you'd, ah, *ghosted* Michael—'

'Ghosted. Oh my God. Did you actually say that?'

'Well, yeah. Although, let's be honest, he's ghosted you too. It's not as if he's made any effort to get in touch since you left, and now he's screwing Ella.'

'I know, Dom, but God, it's just I need to be so careful. I need this separation period just to pass really, really quietly with no drama and no . . . *things*.'

'I still don't understand why you're not just doing a quickie divorce.'

'No. I know you don't understand and that's fine. I have my reasons, trust me. But look, can you ask Darcy if she knows how Ella and Michael got together? If she knows how long it's been going on?'

'God, yeah, absolutely. I'll do that right now. But, Rach . . .' She pauses. 'Are you OK about this? I mean, I know you and he had a big fall-out and I know you've said you don't love him any more and all of that, but that doesn't mean it doesn't hurt to see him moving on.'

'It doesn't hurt, Dom. Trust me. It really really doesn't.'

'Well, good. I'm glad. And, Rach, I am so so so sorry for

shooting my mouth off. I was just so proud of you and wanted to tell people how amazing you are and how well you're doing and I promise that next time someone asks after you I will totally do the zip-face emoji.'

Rachel smiled. 'It's fine. I love you.'

'I love you, too.'

Rachel put her phone back in her bag and headed to the meeting with Lilian and Rosie, arriving ninety seconds late and with a sense of disquiet that she could not quite explain.

The Rachel Gold Jewels range launched at Liberty on a blowy Tuesday night a few weeks later. Some press and social media influencers were invited and there was champagne and tiny mouthfuls of food on trays and Rachel wore black velvet trousers and a white blazer and her hair was professionally blow dried and her dad was there in a black polo neck and jeans looking so proud and so dashing that it made Rachel's heart hurt.

Paige clutched Rachel's arm and talked into her ear over the din about a guy across the room who was at college with her and used to stalk her and was now studiously ignoring her as he recorded voice notes on to his phone. 'As if he's reporting back on the G7 Summit, for God's sake,' said Paige, and Rachel laughed out loud. Lilian gave a sweet speech a few minutes later, then there was a photo call and by 7.45 p.m. people had begun collecting their coats and the event started to wind down. Rachel was looking for her handbag, ready to head for dinner with Lilian, Rosie, Paige and her father when she saw a familiar shape entering the store from the street: a grey woollen coat, a burgundy-and-navy-striped scarf, a beard.

'I subscribe to the Liberty email newsletter,' Michael said, striding across the room towards her, unlooping his scarf, his face warmed by a megawatt smile. 'What a perfect surprise to see that your range was being launched today, the same day I was in town! I just thought I'd drop by and have a look. Never thought there'd be all the razzamatazz! And did not expect to see you either! Wow! You look incredible, Rachel. Really.' He took Rachel's father's hand in his and squeezed it and said, 'So good to see you, Brian, you're looking amazing.' Then he glanced around at the remnants of the party and turned back to Rachel and beamed. 'So,' he said. 'Let's have a look at these things of great beauty!'

Lilian and Rosie threw Rachel a questioning look and Rachel shook her head and shrugged and they followed Michael across to the cabinet containing Rachel's jewellery.

'Wow,' he said, his hands deep in his coat pockets. He turned and looked at her. 'Rachel. These are all just exquisite. Look at these, the way they glitter under these lights. Intoxicating! These gems' – he turned to Lilian who stood at his shoulder – 'are they all real?'

Lilian glanced at Rachel and then answered, 'Yes. Precious and semi-precious. Everything from the orange diamond in this pendant to rare stones like the black opals in this ring. Isn't it exquisite?'

'My God, yes, it really is. Rachel, you really took it up a gear. I'm imagining some heavy-duty financing going into this?' His gaze went to her father as he said this. 'Brian, you really are the greatest dad in the world.'

'Michael,' Rachel began. Her voice stuck halfway up her throat on the second syllable and she swallowed. 'This is wrapping up now. The staff need to clear away and lock up. Thank you for coming, but . . .'

'Sure,' he said. 'Of course. I get it. I was just passing. I just really, really wanted to see your work. You know I always thought you were the most incredibly talented person I know. And I mean that. Insanely talented. And now look at you. Finally getting the recognition you deserve. I'm in awe. Honestly.' He put his hands together into a gesture of prayer, whisked a canapé off a tray, put it in his mouth, said goodbye to everyone and left.

Rachel grabbed her handbag, ran to the toilets and threw up.

By the week before Christmas the entire range had sold out at Liberty and there was a waiting list for orders going into early spring. Rachel renewed the contracts with the two goldsmiths and took out another loan, this time in her own name, to buy in more stock. Dominique threw her annual Christmas party, this time with an eight-month-old baby and no time limit on the invitation. Rachel came just to be polite. The ghosts and echoes of the year before when she was madly in love, when she was moments from getting engaged, when she had walked in on the arm of a man who matched her in looks, in gloss, in hopes for the future and who had turned out to be a sadistic rapist were just too much for her to stomach. But before she left, she cornered Jonno, who was making cocktails in the kitchen and asked him to make her a Negroni.

'Jonno,' she said as he pulled a low-ball glass from a shelf and filled it with ice. 'Remember when you did that digging around about Michael? All that stuff you were telling me about his business affairs? How did you get that information?'

'Well. I have weird contacts, I suppose you might say. Former coppers. Former criminals. Journos who've infiltrated certain rings and sub-cultures. I just know a lot of randoms and we all owe each other favours.' Jonno shrugged and unscrewed the lid of the gin bottle, tipped a slug into her glass.

'So would you know people who could trace someone's ex-wife, maybe?'

'You talking about the street wench Michael took under his weird rapey wing?'

Rachel shuddered slightly and shook her head. 'Rapey? Why did you say rapey?'

'I dunno. Just a vibe I got. The way he was.'

'The way he was? With you?'

'No! Ha, no. With you, I thought. I dunno. I may be misspeaking. Sorry.'

'No. I mean – no. It's fine. I just thought – I thought everyone kind of liked him?'

'Yeah. I kind of liked him. But I also thought he was kind of sinister too. Dark undercurrents. So yeah. What do I know? Anyway, the street wench?'

'Yes. Lucy. Would you be able to find out anything about her?'

Jonno threw her a quizzical look and opened the Campari bottle. 'What for?'

'I don't really know. I just – I sort of want to talk to someone, someone who's been through the Michael thing. It got a bit toxic towards the end. I want to find out what it was like for her.'

'Well, apparently, she disappeared in the night with their kid, and nobody knows what happened to her next. She genuinely disappeared.'

'But the kid. What about the kid? He must be at school some-where or registered with a doctor. Surely?'

'Yeah. I guess. But needle-in-a-haystack situation. He could be anywhere. He could be in another country. He might have been taken into care. He might be living in a cave with her for all we know. What's his name? Did you find out?'

'Yes. It's Marco. Marco Rimmer. He's about eleven, I think.'

'Well, I can have another sniff around. But it's unlikely, to be honest.' Jonno passed her her drink and looked at her for a moment. 'What really happened?' he began. 'Between you and Michael? Did he hit you?'

Rachel shook her head and said, 'No. He never did that.' And that, at the very least, was true.

47

June 2019

Samuel

I live in Enfield. I have a very nice house. Although after the houses I have seen these past two days I now see it a little differently. I do at the very least need a new kitchen.

I have not had a meal at home for four days and I feel happy as I unpack my Tesco bag on to my (now unsatisfactory) kitchen worktop: fresh pasta, some broccoli, garlic, a very large tomato with just the right amount of give around its girth. A vegetarian meal. I try to eat meat only once a week. For the planet, mainly. But also for the animals. Any animal if brought into your home as a baby would behave like a pet. I have seen very loving turkeys on the internet. I try to think of them when I shop, but sometimes all I want is a chicken salad sandwich or a charred burger fresh from a barbecue and I forget about the turkeys that hug their owners.

Donal and I spoke with Libby Jones again this afternoon. We confronted her with what we knew about her bank transactions, and she replied – with very high colour in her cheeks – that Marie Caron and Phineas Thomson were her friends. I asked her where her friends were and she told me that they were on holiday, that she did not know where, that they did not have their phones with them. I asked her why she'd given two-thirds of her money away to friends who go away on holiday without telling her where they are going, and she said that they were very good friends and that she wanted to share her good fortune with them. I asked her if they'd invited her to join them on their holidays (paid for, one assumes, with the proceeds of Libby's charitable act) and she said no, they didn't.

I asked her if she'd noticed the graffiti in the house on Cheyne Walk that said 'I AM PHIN'. She said that no, she had not noticed. I said: It is quite a coincidence that this unusual name was on graffiti inside a house you inherited and is also the name of your very, very good friend. She agreed that it was a coincidence. I asked her why she was here at her friend Dido's house when she had a flat of her own to be in. I asked her if she had been hiding from me. She said: Not at all, I just wanted to let the dog have a run around in Dido's garden.

It was all lies. Of course it was all lies. So. We will get her into the station tomorrow for some proper questions at a hard table on an uncomfortable chair and see if we can persuade her to stop telling us so many lies.

I make my pasta and I watch a detective show on the TV. I like detective shows, even when they get it all wrong.

At around 9 p.m. I get a message on my phone, from Philip Dunlop-Evers.

Samuel. Sorry to bother you. Are there any updates?

I reply that no, there are no firm updates, but that tomorrow promises much news. We have a possible last-known address, I tell him. We are trying to track down two people who may have lived in the house at the time of Birdie's death. We have a lot going on. We will speak tomorrow.

Thank you, he replies.

In the shower I think of the case as if it is a spherical thing, a world spinning in three dimensions inside my head. I look for the holes in it and try to find ways to fill the holes or pull something from one side of the sphere to the other side to make sense of the hole. It's all about completion. This story is so very nearly complete, but the holes are bizarre and infuriating. I think about what I know:

In the late eighties a young woman called Birdie Dunlop-Evers found herself living temporarily in a large house where her band had filmed a pop video.

The large house was owned by Henry and Martina Lamb who had three children: Henry Jr, Lucy and Serenity.

(As an aside, I am confused that parents who would name their first two children in such a traditional fashion would choose such a bohemian name for their lastborn. As if there were other influences at play. The nameless, formless cult they died for, perhaps.)

At some point after moving into the house, Birdie was killed by a blow to the head. She was then mummified in expensive towels and hidden on a rooftop behind a chimney stack for many, many years, before her remains were thrown into the Thames in a timescale that is roughly commensurate with events since Libby Jones took ownership of the house on her twenty-fifth birthday.

At around the same time as Birdie was killed by a blow to the head, Henry and Martina Lamb poisoned themselves on their kitchen floor alongside a mysterious man whose initials were DT. Shortly thereafter (close enough in time for the baby Serenity/ Libby to have been recently fed and changed when the police arrived), somewhere between two to six teenagers, depending upon whose account you believed, fled the house and were never to be seen again.

Two of these teenagers were Henry and Lucy Lamb, we can assume. Another might have been PHIN of the graffiti.

I stop soaping myself as I feel a small hole fill itself in.

Phin Thomson.

DT.

Could the mysterious DT have been the father of Phin Thomson?

It seems almost certain to me that this could be the case.

So let us assume that 'Phin Thomson' was also resident in the house at the time of Birdie's death.

And is now in receipt of £2.48 million from the sale of the house.

I turn the sphere inside my head a little to see it from another angle. I turn it back to Birdie.

Birdie did not arrive at Cheyne Walk alone. She arrived with a boyfriend. Justin Redding, the percussionist. No trace of him was found. No one remembered seeing him. Was he still there the night that Birdie died? Or had he left before? No one I've spoken to seems to think he could have had anything to do with the three so-called suicides or the death of Birdie, his girlfriend. He was too soft, apparently. But to me, right now, he seems a likely culprit. We will need to reel him in from wherever he has been hiding away these past twenty-six years to prove that he is as innocent as those who knew him seem to believe he is. Justin Redding, I realise overwhelmingly, could be the key to everything.

I turn the sphere again to Libby Jones and her red-faced lies, the lies that she does not want to tell, but that she has no choice but to tell.

The dog comes to mind. Her *mother's* dog.

Another job for tomorrow. I make a mental note. Because if the dog does not belong to her adoptive mother in Spain (quite apart from Libby's vivid physical tells when she explained the situation to me, who shares a dog with a mother in Spain? Nobody), then Libby has another person she considers to be a mother. Might this be Marie Caron, the female beneficiary of a third of her inheritance who is now 'on holiday' without a phone? And might Marie Caron be another of the indeterminate number of teenagers who disappeared from 16 Cheyne Walk in April 1994?

My head loops round and round the sphere, trying to find another way to complete it, but this feels like enough for now.

Justin.

The dog.

A man called D. Thomson.

I set my alarm for 5 a.m. I have much to do.

48

Marco orders a Coke and drinks it through a straw, his eyes flicking constantly from the street to his phone and back again. Kris Doll is running late. He said he'd meet them here in their hotel lounge at two thirty, and now it is nearly 3 p.m. But finally Marco hears the sound of a motorbike's thrumming engine and through the window on to the street he sees a man removing a crash helmet and running his hands through ropey dark hair before heading towards the revolving door.

Marco feels himself flush. The man is very masculine-looking and Marco feels some sense of responsibility for this situation. It is he, after all, who has been messaging Kris for the past three days, it is he who organised this meeting, but now he feels suddenly young and out of his depth and he throws a look at his mother that he hopes she picks up on.

'Marco?' says the man, striding towards them. 'And you must be Lucy?'

Marco nods and half rises from his seat. He glances again at his mum as he does so and notices her flushing slightly. There's something strangely glamorous about this man even though his hair is a mess and he looks a bit weather-beaten.

'Nice to meet you,' says Lucy, standing up and shaking his hand. 'This is Stella.'

'Great to meet you, Stella. Can I get anyone a drink? Anything from the bar?'

They all demur and Kris says he doesn't want anything either; then he takes a seat to Marco's left.

'So.' Kris looks from Marco to Lucy and back again, wearing a wry smile. 'What the heck is going on here, then?'

'I don't know where to start,' says Lucy.

'Shall we start with who the hell is *Mike*?'

Marco squirms slightly under Kris's teasing gaze and says, 'He's no one. He's just made up. He's my friend, Alf.'

'And where is Alf?'

'Alf is in London. That was where we were when we called you.'

Kris peers at Marco questioningly but doesn't say anything, a cue for him to explain a little more. Marco sighs and wriggles in his chair. 'My mum is Henry's – or Joshua as you call him's – sister. Henry disappeared in the middle of the night last Thursday and didn't tell anyone where he was going or why. My mum tried calling him and messaging him, but he blocked her, then *I* tried to message him and call him and he blocked me. And so, me and my friend Alf hacked Henry's Google account and found his browsing history and that was where we found you. And you said you were going to meet a British guy who was staying at the Day-ville, which was our first clue to where he was. So we came over here and since we got here we've found out that he checked out of this hotel three days ago and now we have no idea where he is. But we think he came here to find someone. Someone called Phin.'

Kris smiles at Marco. 'Exactly. Yeah. And I know someone called Finn and that is what's freaking me out. I thought this guy, this Joshua, had just found me randomly on the net and was a regular customer. But now I'm starting to think he targeted me because he knew that I knew Finn.'

'Yes,' says Marco. 'Me too. What did you tell him, about Phin?'

'Well, not very much really. Just that Finn and I had . . . well, we'd . . .' Kris's eyes go to Lucy. 'We'd had a friendship. Quite intense. But it had fizzled out and then he'd gone off to Africa to do his game work.'

'What was he doing in Chicago before that?' Marco asks. 'Before he went to Africa?'

'He worked at the Lincoln Park Zoo. With the big cats. But he always wanted to work as a safari guide and then he got a chance at a job out in Botswana a few years back and he just ran. Rented out his apartment. Didn't look back.' Kris rubs his chin with his fingers and turns to Lucy. 'What's the deal with your brother and Finn? Why is he so keen to trace him?'

Lucy sighs. 'Oh,' she says. 'It's a very long story. I think maybe he just misses him. We grew up together and we thought he was dead, actually, and recently found out that he was still alive and yeah, I think maybe he just misses him.' She smiles tightly. 'What else did you tell my brother? About Phin?'

'I told your brother – and remember, I had no idea at the time that he was deliberately staking me out – I told him that Finn was in town. I told him I thought he might be staying in an Airbnb. And I told him that I was hoping to be meeting up with him soon.'

'So Phin is here now? Definitely?' Lucy presses her hand hard against her heart.

'Yeah. At least I thought he was. But I've been calling him and calling him, messaging and messaging. Not heard a word back. And I don't have an address for him.'

'Do you have any mutual friends who might know where he is?' Lucy asks.

'Yeah. We have one friend in common. A woman called Mati. But I'm not allowed to talk to her, otherwise her boyfriend will probably hit me and then hit her, too.'

'Was she Phin's girlfriend?' asks Marco.

'Yeah. She was. Kinda. For a short while, anyway. And she was mine, too. But she also has a very jealous boyfriend so I keep my distance now.'

'And what about the zoo?' asks Marco, whose brain has been fizzing with other possible avenues to explore. 'Did Phin have friends there who he might see when he's here?'

Kris shrugs. 'Yeah. I guess. He worked there for quite some years. I suppose he must have stayed in touch with some of them. It could be worth asking around there.'

Marco swirls his straw around the melted ice cubes at the bottom of his glass with one hand whilst searching Google Maps for the Lincoln Park Zoo with the other. He turns the phone to show his mother. 'Look,' he says. 'It's only two miles from here. Eight minutes in an Uber. We should go there now.'

He glances across at Kris, but sees that he is deep in thought.

After a short silence Kris looks at Lucy and says, 'So, what's the deal? Once your brother finds Finn? I mean – what are his intentions? Because, and please don't take this the wrong way about your brother, I mean' – Kris touches his heart – 'he seemed like a straight-up dude, like, totally a nice guy. But there was something quite intense about him, I thought, and there was a moment when we stopped at the lake to watch the sunset where he was kind of crying? He didn't think I saw it, but I did. And it's strange, maybe, that Finn has gone radio silent the same time your brother is looking for him. The timing. It feels kinda . . .' He trails off and then slaps his legs. 'Anyway. I'm sure the mystery will soon be solved – and hey! Marco! If you're up for it, I could take you to the zoo on the back of my bike? If that's OK with Mom? Mom, that OK with you?'

Marco clasps his hands together in a prayer gesture and widens his eyes at his mother. His gaze has been going to the monster of a bike parked outside the hotel on the street since Kris first arrived; he's noticed passers-by eyeing it; someone even took a photo of it. It is quite possibly the coolest thing Marco has ever seen and he's walked down La Croisette, gawping at its lurid parades of fluorescent performance sports cars and gold-leafed Bentleys, many times in his life.

'Er, yes,' says Lucy. 'Sure. I mean, you won't be going fast?'

'No. My word, no. I drive tourists around for a living, so I am very circumspect when I'm on the road. I'm not in the business of scaring people or getting into accidents.'

He hits Lucy with a very convincing smile and then they all head out of the hotel and wait for Lucy's Uber to arrive. Kris passes Marco another helmet to put on and helps him into the throne-like seat at the back of the bike and Marco can see people watching and feels simultaneously incredible and mortified.

The feeling as they sail through town is immense. He holds his phone out in his hand and takes a selfie, just before Kris turns and says, 'Hey, dude, hands on the bars, remember?' and then he tucks his phone quickly back into his pocket.

A few moments later they pull up outside the zoo. Lucy has just exited her Uber and is standing waiting for them, hand in hand with Stella, who looks suitably awed at the sight of her big brother on a monster bike in a helmet.

'Stay in touch,' says Kris as Marco passes him his helmet. 'Let me know if you uncover anything. And meanwhile I'm going to keep trying to contact Finn. We can have a race,' he says, 'see who finds him first!'

Marco watches Kris Doll mount his bike and reverse back out into the parking lot before changing gear and leaving, one hand raised behind him in farewell.

'Right,' says Lucy, 'who wants to go and see the animals?'

They ask a member of staff where they might find the lions and are pointed towards the Pepper Family Wildlife Centre. Lincoln Park Zoo is a bit like London Zoo, Marco thinks, modern and close to the city with lots of windy paths and nice enclosures. They find the lions and look around for someone to talk to. There's only one person here wearing a uniform and she looks really, really young, but Marco's mum approaches her anyway.

'Hi! Strange question but I'm trying to find someone who was working in this enclosure about five years ago. Do you know anyone who might have been working here then?'

'Five years ago?' replies the girl. 'Well. I was still at high school five years ago! But let me think. I'm pretty sure that Peter Lilley would have been here then. Although this enclosure is quite new. But he's always worked with the lions.'

'Is he around today, do you know?'

'Yeah! I saw him just a minute ago in fact. What did you say your friend's name was?'

'Phin. It's Phin.'

'Hang on.' She opens a door behind her that's sort of invisible and disappears. A moment later she reappears. 'Pete's just dealing with some kind of drainage emergency in the panda enclosure. He'll be along in a minute. You can just wait here. He says he knows Phin! So you're in luck!'

Marco and Lucy glance at each other and Stella runs off to look at the lions, three females and a male who are stretched out in pools of sunshine looking as though they have not a care in the world, and then Pete emerges from the secret door in the wall, wiping his hands down on a towel and smiling. He is tall and slender with soft, sparse blond hair that sticks up like a newborn baby's and a neatly shaped goatee.

'Hi,' he says. 'Pete Lilley. I hear you're looking for Finn?'

'Yes. Hi. I'm Lucy. A friend of Phin's from London. From years and years ago. He told us he was going to be in an Airbnb in Chicago for a few days. We were meant to be meeting up and I've been trying to get hold of him ever since we got here but he's not answering his phone or his messages and we're a tiny bit worried actually. I just wondered if he'd been in touch with you at all, since he got back from Botswana?'

'Yes! Yes, he has. I collected him from the airport, in fact, just over a week ago. Tuesday before last. I always go and collect him when he's in town because I live out that way. He came back to ours for dinner and then I drove him back into the city.'

'Into the city? So, you mean, you dropped him at his Airbnb?'

'Yes. That's right.'

'So you know where he's staying?'

'Well, I know which building he's staying in but it's a pretty big building. I don't know which apartment it is. And it's funny because I've sent him a message or two myself these past few days, wondering if we were going to get together again before he goes back to Africa, but he didn't reply, and I just thought maybe, you know, he was busy doing whatever that boy does. He's a bit of a riddle, as I'm sure you know. Hard to get a handle on, except when he's taking care of animals. His lifestyle never made much sense to me, so I didn't push it.'

'Would you be able to tell me where the apartment block is? Maybe we could go round now and see if we can rouse him. Make sure that everything's OK?'

Peter Lilley nods. 'Sure,' he says. 'Though I can't remember the street number, just the location.' He gives them a street name and tells them that it's opposite a 'brasserie kind of place with a one-syllable name, tables on the sidewalk' and a few doors down from an organic supermarket called Organic Delightful.

Marco sucks in his breath but doesn't say anything. *Organic Delightful!* The same shop that he and Alf had noticed Henry had googled when they were searching his browsing history. His skin flushes with the thrill of the connection.

'Let me know if you find him, won't you? You've got me a little worried about him now too!'

'Yes,' says Lucy. 'Yes, of course I will.' She takes a piece of paper from Peter Lilley with his phone number on it and tucks it in her bag. Then they get ice creams and sit in the sun for a while, waiting for an Uber to arrive to take them to their next destination.

The building that Peter Lilley directed them to straddles four shop fronts. It's got an old-fashioned wooden front door with stained-glass windows and curly brass bits and a panel to the left of the doorway with about fifty brass buttons on it and for a moment they all stand there staring at the brass panel in silence.

'Now what?' says Marco.

Lucy casts her eyes upwards towards the four floors above them.

But just as she is about to reply there is a shadow of movement on the stairway and a young mother appears carrying a toddler in her arms. As she comes to the door Lucy moves out of her way and then, as she opens it she says, 'Excuse me, I'm looking for someone who's staying in this building. In an Airbnb? You don't happen to know which apartment that might be?'

'Sorry. No clue. Half of them are probably set up that way, I reckon. You should just check the site.'

She brushes past them then, and boards herself and her toddler into the Uber that's just pulled over on the street outside. Lucy holds the door in her wake, and they slip inside. The floors are grey granite with sparkly bits and the stairs are made of stone with a metal handrail. There's a lift with a gate that pulls across and floral mosaic panels around it. They climb the stone stairs to the first floor where the landing spreads left and right with rows of identical doors on both sides. The walls are clad in dark wood carved to look like curtains.

'Such a beautiful building,' says Lucy, running her fingertips along the wooden folds, but Marco, who prefers his buildings white and modern and well lit, does not particularly agree.

'What shall we do?' he asks.

'I mean, I suppose we could just start randomly knocking on doors.'

Stella looks up at Lucy and shakes her head. 'No,' she says. 'I don't want to do that. It's scary.'

'Why is it scary?' says Lucy, leaning down to meet Stella's face.

'People might get angry. People might shout. And look,' Stella says, trailing her right arm in both directions. 'Look how many there are. And he might not even be here.'

Lucy breathes in and stands upright. She glances at Marco and nods. 'She's right. We could spend an hour knocking on every door and it could turn out Phin's not even here. We need to find out which apartment he's in some other way.'

Marco nods back, his gaze firmly on his phone as he scrolls through Airbnb rentals advertised on this street. And then he stops scrolling and turns his phone to his mum and says, 'Look. There are two in this building on here. They're both booked at the moment, one of them for another week, the other for another ten days.'

His mum tries to take his phone from his hand, but he pulls it back. 'You don't need to touch my phone, Mother!' he says. 'Just let me hold it.'

He scrolls through the pictures of the first apartment. It's kind of bland: cream sofas, wooden coffee table, a divan bed dressed with pale floral bedding, a shiny gold chandelier. It has a view from the bedroom window of a wall with metal fire escapes attached to it. Then he clicks on the second apartment. This one is much nicer, lots of bright colours and pretty furnishings and a view from the living room across the street. He scrolls and he scrolls looking for something to identify the apartment somehow and then stops and holds his breath. A photograph of a front door painted a kind of greeny-blue with a doorknocker in the shape of a fox's head.

'Come on,' he says. 'let's find the fox.'

49

February 2018

Rachel dropped her sunglasses from her head to her nose and grabbed the handle of her pull-along case. The winter sun was noticeably warmer here in Nice, with its extra few degrees of proximity to Africa, than in London. She held her face up to it and closed her eyes for a moment, soaking it in. Then she turned and headed into her hotel. The time was 10 a.m.; Michael's son's school day ended at 4.30 p.m. She had all day to meander, to shop, to eat, to relax.

As she unpacked in her hotel room she remembered where she was this time last year: the wooden stilt house in the Seychelles with the bed that was wider than it was long. She thought of the silly little props she'd packed into her suitcase that had seemed innocuous at the time, a bit of fun, but that had fractured her marriage. But she knew that if it hadn't been then, it would have been another time, another trigger, another 'mistake'. Michael Rimmer was a timebomb waiting to go off and now she just wanted to know that she was not alone in this world.

She wanted to know if he had raped Lucy too.

Marco's school was in a rough suburb called L'Ariane that looked nothing like any part of the south of France that Rachel had ever seen or envisaged before. Tower blocks loomed overhead, freeways knitted together in angry graffitied tangles, empty shops were shuttered behind cold metal grilles. She pulled her puffa coat together and zipped it up to cover her expensive-looking outfit, then she pulled up her hood, even though the sun was still warm.

The school was behind a high brick wall, the sun glowing gold between two six-storey blocks. The campus was huge and looked more like a prison compound than a school. A sign by a gated entrance said 'COLLÈGE' with an arrow pointing ahead. Other parts of the school were signposted at two other entrances. One said 'PRIMAIRE'. The other said 'PETITE ÉCOLE'. Rachel realised she had no idea which part of the building she was meant to be waiting outside; all she knew was that Michael's son was around eleven. She didn't know what class he'd be at in school in the UK, let alone in France. It was nearly four thirty, and groups of parents were beginning to cluster around each entrance. She turned on her phone and looked again at the photo that Jonno had sent her. A shot taken from the school's online newsletter, accompanying an article about a class trip to the aquarium. He was third from the right, taller than his peers by two inches and with a thick

mop of dark wavy hair and a somewhat arresting attitude.
M. Rimmer.

Rachel had assumed that Michael's son would be at a private
school, or an international school, a school with views of the ocean
and palm trees in the grounds and children in uniforms clutching
folders. She had assumed that Lucy would be like her: alone, but
comfortable. She had pictured her playing her violin in an ensem-
ble, her hair held back in a chignon, seated in front of red velvet
curtains. She had imagined her to be bohemian, arty, shabby chic.
But this school did not speak of bohemia or shabby chic, it spoke
of poverty, and for the first time it occurred to Rachel that maybe
Lucy was poor.

She saw some children start to emerge from the gate nearest
her and watched quietly from under her hood. They looked around
the right age group, early teens, so she waited where she was, her
eyes not missing a child as they passed. And then she saw him. It
was definitely him. Taller than his friends. Better-looking than
them too. A hint of Michael, but much more of someone else with
his thick mop of hair, the slightly wild, uncaged look of him. There
was a boy on his left with a shaved head, carrying a Minecraft
rucksack. To his right was a small blond boy wearing a dark woollen hat and a red puffa coat. Marco bumped fists with both of them
in turn and then peeled away. He didn't look around for a parent
as some of the other children did but headed instead towards the
entrance labelled 'Petite École', where he smiled at a teacher
standing at the gate and held out his hand for a tiny girl with golden-
tipped ringlets and took from her a pink and gold rucksack with
tiny furry animals hanging from it.

Rachel flinched. A sibling. Marco had a sibling. That was another thing that Rachel hadn't expected. But why not, of course why not? Why wouldn't Lucy have another child? Or maybe more? She wondered if Michael even knew about this girl.

She fell into step behind them and followed them to a bus stop and then on to a cold, creaky bus that travelled for over half an hour before finally pulling off a highway and on to the bustling back streets of Nice, where the children disembarked. They walked for nearly twenty minutes through the city until they reached the far end, by Castle Hill, and she followed them to a scruffy blue house, built high up the winding coastal road, with grimy, sea-salt-encrusted windows overlooking the ocean on one side and grimy, car-exhaust-mottled windows overlooking the street on the other. Marco used a key to let them in through a scuffed, peeling door painted with the words 'Maison de la Mer' and then they were gone.

Rachel didn't know what to do now. The sun was growing low and fat, tilting lazily towards the horizon. The temperature began to drop. She thought of her warm hotel room with its squishy bed and towelling robes. She thought of a meal in a candlelit bistro or brasserie. Behind the dirty windows she saw moving shadows, lights going on, curtains being pulled across. In the lowest window she saw a small man with a moustache and a scrubby beard sitting at a computer in a scruffy room with peeling paint on the walls, his face lit by the screen. A button by the door said 'Concierge'.

Rachel stood for a moment, her fingertip extended towards it, weighing up her options. She could ask the building manager which room Lucy was in, and then what? Her cover would be blown before she'd even decided what she wanted to do. But she couldn't stand out here all night either. Lucy and the children probably wouldn't be going out now – it was getting dark – but as she thought this, she heard noises behind the front door and quickly moved out of the way; she stood in the next doorway down studying her phone. Glancing up, she saw the children leave the hostel, followed a second later by a willowy woman with long dark hair swept over one shoulder, a velvet coat, lace-up leather boots, and an instrument case slung across her back. On her head she wore a beanie hat with a furry pom-pom. The girl wore earmuffs now and the boy had a thick scarf wound high around his neck and a pair of ski mittens.

She followed behind them for ten minutes as they walked across town towards the centre. Soon they were in one of the central squares, lit up for the evening with streetlights and fairy lights and the inviting glow of restaurants and bars on all four sides. Here Lucy and her children stopped. Rachel took a seat on a bench opposite and watched as Lucy laid out a yoga mat behind her, and then a rug. The two children sat on the rug and opened the bags they'd carried with them. Lucy opened her violin case and brought out her instrument. She pulled off her woolly hat and tidied her hair. She applied some lipstick and took off her shapeless coat, revealing a fitted black dress, tiny at the waist, with a soft grey cardigan and a silky neck scarf.

Rachel stared at her, hungrily. There she was. There was Lucy. The apparition turned flesh and bone. Although even here, in three dimensions, there was something diaphanous about her, something not quite real. She looked as if she could fade away into the cold night air, like a frozen breath. And she was beautiful. So beautiful, in a way that Rachel, who had always considered herself to be fairly good-looking, had never been beautiful.

It was five thirty. The day was growing dark now. The restaurants were beginning to fill. The townsfolk and a smattering of out-of-season tourists were beginning to promenade. She watched Lucy angle the violin to her chin and then apply her bow to its strings and burst into a rousing version of 'Titanium'. This was so unexpected to Rachel that she almost laughed out loud. She'd been imagining Beethoven, Vivaldi, not David Guetta.

After that Lucy played a very snappy version of 'Valerie' and then an Adele song and she played these poppy songs seriously, with her heart and her soul. Nobody stopped, nobody threw any money into the upturned bowler hat at her feet. Rachel pulled her purse from her handbag and took out a twenty-euro note. She stood in front of Lucy and watched her until she hit the last notes of the Adele song and then she clapped her hands together and smiled and said, 'Wow. You are amazing.'

Lucy smiled, but it was a guarded smile, the sort of smile that someone who feels constantly under threat would use. 'Thank you. I appreciate that.'

Her accent was cut-glass English, like the girls at Liberty, like all girls who've never tried to fit in anywhere by flattening, lengthening, twisting their basic elocution, because it never occurred to them that they needed to.

'Here.' She handed Lucy the twenty-euro note.

'Oh,' said Lucy, looking at the note in surprise. 'That's very generous.'

'Not at all. You're very talented. And I guess business is slow this time of year.'

'Painfully.' Lucy stared at the note in her hand for a moment, before folding it in half and tucking it into the pocket of her dress.

'Can I get you a drink?' Rachel asked. 'Something warm, maybe. A *vin chaud*? Something for the children?'

'Oh. Actually. Yes. A *vin chaud* would be amazing. That's so kind. Thank you so much.' She turned to the children behind her and said, 'This kind lady has offered to get you a drink. Would you like hot chocolates?'

The children both nodded and Rachel smiled and said, 'Right then. Two *vins chauds*, two hot chocolates. I will be right back.'

As she waited for her order, she watched Lucy put her violin back to her chin and then play 'The Whole of the Moon' so beautifully that it made Rachel want to cry.

She took the drinks back to Lucy's pitch and handed the hot chocolates to the children who both said *thank you very much* with a hint of French in their accents, and she placed the wine on the pavement by Lucy's feet, who smiled at her over the top of her violin. Rachel applauded again at the end of the song and Lucy gave her a small bow.

'That was so beautiful,' said Rachel. 'Did you have a classical training?'

Lucy laughed wryly. 'No. Most definitely not. I was taught by someone who had a classical training, but she preferred to play pop, so that was what she taught me.'

'Well, she was an excellent teacher. Cheers.' Rachel touched her paper cup against Lucy's. 'Where are you from?'

'London originally. Born and bred. But I've been in France since I was a teenager.'

'What brought you here?'

'Oh, you know, *family*.' Lucy took a sip of her wine and then cocked the paper cup towards Rachel. 'What about you? Do you live here?'

'No. No. I live in London. I'm just . . .' She licked her lips quickly. 'Having a break by myself. This time last year I was on honeymoon. Now I'm separated. Just fancied getting away from reality for a few days.'

'Funny,' replied Lucy. 'How people think that this isn't reality.' She gestured around the square. 'When every inch of it to me is nothing but.'

'Yeah. I guess. I mean, this . . .' Rachel pointed at her violin, resting in its box. 'Is this a lifestyle choice for you? Or is it . . .'

'Necessity? Yes. It's necessity. Believe me. I would much rather be wrapped up snug somewhere now in a lovely apartment with a TV and a fire and money in the bank. This . . .' She sighed. 'This was not a plan. Nope. This was not a plan.'

'So, you're a single mother?'

'Yes. Yes, I am. Didn't expect to be. But there you go.'

'What happened to their fathers?'

'Well, one up and disappeared. Left me in a flat in L'Ariane with six months of unpaid rent. The other—'

Rachel watched her face, keenly, painfully.

'The other was – well, he was the worst person in the world.'

A muscle twitched in Rachel's cheek. 'God. Really. In what way?'

'Well, just in the usual ways in which some men are the worst people in the world. You know.'

Rachel looked into Lucy's eyes. She saw a chink of fear, a chink of pain.

'*You mean he hit you?*' She mouthed this so that the children would not hear.

Lucy nodded, her eyes flicking to her children and back.

'How many years?'

'A few. Long enough. Too long. You know.'

'Yes,' said Rachel. 'Yes. I do know. My ex, he didn't actually . . .' She mouthed *hit me*. 'But he was violent. In other ways. And if I'd stayed longer, it would only have been a matter of time.'

Lucy nodded, her eyes wide. Rachel saw tears shimmering on their surfaces and then Lucy clutched Rachel's arm and squeezed it. Rachel looked down at Lucy's hand and blinked. 'Is there anything I can do?' she said. 'For you? For your children?'

'Oh. God. No. You've been more than generous. But thank you.'

Rachel opened up her handbag and pulled out her purse. She slid out two more twenty-euro notes. 'Here,' she said. 'Take these. Go home. Order a pizza. Get the kids into bed. Take the night off. It's getting cold.'

Lucy gazed at the two notes for a few seconds. Rachel expected her to push them away, but she didn't. She took them and she put them in her pocket. Then she wiped some tears from her cheek with the back of her hand before pulling back her shoulders, picking up her violin and saying, 'I'll play a song for you. Any song you like. Just name it.'

Rachel sank her hands into her pockets and breathed in hard to control a wave of tears.

'For us?' she asked.

'Yes. For us.'

Rachel thought for a moment, cast her eyes to the sky, looked back at Lucy and said, 'How about "Firework"? Katy Perry?'

Lucy nodded. Knowingly. Then she put her bow to the strings and played and for three minutes Rachel stood and listened, tears coursing down her cheeks, the lyrics playing silently inside her head, overwhelmed by the sense for the first time in months that she was not alone in this world.

50

June 2019

Marco knocks the fox's head against the glossy blue-green door. He looks at his mum and she looks at him. After a moment he knocks again. Then he steps forward and puts his ear to the door. There is nothing. No sounds of breathing or of footsteps or of a TV set or radio or food being prepared or phone calls being made or anything. Just silence.

'Uncle Henry!' he calls out to the silence. 'Uncle Henry. It's me. Marco. Are you in there?'

He knocks once again, twice, three times. Then he sighs. 'Now what?' he asks his mum.

She looks at the time on her phone. 'We could just go and get something to eat?'

They haven't really eaten anything since the Quik E Burger

at breakfast time. Just the ice cream at the zoo. Marco nods and they head across the street to the brasserie that Peter Lilley had told them about, the one with the one-syllable name that turns out to be Blanche.

They sit outside on a terrace on the sidewalk and are handed large menus by a smiley girl with plaited blonde hair. 'Can I get you guys anything to drink?'

His mum orders a glass of wine and the girl says, 'You're British?'

'Yes.' Marco's mum smiles. 'Yes, we are.'

'What brings you to Chicago?'

'Oh, just trying to find an old friend.'

'Really? You're the second person in a row from Britain to tell me they were here trying to track someone down. I wonder if he was looking for you!'

Marco sends his mum a wide-eyed look.

'Oh,' she replies coolly. 'What – what did this guy look like?'

'He was kind of your age, I guess. But fair, blond hair. I'd say tinted though. Very nicely dressed. Very polite. Do you know him?'

'Well, yes. I think I might. I think he might be my brother.'

'No way! Wow! And you're both looking for the same person?'

'Yes, I believe we are. Though now I've lost track of my brother too.'

'Oh my goodness! Well, I'll keep an eye open for him for you. Let him know you're looking for him if I see him.'

'Just ask him to call me. He knows I'm here. He just needs to call me.'

The waitress leaves to get their drinks and Marco stares at the windows of the building opposite.

'Which window is the one with the fox's head?' he asks.

'That one roughly.' Lucy points at a window on the first floor.

'We should sit here for as long as possible.'

'Yes,' his mother agrees. 'We should. But first decide what you want to eat.'

He looks down at the menu and sees schnitzel and he remembers something: a similar moment on a pavement in the summer heat. Just before they left France a year ago. 'Remember', he says, 'when we were still in France and your fiddle was broken and we had no money? Remember we had that last dinner? And I didn't want to eat my schnitzel because I was so cross with you for not telling me why our lives were so shit?'

'Yes,' Lucy replies with an edge of sadness in her voice. 'I do remember that. And we had to use the showers in the beach club and you and I slept under the underpass in the rain. Remember that storm?'

'Yes. It was insane.'

'Where was I?' asks Stella.

'You were at Mémé's.'

'Why was I at Mémé's and not you?'

'Because she didn't have room for us. And because Fitz was too smelly.'

'I didn't like it when you left me at Mémé's. I used to cry.'

'I know you did. I know you did, baby. And I hated leaving you there. But we didn't have many options back then. We were in as bad a place as it's possible to be.'

'Worse than now?' asks Marco.

He watches his mother's reaction carefully, needing to understand exactly how bad things are.

'In some ways, yes,' she replies. 'When you are a parent, not being able to feed your child is just about the worst, most soul-destroying thing imaginable. And now I can feed you. I can clothe you. I can give you warm beds to sleep in—'

'But they're not our beds.'

Marco sees his mother breathe in sharply. 'No. Not your beds. Your beds are waiting for you in England.'

'But even those aren't our real beds.'

'No. Your real beds are in a furniture shop waiting for us to buy them and put them in the house I'm going to buy when we get back.'

'But we haven't got a house to put them in.'

'Well, actually, that's not entirely true. There *might* be a house to put them in when we get home. I put an offer in on a house last week. It was accepted. I'm waiting to hear back from the estate agent about getting surveys done. That kind of thing. But if everything goes according to plan, we might be moving in by the end of the summer. Maybe even earlier.'

'What sort of house is it?' asks Stella.

'It's an old house.'

'Urgh,' says Marco. 'I hate old houses.'

'I know you do. But I promise you a very large budget for your bedroom to make it as white and modern and featureless as you like.'

'Will I have my own bathroom?'

'Yes, you'll have your own bathroom.'

Marco remembers the tiny, mouldy shower room at the bottom of their corridor in Giuseppe's building in Nice that they had had to share with two other families. He remembers the feeling of his stomach rumbling at night with no food in it. He remembers his sister's feet in his face every morning in the bed all three of them had once shared. He remembers the cold of the pavement through the yoga mat in the city squares where they'd once spent every night while his mum busked for the tourists. And then he thinks of the last year of his life, which has been so perfect, from the moment he first laid eyes on his sister, Libby, and his Uncle Henry, from the moment they first walked into Henry's beautiful apartment with its silken sheets and marshmallow mattress toppers, security panels and plasma-screen TVs, its computerised fridge full of fresh food, double-glazed windows that stoppered the room from the noises outside, cats that lived on cushions and beds, not on street corners, steamy showers that tumbled water like tropical downpours heated to forty degrees. For a whole year Marco has had a place to be, a family, friends he can bring home, freedom to explore, regular meals, new clothes, warmth and shelter and security. And now, here, on this Chicago street, Marco discovers that his life is about to change yet again and it feels once more like a thing that teeters helplessly on a tightrope over a crevasse.

51

Samuel

It is 6 a.m. and the train is full of the dead-eyed people who head home from work at this ungodly hour and the people who head out to work at this ungodly hour and I am among their number today. But my eyes are not dead. My veins flow with adrenaline, with purpose. I am feeling propulsive.

At my desk I switch on my computer and I sip the bad black coffee for which I have a strange fondness. There is no more news about the whereabouts of Marie Caron and Phineas Thomson in Chicago. I have a contact on the force in Chicago, from a case on which we partnered with them a few years back. As a favour to me he has said that he can bring Phineas and Marie in for remote questioning, once Interpol have their precise location. I write to him and update him on the situation. Then I spend some time immersed in my ongoing search for Justin Redding, the tambourine-playing man who is too soft to kill someone. I have asked for database searches of every music college in the country, and nothing has come back. I have asked for searches of hospital and GP records and again, nothing has been returned to me. It seems that Justin Redding (*a*) is dead, (*b*) is a recluse or (*c*) has, like everyone else in this case, changed his name. Maybe Redding was his stage name. And if that is so, then I cannot see how we are ever going to be able to track him down. I had hoped that the news reports about Birdie's death might have rattled some cages, dislodged some memories, opened up some doors into dusty corners. But nothing. Nobody. Silence. Who was this man who lived for a while in Cheyne Walk over twenty-five years ago with a young woman who is now dead?

Next, I turn my mind to Libby's mother's dog. How can I learn the truth about this? I search for Libby's mother on Facebook. Her name is Alyssa Rutherford Jones. She is easy to find and also, happily, has an open page. I scroll through her many, many photographs. Her life is very bright. She wears bright clothes and drinks bright drinks and eats in bright restaurants and sits among bright cushions under bright blue skies. She has a partner who looks very young and wears a white shirt most of the time and has had too much tooth whitening. Libby's mother lives a nice life in Spain. But one thing Libby's mother does not do is enjoy the company of a dog. In particular, she does not enjoy the company of the small brown and white dog that Libby looks after. I feel that this is as much as I need to do here, that my suspicions have been borne out. I now have a greater confidence in the path that I am pursuing.

This leaves the last item from last night's shower: D. Thomson.

I come back once again to the journalist, Miller Roe. He found a missing person with the initials DT but it proved a dead end. I wonder if the man that he found ever went by the name of Thomson. I decide that I have had enough of waiting for Miller Roe to make an appearance. It is time to drag him from his hiding place. I make a call and ask for his phone to be located. An hour later we have it. And it comes as only a very slight surprise to me to discover that Miller Roe is currently somewhere in the very close vicinity of Dido Rhodes's house.

I wait until 8 a.m., to be polite, and then I call Libby.

'Good morning, Miss Jones, I hope I have not disturbed you?'

'No,' she says, sounding tired. 'I'm awake. It's fine.'

'Good. I am glad. I want to ask you, are you still staying at your friend Dido's house?'

'Yes. Yes, I'm still here.'

'Ah. OK. I know we are seeing you later on today, Miss Jones, for which I am very grateful. But I have cause to believe that you have a guest? Currently? A Mr Miller Roe?'

Oh, the silence is so long and very sharp. I wait for it to end.

'Miller . . .?'

'Yes. Miller Roe. He is an investigative journalist. He worked on the article we discussed, the one that was in the *Guardian* four years ago. And I have been searching for him high and low. I have sent him messages and emails and he has replied to none of them. I have been to his house and his neighbour told me he has not been home for days. That he mainly stays with his girlfriend. And now it transpires that in fact he is very close to you. Which makes me wonder if maybe *you* are in fact that girlfriend. So, please, Miss Jones, if he is there, could you put me on the line to him? I would be most grateful.'

There is another terrible silence. I picture it filled with Libby Jones's beseeching eyes, Miller Roe's stern shake of the head.

'No. He's not here,' she says at last.

'Well, his phone is definitely in very close proximity to you. So maybe he left it behind?'

'No. I mean – I don't know.'

I leave more silence, hoping that Libby Jones will come to her senses and realise the futility of her stance and then, sure enough, a moment later I hear the phone pass across to somebody else and there is a man's voice on the line.

'DI Owusu? This is Miller Roe.'

'Ah. Mr Roe. At last. It is a joy to hear your voice.'

'What can I do for you?'

'So much, Mr Miller. So much. I am looking forward to the pleasure of Miss Jones's company here at the station later on today and I would be very grateful if you could join her. Do you think that would possible?'

'What is this about?' Miller Roe sounds gruff and agitated.

'Oh, I'm sure Miss Jones has told you what it is about. But in a nutshell, it is about the Mysterious Case of Serenity Lamb and the Rabbit's Foot. I have some theories that pertain to your newspaper article and a sincere hope to unblock some of the dead ends you bumped into along the way.'

I hear Miller Roe exhale loudly. 'Fine. Yeah. Sure. What time do you want us?'

'Oh. Thank you. What time could you be here?'

'Three p.m.?'

'Yes. That would be perfect. Thank you, Mr Roe. I look forward to it.'

I realise as I put the phone down that now Miss Jones and Mr Roe have more than half the day to decide on new ways to lie to me.

But that is fine. I will be ready for them.

52

February 2018

Rachel was haunted for days after her visit to Nice. Haunted by Lucy. Beautiful, ethereal, broken Lucy; the children stoic in the cold and the dark; the empty bowler hat upturned on the ground by her feet. She was haunted by the thought of the things that Michael might have done to Lucy. She was haunted by the idea that she couldn't do anything for Lucy. That she couldn't rescue her. That she couldn't save her.

But she went back to London and got on with her life. There was a range review at Liberty, some items were taken out, some were added, and Rachel employed a new goldsmith and extended her bank loan. A man asked her out for dinner in the queue for coffee at her local café and, even though he was gorgeous and asked her with charm and appeal, she said no. She said, 'I'm married.' He said, 'The good ones always are.' For a moment afterwards she felt a pang of regret. Had she just let her soulmate walk out of her life? But then she thought of a day, under a year from now, when she would be able to cut herself off from Michael forever and never have to set eyes on him again and she filled her soul with resolve and moved on.

She went to nearly all her yoga classes. She had a dramatic haircut and regretted it. She almost adopted a dog and then realised that was mad and didn't go through with it. She started work on a silver bangle for Dom's baby's first birthday. And then, around the middle of April, she felt the spectre of the anniversary of the day she left Michael and tried to ignore it, but as it drew closer she realised she couldn't, that it was raw and ugly and would swallow her whole if she didn't distract herself from it so she invited her team for dinner at her house: Paige, the three goldsmiths and her father.

She left work early and came home via three different food shops. She put an up-tempo playlist on Spotify, poured herself a glass of wine and smothered her thoughts with the following of complicated recipes and the singing of jolly songs and the slow, sweet bleed of alcohol through her veins.

Her father arrived first, clutching a bouquet of lilies and a bottle of champagne.

She hugged him and felt that there was less of him inside her embrace and then she took his coat and thought he looked thin, and she said, 'You've lost weight.'

'No. No, I don't think so.'

She looked at him and saw something pass across his face. It looked like pain. Her blood chilled. 'Are you OK, Dad? Are you ill?'

'No. God, darling, no. I'm fine. I am absolutely fine. Get this in the fridge now, let it chill.' He passed her the champagne and she glanced at the label and saw that it was not in fact champagne but that it was a sparkling wine from Spain and even though Rachel liked sparkling wine from Spain very much, she had never once, in all her thirty-four years, known her father to bring anything other than proper champagne to a party or a meal.

'What's with the cava?' she asked.

'Oh. Ha!' He gave a small nervous laugh. 'A nice lady at the supermarket told me I should get it. Said it was better than champagne and half the price. I didn't want to argue with her.'

She unwrapped the lilies from their plastic packaging in the kitchen. Normally her father bought all his flowers from the florist on St John's Wood High Street that charged eight pounds for a single hydrangea bloom, but these were from Tesco.

'Did she tell you to buy your flowers from there too?' she asked teasingly.

'Oh. No. That was me. I just thought they were rather lovely.'

'Well, they are rather lovely. And thank you so much.'

'My pleasure, darling. Always. You look well.'

'Thank you.' She glanced at him as she fanned the flowers out in the vase. 'Is everything OK, Dad? You seem a little . . .?'

'I told you. I'm fine. Maybe a little tired. That's all. What's for dinner?'

She talked him through the menu, and he made all the right noises and pretended he was starving but Rachel could tell he wasn't starving; she could tell he had no appetite at all. She gave him crisps to put into bowls and asked him to put out some wine glasses and she watched him as he moved and she was sure, certain in fact, that her father was not well, that he was ill, and at the thought of her father being ill she felt a stab of anxiety in her gut. If her father died, she would have no one.

'Oh,' he said, turning from the dining table towards her. 'By the way – and I hate to bring this up, but Michael, has he – since the time he appeared at Liberty – has he bothered you at all?'

'No, actually. No, he hasn't. I haven't heard a thing from him. I get bits of gossip from Dom from time to time. He's still going out with Ella.'

'Ella?'

'Remember? The girl I told you about who was flirting with Michael at Dom's party two Christmases ago, and then snapped him up the minute I was gone?'

'Yes. I think so.'

'Apparently he's been splashing the cash again. Wining and dining. Mayfair restaurants. All of that.'

Her father caught his breath sharply. 'Oh, darling.'

'Yup. It's fucking gross. He's gross. Everything about him is gross. And God knows where he's getting the money from. It doesn't bear thinking about.'

'It's disgusting that he's spending all that money on another woman when you think how he treated you. It's absolutely disgusting.'

Rachel glanced up at her father in surprise. His voice broke as he spoke, and she saw now that there were tears in his eyes. 'Oh, Dad,' she said, going to him and placing an arm around his shoulders. 'Please don't cry, you silly bugger. It's not that bad. It's fine. Whatever money he's spending on her, I can assure she will be paying for it, somehow or other.'

'I know. I know. But still. When I think of how he treated you. How bad he made you feel. How he lied to you about everything. And now he's out and about, gallivanting with another woman. It just sickens me, Rachel. It really sickens me.'

Rachel gazed at him. He appeared overwrought, his eyes blinking against unspilled tears. 'Dad?'

'Oh. It's fine. It's all fine. Let's talk about something else. Tell me exciting things. Tell me about the business. How's it going?'

Rachel wanted to push back into the previous conversation. There was a sub-text, a backstory, something behind her father's extreme emotional reaction, but she knew it would be a waste of time to pursue it. So she replied with news about the latest sales figures, about a special commission that had come in that morning via her website for a woman who was married to an Oscar-winning film star and she chopped and stirred and drank more wine and then at 8 p.m. the intercom buzzed and Paige arrived bearing a small bottle of tequila and a cactus. Then came the three goldsmiths, bearing four-packs of beer and a small chocolate cake. She watched her father as the evening unfolded, the sweet pleasure that always suffused him when in the company of younger people. For a while Rachel could believe that she'd completely imagined the early moments of the evening, the sadness behind his eyes, the diminished form of him, the brittle anger, the sense that he was sick in some way. For a while she could believe that she wasn't missing something vital.

*

'I'm thinking of putting the house on the market.'

It was a month later, mid-May, the best part of the year. Her father was taking her for lunch. He said he'd heard of a new place that he wanted to try. *A nice little pizzeria.* Rachel's father didn't do nice little pizzerias. He did brasseries and restaurants where people kept your water glass topped up and butter came in interesting shapes on silver dishes. Here the butter came in oily foil wrappers and the sound system played Italian pop music.

Rachel jolted at her father's announcement. 'What?'

'Yes. The house. It's so big, just for me. I suppose I'd always held on to it imagining . . .' He tailed off but Rachel knew what he was implying. He'd imagined it filled with grandchildren. 'Anyway. It's too big and I could do with freeing up some capital.'

Rachel shook her head slightly. As far as she was aware her father had loads of cash in the bank. 'What for?'

'Well, for living. I mean, I have another twenty good years. Possibly another ten bad years after that. They'll need to be paid for.'

'But—' She stopped. She wanted to say, 'But, Dad, you've got loads of money,' yet that sounded crass. She had no idea, really, about her father's finances. He didn't talk about them. He just displayed them in the way in which he lived his life. And he had, she noticed, stopped displaying his finances in quite the same way lately: the sparkling wine, the supermarket flowers, the nice little pizzeria. 'Well, whatever you need to do, Dad. But I think if you held out for a few months you might get a much better price for it. The property market is—'

Her father interjected, his face serious, his hands clasped together. 'No. I can't wait around for the property market. It's fine.

If I lose a few thousand so be it. I just . . . It's time, Rachel. It's time for me to face the fact that I'll be old soon. I'll need to think about things like stairs.'

'Oh come on, Dad. You're only sixty-four!'

'Yes. Now I am. But I need to be ahead of the curve. Get my affairs in order. Get some more money in the bank and buy a place that will be manageable when – *if* – I'm infirm. Give you less to do, less to worry about and think about. I need to downsize. Simplify. I need to be ready.'

Rachel stared across the table at her father and felt a sickening thud of dread hit the base of her gut. 'Oh my God. Dad. Are you ill? Is that what this is? Are you ill? Is that why you've lost so much weight? Please, Dad, please be honest with me.' Her heart raced painfully as she waited for her father's reply.

He shook his head. 'No. No, darling. I promise you. I am not ill. I am perfectly healthy. I just need to be prepared. Prepared for anything.'

'Do you swear?'

'I do. I swear. On your life, Rachel. On your life.'

The house went on the market the following week. Her father had clearly been doing more than thinking about it when he took her out for pizza. The first viewing was conducted within hours of it going on the estate agent's books and an offer was placed and accepted before May was over. In early June he put down a deposit on a one-bedroom semi-retirement flat in a glamorous block near Regent's Park and for the next few weeks Rachel spent all her spare time at the house, helping her father to start boxing things up.

Her father's house was huge, but very neat and organised. Since her mother died, her father had had a lady who cleaned and kept house for him, so there were no nasty secrets hiding behind cupboard doors or under beds, just reams of neatly folded laundry, stored in size order and ready to slot straight into boxes, folders of paperwork labelled and kept in chronological order, family mementoes already boxed and sealed and in the loft. The only room that lacked order was her father's study, a tiny snug room overlooking the garden where he'd tended to spend most of his time since retiring from full-time work. Here he watched TV on his laptop and lit gas fires in the winter and brought his meals to eat. The back of his office chair was always slung with layers of discarded jackets and ties and cardigans. There were always a few pairs of shoes under the desk and abandoned coffee cups here and there with the screwed-up paper wrappings from his favourite sweets from Marks & Spencer inside. It was what he called his 'old man cave', a place where he felt safe and happy doing nothing. The cleaner wasn't allowed in here and neither, really, was Rachel, but she'd run out of parcel tape and hoped she might find some secreted somewhere.

She pulled drawers in and out, feeling around inside them with her hands. She moved his paperwork about and studied the bookshelves. And then her eye was caught by a sheaf of bank statements protruding from one of the shelves, almost to the point of sliding off completely, so she picked them off the shelf and looked for a spot on her father's desk to place them, and as she put them down, she did a double take. There were numbers on the bank account that made no sense. Two payments made into a bank account with a strange, abbreviated name: PMX Acc.dx, one three weeks ago for £100,000, and another just three days ago for £250,000. She flicked through the papers quickly to get to the final balance: £12,200. Immediately she went through her father's drawers again, looking for earlier statements. She found an unopened statement in amongst a pile of junk mail, and she ripped it open. Another two payments, these from April. One for £150,000. Another for £100,000. She got out her phone and ran a Google search for PMX Acc.dx but it brought up nothing. Then she ran a search for just PMX and it brought up so many results, from specialist school software companies to punk music websites and social media marketing companies, that she didn't know what to look at first.

Her father was in the garden shed, clearing it out entirely as he would no longer have a garden when he left this place. She gathered the papers together and headed out. 'Dad?' She tapped lightly on the wall of the shed.

He turned and beamed at her. 'Yes, darling!'

'Erm, can I talk to you? About something sensitive?'

'Oh.' Her father put down a box of tomato seedlings held in his hands. 'Yes. Of course.'

He followed her towards the garden table and they sat opposite each other.

'Dad,' she said. 'What is PMX?'

'PMX? That's what ladies get? Isn't it?' He flushed as he said this, as if he were eight years old and being asked in front of his class.

'No. No, that's PMS. PMX. It's on your bank statements. Look.' She spread the statements out on the table between them.

'It's a company and you've paid them six hundred thousand pounds over the past three months.'

'What? No. Surely not?' He slipped on his reading glasses and cleared his throat. Then he scanned the bank statements blankly before tapping them with two fingers and removing his reading glasses and saying, 'Ah, yes. Just some investments. My financial adviser told me to put my cash there. Make it grow.'

'But, Dad, you've put *all* your cash there. I mean, you only have twelve grand left.'

'Well, yes. In that account. But I have more money in other accounts. And obviously a whole lot more once this house is sold.'

'Dad, that's so much money! Who are these people? What's the name of the company? So I can check them over?'

'Oh, I can't remember.'

'Well, can you give me the number for your financial adviser so I can speak to him and find out more about them, because I'm worried that this might be something dodgy. These don't look like investments, Dad, they look like straight-out payments. And why would you leave yourself with so little cash?'

'I told you, I have other accounts.'

'Where? Please, Dad, show me the other accounts. I want to see them. Do you have an app? On your phone?'

'Well, yes—'

'Can you get into it, please, and show me?'

'Well, not now. No, darling.'

'Please, Dad, please. I want to make sure you're all right. I want to make sure that nobody's taking advantage of you. Let me see.'

Her father's head collapsed into his chest and then he looked up at her and sighed and he said, 'I have a little. I have enough. Don't worry about me.'

'I am worried about you! You're thin and you're not yourself. You're doing things that are out of character. Please just let me talk to your financial adviser. Let me check this out with him. Because I'm pretty sure that there's no IFA in the world who would advise you to put virtually every penny you have into investments. Please, Dad, let me talk to him.'

'No, darling, I don't want you to do that.' His voice had become hard. 'I want you to . . . to . . . *back off*. I really do. Just back off. Please.'

And then her father, her lovely soft father who had never once raised his voice to her in all of her thirty-four years, forced back his chair and strode angrily away from her without a backward glance.

Rachel ran back into her father's office. She hunted through his desk until she found his Rolodex and then she spun it round until she got to a name she found familiar. Fred Kleinberg. She remembered her father talking about him in the past. She called him and she asked him about her father, about a company called PMX who had taken receipt of £600,000 of her father's money since April and, as she had so very strongly suspected, Fred Kleinberg knew nothing about it.

'I have not spoken to your father for a couple of years,' he said.

'Do you think it's possible that he found a new adviser, maybe?'

'It's possible. Yes. But I would be surprised. Your father, he never really wanted to invest. Especially once he stopped earning an income. He wanted to keep his money safe, he said, safe where he could see it. I started him a little pension, but that's as far as it went. I'm really sorry, Rachel. I truly hope you find out what's going on.'

Rachel thanked him and hung up. And then she called Jonno.

53

June 2019

Samuel

Donal's face appears framed within my doorway, his hand over the receiver of his phone. 'Boss. I have a woman on the line. Claims she has something for you on the Birdie case?'

My gut fills with joy. This – I can feel it – this is it. This is not a case that has brought about the usual rash of crazies and fantasists and time-wasters. Cold cases don't tend to attract these types. The crazies and the time-wasters like to dance in the burning flames of the moment, when things are fresh and hot and volatile, when every second counts. So this call will mean something, I just know it.

'Put her through please.'

I clear my throat and pick up a pencil. 'Good morning. This is Detective Inspector Samuel Owusu. How can I help you?'

'Oh, good morning, my name is Cath Manwaring. I'm calling from near Cowbridge. In Wales. It's about the body you found. The young woman from the pop band. Birdie . . .?' I can hear paper rustling as she consults her notes.

'Birdie Dunlop-Evers?' I offer.

'Yes. That's the one. And it says in this article here in the *Guardian* that she was last known to be living with her boyfriend, a Justin Redding?'

'Yes.'

'Well, I don't know if this is helpful in any way, I could be tot-ally barking up the wrong tree and about to make a complete fool of myself. But I'm pretty sure the guy who gardens for me is him. Except his surname isn't Redding. It's Ugley.'

'I beg your pardon?'

'The man who gardens for me, his surname is Ugley. With an "e".'

'Justin Ugley?'

'Yes.'

I stifle an urge to say something flippant about how it is no wonder he chose to use a stage name and I clear my throat and say, 'And how old is Mr Ugley, roughly?

'I'd say, mid-fifties?'

I nod to myself. This would be correct.

'And for how long has he been doing your garden?'

'Oh, about a year or two.'

'And what makes you think it is him?'

'Well, his face, really. The photo on the article. Of the pop group. I remember the pop group, but I really only remembered the face of the lead singer. I'd never really looked at the other members before but when I looked at him in that photo, I just had a jolt. You know? Caught my breath. It was him. It was Justin.'

'And this Justin, do you know where he lives?'

'Well, he's something of an itinerant, I would say. I have a strong feeling he lives in a camper van. But I've also seen him leaving a cottage on occasion, in the village.'

'And this camper van. Where would we find it?'

'It's in one of the fields up behind the business centre.'

'Which business centre is that?'

'Cowbridge Business Park. On the A4222. About a five-minute drive east from the village centre.'

'And if I were to come now, would I be able to find him there, do you think?'

'Well, I have no idea. He works for me on Tuesdays and Thursdays. I have no idea what he does on Fridays. I have no idea about him at all really. He's a very nice man. But I think he has some issues.'

'What kind of issues?'

'Well, drink, mainly. He's a drinker. Spent some time in prison too over the years, I believe. And just generally a bit of a loner.'

'And has he ever said anything to you about having been a musician? In his youth?'

'No. No, he hasn't. But I have seen him once or twice in the village pub playing the tambourine with a local band. It wasn't his tambourine, he just picked it up and joined in. As if he was sort of *drawn* to it, you might say. So that's something that makes it seem likely, don't you think?'

'Yes. I think it does.'

'And there was another thing in the article that caught my eye,' Cath Manwaring continues. 'It said something about the house where they think Birdie might have died, about a suicide pact and people poisoning themselves with a homemade tincture. And Justin has offered on occasion to resurrect our herb garden. He says he used to be an apothecary. That he spent years living on a smallholding growing herbs and making potions. I tried to find out more about it, but he didn't seem to want to expand on it.'

I make some noises down the line to express my interest in what Cath Manwaring has just said, and I make notes that are not actually notes but lively pencil doodlings which express the thrill that is beginning to consume me. I believe that this man *is* Justin Redding. I believe it with every iota of my being.

'But listen. Like I say, he's very nice man. But very damaged. A man on the edge, you might say. And if it is him, if he is Justin Redding, I wouldn't want him getting hauled in and dragged over the coals for something he didn't do. I would feel terrible. I mean, do you really think he did it?'

'Mrs Manwaring, at this point, I really cannot say. But I strongly suspect that he will know something about the house where Birdie died and, at the very least, he will be able to help us move our investigation along.'

'Are you going to come out? To Cowbridge?'

'Yes. I am going to come out to Cowbridge.'

According to Google Maps it will take me three and a half hours to drive from here to Cowbridge. A seven-hour return journey. But Libby Jones and Miller Roe are due to meet me here at the station at 3 p.m. and even if I were to leave right now, I would have no time to do anything other than turn right round and come straight back if I want to stand any chance of making the meeting. I call Donal.

'Donal. I have a big request. When Miss Jones and Mr Roe arrive this afternoon, please could I ask you to step in and oversee the conversation? I have to go to Wales. I will be back to join you as soon as I possibly can.'

Donal of course says yes. He loves to interview. And I take the car from outside the station, type the name Cowbridge Business Park into my satnav and go.

The British countryside is a beautiful thing, especially in June. The blinding fields of rape. The puffball trees on swollen hills. The tumbling baskets of flowers hanging outside country pubs. I have some music playing, a mix of pop songs and some jazz from the 1920s; you can hear the crackle of the needle on the vinyl. I have my window open, and my heart is full of anticipation. I asked Cath Manwaring if she perhaps had a phone number for Justin Ugley and she told me that, as far as she is aware, Justin Ugley does not own a phone. So I am coming to him unannounced and he will be unprepared and, really, that is the best way for me to find him. Newly born.

I pull off the A road a few metres past the business centre and take a farm track as described to me by Cath Manwaring in the closing moments of our phone call. After a few minutes I see the shape of a van reveal itself to me over the top of a hedgerow and I know that I am there.

The camper van is painted black and gold and has a canopy

attached, under which there is an armchair, a threadbare rug and a table piled with books. Also the remains of a lunch: an apple core, an empty crisp packet, some crumbs and a crumpled napkin.

I see movement behind the tiny letterbox windows at the back of the vehicle and step out of my car. The movement stops at the sound of my car door closing. I fold up my sunglasses and I walk towards the van. The side door is open so I call out: 'Justin Ugley?'

It takes a long moment for him to appear and then when he does, I am taken somewhat aback by his appearance. Equally, I can see that he is very taken aback by my appearance as I strongly suspect that there are not very many men of colour to be seen in this corner of the world. Justin's appearance is alarming because he is very dirty. Not dirty like a person who doesn't wash, but dirty like someone who has been in dirt. His clothes, his face, his hair, his hands.

'Hello?'

'Good afternoon, Mr Ugley. I am DI Samuel Owusu. I work in the special crime division at Charing Cross, in London. I wondered if you had time to answer some questions?'

'What about?'

He wipes his hands on a wet rag and I see tattoos reveal themselves. I notice pieces of jewellery on his face that catch the light, in his eyebrows, his nose, and in his ears. His hair is long and tied away from his face with a rag. He looks like a man from another time, another age. But even beneath the dirt and the hair and the piercings I can see that Cath Manwaring was correct. This is clearly the man in the photographs of Birdie's band, the Original Version.

'About a woman called Bridget Dunlop-Evers. Or Birdie. I believe that you were once in a relationship with her?' I say.

'How the hell do you know that? I mean, how did you find me? I don't understand. I haven't seen Birdie for, like, twenty years. Longer. What's happened to her? Is she OK?'

'No. I'm afraid not, Mr Ugley. She was reported missing by her family in 1996 and was never found. About two weeks ago her remains were found on the bank of the River Thames.'

I watch his face. He looks genuinely shocked. But whether that is because his former love is dead or because a crime he committed twenty-five years ago and thought he had got away with has come back to catch him out, I cannot tell.

'Seriously?'

'Yes. I'm afraid so.'

'How did she—? I mean – what . . . ?'

'A blow to the head,' I reply.

He flinches. 'But you know, I mean, I haven't seen Birdie for so long. The last time I saw her she was, well . . . *alive*. I don't think I can really *tell* you anything. Or help you. Not really.'

'I appreciate that, Justin. Of course. But it would be very helpful to talk to you about what you remember from the time you lived together in Chelsea.'

He nods, which confirms that my working theory is correct, that Birdie and Justin did move into the big house in Cheyne Walk back in the late eighties.

'You want to talk . . . now?'

'Yes. Please. If you're not busy.'

'I could do with a few minutes. If that's OK. Just to wash up.'

'Of course. I can wait here. Take your time.'

He emerges five minutes later in new clothes, a T-shirt and some jeans, and his hair has been brushed and tied back neatly. His face is interesting, with a hooked nose, and his eyes are very bright hazel and the saddest I have ever seen, and I have seen some very sad eyes. The tattoos on his hands run all the way up his arms and into the sleeves of his T-shirt. Many snakes and skulls and crosses.

'Sorry about that,' he says. 'Do you want a cup of tea or something?'

'I'm fine, thank you. I have my water.'

He gestures towards a folding stool, and I sit on it.

'I am going to make some notes, I hope that's OK?'

'Yeah. Sure.'

'So, please, tell me in your own words about how you found yourself living in this house on Cheyne Walk and what happened when you lived there. I believe there was a pop video filmed there?'

'That's correct. Back in '88, I think. Bloody Birdie got a bloody cat and we got kicked out of our flat and that woman, Martina, offered us a room and I genuinely thought it was just going to be for a few days. But it ended up being for . . . God, ages. And it was really fucked up. Really, really fucked up.'

Here, I think, here it is. Here is what I've been waiting for.

'In what way was it . . . messed up?' I ask.

'Oh, Christ. I wouldn't know where to start.'

'Well, maybe you could just start at the beginning?'

And then this man with his metal face and scribbled arms and scarred legs and sad, sad eyes tells me about a spoiled family with untold wealth, bored to death inside a pretend castle on the banks of the Thames. And then the father, a lazy, indolent man with no redeeming features, becomes ill. A woman called Birdie who is living inside the pretend castle brings a healing man into the house in order to help the lazy man. And this healing man brings with him a wife and two children, and then there are ten people living in a house where once there had been four and slowly the healing man who had been brought into the house to treat the lazy man had taken everything from him: his wealth, his wife, his freedom, his dignity.

'I left after two years or so,' Justin says. I hear pain in his voice as he utters these words. 'I shouldn't have. I should have stayed, for the children. But I couldn't bear it. Not for another moment. It was insane. Birdie turned into a psycho. She got off on all the twisted stuff that was going on.'

'What sort of twisted things?'

'Oh, the kids mainly. Keeping them contained in the house. Hours of physical exercise every day. Hours of learning the violin. They weren't allowed to wear normal clothes or do normal things. No television. No friends. Strange punishments. It was just . . . everything just felt wrong. And Birdie was clearly obsessed with him.'

'With who?'

'David. The healer.'

'David – what was his surname?'

'Thomsen. David Thomsen.'

I feel a bloom of sweat break out on my fingertips where they grip the pencil and I wipe them against my trouser leg then return them to my pencil and write the word 'Thomson'.

'With an "e",' Justin says, peering at my notepad.

334

'I beg your pardon?'

'It was Thomsen with an "e".'

'Oh. Thank you. And what were the names of his family members?'

'His wife was called Sally. His daughter was called Clemency. His son was called Phineas.'

There, yes. I feel it as pieces of metal locking into place; I can almost hear the sounds they make as they do so. These names are biblical; they are spiritual. They share a sensibility with Serenity, the birth name of Libby Jones. There is something there that ties everything together.

'And do you know what became of this family?'

'I don't know what happened to any of them. I just knew I'd had enough, that I needed to get out. I met a woman at the market where I sold my oils and remedies and she was buying a small-holding in Wales, asked me to come and join her team. I fled. Couldn't get out of there fast enough. Felt horrible about leaving the little ones, you know. But I just really needed a clean break. From Birdie. From David. From London. From all of it. I should have come back, y'know. I should have come back. Checked that they were OK. The kids. But I was just . . .' He sighs and I see a sheen of tears across his eyes. 'Do you know?' he asks softly. 'Do you know what happened to the children?'

I shake my head. 'No. Not yet. We're still trying to trace them.'

'But they're alive?'

I smile sadly. 'I'm afraid, Mr Ugley, that we don't know that yet.'

He nods and I see a tear run down his cheek, which he wipes away with the back of his tattooed hand.

'And you and Birdie,' I continue. 'Did you stay in touch after you left?'

'No. I never spoke to her again. Never heard from her. Never saw her. Have thought about her a lot though. But I had no idea she'd gone missing, had no idea about . . . any of it.'

'So you didn't see any of the stories in the press at the time about the house, the suicides?'

'The suicides? God. No. At the smallholding it was kind of, I suppose, a commune, in a way. We didn't have a TV. We didn't look at newspapers. We lived completely self-sufficiently.'

'And for how long was this?'

'Oh. I lived there for . . .'

I see Justin dry swallow and blink twice. He is experiencing some harsh emotion.

'For about ten years? I was, erm . . .' Another dry swallow. Then he clears his throat and shifts in his armchair. I watch his fists clench and unclench, his lower lip wriggle. 'It wasn't the answer to my problems. I kind of lost the plot there, I think. Too many drugs. Too much scrumpy. Trying to black it all out. Ended up in prison a few times. Then two years ago, the last time I got out of prison, I bought this van and I've been trying to lie low, y'know? Trying to keep away from triggers. Live a quiet life. And yeah, I have no idea about the Thomsens or about Birdie or about anything really. All I know is the weather, the soil, the seasons, what I'm going to have for lunch. And now . . .' He gestures at me.

'Now,' I say, 'a detective from London.'

'Yes. A detective from London. Who I'd really love to help.

But I really don't think I can. Because whatever happened back then, I wasn't there. I'd already fucked off.'

I pick up my pencil as I feel the dark scudding clouds of his grief and guilt move on for a while, see the horizon become clear again.

'When you lived there, in Chelsea, you grew the plants, yes, in the garden?'

'Yes. I did.'

'And there was deadly nightshade, amongst the things you grew?'

'No. No, I would never have grown such a thing, there would be no reason to. Especially not in a house with children in it.'

I rearrange myself on the folding stool as I frame my next question.

'Deadly nightshade was found in the remains of the garden. And that was what was used to poison the adults. Do you have any theories about how it might have found its way into your herb garden? Who might have grown it?'

This question lands on his face like a punch.

'No. No I don't.'

'So nobody else in the house was capable of planting or growing these things?'

He lets one beat of silence pass before he replies. 'Not that I was aware of. But who knows? If they were planning a suicide pact then maybe one of them worked out how to grow it? I left a book behind, in my room. A book of spells and potions. I left my cabinet behind, which was full of seeds. I don't even know what half of them were. Might have been some *Atropa belladonna* in there, I suppose.'

In his reply to this question, he shows me three separate signs that he is lying, but what I am not sure about is if he is lying to protect himself, or to protect somebody else.

'So, it could have been anyone in the house?'

'Well, yes. Apart from the children, of course.'

'Ah yes. The children. And what is your theory about the children? They all disappeared. From what you knew of them, why might they have fled, where might they have gone?'

'As far away from that house as they could possibly get, I hope. If they had any sense.'

'But they were quite young, some of them. Who might have helped them?'

'I really don't know. Maybe Phin and Clemency's mother, Sally? I don't know what happened in that house after I left; I don't know who came or who went. I wish I did. But I really don't know.'

My phone buzzes at that moment from inside my trouser pocket. I excuse myself to Justin and I look at it. It's a message from Donal. Interpol have now supplied images of the people who entered the United States under the names of Phineas Thomson and Marie Caron. I open up the picture of Marie and I turn it to Justin. 'Do you recognise this woman?'

He peers very closely and opens up the image with his fingertips.

'God. Is that—? Yes, that is. It's Lucy Lamb. Henry and Martina's daughter. She looks exactly the same as she did when she was a child.'

My phone buzzes again and I take it back. There is another file attached. This one is CCTV footage of the man leaving the airport. I play it to Justin. He watches it three times.

'This man's passport says that his name is Phineas Thomson.'

'That's not Phin,' Justin says. His whole demeanour has changed at the sight of Henry Lamb. I see him straighten and become animated. 'No. Definitely, not. That's Henry. I'd recognise the way he walks anywhere.'

'The way he walks?'

'Yes.' He points at the screen. 'His feet sort of *slap* the floor. See. That's Henry. Except when I knew him, he had brown hair, not blond. So his hair is dyed. And, you know it's almost . . .' He peers closer again. 'It's almost as if he's tried to make himself look like Phin. Because when he was young, he had the most almighty crush on Phin, you know? He was infatuated with him. And now it looks as if he's almost turned himself into him.'

I feel a shiver pass through me at this idea. But I don't yet know what it means.

I need to get back to the station to join Donal interviewing Libby and Miller and so I make movements towards leaving. My pencil goes into my pocket with my notebook. Our conversation appears to be over, but then Justin asks another question.

'You know, I don't really understand. Are you looking for the person who killed Birdie?'

'Yes, we are.'

'But surely it's obvious who killed her?'

'It is?'

'Yes. It must have been David Thomsen. He was a violent and twisted man. He had the motive – a tangled love life, between his wife, Martina and Birdie. He must have killed her, and then killed himself. Surely?'

I nod as I get to my feet. 'Well, yes. That would of course be the obvious conclusion to have come to, were it not for the fact that Birdie's remains were removed from the property at Cheyne Walk only a year ago by someone who knew where the body was, and knew that if it wasn't removed the new owners would find it there and old secrets would be uncovered. By someone, we must conclude, who was worried that they might get caught.'

Justin takes a moment to absorb this. His face tells me nothing during the silence. He nods. He inhales and exhales. 'Yeah. I see. Yeah.'

Then he rouses himself and brings down his hands firmly against his thighs. 'Well, if there's nothing else?'

'No, there is nothing else. You've been very helpful. I have so many new leads.'

'Is Henry one of them?'

'Yes. Henry is one of them.'

'Poor Henry,' he says.

'Was he a poor Henry?' I reply.

'Yes,' says Justin with feeling. 'They all were. They were all victims. Whatever happened inside that house, none of them deserves to be punished for it. None of them.'

54

June 2018

Rachel sat in her father's kitchen, the bank statements still in her hand.

Her phone buzzed and she saw that Jonno was returning her call.

'Jonno. Hi.'

'Hey. Listen,' he says. 'I've got the intel on the company on your dad's bank statement. Are you ready for this?'

'Yes. I'm ready for it.'

'Well. It is in fact a wealth management company.'

Rachel breathed a short sigh of relief. Her father still had control over his money. He could get it back.

'But—'

'Oh God. What?'

'It's been paid into another person's account.'

'Sorry, what?'

'Yes. Another person's investment pot.'

'How do you know this?'

'I just do. But what I don't know is whose pot it's gone into. And I have no idea how you would find out other than by contacting the company directly and emotionally blackmailing them into telling you. But they won't. Because they're not allowed to. So, yeah. Over to you.'

Rachel ended the call and rested her phone on the counter in front of her. She stood up, and then she sat down again, then she picked up her phone, googled the name of the wealth management company and called the number.

'Erm . . . hi.' She sounded shrill and intense even to her own ears. 'I wondered if I could speak to someone in customer service?'

'Can I ask what it's regarding?'

'Yes. It's regarding my father. He's a retiree, and I've just been looking at his bank statements and seen that he has, over the past few months, transferred all his money into an account held by your company. But it's not in his name. And I'm worried that he's being scammed or blackmailed. How could I find out, please? I'm really very worried.'

'Hold the line, please. I'm going to transfer you.'

The line went quiet and then there was music and a very posh automated recording telling her that her call would be answered shortly, and she paced the room for five minutes growing increasingly stressed and impatient until finally the music stopped and a voice said, 'Client security services, how can I help you?'

Rachel began to retell her tale of woe and halfway through, as she uttered the word 'blackmail', she turned and came face-to-face with her father who had entered the room without her noticing. He stared at her and shook his head.

'Sorry, could you hold on, just for a moment?' she asked the woman on the line.

She pulled the phone from her ear and stared at her father.

He looked at the floor. 'Hang up,' he said. 'Just hang up. I'll tell you everything. Please just end the call.'

She ended the call and sat down on the arm of the sofa.

'Oh God. I've been such an idiot,' he said. 'I know I have. But I didn't know what else to do. I just panicked. Everything was going so well for you. I couldn't let anything mess it up.'

'Dad, I don't understand what you're saying.'

'I'm saying . . .' He sighed and started again. 'I'm saying that someone has somehow got hold of some – images of you.'

'Images?'

'Yes. Pictures of you. Nudes. Some film footage. And they have been sending them to me and making me pay them money to delete them.'

'I'm sorry – *who* ?'

'I don't know. An anonymous emailer. I just kept thinking it would stop. That he would go away if I gave him the money. But then he'd be back again a couple of weeks later with another picture. Another film. And now, well, as you've seen – there's no more money left to give.'

Rachel screwed up her eyes and looked at the ceiling. Then she looked down again and exhaled. 'Have you still got them? These . . . nudes?'

Her father nodded sheepishly. 'I thought I should keep them in case this ever went to the police.'

'Show them to me, please.'

'Oh, no. You don't need to—'

'Just show them to me.'

He sighed and then indicated for her to follow him into his study, where he flipped open his laptop. 'Here,' he said, turning the screen towards her and then moving to the other side of the room.

Rachel took a deep breath, readying herself. Her father had put them in a folder named 'Recipes'. She clicked on the first one and then immediately had to close it again. She knew instantly that it was one of her own photos, from her own phone, and she knew instantly that it had been taken when she was with a guy called Travis whom she had met online about three years ago and had enjoyed a very brief, very intense, very sex-based liaison with before he'd dumped her without any explanation. Her first instinct was that it was him, it was Travis, that he'd somehow reappeared, out of the blue, found her father's email address and decided to blackmail him. But then she remembered that this was her photo, taken on her phone, that Travis would not have had access to it. And it was not a pretty photo. Not a pretty photo at all. She could see that now. Back then it had looked raw, extraordinary, exquisite, erotic. Now it looked sad, regressive, a little bit tragic.

She opened the next one. This was the time that Travis had brought his friend. Rachel couldn't remember his name but staring at the image now she saw a look on his face that turned her stomach sour. She shuddered and opened the next. This was an MP4 and she gulped drily before pressing play. Her, Travis, his disgusting friend in her bedroom in Camden Town. Her finger went straight for the mute button as the sound came through. She looked at herself on the video and saw a woman who was lost. She wondered what the hell she'd been looking for.

She didn't open the next file. She closed her father's laptop and threw herself back into the chair. 'Fuck.'

Then she looked at her father and said, 'Dad. I am so sorry. I am so, so sorry. I want to kill myself. The thought of you, seeing that. It makes me want to kill myself.'

'Please don't do that, darling. Please don't. It's nothing. It's forgotten. But is it him? Is it the man, in the photos? Who is he?'

She shook her head. 'No. It's not him. I haven't seen him for over three years and he didn't know anything about me, least of all that I had a rich dad. He just wasn't the type, you know. He wasn't . . . *clever* enough.'

And as she said that, she knew. She just knew. Her stomach flipped and her blood ran hot and violent through her veins. She picked up her phone and she scrolled through her camera roll, way back to 2015, then she scrolled and scrolled to the beginning of the year, to February, just after she met Travis, and she scrolled all the way up to July and then down again and she knew, she knew that she and Travis were over by July, and she knew that they had met at the end of February and that that was where the photos and the films would have been, and they were not there, they were not there and there was only one person who might have been able to access her phone, only one person who would have wanted to go through her camera roll, only one person who was desperate enough, clever enough, horrible enough to do something like this to her.

55

June 2019

Libby had called in the middle of the night, the ring tone of Lucy's phone bleeding into her dreams.

'Libby,' Lucy had replied in a loud whisper, seeing 2.15 a.m. flashing on the clock radio. 'What is it?'

'Mum! I'm so sorry I woke you up! I'm so sorry! But the police have been on the phone again. The detective guy. And he knew that Miller was here. They traced his phone. And now we both have to go to the station this afternoon, to answer questions.'

'Wait. They aren't arresting you, are they?'

'No. But they know so much now. And they're going to keep asking us questions until we run out of ways to avoid the truth and I can't lie any more but I don't know what to say. What shall we say, Mum?'

'What time is it there?' she'd asked.

'It's just after eight in the morning.'

'What time are you supposed to be going to the station?'

'Three p.m. Miller's getting legal advice from a friend. But, Mum, you need to find Henry and you need to get your story straight. This is all about to explode. Seriously. We can't keep this at bay for much longer.'

It's gone 3 p.m. in the UK now, and Libby and Miller will already be at the police station.

Lucy feels impotent and sick.

She hates herself for putting Libby in this position, for coming into Libby's blameless, uncomplicated life and tainting it with lies and subterfuge and darkness. She hates that there's nothing she can do to help her oldest child, that she can't be there by her side, holding her hand, protecting her from all of this. And she hates that even if she and Henry can somehow navigate their way through this sickening leg of their journey and find their way to the other side, even once this dense shadow has dissipated and cleared, she still has another dark shadow hanging over her, the shadow of what happened in Antibes last summer, and that she will never, ever feel free.

Tears are rising to the base of her throat when Marco suddenly appears.

'I've had an idea,' he says, bouncing on to the bed beside her. 'Let's get Kris to ring Henry. He'll answer if it's Kris. Let's do it now.'

Lucy's head is spinning too fast for her to properly process what Marco is suggesting. But she forces a smile and says, 'OK.'

He types a message and a moment later his phone buzzes with a reply.

Lucy draws herself into a sitting position and rubs her face with her hands. 'What did Kris say?'

'He said he'll do it. But he wants to know what he should say. I said he should just pretend that he wants to hook up with him.'

Lucy gives her head a small shake. 'Sorry?'

'Well, Kris said that apparently when Henry messaged him on Tuesday night when he was really drunk, he was trying to hook up with him.'

'Wait, is Kris gay?'

Marco shrugs. 'Doesn't really matter, does it, if Henry fancies him? We're going to do a sting on him. Pretend that Kris wants to hook up, arrange a meeting place. We'll all turn up. Pow!'

Lucy nods, a smile breaking through her heavy mood. 'A tiny bit genius. And when will this *sting* take place?'

'As soon as Henry replies to him and – oh!' Marco stops and looks at his phone as it pings with an incoming message. 'Here he is now. Hold on . . .' He reads the message and then turns it towards Lucy so that she can read it too.

We've arranged to meet for brunch, 11, at Blanche.

'Blanche?' says Lucy. 'That's the place opposite the apartment block where Phin might be?'

Marco nods. Then he beams and he says, 'Oh my God. We're going to see Henry!'

Lucy calls Libby six times between awakening and heading to Blanche. All six calls go to voicemail, and she feels her chest grow tighter with each attempt, as she tries to imagine what Libby and

Miller are being forced to reveal on the other side of the world. But now her focus is fixed firmly on the next few moments. She has dressed carefully, neatly, and shampooed her hair and Stella's. She notices, as they leave the hotel, that Marco has also made himself look smarter than he usually does. His hair is neatly combed, and he is wearing shoes, not trainers.

They sit silently in the foyer of their hotel and wait for Kris to message them from the restaurant. Marco's phone buzzes at eight minutes past eleven and they all jump.

We are in the back left-hand corner, near the bar. He looks like shit.

They get to their feet, ready to leave the foyer, when two men in dark clothing bowl through the front door and head sternly towards the front desk. Instinctively Lucy moves herself and the children out of view and watches as one of the men pulls a badge from his pocket and asks the receptionist, in a low rumble of a voice, if they have a guest by the name of Marie Caron currently staying with them. Lucy herds the children quickly from the building, her eyes taking in the shape of an unmarked police car parked outside, before swiftly bundling them all around the corner and into a waiting Uber.

She's about to shut the door when she feels a force being exerted from the other side, sees a man's face at the window, a police badge held against the glass.

56

Samuel

I get back to Charing Cross at 6 p.m. Donal called me an hour ago to say that the interview was not progressing. I told him to keep going. Just keep going.

As I enter the interview room, I can see Libby Jones is tired. And so is Miller Roe. Donal has some juice left in him, but even he, I can see, is beginning to flag, after three hours of fruitless interviewing.

But I have something new to introduce to the room. I sit heavily on the spare chair and I look from Libby to Miller. I slowly pull my phone from my jacket pocket, and I turn it on.

'Here,' I say, turning it towards them. 'See this?' I tap the screen. 'This is Lucy Lamb, checking into a hotel in Chicago three days ago with her children. What is she doing there?'

I fully expect Libby Jones to defer to Miller, but she does not. She takes the phone from my hand, quite suddenly, and she stares at the image on the screen. I see that she is close to crying and I do not breathe while I wait for her response. But then she rallies. She pulls back her shoulders and hands me the phone.

'I told you. She's on holiday.'

'So this is Lucy Lamb. Your sister?'

She nods stiffly.

'Not Marie Caron, your friend?'

She shakes her head.

I feel Miller Roe bristle. He is very protective of Libby Jones, this big, hirsute man. He cares more for her than he cares for himself.

'On holiday? With her children?'

'Exactly.'

'But without a phone?'

'Yes.'

'She went on holiday to Chicago with her children, in the middle of school termtime, and she didn't take a phone?'

'I told you this all before. She wanted it to be a proper holiday with no distractions.'

I sigh so hard that it moves a sheet of paper on the table.

There are many things I want to say but I pull myself back, because I am feeling annoyed, and I have had enough now, enough of this stuff and nonsense.

'Libby, please, just be honest with me. We now know where Lucy Lamb is staying and there will be local operatives there even as we speak. I am certain that the moment you leave here, the first thing you will do will be to call your sister or your brother to warn them that we are coming, but it will be too late. So please. Just save us all the stress and bother of this pretence. Just tell me. Now. Why is your sister in Chicago and what is she running from?'

'Fine. Fine,' she says. 'I'll tell you. She's not running from anything.'

Miller stands and puts a big arm out towards Libby as if he is about to usher her from the room, but she pushes it away.

'It's pointless now, Miller,' she says to him. 'They know where she is. It's pointless.' And before he can interrupt her again, she starts to talk.

'Lucy is not my sister. She's my mother.'

I am felled slightly by this pronouncement. It is a killer twist that I did not see coming.

'She gave birth to me when she was fourteen. And the reason she's gone to Chicago is to find my father.'

'And who is he, your father?

'My father is Phineas Thomsen. The real Phineas Thomsen. Not the one that Henry pretends to be. I've never met him, and Lucy, my mother, hasn't seen him since she was eighteen. But Miller managed to track him down for me and we thought he was in Botswana but it turned out he wasn't in Botswana, that he was in Chicago. So first of all Henry went over and then my mother followed him.'

'Just to see Phineas?'

'Yes.'

'And? Have they seen him?'

'Not as far as I'm aware.'

I shift my position. This still makes no real sense. 'I understand that your brother, Henry—'

'He's not my brother, he's my uncle.'

'Yes,' I say. 'Of course. Your uncle. I understand that he was infatuated with Phineas. When they were children. To the extent of changing his appearance to make him look more like Phineas? And now of changing his entire identity?'

'I have no idea. I wasn't there.'

'No. No, of course you weren't. When did you first meet them? Your mother, your uncle?'

'Last year. Around about this time. A few weeks after my birthday.'

'And before that you didn't know about them?'

'Well, no. Only what I'd read in Miller's article. I mean, I knew they'd existed once. But that was all I knew. And then one day after I inherited the house, I came to visit it and Henry was there. And then Lucy came and since then – well, they're just family now. They're just a part of me.'

'And do they ever talk to you, of what happened in that house? Of the abuse?'

'Not really.'

'Not really?'

'I mean, I know that things were difficult. I know that it wasn't a dream childhood, for any of them. But they haven't gone into detail about it.'

I sigh. 'Miss Jones, before I let you go, can I ask you – why all the lies? What are you trying to protect your uncle and mother from?'

'I wasn't trying to protect them. I just didn't want – I don't know. They've been running scared their entire lives. Since they were children. Running.'

Libby Jones is crying, and Miller Roe has his arms around her and is pulling her into his big chest. He looks at me angrily.

'I think we're done here,' he says.

'Yes. I agree. We are done here. I am sorry to have upset you, Miss Jones. But what we mustn't forget, whatever the truth of this situation, a young woman was killed in that house. Violently killed. This must remain the focus and I will keep making people cry for as long as it takes to find out who did it and why.'

57

July 2018

Michael was not in the UK. Rachel had established this by metaphorically holding her nose and calling Ella.

'He's in Antibes,' Ella said.

'Where is he staying?'

'Well, in his house, I suppose.'

'How long is he going to be there?'

'The whole summer. He's writing a book, you know.'

'He's—?'

'A novel. Loosely based on his life.'

Rachel had swallowed the urge to laugh out loud. 'Really,' she'd said. 'How bizarre.'

*

A few days later Rachel got on a plane and flew once again to Nice, from where she took a taxi to Antibes, and on a hot July morning she pulled her rucksack over her shoulders, put on her sunglasses and started to walk.

She didn't know where Michael's house was, precisely. She knew that it was *a stone's throw from the sea.* She knew that it was *the colour of dead roses.* She knew that it was *a two-minute walk from the best seafood restaurant in Antibes,* and that it was tucked down an alleyway with its own private driveway and off-street parking, *a godsend in Antibes.*

The best seafood restaurant in Antibes did not seem to be a singular thing. There were numerous best seafood restaurants in Antibes. Rachel decided to visit them all using a Tripadvisor list, starting with their number one. By the time she had got to number five on the list it was afternoon and she had done nearly twenty thousand steps. But as she neared the sixth best seafood restaurant she turned and saw behind her a sparkle of ocean and a suggestion of steps built into the sea wall, and ahead of her were small lanes and cobbled alleyways leading off the main road, and she drained the last of the water from her plastic bottle, dropped it in a bin and headed down the first lane, her instincts fully engaged with a sense of rightness, and there, around a small bend at the top of the lane, was a turning into a driveway in front of a beautiful house the colour of dead roses.

There was a sports car parked on the driveway. Not a cheap, runaround sports car, but what looked like a performance car, a Maserati in fact, the sort of car that costs tens of thousands of pounds. Rachel felt bile rise and fall in her gullet. Her fists compressed themselves into hard lumps. She passed the ugly car and headed for the front door.

A middle-aged Asian woman answered the door. 'Hello?'

'Oh, hello. I'm Rachel. I'm Michael's wife, could I come in?'

The woman's face blossomed. 'Oh! Rachel! Michael's wife! Yes. Please. Come in! Please.'

'Is he here?' Rachel asked, casting her eyes around the house, this mythical place that had been such a huge part of Michael's allure when she first met him and yet he had never once brought her here. It was a beautiful house with the same cosy charm as Michael's London apartment: arches led from the hallway into an airy open-plan living room and kitchen, with tall black-framed doors leading on to a lush-looking garden filled with banana trees and palms.

'Yes. He is here. I think he has a siesta. I can check?'

'No. No, that's fine. Don't wake him. I'll just wait here for him, if that's OK?'

'Of course it's OK. I keep asking him where you are, where is your wife, why you aren't here. He keeps saying that you are very busy working in London. Making jewellery. Too busy to come. But now you are here and he will be so happy to see you! I'm Joy. Please sit down. Let me get you some water and snacks.'

'Could I use the bathroom? Where would it be?'

'Just here, Mrs Rimmer.'

'Oh, please don't call me that. Call me Rachel. Please.'

Rachel locked the door of the bathroom and sat down on the closed toilet. Her heart was racing, and she was hyperventilating slightly. She stood up again and ran her hands under the tap, turned them over and let the cold water run over her pulse points until her wrists felt numb. She splashed water on her face, and she talked herself down from pure panic, muttering under her breath, *Be cool be cool be cool.*

She used her wet hands to smooth down her heat-frazzled hair and she tucked some loose strands behind her ears. She wanted to walk out of the front door. She wanted to run. But then she remembered that gross sports car, the car that her father had paid for, and then she remembered that she was not scared, that she was angry, that she was filled with a dark burning hate and that there was nothing this man could do to her that would hurt her more than what he was doing to her father.

She left the bathroom and peered down the length of the hallway. There were two more doors off it, one of which led into a small study overlooking the driveway with a clear view of the Maserati. She tiptoed in and quickly leafed through the paperwork on the desk. She opened the camera in her phone and took photos of as many things as possible, her hands shaking slightly, her heart still racing. She opened drawers and ran her hands under the desk. She opened a folder and took more photos of statements and letters. She didn't know what anything was. She had no idea if any of it had any meaning, but Jonno had said to get as much evidence of his business activities as possible, so she was going for quantity over quality.

She tugged at a drawer in the bottom of the desk that finally came loose at her third attempt. She recoiled at what she saw inside, her hands clutching her chest.

'Oh my God,' she muttered to herself. 'Oh my God.'

A gun.

A handgun.

Just sitting there.

She took a few photographs of it and then slammed the drawer closed again.

'Are you OK, Mrs Rimmer?'

She jumped, hard, at the sound of a voice behind her.

It was Joy.

'Yes. God. Sorry. You made me jump. I was just looking for something.'

'That's OK! No problem! Just come through when you're ready.'

'Thank you, Joy.'

She turned back to Michael's desk and moved the mouse of his computer. The screen came to life: a photo of Michael on the back of a speedboat, a young woman under each arm, a bottle of champagne in the foreground of the shot in a silver bucket. Rachel had no idea who the girls in the picture were, or when it had been taken, but Michael was clean-shaven in it, so she assumed it had been taken before he met her. She tried his birth date for the passcode, but it failed. She tried it backwards, but it didn't work. Then her eye went to the stupid car parked in the driveway, with its stupid personalised number plate: MR74.

On her fingers she counted up his initials, then condensed them down to one-digit numbers. A 4 and a 9. Then she added the 7 and the 4 and pressed enter. The screen opened up. Her heart galloped.

She clicked on his email and scanned the inbox with her eyes. And there it was, four days ago, PMX Wealth Management, entitled *Your PMX: July Accounting Update*. She opened it and pressed 'Forward', sent it to her own email address and then deleted it from the sent folder and from the trash folder. She closed the email and went back to his inbox. Lots of 'Thank you for your order' type emails; clearly Michael had been shopping. Menswear. Wine. Books. Jewellery.

She felt her throat pulse with anger. Her father's money funding this monster's five-star lifestyle.

There were sub-folders on his email account, and she was about to click one open when she heard a man's voice.

She shut down the email account, slipped her phone back in her pocket and quickly strode back towards the living room, just in time to see Michael descending the last stair.

'Oh my God. Rachel! Wow! How wonderful! What are you doing here?'

The beard was gone, his face was smooth with afternoon sleep, and he had a very nice tan.

'I was in town. Thought I'd finally check out the legendary "house in Antibes"! Not renting it out this summer, then?'

'Er, no! No. I had a few bookings, but I cancelled them. So good to be back! Can you stay? Are you in a rush?'

'I can stay, sure, for a few minutes. Why not?'

Joy had laid out crisps, salami slices, olives and salted crackers on a plate, with a jug of iced water and two cut-crystal tumblers.

'Thanks, Joy,' Michael called out towards a room behind the kitchen.

'My pleasure, Mr Rimmer,' came the disembodied response.

'Is she here full-time? Like, a housekeeper?'

'Yes. But not a live-in. Eight 'til eight, Monday to Saturday.'

'Wow! Get you with staff!' She said this in a tone filled with bitterness but was not surprised when he didn't pick up on it.

'Well, you know, it's a different lifestyle here to London. It's more—'

'Expensive?'

He laughed. 'Yeah. That's not what I was going to say, but yeah.'

'So, how did you manage the turnaround in your finances? I mean, a year and a half ago I was having to do all our food shopping because you were penniless. And now look at you! And the car! Wow!'

'Oh, so, I sorted the shit out with the lost shipment. It was found. Thank God. So yeah, all back up and running.' He eyed her sheepishly, curiously. 'Is this – are you here to discuss divorce?'

'No. No, I'm not. I told you, I just wanted to see this house. Ella told me you were here. I was coming anyway. Just being nosey.'

'But do you actually want a divorce?'

'I don't know. Do you?'

'No. I mean, I hadn't really thought about it. I guess so? But I kind of liked being married to you, Rachel.'

He looked at her, flirtatiously, affectionately, as if all that lay between them were a failed romance, not rape, not blackmail, not the risotto crawling down the kitchen wall.

'Michael. You raped me.'

'Oh, come on, Rach. *Hardly.*'

'I was asleep. You put your hand over my mouth. Around my throat. You fucking raped me.'

'Rachel. Come on. You and I both know that you'd been waiting for me to take control. To dominate you. It was what you wanted. You know it was.'

Rachel pulled in her breath against the wave of pure rage that was throbbing around her rib cage. 'Do you understand, Michael, the subtlety, the nuance of BDSM? Soft BDSM in particular? It's a game between two people who both understand the rules. And you, Michael, did not understand the rules, and what you did to me was not a game. It was violent and it was misogynistic and brutal and animal. It was all about you, Michael, and nothing to do with me, and if you enjoyed what you did to me that night then you are not just a rapist, Michael – you are a fucking monster.'

He smiled at her then. It was his good-old-boy smile, the one he used to pull people into his orbit, that made them feel safe and golden. 'Whatever you say, Rachel. Whatever you say. We both know the truth about that night.'

'It's called gaslighting, you know? What you're doing? It's a classic abuser technique.'

Michael snorted. 'Abuser? Fuck's sake, Rachel. I put you on a fucking pedestal. I worshipped you. I would have given you everything, if you'd let me. But no, one thing doesn't go your way and *boom*, you were out of there. Like the princess I always secretly knew you were.'

'You were lucky, Michael, that I didn't go to the police.'

'Yeah, Rachel, why *didn't* you go to the police? If you were so sure you'd been "abused".' He made quote marks in the air.

'Raped, Michael. Not abused. Fucking *raped*. And I did not go to the police because for so long I wanted to pretend it hadn't happened, because if it had happened then that meant that I wasn't me any more, and more than anything I needed to be me. But now I know that the two things can both be true; it can be true that I married a man who violently raped me, and it can also be true that I am strong and special. Just like it was for Lucy.'

'Lucy?' Finally she saw the smug smile fall from his face.

'Yes. I met Lucy. A few months ago. She told me that you abused her too. Yet, wow, she is some woman. Isn't she? Just beautiful. And holding it all together single-handedly with two kids.'

'Two kids?'

'Yeah. Her life didn't stop after you. And neither will mine. Anyway, it's been lovely seeing you, Michael. I just really, really wanted to see this house. I always thought you and I would spend time here together, but then it turned out you were a crook and liar and a total fucking loser. So yeah. Never mind.'

Rachel got to her feet and pulled her rucksack on to her shoulder. 'Bye, Michael. Have a good summer. And good luck with the novel. Don't forget to put the bit about raping women in it, will you? Your readers will be fascinated by that.'

She put her head around the corner at the back of the kitchen and called out to Joy: 'Thanks so much, Joy, lovely to meet you!' and then she left Michael's house, slamming the door behind her, her feet hitting the sun-baked cobbles with a satisfying thud.

58

June 2019

The Chicago police give the children drinks from a vending machine and settle them in another room. In the room where Lucy sits there is a computer screen and on the screen is a pair of British police detectives, one black with close-cropped hair, wearing a short-sleeved linen shirt, and the other white with a thick fringe of brown hair, wearing a fitted green polo shirt. They introduce themselves to Lucy as Detectives Owusu and Muir and tell her they are talking to her from a room at Charing Cross Police Station. They tell her that they have just spoken to Libby and to Miller. The detective called Samuel Owusu says he has also spoken to a man called Justin Ugley today, whom Lucy may have known by the name of Justin Redding, and that he had told them that life in Lucy's childhood home had been unpleasant, maybe even traumatic, and was there anything, he wants to know, that Lucy would like to tell them about the period of time when Libby was a baby, just before she and her brother Henry disappeared?

Lucy gulps drily and takes a sip of water. She is astounded that these detectives know so much. She is astounded that they have somehow found Justin, who for her feels like a sub-plot in a distant dream. She can't even really remember what he looked like; he was always much more Henry's friend than hers. She is astounded that they know her real name and that she is Libby's mother.

'What did Libby tell you?' she asks now.

'She told me very little. Because of course she was only a baby when these events occurred and so was not party or witness to them; all she would know would be what you and your brother might have told her. And what she would have read in her boyfriend's magazine article. She didn't know Birdie, she didn't know Justin, she didn't even know you, her own mother, until a year ago. Her insight was limited. Which is why we need to talk to you, Miss Lamb.'

'I'm not sure what I can tell you. It was such a long time ago.'

'Well, for example, maybe you could tell me about David Thomsen. About what sort of man he was.'

Lucy feels her insides compress, empty of every atom of air, collapse.

David Thomsen.

Dark interference swarms around her peripheral vision. She grips the underside of her chair and breathes in hard.

'Are you OK, Miss Lamb?'

'Mm-hm.' She nods. 'Yup.' Then she says, 'Should I have a lawyer present for this? I mean, am I under arrest? Or—?'

'No, Miss Lamb. No. You are not under arrest. We're merely trying to find our way through the tangled web of Birdie's history in your childhood home and how she might have met her end there. Unless – maybe you already know the answer to the question? Maybe you could tell us, right now? Then you will be free to leave and enjoy the rest of your time in Chicago with your children.'

'I don't know what happened to Birdie.'

This was almost true. She was pretty sure that Henry had hit her with the elephant tusk. But then again, she'd been holding Libby, the baby, she'd been crying, everything had happened so quickly, she didn't know, she really didn't know.

'She was evil,' she says now, the words tumbling from her outside her control. 'Birdie was pure evil.'

She watches the detective's face on the screen. Nothing moves, apart from one eyebrow.

'In what way was she evil?'

'She groomed me to have sex with her lover when I was thirteen.'

'Her lover?'

'David Thomsen. He was forty-six. Maybe older. She wanted me to get pregnant by him because she wasn't able to. So she groomed me. She left me alone with him. Made out it was romantic. Made out I was doing something noble and beautiful. And then . . .'

Tears form in the back of her throat and threaten to spill down her cheeks. She chokes them back, compelled now, desperately compelled, to tell someone about this thing that happened to her when she was just a child, to throw it at someone, to hurl it hard, to make it land somewhere and for someone to see it, to recognise this thing that she has never told anyone about, not even Libby.

'They stole my baby when she was weaned, and they didn't let me touch her. They kept her, Birdie and David, they kept her, they called her "their baby". I could hear her cry, but I wasn't allowed to go to her. And it was Birdie, she was the one. She had this way of looking at you, with those eyes she had, they were so pale, they almost weren't blue, they were almost like chips of glass. Her hands, they were always cold. She would never touch you softly, only hard. When she taught us the violin – her hands around our wrists, like metal clamps.' She subconsciously forms her hands into cuffs around her own wrists as she speaks. 'The smell, she had this smell. Of sex. Often. Of hair. She had so much hair. She never washed it. She never smiled. She took my baby and pretended she was hers. I *should* have killed her. If I had killed her, I would have been *proud*.'

Lucy's heart pumps hard with adrenaline and she takes a deep breath to try to control it.

The detective stares at her for a second and then says, 'So, you are telling me that even though you wanted to kill Birdie Dunlop-Evers, you did not.'

'Yes. That's what I'm telling you.'

'So, who did kill her?'

'I don't know.' She flinches with the lie and hopes that the detective in London will miss it on the screen.

'Did you see her die?'

Lucy swallows. An image flashes through her mind. The elephant tusk in Henry's hand. Birdie on the floor. But the bit in between is blank, voided. She looks up at the detective and says, quite firmly, 'No.'

'What happened that night, Miss Lamb? What happened when the adults died and your baby was left behind?'

'I don't know. They died. They killed themselves. Probably because they knew they were evil.'

'But Birdie did not kill herself.'

'No. They probably killed her. David probably killed her. And then killed himself. And took my poor stupid parents along with him.'

'That would indeed be the obvious explanation, Miss Lamb. I agree. But it's much more complicated than that, you see. Because someone has tried to dispose of the remains. Has taken them from the roof of the property and thrown them in the Thames. And this within the last year. It could not have been David Thomsen covering his tracks because he is dead. So, it is someone else. Covering their own tracks.'

Lucy flinches. Fucking Henry. He said he'd got rid of them, that no one would ever find them. What was he thinking, dumping something that incriminating in the River fucking Thames? Did he honestly think that they would never be found? But she can't let this unravel so easily. She straightens her neck and says, 'If you found the bones in the Thames then she could have been killed anywhere. What makes you think she was killed in our house?'

'A small thing called forensics, Miss Lamb.' The detective smiles benignly as he says this, and Lucy nods, tersely. *Of course.*

'So, the person who removed the bones from the roof of the house in Cheyne Walk, this person needed to have had access to the house in the past few months to a year. And we know that Libby took ownership of the house around a year ago and that thus, it could only have been you, Henry, Libby Jones, Miller Roe, or the solicitors. Libby tells me that Phineas Thomsen is currently there in Chicago but that he works as a game ranger in Botswana, and we have spoken with his employers, who confirm that he was in Botswana every day for the previous two years. So you see, don't you, that – unless it was Libby who moved the bones, which seems unlikely as she didn't know they were there – something else is at play here. Something beyond a suicide pact. That a crime has been committed and that really, in all reasonable probability, Birdie's bones were moved and disposed of by either your brother or yourself. So if it wasn't you, Miss Lamb, then please, can you tell me where will we find your brother?'

Lucy glances up at the man on the screen. He is staring at her, and where she expects to see dispassion, she sees great compassion. He is not out to get her. He's just out to solve a puzzle. But still, she thinks, still, if in order to solve his puzzle he unlocks too much of her, follows her too far down this path, who knows where it will end up? It could, she realises with a cold shudder of dread, end up in the basement of Michael's house in Antibes, and then she would lose everything. Absolutely everything.

She glances up at the man on the screen, and she nods, just once.

PART FOUR

59

I pull down the cuffs of the very nice Reiss shirt I bought at Heathrow on my way here, what feels like a hundred years ago, but was in fact only a week. Kris sits opposite me looking incredibly handsome and fiddling with his phone. He is very distracted and I'm starting to wonder if maybe there was an ulterior motive for his sudden and very thrilling invitation to join him for brunch this morning.

'Are you OK, Kris?' I ask, dropping my eyes to his phone.

'Yeah. Sure. Sorry, Josh. I'm expecting an, er, something from a client. They'd provisionally booked a two p.m. tour, but said they'd get back to me to confirm. Just want to know how long I've got.'

I glance at the time on my phone. It's 11.33 a.m. 'We have plenty of time. I might just order myself a Bloody Mary. How about you?'

'Oh, no. Not if I'm out with a client later. Need to stay sober.'

'Of course. Do you mind—?'

'No. Of course not! Go ahead.'

I order the Bloody Mary and turn back to Kris to see him staring at me intensely.

'So, what have you been up to since I last saw you?' Kris asks, taking a sip from his water glass.

'Oh,' I say airily. 'This and that. Just having a really quiet time.'

'Where are you staying now?' His eyes go to his phone again.

'I moved into an Airbnb. Not far from here, actually. Just wanted to feel like I could stretch out a bit, cook for myself, that kind of thing.'

'And when are you planning to head back to London?'

'Soon, I expect, but I haven't booked a flight home yet.'

'Do you not have anyone at home waiting for you?'

I smile wryly. 'Just two slightly ridiculous cats.'

'So you don't live with anyone?'

'No. Just me, all alone in a beautiful apartment.'

'And family?'

'Yes. I have "family".' I laugh hoarsely. I'm not sure why I've just put the word *family* into invisible quotes. I lose the smile and correct my stance. 'Yes. I have a sister, two nieces, one nephew. No parents. Bijou.'

'And what does she do, your sister?'

'Oh. God, nothing really. I mean she's a musician, I suppose, but she's not really doing much musicking at the moment. She's dealing with some financial jiggery-pokery, looking for a new house. It's all very complicated.'

My Bloody Mary arrives, and I hold it aloft. 'Cheers to you.

And thank you so much for being a part of my Chicago experience. And, oh, talking of which, I wanted to apologise, wholeheartedly, for that quite crude message I sent you on Tuesday night. I was a little the worse for wear. And that is putting it extremely mildly. I don't even remember sending it.'

'Yeah, I could tell from the typos that you were probably not sober. But it's fine. These things happen. I understand.'

Kris looks at his phone again. Then his gaze goes to the doors of the restaurant and suddenly I know. *I know.* Someone else was supposed to be here. But who? Who the hell does he know who would want to meet me here? Not my sister, surely. There's no way her path could have crossed with Kris's. But then I remember. Marco. He accessed my browsing history. He could have seen my search for Kris's tour-guide service. He would have had access to Kris's phone number. And then I know. I've been set up. I've been completely and utterly set up. I resist the urge to turn and look at the front door, and say, 'So, did you ever find your British friend, Finn?'

He shakes his head and grabs the back of his neck, nervously. 'No,' he says. 'Still trying to track him down. He's gone very quiet. I'm a bit worried about him, actually. And you know, Joshua, something hit me the other day. Remember when we were talking that day, by the lake, and you said you'd been brought up overlooking the banks of the Thames? It didn't occur to me at the time, but yeah, weird, so was my friend Finn! I may be barking up entirely the wrong tree, but it seems like kind of a coincidence. And it's kind of made me wonder about you, Joshua Harris!' He says this in a mock-playful tone, but I can tell his bloodstream is fizzing with adrenaline.

I gaze at him, echoing his faux playfulness with a cheesy smile. 'And what exactly does it make you wonder, Kris Doll?'

'I don't know. That maybe you're the guy? The guy Finn told me about?'

'Remind me which guy that was?'

I see a muscle in Kris's cheek twitch before he speaks, 'The guy who was obsessed with him. Who kept him locked in a room.'

'Kept him locked in a room?' I say. 'That sounds horrible. Your poor friend. But I can assure you that that was not me.'

'Are you sure?'

My expression freezes. 'Yes. I'm quite sure. And you know, actually, I have a few things I need to take care of. I think I should probably get going.' I drop a few ten-dollar notes on to the table to cover my scrambled eggs on toast and Bloody Mary and pull my jacket from the back of the chair.

Kris gets to his feet suddenly and puts his hand out towards me. 'No,' he says, a note of panic in his voice. 'Don't go. I'm sorry. I didn't mean to freak you out. It was just – it seemed, I don't know – please, stay, finish your drink at least.'

His eyes go to the door again and mine follow them. I see a dark car pull up outside and park haphazardly in the road. I see two doors open in unison, two men in dark clothing step out.

I turn and look at the back of the restaurant, see a corridor leading to the kitchens, and run.

60

Samuel

Donal and I return to our desks. For a minute we sit in a stunned silence, unable to believe what has just happened.

Lucy Lamb has just delivered us her brother.

My contact in Chicago is on his way with a colleague to the restaurant where Lucy informed us that Henry Lamb would be breakfasting with a male friend. Very soon we will find out whether or not we will be able to question him about what happened to Birdie Dunlop-Evers. Very soon, I hope, we will be able to put away these files and these papers, put away the world that the bag of bones found by Jason the mud-larker on the banks of the Thames two weeks ago has built inside my head, the world that fills my quiet moments and my sleep and all the gaps in between, this world of abuse and darkness and wealth, this world that spewed four vulnerable children out on to the streets and left them to fend for themselves.

But first we need to hear from Henry and for now there is nothing for Donal and me to do other than sit here and stare at the wall.

'Kind of hot, don't you think?' Donal pronounces, suddenly.

'I beg your pardon?'

'Lucy Lamb. Those dark eyes. The sunken cheeks. Very . . . *hot.*'

I roll my eyes at him. His live-in girlfriend left him about three months ago and he has gone from being the sort of man who tells you all about putting up shelves at the weekend and taking the kitten to the vet to the sort of man who talks only about hot women. He needs another girlfriend, very soon. This lasciviousness does not suit him.

I open up my email for something to do other than discuss Lucy Lamb's cheekbones with Donal. There is one from Philip Dunlop-Evers. He writes every day. *Just checking in. I know you're busy. I'm sure you'll let me know when you hear anything.*

I press reply and type.

We are very close to interviewing a prime suspect, a man who was a teenager living in the house at the time of Birdie's disappearance. We have also tracked down Justin Redding, who was very helpful but was not, it seems, living in London at the time. I am hoping to have something to share with you by the end of the day. I will send you an update, or please feel free to call me.

He won't call me. He's too polite. He imagines that I am too busy to take phone calls. He is a very nice man. Nicer, so it seems, than his sister, who has been painted in very troubling colours by both Lucy Lamb and Justin Ugley. I think of those tiny bones, so delicate that we thought at first that they belonged to a child. But now it appears that they belonged, quite possibly, to a monster.

Donal and I both jump then at the sound of my ring tone. I grab my phone and press reply.

'Hello. DI Owusu. This is Agent Jacobs calling from Chicago. We have your interviewee ready for you. Are you ready to join us on video?'

'Yes. Yes, we are. Give us three minutes. Thank you so much.'

I glance at Donal and I nod. He nods back and we head once again to the interview room.

61

July 2018

Rachel checked into her hotel in Nice and immediately threw off her clothes and took a ten-minute shower, to wash off not just the sweat of the day, but the feeling of Michael's company. She had not intended to say all she'd said, she'd been planning to play it cooler, stay longer, talk more, find out more about his finances. But she'd managed to gather quite a lot of information during the fifteen minutes or so she'd had alone in his office, more than she'd expected, and she felt an extraordinary glow of centredness after what she'd said. Not closure. Nowhere close to that. Not while Michael had £600,000 of her father's money. Not while that red Maserati sat obscenely on his driveway. Not while every time Rachel closed her eyes she saw the imprint of those hideous photographs in her consciousness, and the shamed outline of her father's back to her as she looked at them on his laptop in his cosy little study.

She put on a silky blue skirt that skimmed her ankles and a black vest top, slung her bag across her chest and headed out into the sultry night air. The centre of Nice felt like a different world tonight to the one she'd experienced back in February. The air was loud with music from restaurants, from fairground rides, from the dozens of buskers and street entertainers that lined every square. Men stood outside restaurants waving menus and trying to entice her inside to eat and she allowed herself to be tempted into one of the restaurants on the main square by a man with tumbling grey locks and a white shirt straining over a wide girth. She ordered a minute steak and frites and a carafe of white wine. The middle-aged waiters buzzed around her, feigning attentive service, oozing paternalistic sexual predation, but she didn't care. She was like a smooth stone at the bottom of a lake teeming with fish. She was solid, immovable, centred. She looked at her phone when it buzzed. An email from Jonno. His 'contacts' were still going through all the information she'd sent across earlier on. Nothing to report yet.

She ordered an extra glass of wine and a slice of chocolate tart, and then, through the aural chaos of the square, came a familiar sound. The opening notes of 'Titanium' played on a violin. Rachel pushed her cake away, downed her wine, paid her bill and strode away from the restaurant.

Lucy looked terrible. So thin. Bedraggled. Her lips were dry. The children looked terrible too. Rachel moved a few steps closer, her arms wrapped around her waist. A small crowd started to gather around Lucy. Rachel saw coins being thrown into her bowler hat. She passed quickly without making eye contact and threw a twenty-euro note into the hat. She heard a shouted *thank you* from Lucy and then Rachel moved away again, watched her from across the square until finally, at nearly ten o'clock, she clipped her violin case shut, tipped the money from the bowler hat into a purse, handed the violin, the yoga mat and the dog to her son, roused her sleeping daughter and headed back to the blue building on Castle Hill where Rachel watched her knock on the door, saw the concierge's face in the lower window light up at the sight of them, saw him fling open the door and say, 'My girl. My children. My dog! Come in!'

Rachel's flight on Sunday was not until the evening so after a late breakfast she packed her bag, left it behind the front desk of the hotel and set off in a taxi to Antibes. Jonno had come back to her an hour ago with confirmation that the recipient of the PMX account was closely affiliated to a company called MCR International: Michael's business operation.

'So, it's definitely him then?' she asked Jonno.

'Yes. One hundred per cent definitely him. Do you want me to call the police?'

Rachel had paused. 'No,' she'd said, 'not yet. I'm not sure what I want to do just yet. I need to think about it.'

But now, Rachel knew exactly what she was going to do. She was going to go to Michael's house, right now, and she was going to take the gun from his desk drawer, and she was going to press it hard against his head until he had paid back every last penny of her father's money. *Every last penny.*

The housekeeper, he had told her, did not work on Sundays.

They would have the house to themselves.

The taxi dropped her on the main road and she headed down the cobbled turning towards Michael's house. The red Maserati was there. The shutters were open. The air smelled of barbecue smoke. Rachel peered through the windows to either side of the door and saw a suggestion of movement and ducked.

She almost called out. But she didn't. She waited for a few minutes and then went to the gate at the side of the house and opened the catch. It led her to the garden, where she saw the sparkling teal of the swimming pool, colourful birds flitting through the flat arms of the banana trees and tiny hummingbird moths hovering around lavender bushes. It was a perfect, beautiful oasis in the city, but the air felt heavy and black somehow.

She peered through the tall glass doors that opened into the kitchen and for a moment she assumed she was watching Joy, the maid, cleaning the kitchen. A woman with dark hair, wearing rubber gloves, spraying bleach on to surfaces, scrubbing hard. She saw the woman pick up a handful of what looked like red fabric, but then she saw it was not red fabric but was something that had been stained red and she followed the red patch on the floor with her eyes and saw it led to what looked like a foot. A bare foot, tanned, with a suggestion of hair.

Rachel knew whose foot it was. She would recognise it anywhere. Such lovely feet he had, Michael. Then the woman turned slightly and Rachel saw, with a hard jolt of recognition, that it was not Joy, that it was Lucy, and she watched, transfixed, sickened, euphoric, as Lucy wrapped Michael's lifeless body up in a sheet, and then rolled him on to two bin bags laid out side by side. She watched Lucy drag him across the cool white granite tiles out of the kitchen and into a room at the back, the room that Joy had gone into the other day when Rachel had been here speaking to Michael. A few moments later Lucy returned and began once again to scrub, to spray, to bleach, tossing endless scarlet-stained bundles of kitchen towel into an open bin bag on the floor. Then finally, after another half an hour or so, she peeled off her rubber gloves, dropped them into the bag and tied a knot in it.

A moment later Rachel heard the front door slam closed. She stood silently, her breath caught somewhere between her gut and the back of her throat. What had she just seen? Was it possible? Really? Had Lucy murdered Michael? Surely not? Surely not?

Finally, she moved, shook out her frozen shoulders, took a few steps closer to the house. She took a tissue from her handbag and used it to try the handle of the garden door. It slid open easily. She spied a pair of Michael's flip-flops by the back door and changed into them from her sandals, which she left in the garden.

Slowly, quietly, she tiptoed around the house, trying to piece together what might have just happened. But it was perfect, immaculate: the kitchen gleamed, the dishwasher thrummed quietly; there was no sign anywhere of anything being awry. Rachel's heart raced with a sick excitement. The drama of it. The wonder of it. The sheer fucking kick-ass-ness of it. Lucy had killed him. She'd bided her time and then she'd come to him, and she'd killed him, and now – now he would never be able to hurt another woman again. Rachel's heart pounded with relief, with adrenaline, with nausea, with awe.

And as she thought this it occurred to her that if Lucy had

reason to kill Michael, then so too did she and that she should not be here, *she should not be here at all*. But she needed to see him. She needed to know for sure that he was gone. And so, quickly, stealthily, she went to the room behind the kitchen, which turned out to be a kind of utility room, and in there was a narrow staircase leading down to a basement. She turned on a light and descended quickly. The basement was used as a wine store; the walls were hung with framed prints of grapes and vineyard insignia. There was a small glass bar with two wooden stools and a row of wine glasses on a shelf, behind which hung a vintage-style etched mirror with an art nouveau image. And there was Michael, in a black plastic cocoon. The bags were not sealed and Rachel bent down to pull back the black plastic with the tissue. She saw his midriff, the whorls of soft hair encrusted with blood. She saw the deathly tips of his fingers. She saw his T-shirt, bunched up around his chest, the dip in his throat and the slack jaw, his mouth hanging to one side, his eyes staring through her.

She pulled the bag over him and left him there, stopping briefly at the top of the steps to look back at him. Pathetic, she thought, pathetic.

In the kitchen, she kicked off Michael's flip-flops, put her own shoes back on, pulled the sliding door closed again with her covered hand and headed down the cobbled lane, into the busy streets, towards a taxi rank and then to her hotel, where she collected her bag from the receptionist and headed to the airport.

62

June 2019

I stare at the screen. There are two detectives, one black, one white. The black detective is called Samuel and appears to be the man in charge. He rests his elbows on the table in the room in London he's talking to me from and smiles at me, warmly.

'Henry Lamb,' he says. 'We meet at last.'

'I hadn't been aware that you'd been looking for me,' I point out.

'Well, no. I suppose not. You've been somewhat incognito.'

'I've been under a lot of stress at work. I needed to get away. Properly.'

'And also, of course, you have just come into quite a large sum of money?'

'Yes. Although that had nothing to do with it. I already had a large sum of money before I acquired this large sum of money. I just needed to escape. To let off some steam. I've been squashed into a flat with my sister and her children and her dog for over a year and I needed some space.'

'Which explains why you haven't been answering your phone or replying to any messages?'

'Precisely.'

I glance at the white detective. I can tell he despises me, that I am everything he hates. I throw him a slightly flirty look, just to watch him squirm. He does.

Samuel, the black detective, runs the results of his investigation past me briefly. He's very pleased with himself, I can tell. And to be fair to him, he has just cause. But really, I made this all so easy for him.

Over and over again I replay those moments through my mind: The day in June last year, just after I'd seen Libby taking ownership of 16 Cheyne Walk. The warm evening sun beating down on my shoulders as I climbed on to the roof, pulled back the tarpaulin behind the chimney stack and scraped away the dead leaves, the broken twigs and the branches scattered by winter storms long past, and stared blindly for a moment at the dirty sarcophagus of old towels and sheets hidden underneath. I see myself peeling away the fibrous layers and staring in shock and awe at the tiny skeleton within, then quickly dropping the bones, one by one, into a black plastic bin bag. I remember clambering back through the house and then sitting for a while with a cold beer, which I opened and sipped in the sun, with Birdie's bones at my feet, then lighting a small fire to burn the towels.

I recall how I waited for the day to grow darker, then took my two empty beer bottles and the small black bag and stood for a while down by the Thames, watching the sun setting over it, wreathing the surface of the water in vibrant ribbons of colour. I waited for a pause in the river traffic and was about to open the bag and toss the bones into the water when a barge somewhere out of sight hooted its horn and I jumped and I lost my footing and the bag fell from my hands and into the water. I stretched to reach for it, but it drifted away from me and then there was nothing I could do but stand and watch as it bobbed its way downriver, the whole of Birdie, every last bit of her, and all the forensic bits and pieces that were probably still attached to her, and off she went. Would she be found? I had no idea. I could only hope that if she was, that it would be by fish or by birds, that she would be picked apart ten years, a hundred years, a *thousand* years from now, and that I would never hear from her again.

But as it transpires, she lasted a year before making her presence felt once more and that, annoyingly, is my fault and only mine.

'So, Mr Lamb—'

This is the first time, possibly in my whole life, that I have ever been called Mr Lamb and I almost turn to see if my father has somehow appeared in the room. *Mr Lamb.* For that is me, whatever other names I may have ascribed to myself. But I had almost forgotten.

Samuel continues: 'Someone returned to the house on Cheyne Walk at some point last summer and removed the remains of Miss Dunlop-Evers from the roof and disposed of them in the Thames. Do you have any idea who that might have been? Assuming of course that it wasn't you?'

Samuel looks at me and even from all these thousands of miles away, even on a screen, I can see the hot burn of human understanding in his eyes and I know that he could read me, every inch of me, every atom, if I let him. But he underestimates me. I have spent my whole life finding ways to tamp down my body language, to hide the truth of who I am and what I am. He will get nothing from me. Nothing.

'Well. It wasn't me. And it wasn't Lucy. Have you considered the possibility that it might be someone else who was present at the time?'

'Ah, yes. You mean, for example, the Thomsen children. We have accounted for their whereabouts since the beginning of last year. They were not in London. And even if they were, they could not have gained access to the house without a key. And it seems, according to everyone we've spoken to, that only you, your sister and Libby had access to keys.'

'You're wrong,' I say triumphantly.

'In what way exactly am I wrong?'

'You're wrong that the only way into the garden is through the house. There's a gate.'

I see both detectives flinch slightly as their watertight theory starts to leak.

'A gate?'

'Yes. In the back wall. It leads into the garden of the house behind. It's totally overgrown with wisteria. You may not have noticed it.'

'So, you're saying that someone who lives in the house behind may have used this gate to enter the garden of your house, climb on to the roof and remove Miss Dunlop-Evers?'

'No. I'm not saying that. That house is converted into flats and the back garden has actually been turned into a small car park. Easily accessible from the street. Anyone could get through it.'

I relish the small silence that falls after this pronouncement.

'May I get back to my holiday now please, Detective?'

'Sorry, excuse me, Mr Lamb. Just a few more questions, if you don't mind.'

'I'm pretty sure there's nothing left to say. You know everything. Birdie Dunlop-Evers was a sociopath, she terrorised our whole household for more than five years, she groomed my sister for sex with a grown man when she was only thirteen, she stole my sister's baby, she was part of a suicide pact with my parents and David Thomsen and somehow ended up dying from a head injury that was probably very well deserved and which could have been delivered by any of a number of people as she was universally hated and very dangerous. And now we've established that absolutely anyone could have got into the back garden to, as you say, remove her remains from the roof and toss them in the river. I think, Detective, that your lukewarm case just ran cold again. And to think that you got *Interpol* involved in this. How embarrassing!'

Samuel rests his gaze upon me for a few seconds, before adjusting his position slightly and looking at his paperwork. 'Just a few more questions. If you don't mind.'

I throw him a hard stare. What else has he got?

'You were the last person to see Libby Jones – or Serenity as she was then known – when you left the house. Yet by the time the police arrived, the bodies of your parents and Mr Thomsen had been lying on the kitchen floor for three to four days. What happened, please, during those days? Who was there and what were they doing?'

I sigh. 'No one was there. Everyone else ran away and left me to deal with all the shit. Lucy left me with her baby. It was all down to me. I stayed as long as I could.' I deliver my best martyr face and sigh again.

'But what I don't understand, Mr Lamb – and I appreciate that you were only a child at the time – is why did you not call the police? Here you were, as I now know, four young teenagers, trapped in a house with evil people, sexual abuse was happening, child abuse was happening, and finally your captors were all dead and you were free. Why did you not call the police then? Call them and let them take you to safety?'

A good question. I rearrange myself in my chair and then look straight into the screen. 'We were traumatised,' I say. 'We were broken. We were damaged. I have no other explanation for you. Decisions I made when I was sixteen years old feel so distant as to be almost alien. If I had my time over again, I would have called the police. But as it was . . . I did not.'

Samuel exhales and I can see I have beaten him.

'Well, I am going to thank you for your time, Mr Lamb. But I will need to stay in touch with you and this is still an active investigation. So please, I would appreciate it if you and your sister could return to London immediately and do not disappear again.'

The screen goes blank a moment later and I turn to the operative in the room with me. 'It appears I am free to go?'

'It appears you are. Yes.'

Back on the street I turn on my phone. I pause for a moment. I can feel a thrum of tears at the base of my throat. I can feel a restlessness, a need for something, but this time it is not a need for oblivion, it is quite the opposite. It is a need for a hug from my sister. To be with my family. To be safe. I want to see my cats. I want to see my colleagues. I want to go for a jog around Regent's Park. I want to go home.

I press some buttons and unblock my sister's phone number. Immediately an array of notifications from her appear on the screen. I open the newest one and read it:

I'm sorry. I just wanted it to end. I hope it was OK. Please call me.

I call her. 'Well, hello.'

'Oh my God, Henry. Are you OK? What happened with the police? Where are you?'

I tell her that I am fine, that I am free. I tell her where I am, and she tells me that she is at the same hotel that I was staying at only a few short nights ago.

She's waiting for me in the lounge with Marco and Stella and to my surprise all three of them throw themselves at me when I appear, and I am momentarily subsumed by people who smell familiar, and it is a strangely wonderful feeling. I gently squeeze them back.

And then we order something to eat and I can feel it, I can feel it lift, and although I know it is not fully over, although I know that DI Owusu is at this very moment in London thinking of new paths to pursue, new questions to ask, although I know I am not yet out of the woods entirely, I can, for the very first time since that April morning back in 1994 when I left my parents dead on the floor and Libby asleep in her crib and strode into central London with a thousand pounds in the pocket of my father's Savile Row jacket, see what lies beyond, and it looks good to me and now I just want to get there. I am feeling healed, somehow, and please excuse the woo-woo nonsense, you know I don't normally subscribe, but I really do feel reborn.

Chicago has healed me. Lucy and her children have healed me. And now this unctuous *pasta aglio e olio* is also healing me. When I get back to London, I will reclaim my identity. I will reclaim Henry Lamb. I will own the little boy who I last saw looking at me in a mirror in a Chelsea townhouse all those years ago. I have no reason to pretend not to be him any more. No reason whatsoever.

'Oh,' says Lucy, breaking into my thoughts. 'I can't believe I didn't ask. But Phin? Did you ever find him?'

I cough on a mouthful of pasta and bring my napkin to my face.

'No,' I say. 'No, unfortunately not. But not for lack of trying.'

I see something pass across her features then. I'm not sure what it is. Disbelief? Fear? But it's gone before I can grab hold of it to analyse and then she smiles again.

'Ah, well,' she says. 'Maybe it wasn't destined to be.'

'Maybe not,' I say. 'Maybe not.'

PART FIVE

63

Samuel

The screen goes blank, taking Henry Lamb with it. I run my hands down my face.

Donal glances at me.

'Pub?'

My head says, No, go home, Samuel, sleep. But my heart makes my mouth say, 'Yes. Pub.'

The pub is busy, the pavement teems with Friday-night drinkers, the night is warm and still almost light. Donal braves the queue at the bar, and I sit on a stool at a tall table that has just been vacated. I try to let the day's stress pass through me in a Zen-like fashion, from my core, via my breath. But it has been such a long day. I have driven to Wales and back, even before conducting three back-to-back interviews. My body holds on to its stresses stubbornly and I know that only alcohol will help me to release them. While I wait for Donal, I switch on my phone. There is a message from Cath Manwaring. She wants to know how I got on with Justin earlier. I assume that she is being nosey, wanting to get full value from her Good Samaritan phone call of earlier today. But then she says that she is worried about him. That he normally comes to the pub on a Friday night but that this evening he's not there and does Samuel know anything about his whereabouts.

Have you arrested him? she asks.

I reply quickly: *No. He was not arrested. I left him in his van, at around 2pm.*

Did he seem upset?

No. He seemed OK.

I think I'll send my husband up there. I'm worried. I feel guilty.

Please, Mrs Manwaring, don't feel guilty. You did the right thing. Justin's recollections were very, very helpful.

I hope you're right, Detective, I really do.

Donal appears with my pint. It looks miraculous as he sets it down on the tabletop, a golden, beautiful thing that I could not have dreamed of at any point during this day that has felt endless and resulted in nothing. Henry Lamb has shown me how impossible this case is. We cannot prove anything. It is all anecdotal. The case is thick with dust and I cannot cut through it and now, as I take my first large sip of the ice-cold beer that I deserve so much, I feel my grip, my resolve start to weaken. How much more of the taxpayers' money can I throw at this thing? An evil woman. A woman loved by nobody, missed by nobody, a woman with shards of ice in her heart. A case of child abuse where no evidence remains, where numerous people were in the house, where no records of any description exist for an entire six-year period of time, where a family of itinerants moved in and took over without anyone ever knowing. It's impossible. It's terrible. It's going to kill me if I keep fussing at it. I think maybe I must let it go. Maybe. But first I will finish this beer and talk nonsense with Donal and then I will go to bed and tomorrow I will decide if there is anything more to be done here.

Because there is something still niggling and nagging at me and that thing is Henry Lamb. He is more than just a damaged child. There is something else about him, something twisted. Something wrong. I have not drawn the US authorities' attention to the fact that both Henry and Lucy entered the country on fake passports. I need them both to return. I need them here, in London, close at hand, because there's more to this story, I know there is.

I am halfway through a second pint of lager when my phone buzzes. It's another message from Cath Manwaring. I read it and my heart stops beating.

Please. Call me. It's about Justin. Something terrible has happened.

64

July 2018

Rachel returned to Antibes a few days later. Michael's body had been discovered by Joy, his housekeeper, and the police, of course, wanted to speak to her. Yes, she told them, she had visited him just a week ago. Yes, they had left on bad terms. Yes, they were separated. Yes, there were some financial issues they'd been trying to iron out. But no, she said, no, I had no real reason to kill him. None whatsoever. I left his house, she told them, determined that I would never see him again.

He was an abuser, she told them, a criminal, a man who sold equipment to drug manufacturers, who operated inside a netherworld of darkness and subterfuge and kept a handgun in his home office. He was a bad man, and she was glad that he was dead, but no, she had not killed him, and she had no idea who might have done so. He owed a lot of people a lot of money, she told them. He knew some very bad people. There were a lot of people in this world, she told them, who might have cause to want Michael Rimmer dead. A lot of people.

'What do you know about his first wife?' they asked her. 'Lucy Smith?'

'Nothing,' she replied. 'Michael never talked about her. All I know is that they split up acrimoniously many years ago and he hadn't seen her again since.'

'Interesting,' they said, 'because according to Mr Rimmer's housekeeper, he had seen Lucy Smith recently. Very recently, in fact.'

Rachel's heart had skipped a beat. How could Joy know about Lucy being there? She didn't go to Michael's house on Sundays.

'Apparently Miss Smith visited Mr Rimmer about five days before his death. The very same day, in fact, that she said you visited Mr Rimmer. She came with her children and her dog and spent fifteen minutes or so in the garden with him. The housekeeper said it all seemed very convivial.'

Rachel tried not to let her confusion show and nodded, thoughtfully. 'Well,' she said, 'maybe Michael lied to me about Lucy. He lied to me about everything else, so it makes sense.'

With no physical evidence to detain her, the police let Rachel go a few hours later. She pulled down her sunglasses and walked across this now familiar town towards the beach. Rachel resisted the overwhelming urge to walk the coast road up to Castle Hill, to knock on the door of the shabby blue building, and to see Lucy and tell her she was her hero and that she would protect her with every fibre of her being from here until the end of time. But she could not, in case it led the police to her. So instead she sat at a table overlooking the ocean and drank an Aperol Spritz served to her by a young man who looked like an aftershave model. She raised the glass to Lucy and prayed silently for both of them.

For many months afterwards Rachel was kept informed of updates in the case by the French detective called Avril. For many months afterwards Rachel knew that she was still considered a potential suspect and she also knew that the police had not yet given up on their search for Lucy. They had tracked down her last-known address via her children's school and been told by the building manager there that they had gone on holiday to Malta, but no trace of her or her family was ever found on Malta or indeed anywhere else. Lucy had simply disappeared into the ether.

For many, many months Rachel slept restlessly at night, waiting for the phone to ring, for her presence in Michael's house after his murder to have been uncovered. But also with the cold dread of them finding Lucy. She thought of the serious young boy, the angelic young girl, their tired eyes as they sat beside her in the square. She even thought of the dog and she feared for all of them if Lucy was ever to be caught. And then, one morning in early June, just under a year after Michael's body was discovered by Joy in his basement, Rachel's phone rang.

It was Avril the French detective.

'We have an update for Michael's case, Mrs Rimmer,' she said. 'Are you able to talk?'

65

June 2019

They arrive in London at 7 p.m. on Saturday night, Lucy, the kids and Henry. The stern-faced men at passport control waved them through disinterestedly at both ends of the journey, just as Henry had said they would. 'That detective won't have told anyone,' he'd said to Lucy as they sat in the Uber heading to O'Hare. 'He wants us in London, not stuck out here indefinitely.'

At nine o'clock they peel themselves out of the black cab they'd taken from Paddington Station and let themselves into Henry's apartment block. The porter, Oscar, is not there – he finishes early on the weekend – and they move silently with their suitcases into the lift and up to the third floor.

Lucy drops her rucksack on to the floor in the hallway and glances around. Can it be only four days since she was last here?

Only eight days since she was making fairy cakes for Stella's cake sale? How is that possible? she wonders. How? She feels she has lived a thousand lives since then.

The cats appear at the sound of humans like ghostly shadows curling around the walls of the flat. Henry scoops them both up: the nice one rubs his face against Henry's; the horrible one yowls and scratches him and Henry lets it drop to the floor. The cleaner has been and every surface is immaculate and clear.

That night they order fried chicken from Deliveroo and watch TV lined up on the sofa and Henry is different somehow, softer, as he sits with the nice cat on his lap, feeding fried chicken into his own mouth and joining in with Lucy and the children's jokes. Stella at one point removes all the cushions from behind her back and puts them on the floor to sit on, and Henry doesn't even notice.

They all go to bed as early as they can given the jetlag, at just after 2 a.m., and Lucy lies and listens to the sounds of London traffic outside the bedroom window and she feels it again, this awful feeling that has followed her for over a year, the tightness around her skull, the dull dread that blunts everything with its incessant chipping away at her sense of security. If the police can somehow find out that Henry was responsible for killing Birdie Dunlop-Evers with a single blow to the head a full twenty-six years after the crime was committed, then what else are they capable of uncovering? I am home, she thinks, I am in clean pyjamas in a big soft bed in a luxury apartment block in central London. But I will never ever feel safe, not until I know that the French police are not still looking for me.

66

'Welcome home, Henry.'

I hold the door ajar, somewhat petulantly, and let DI Owusu into the apartment. It had been quite a shock to my system, I can tell you, to see his face on the intercom screen a moment ago, this man who I had last seen on a laptop in an interview room in Chicago, this man who I thought I had dispensed with on Friday, this man who really should have just shut up shop now and found a new and more thrilling case to investigate, a case in which he might experience some semblance of success. But no, here he is again, and on a Sunday morning of all the godforsaken times for an overly persistent detective to descend upon a person.

'Thank you,' I say and let him into my apartment, apologising for the mess, chucking cushions back on to the sofa as I say, 'What can I do for you today, Detective?'

'Actually, Mr Lamb, I have come to you this morning with

some sad news. I wanted you to be the first to hear this, before it hits the newsstands, because, Mr Lamb, I'm afraid this is very much about to hit the newsstands in a big way. You may wish to sit down.'

I blink slowly. I have genuinely no idea what it is that Detective Owusu is about to tell me. All the people I love surge through my head in one go: Lucy, the children, Libby, even Miller Roe. I sit down slowly and stare at the detective. 'OK.'

'So, on Friday I went to Wales to talk to Justin Ugley – or Redding, as you may have known him as a child.'

I nod, and gulp.

'Well, unfortunately, Mr Lamb, Justin was found dead on Friday night, by one of his neighbours. He had, I'm very sorry to say, taken his own life.'

'Oh my God.' I clap my hands over my mouth and feel a genuine sucker punch of sadness in my lower gut.

'He left a note and I thought it right that you should see it, as it concerns you. Would you like to read it?'

'Oh. Yes, yes, I suppose I would.'

The detective passes me a printout of the note and I unfold it. The handwriting is immediately and overwhelmingly familiar – it is the same handwriting that was in all the notebooks we once pored over together in the garden, the neatly inscribed Latin names of all the plants and herbs and fruits we grew together, the seasonal planting plans. Justin's lovely handwriting.

I start to read:

To whoever finds me like this – please, first of all, know that
I am so sorry. It is of course a selfish act that will result in

pain for whoever is first to get here. Please be assured that I am happy now, or at least that this was not an act of violent desperation, but an act of spiritual release. I have been very unhappy for a very long time. I have made bad decisions and dreadful choices. I have hurt people. I have let people down. I am hollow and what you see of me now, the empty husk that remains of me, is all I have been anyway for the past twenty years. I have been haunted now, for so long, by what I was witness to back in the late 80s and early 90s in that house in Chelsea, the terrible child abuse I saw being perpetrated by David Thomsen and Birdie Dunlop-Evers, and not only that but their embezzlement of the Lambs' money and personal possessions, under the guise of 'saving their souls' but, in reality, to line their own pockets. The things that happened behind the closed door of that house were appalling, and like a coward, I did a flit. I left them to it.

But the guilt overwhelmed me and ate away at me. I thought about those children all the time. In particular, I thought about Henry. Henry was the black sheep in that house. The girls had higher status and Phin was the alpha boy, son of the alpha male. Henry was at the bottom of the pile, desperately looking for whatever human connection he could find. Such an interesting little boy. So quick to learn. Such a strong sense of right and wrong. More than anyone else in that house Henry knew where the moral high ground should be and was constantly begging the grown-ups to try to find it. But to no avail.

One day in 1994 I came back to London. I'd written numerous times to Henry, but never heard back from him and I wanted to make sure that everything was OK. I rang the bell, but nobody answered. So I came in through the back gate, via the house behind, and I saw Henry through the kitchen window. He looked so thin. So weak. So broken. I saw David and Birdie and they were laughing. Henry caught my eye through the glass, and I gestured to him to come into the garden. He told me terrible things. I said I would tell the police. That I would get them out of there. I was going to rescue them, that's what I told Henry, and he held on to me, sobbing, and at that moment, Birdie appeared, and a tussle began and I'm afraid that in the course of that tussle, Birdie died.

We hid away her body, Henry and I. That was wrong. I know that now. I wish I'd called the police and confessed to my crime; the children would have been saved and their lives would have been so different. And so I suppose that when Henry – if it was him, and I suppose that is something we will never know – moved Birdie's remains, it was to save me, to protect me. So please, if you find Henry, know that he has done nothing wrong. Please tell him that he is and always has been the best of boys. And that I am so sorry I let him down. For that, more than anything, I will never ever forgive myself. But I hope that one day maybe he will find it in himself to forgive me.

Yours,

Justin L. Ugley

PS: Please call my mother on this number to let her know what has happened. She is very elderly and may not remember who I am, but I suppose someone should be informed of what I have done.

I reread the last two paragraphs, to be sure of what they say. It is all a lie. Of course it is a lie. But I must not let the detective know. He must assume that all I have just read is a true and accurate retelling of real-life events, and so I look up at him with tear-filled eyes – to be truthful, the tears are real; Justin was a jolly nice man, a golden spot in those dark, dark years, I am very sad that he has taken his own life, I am very sad that his life held so little value to him that he was prepared to sacrifice it to save me – and I say, 'I can't believe this. I can't believe he's gone. He was my best friend. My only friend. And he tried so hard to rescue us. Poor, poor Justin.'

And then I realise, inside a sickening tidal wave of knowing, that Justin has sacrificed himself for me. That he has given himself to *save* me. Me. Henry Lamb. Pathetic loser that I am.

But for some reason he thought I was worth his own life. And only then do I cry proper tears. Tears of wonder and gratitude, and also tears of relief, because even though the letter is a lie it also could be true. Quite easily. Just as I have recalibrated my own personal history to rewrite the part where I grew deadly nightshade in the garden of 16 Cheyne Walk and used it to poison to death my parents and David Thomsen and have come almost to believe that they really did kill themselves in a suicide pact, then so too in a parallel world maybe Justin *did* send me letters that I never received, maybe he did come to London to rescue us, and maybe it was him, not me, who bashed Birdie on the head with an ele-phant's tusk and robbed her of her life. Why not, I think, why ever not? And immediately the nuts and bolts of the story shift and fall into new places in my head and within moments I have recali-brated everything, the whole fucking thing, and I *did not* kill Birdie, but I might have moved her bones, and really, would that be such a crime, to protect a man like Justin? A fine man. Really?

'Does this match up with your memories of events?'

I nod, pathetically, and run my hand under my snotty nose.

'Yes,' I say, in a teeny tiny voice. 'Yes. It does.'

DI Owusu sighs and leans back into his chair. He stares at me. 'We went back to the garden at Cheyne Walk,' he says. 'The gate in the back wall you told us about. We found it. But it is still grown over with wisteria branches. The branches are mature and intact. There is no way that anyone would have been able to access the garden on number sixteen Cheyne Walk through that gate within the past few years. It is impossible. So, Mr Lamb, I have to ask. Was it you? Did you move those bones?'

I nod, pathetically. Then I glance up at the detective and say, 'Are you going to arrest me? For what I did with Birdie's bones?'

'I don't know, Mr Lamb. Do you think that I should?'

I shake my head. 'No. I don't.'

For a long moment Detective Owusu stares at me. I see what is in his eyes: the truth. He knows that Justin's suicide note is a fiction. He knows that my tears are theatrical. He knows that I killed Birdie. And he knows that I know he knows. We are both still and silent in a glittering, crystalline moment of reckoning. I wait for him to throw something more back at me, to make one last attempt to dislodge the truth from me. But he doesn't. Instead, he smiles.

'Well.' He starts to get to his feet. 'We shall see. But for now, I think our business here is done. Oh – but there is one thing. Only vaguely connected with the case. It has been mentioned a couple of times in my investigation that you had been trying to find Phineas Thomsen. The *real* Phineas Thomsen, that is. I wonder – did you ever find him?'

I can feel a violent flush blooming through my body, radiating outwards from my stomach, and I try to catch it and halt it before it reaches my face. 'No,' I say. 'Sadly not. It looks like he's determined never to be found.'

'He was very important to you?'

'Yes. He was something of a role model, I suppose. As you can tell from me using his name all of these years. But also, Phin was Libby's real father. Did you know that?'

'Yes,' says Samuel. 'I did know that.'

'That was my real incentive for wanting to find Phin. To bring about a reunion. For him to finally meet the daughter he hasn't seen since she was a baby in a crib. But there you go, his loss. He was never really the dad type, I suppose you might say.'

I'm gabbling and I can tell that DI Owusu is reading my body language constantly, so I stop. I breathe in and out and I say, 'It's a shame. He's missing out on such a wonderful relationship with such a wonderful girl. He really is.'

DI Owusu leaves a moment later. I press my back against the door as I close it behind him and let myself sink down on to the floor where for a few minutes I sit and shake.

67

July 2019

Lucy gazes up at the strange building. It looks like a fridge that has been tipped on to its side. She stands by the main door and regards the buzzers, trying to remember which number Rachel had said it was. Thirty-one, she thinks, before pressing the button.

'Hi,' she says, 'this is Lucy. Could I come in?'

There's a tiny silence before the latch buzzes and Lucy pushes the door and steps into the entrance. Rachel meets her outside her apartment door. She's wearing short pyjamas and her dark hair is piled up on top of her head. Her legs are endless and smooth and for a moment Lucy feels thrown by the sheer perfection of this young woman; for a moment she thinks no, Michael would not have hurt this woman, no man would ever hurt this woman because she is a goddess. She turns for a second, considering an escape, but then Rachel smiles and says, 'Christ. Thank you. Thank you so much for coming. Come in.'

Rachel had pushed a note through the door of Henry's apartment block two days ago: 'Lucy, I have news for you re the investigation in France. Please, please call me.' Rachel had seen the story in all the papers last month, she'd said, about the pop star who'd died in the big house in Chelsea. She'd seen the paparazzi photos of Lucy leaving Henry's apartment with her dog and she'd tracked it down.

Lucy follows Rachel, now, into her apartment. It's messy and modern with a teak kitchen counter suspended from the ceiling. The living room overlooks the canal at the back and the whole room is filled with sunlight. It is, Lucy considers, exactly the sort of flat she would love to live in if she were a single woman with no dependants.

'You know,' Rachel begins, as she fills the kettle from the tap. 'We've actually met before?'

'We have?' Lucy peers at her, trying to find something familiar. And then it hits her. 'Oh!' she says. 'Was it you? In Nice last year?'

'Yes. February 2018. I was there. You played me "Firework" by Katy Perry.'

Lucy nods. 'I remember,' she says. 'I remember now. You were very generous. Very kind. Why didn't you—?' She pauses. 'Why didn't you say something?'

'Oh,' says Rachel, pulling tea bags from a jar. 'I don't know. I suppose I'd come looking for answers and you gave them to me and I didn't want to intrude any more. I didn't want to make a mess.'

'What answers?'

Lucy sees a film of tears cover Rachel's eyes.

'Oh, just that it wasn't only me, I suppose. That *I* hadn't done that to him, that he was already like that.' She laughs nervously and drops the bags into huge mugs. Then the smile leaves her mouth and she sighs heavily and closes her eyes. 'Lucy,' she says, looking at her intently, 'that day. The day Michael died. I was there. I saw you.'

Lucy shakes her head in shock and laughs, nervously. 'What?'

'I saw you at Michael's house. Clearing up the kitchen. Taking Michael into the basement. I saw it all and all this time I wanted to tell you that I'd been doing everything I could to protect you, to keep you safe. Every time I talk to the police, I remind them that Michael was a criminal, that he wasn't a victim of crime, that he was a victim of himself. And I knew that they still had searches open for you, that you were still an active line of inquiry. But then a few weeks ago I got a call from the investigation team in France. And it's official. They've closed the case. It's been recorded as an organised crime murder. They're not looking for you any more, Lucy. It's over.'

Lucy feels a bubble of nervous euphoria pass through her gut. She shakes her head slightly. 'Are you sure?'

'I am completely sure, Lucy. That's what I wanted to tell you. Just that. After all these months, finally. It's over.'

Lucy shakes her head again, not quite able to absorb this pronouncement. 'But what if. . . I don't know. What if someone suddenly unearths some new CCTV footage or someone suddenly remembers seeing me going in there. It could still—'

Rachel interjects. 'No,' she says. 'That's not going to happen.

The investigation was thorough and all-encompassing, believe me. They have left nothing unturned and now it is over. Locked away in a box. Nobody is looking for you, Lucy. Nobody is looking for you ever again.' She smiles brilliantly and Lucy returns the smile.

'Oh my God,' says Lucy. 'I can't get my head around it. All these months, every waking minute of every day, it's been there. Right there. I've been ready to run. You know. Ready to hide. And now . . .'

'Yes . . . it's finished.' Rachel smiles again. 'But I really need to ask you, Lucy, what was it? What made you do it?'

Lucy glances down at the floor and then up at Rachel, her eyes shining with tears. 'I went there to collect our passports. On that Sunday. I knew he'd expect sex in return, I knew that, but I thought it would be worth it to get my freedom back. To get back to the UK to find my daughter. So I was ready for it. Wearing nice underwear. Ready for sex. But that wasn't what he wanted. He raped me in his kitchen. He pushed me into broken glass. Look.' Lucy pulls up her T-shirt to show Rachel the small livid scar that is still there, over a year later. 'I was bleeding and in pain and he kept raping me and there was this knife. The knife I'd been using to slice the tomatoes. And I – Well. You know what I did.'

Rachel takes Lucy's hand in hers and her eyes fill with tears too. 'I know,' she says. 'I know. You don't need to say any more. I know.'

'And you? What were you doing there? When you saw what I did?'

'Ha! Well, I'd come to kill him too!'

Lucy gasps. 'What? Really?'

Rachel smiles. 'No. Not really. But maybe. If it had come to it.'

'Because of how he treated you?'

'Yes. Because of how he treated me. Because, you know, he raped me too. Raped me. In my sleep. I was asleep!' Rachel clamps her hands over her mouth and makes a loud sobbing noise. 'And then' – she smiles apologetically and continues, drawing in her breath – 'a few months later I found out that Michael had black-mailed my father out of all of his life savings by threatening to publicly share filthy photographs of me that he'd stolen from my phone at some point during our brief marriage. I went there that day to get him to pay the money back. I was going to get his gun – did you know he had a gun? And I was going to point it at him until he agreed to pay my father back all his money.'

'And if he'd refused?'

Rachel looks directly into Lucy's eyes and after a beat of silence says, 'I would have shot him.'

'But I got there first?'

'Yes. You got there first. And you, Lucy, you are my *heroine*.'

Rachel leans towards Lucy then and takes her into her arms. 'Thank you,' she whispers into her hair. 'Thank you for what you did.'

'But what about your father's money?' Lucy asks. 'Did you ever get it back?'

Rachel nods and smiles. 'The wealth management company who'd been holding it for Michael really did not want the bad pub-licity, so they paid it all back to my father, no questions asked. So. Happy ever after.' She smiles again and slaps her hands against her bare legs. 'Is ten thirty in the morning too early for champagne, do you think?'

Lucy blinks in surprise. Then she smiles and says, 'I'm fine with that.'

They take the champagne out on to Rachel's balcony and make a toast to each other, to safety, to bad things happening to bad people and good things happening to good people, and Lucy tells Rachel about the old vicarage in St Albans and Rachel says she'd love to see it and Lucy says she'll invite her for drinks when it's fit for visitors and Rachel tells Lucy about her designer jewellery business and shows her some exquisitely pretty pieces on her website.

'I'll make you something, Lucy,' says Rachel. 'Whatever you want. Just choose something and it's yours.' But Lucy shakes her head and says, 'No. I don't need anything.'

'What about for Libby, then? For your daughter?' and Lucy smiles and says, 'Oh. Yes. Thank you,' and they don't talk about Michael because Michael is dead and they are alive and they are safe and the sun shines on them as the barges pass down below.

68

August 2019

Max Blackwood, the estate agent, stands outside the vicarage in St Albans on a cool August morning, wearing a sweater over his business shirt. 'Good morning, good morning!' he sings to Lucy as she steps out of her car. 'It's D-Day!'

Lucy waits to oversee Stella as she clambers out of the back, while Henry joins her from the passenger seat and Marco climbs out of his side and the four of them stand and survey the house.

'Fuck me,' Henry stage-whispers to Marco. 'I see what you mean.'

'I told you, didn't I?' says Marco, who hates the house with a passion. 'Clapped.'

Stella meanwhile grabs hold of Lucy's hand and squeezes it excitedly. The whole journey she has been clamouring to get here so that she can see her room again. The children have been here only once before, just after the sales contracts were exchanged. Today is completion day and Lucy strides towards the estate agent and takes the keys from his outstretched hand.

'Thank you so much,' she says to him. 'This is pretty much the most exciting day of my life. Can you believe it, forty years old and this is the first home of my own I've ever had?'

The estate agent beams at her and says, 'Better late than never. And worth the wait I'd say. Such a beautiful house.'

They wave him off a moment later and just as he leaves, Libby and Miller pull into the driveway. Libby clutches a huge bouquet of flowers and Miller carries a bottle of champagne. 'Happy house day!' says Libby, running towards Lucy and hugging her.

Libby's seen the house before but Miller hasn't and he eyes it from the driveway and says, 'Wow. It's essentially beautiful, but God you'll have your work cut out for you.'

'Yes, well, I'm prepared for that. And as it happens, the best kitchen designer in Hertfordshire has already drawn up plans for the kitchen and it is going to look incredible.'

Dido is going to be overseeing most of the work. She's assembled a squad of local interior designers and an architect to work with her on it. But first Lucy just wants to be in there, inside. Her first home. Her babies. All in one place. Finally. She turns the key in the door and feels a shiver of pleasure as the door opens under her hand – each time she's seen the house before it's been the estate agent's hand on the keys, pushing open the door – and then they are inside the house and although it is scruffy, broken, badly modernised and falling apart, it fills her heart in a way that is beyond anything she ever experienced before.

Fitz scampers ahead of them and out towards the back door, beyond which he knows there is a two-hundred-foot garden that is all for him. Stella runs up the stairs and into her bedroom with Libby, and Lucy can hear her from here explaining to Libby exactly where her big bed with a ladder up is going to go and how she's going to have tea parties under it with Freya G and Freya T when they come for sleepovers, which will be happening all the time according to Stella. Downstairs Lucy stands between Miller and Henry, surveying the house and talking about what will go where once Dido's plans start to take shape. And then she turns and notices Marco standing quietly in the corner of the hallway, kicking at the skirting board with the toe of his shoe.

'Is it too late to change our minds?' he says.

'Yes,' says Lucy, who has had to put up with two months of Marco canvassing to be allowed to stay at Henry's and at his central London school and not join them out here in the countryside. But then a moment later she notices that Marco is in the garden with the dog and that he has found a tennis ball from somewhere and is throwing it for Fitz, who scampers helter-skelter up and down the lawn chasing it and bringing it back and she sees a flush of colour pass into her son's cheeks, and she knows that he will love it here. Eventually.

Libby orders in a stack of super-sized pizzas and they eat them in the garden with the champagne while Stella jumps up and down on the trampoline with the dog. The past couple of months have been stressful in so many ways. The story about Justin's suicide and the dead pop star and the starving children locked in the Chelsea mansion had gone, somewhat predictably, viral. The papers couldn't get enough of it for a few days. The story was accompanied by numerous pictures of Birdie, of the house, of Lucy leaving Henry's apartment with the dog, of Libby and Miller leaving her house in St Albans, of Martina and Henry Senior when they were newlywed, of the Harrods crib with the blue painted flowers on it that Libby had been found in as a baby, of the camper van that Justin had been living in, of the pub where he was a regular.

There was even a photo doing the rounds of a young man called Jason Mott, a mud-larking guide on the Thames who had been the one to find the bones. He had a thick mop of strawberry-blond hair and a padded gilet with many pockets over a sleeveless vest. He said, 'I've found some strange things over the many years I've been sifting through these mudbanks and shingle shores, everything from false teeth and golf balls to Roman coins and jewellery, but finding this bag of bones was the most shocking discovery of my career. Now a man is dead and I'm wishing I'd thrown them straight back in the river. If I had my time again I would.'

But the glare of the story is starting to fade now. The press has moved on; the public has moved on. Lucy has her house. Henry has his home back. They have been issued their original birth certificates and have reclaimed their given names – the deeds to this house are written out to Lucy Amanda Lamb – and now they are both free from the shadows that have followed them all their adult lives. Neither of them is hiding any longer. The house on Cheyne Walk is finally excised from their psyches. Their lives have begun again.

But there is still one missing piece and as the day spills over from early to late afternoon Lucy's eyes keep going to the time on her phone and the driveway beyond the kitchen window and with every passing moment she becomes increasingly distracted, losing focus on the conversation wheeling around her.

But finally, at nearly five o'clock, there is a crunch of tyres on gravel and the doorbell rings.

'Libby, can you get that for me?' she calls out to her oldest child.

Lucy stands at the edge of the hallway and watches as Libby opens the door to a tall man with dirty blond hair, a scraggy beard and a shy smile.

Lucy's heart lifts at the sight of him and she takes a few steps towards the door, but still keeps out of sight. There's the sound of footsteps behind her and she sees Henry drawing close. She puts a finger to her lips, and he nods and stands behind her.

'Hi?' says Libby, a question in her voice.

'Hello,' says the man. 'Are you Libby?'

'Yes,' she replies. 'Are you—?'

'I'm Phin.'

'Oh.' A tiny breathless syllable. 'Wow.'

Lucy and Henry exchange a look. She feels Henry's hand gently squeezing her shoulder and she takes it in hers.

'I'm assuming that nobody told you . . .?' says Phin.

Libby shakes her head. 'No,' she says. 'Nobody told me.'

'So this is a bit of a shock?'

'Yes, it's a bit of a shock.' Libby laughs. 'Do you – do you want to come in?'

'Thank you,' says Phin. 'I'd love to come in.'

Lucy and Henry pull back a bit as Libby leads Phin down the hallway towards the kitchen. 'I was supposed to be here two hours ago,' says Phin. 'I've been down in Cornwall, with my mother and my sister. The traffic was horrific. I hope I haven't ruined the day?'

'No,' Lucy hears Libby reply brightly. 'No, not at all. We've had a lovely day. And now . . .'

Lucy holds her breath hard inside her chest.

'Now it just got even better.' There's a short pause. 'Anyway. What can I get you? Wine? Beer? Cold manky pizza?'

There's a peel of combined laughter then. The laughter of her daughter and her daughter's father on a Friday afternoon in Lucy's home.

Lucy turns to Henry and smiles. She mouths the words *thank you*.

Then she takes Henry's hand and together they walk towards the kitchen, their family finally complete.

69

Two months earlier

Phin pulls the bolt back on the door of his flat. It's late and he's really not in the mood for making small talk with someone called Jeff. The flat is a mess, and he doesn't really want to show it to him. He sighs heavily and says, 'Hold on.'

Then suddenly there is a foot inside his door and a tall man pushes him bodily into the hallway. The man has dyed blond hair and wild eyes. His breath smells of old wine and old food. His pale eyes are manic.

'What the fuck?' says Phin. 'Dude. What the fuck?'

The man turns and slides the bolt across, and Phin tries to get around him to unlock it. 'Seriously, dude. Get the fuck out of here.'

His heart scrambles in his chest. He'd had a weird feeling about the note from 'Jeff' he'd found pinioned under his door knocker earlier. There'd been something unsettling about it and he'd felt slightly unsafe ever since and now he thinks he might well be about to die.

The guy barrels himself against Phin, down the hallway and into the living room and on to the sofa, where he pins him down by his shoulders, flicks his hair out of his eyes, breathes his rancid breath into Phin's face and says, 'Hello, old boy.'

Phin stares at the man who has come here to kill him, and then recognition dawns.

'Henry,' he says. 'Fucking hell. What the fuck.'

'Fuck me, Phin. You look so different.'

'Henry. You look—'

'Yes. I know. I look like you. Crazy, eh? Can you believe it? What sort of sad loser spends his whole adult life pretending to be someone he was in love with when he was a child? You know, I even call myself Phin sometimes. Isn't that pathetic?'

Phin nods, then shakes his head, then says, 'Yes. That is pretty fucked up. What are you doing here? What do you want?'

'Oh, Phin. That is an excellent question. Truly. And you know, I'm not sure I can answer it. I just – I just had to come. I mean. You disappeared. You left me. And ever since you left me I've been – lonely.'

'Lonely?'

'Yes. Lonely. Pretending to be you has just made me feel closer to you. Less alone.'

Henry finally unpins Phin's shoulders and flops heavily on to the sofa next to him. He breathes out loudly and then turns to Phin and says, 'I'm sorry.'

'Sorry for what?'

'Sorry for being me.'

'Why are you sorry for being you?'

'Oh, I don't know. Because I made everything twice as bad as it already was for you in that house. Because I'm just heavy, aren't I? I'm a deadweight. I know I am.'

'Well, Henry, I haven't seen you for twenty-odd years so I can't say you've been dragging me down.'

'Oh, get me a drink, will you? I really need a drink.'

'I don't have any.'

'Ah. No. Of course you don't. You never needed crutches, did you? You were always enough for you.'

'Well, that's total and utter bollocks.'

Henry stares at Phin questioningly.

'Do you really think that?' says Phin.

'I don't think it. I know it.'

'Well, you're wrong. My whole life has been a search for meaning. My whole life has been about trying to work out what the fuck I'm for.'

'Yeah. Right.'

'Yes. Right. You know, Henry, did you ever stop and think about what it does to a person growing up with a father like mine? You only had him in your life for a few years. I had him in my life for eighteen. I was already fighting for my own identity, for my own survival long before I ever met you.'

'But you made me feel so . . .'

'What? What did I make you feel, Henry?'

'Lesser.'

'That's such bullshit. Come on. You were the one with the big house and the posh school and the bedroom full of nice things. I

426

arrived in your house with *nothing*. Literally just a bag of clothes. And there you were, Little Lord Fauntleroy, with *everything*. Everything a child could want. How do you think that made me feel?'

'I don't know. I don't know how it made you feel.'

'It made me defensive, Henry. It made me turn inwards. It made me want to lose myself in books and dreams and thoughts of worlds that existed outside my own tragic existence. And there you were. Wanting, wanting, wanting. Looking at me like I had the answers to everything. And I had nothing, Henry. Could you not see that? I had *nothing*. And the more you expected me to give you something, the more it reminded me how little I had to give. You were the one, Henry. You were the leader. You were the one who got us out of there in the end.'

'But I nearly killed you. Did you know that? I nearly killed you. It was me giving you the drugs that made you ill. They were meant to make you love me. It was a ridiculous fucking *love potion*, Phin. And it nearly killed you.'

'I wasn't ill from your love potion, Henry. I was ill from mal-nutrition. From dehydration. It was their fault I was ill. Not yours.' Phin sighs and turns to look at Henry, properly. 'Henry, look, mate. We're cool. Do you see? You and me. We're cool.'

Henry looks thoughtful for a moment and nods. But then he becomes agitated again. 'But if we're cool then why did you run away from Botswana when you heard I was coming?'

Phin looks at Henry in bemusement. 'I wasn't running away from *you*, Henry,' he says. 'What on earth made you think I was running away from you? It was the others I was running away from. From Lucy. And . . . well, Lucy's daughter. I just wasn't—'

Phin holds himself together for a moment. 'I wasn't ready for the whole father-daughter reunion thing. I just wasn't. I got scared. I pussied out.'

Phin shrugs and Henry sighs loudly and says, 'Fuck's sake, Phin. Fuck's sake.' Then he pulls his phone out of his pocket and he opens up his camera roll and he scrolls backwards to photos of what looks like a family dinner in a restaurant and he opens up a photo of a young woman with blonde hair and says, 'Phin. Look at her. That's your daughter. That's Libby.'

Phin stares at the photo in a hushed silence. A sweet-faced girl, with a huge smile, a dimple. She looks like him. She looks just like him.

'She's the nicest person in the world, Phin. And I know you weren't a fan of the baby thing, I get that. Babies are fucking terrifying. But look at her. She's not a baby any more. She's a grown woman with a home and a job and a boyfriend and she doesn't need a dad. She doesn't need you. But fuck's sake, Phin.' Henry pauses for a moment and turns off his phone, stares at Phin and says, 'Has it ever occurred to you that maybe you might need her? Come home, Phin. Come and see her.'

Phin closes his eyes. Then he opens them again. He looks at Henry and from somewhere deep inside him comes a wave of certainty, a wave of love. He pulls Henry to him and for a long, drawn-out moment, they hold each other hard.

When they finally come apart, Phin says to Henry, 'OK. I'll come. I promise. I'll come. This year. Maybe August. Just promise me, in the meantime, you won't tell anyone you've seen me.'

Henry looks up at Phin and smiles and says, 'I swear on my life. I won't tell a soul.'

Epilogue

Eight months later

'Can I help you, sir?'

Henry checks his reflection quickly in the plate glass of the showroom window. He tousles his dark, ropey curls and runs his fingertips over the rough three-day stubble on his chin. Then he turns to the hovering salesman and hits him with a personable smile.

'Hi,' says Henry. 'Yes. Thank you. I'm looking for a Gold Wing? Your website said you had some in stock, but I can't see any?'

'Beautiful!' The salesman's eyes light up and he clicks his fingers. 'Follow me, sir, right this way.'

Henry follows the young man across the showroom and towards a display in another area off the main reception. His skin turns to goosebumps at the sight of the huge bikes, four of them lined up diagonally on pedestals, hit from all angles with halogen beams.

'Wow,' he says.

'Yes,' says the salesman. 'Wow indeed. Were you looking for a particular model?'

'Er, yes. The GL1500.'

The salesman smiles and waves his hand towards a red and black bike.

It's the one.

It's exactly the same.

Henry's stomach lurches.

'It's a 1998 model,' the salesman says. 'Virtually immaculate. Only fifteen hundred miles on the clock. Spent most of its long life under tarpaulin. And is now ready and raring to get on with the rest of its life, hopefully on the road. Want to climb on board?'

Henry nods. 'Sure,' he says. 'That'd be awesome.'

The salesman presses a button on the wall and the pedestal sinks into the floor until the bike is flush with the ground.

Henry hitches his leg over the bike and is instantly transported back to the heady streets of Chicago. He runs his hands over the controls, the handlebars.

'Beautiful, isn't she?' says the salesman.

Henry nods, but says nothing. The oneness he has felt with the world since he returned from Chicago, since he and Phin made their peace, since the big family reunion in Lucy's new house, has started to fray at the edges. For months he has embraced being Henry Lamb. The idea that Justin had sacrificed his life not for the glamorous refurbished version of Henry Lamb, but for the original slightly crappy version, has filled his soul with rightness and substance. Henry Lamb was enough, he'd thought, he didn't need to be anybody else. But recently his beautiful apartment has started to feel empty again, and he is aware once more of his aloneness in this world, his strangeness, his otherness. Once he had let his hair grow back to its natural dead ash, let his lip fillers deflate, his cheek fillers disintegrate, once he saw the old Henry staring back at him from the mirror again, he panicked. He no longer wanted to be Phin, but he did not, he knew with a sickening certainty, want to be dull old Uncle Henry either. And his thoughts kept returning, over the weeks and months that followed, to the last time he'd felt anything, the last time he had not felt numb. To the last human being he had met who was worthy of imitation.

'Oh,' says the salesman. 'My name's Theo, by the way.'

'Hi, Theo,' says Henry, tossing his dark hair out of his dark eyes and giving Theo his hand to shake. 'My name's Kris. Kris Doll.'

'Lovely to meet you, Kris,' says Theo. 'You have awesome taste in bikes.'

Acknowledgements

Firstly, I need to thank every reader of *The Family Upstairs* who wrote to me over the past four years to say *please can you write a sequel, I need to know what happens next*! I am very much not a writer who likes to write sequels; I did it once before and I didn't enjoy it. I held firm for quite some time in my refusal to countenance the concept. But then something clicked and I realised that what I wanted more than anything was to spend another year in the head of Henry Lamb. So thank you, readers, for pushing me into doing something that I think I secretly wanted to do all along!

Thanks as ever to my publishing teams in the UK and the US. In particular, thanks to Selina Walker, Najma Finlay, Claire Bush, Sarah Ridley, Laura Richetti and Claire Simmonds at Cornerstone and to Lindsay Sagnette, Ariele Fredman, Milena Brown, Jade Hui and Zoe Harris at Atria.

Thanks to the amazing team at Curtis Brown, my London agency. Especial thanks to Jonny Geller, Viola Hayden and Ciara Finan, and to Kate, Nadia and Sophia in foreign rights. And thanks to my incredible agent in the US, Deborah Schneider at Gelfman Schneider, and to Luke Speed and Josie Freedman, my film and TV agents in the UK and the US.

Thank you to all my foreign publishers. It's been an amazing year for my book sales in foreign markets and I'm so grateful to you for all you do to get my work to your wonderful readers.

Thanks to all the booksellers and all the librarians and to everyone I've met online and IRL at the events you work so hard to organise.

Thanks, as ever, to Richenda Todd, the world's greatest copyeditor. Thank you for the TLC you always show my work.

Thank you to Will Brooker, who shadowed me as I wrote this book whilst writing a book of his own called *The Truth About Lisa Jewell: A Year in the Life of a Bestselling Novelist*. Thank you for being more than a shadow, for encouraging and reassuring me as I sent you my work in progress, and for making the writing of this novel such a memorable and fun experience. Thank you also for so effortlessly supplying me with a neat fix for my plotting disaster back in December.

And lastly, thanks as ever to all of my friends and family for being the best friends and family, and to my writer friends for being the best writer friends and to my dog for being, of course, the best dog in the world.

A note on the character name Oliver Wolfensberger

Last year Spear Camden ran an auction to raise money for their charitable works, and a character name in my novel was one of the lots on offer. The winner of the auction was Oliver Wolfensberger, who is immortalised in this book as the new owner of the infamous 16 Cheyne Walk! Here's a little about the charity:

Spear Camden is one of the charities supported by the Lighthouse London Community Trust. It takes vulnerable local young people aged 16–24 who all have barriers to employment, and puts them through an intensive six-week coaching programme, as well as offering a follow-up year of support. The result is that, despite coming from often difficult backgrounds – out of care, prison, escaping gang violence, struggling with mental health issues or long term unemployment – more than 75% of the young people who complete the six-week Spear programme are in work, training or employment a year later.

And a message from Spear Camden:

The money raised by your auction prize was enough to completely transform the lives of one and a half young people. So huge, huge thanks to you and Mr Wolfensberger!

Bringing a book from manuscript to what you are reading is a team effort, and Penguin Random House would like to thank everyone at Century who helped to publish *The Family Remains*.

PUBLISHER
Selina Walker

EDITORIAL
Joanna Taylor
Sophie Whitehead
Charlotte Osment
Richenda Todd

DESIGN
Ceara Elliot

PRODUCTION
Helen Wynn-Smith
Tara Hodgson

UK SALES
Mat Watterson
Claire Simmonds
Olivia Allen

Jade Unwin
Evie Kettlewell
Neil Green

INTERNATIONAL SALES
Richard Rowlands
Erica Conway
Laura Richetti

PUBLICITY
Najma Finlay

MARKETING
Sarah Ridley
Claire Bush

AUDIO
Meredith Benson